FOREVER A HERO

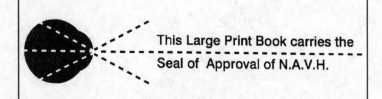

This Large Print Book carries the
Seal of Approval of N.A.V.H.

FOREVER A HERO

LINDA LAEL MILLER

WHEELER PUBLISHING
A part of Gale, Cengage Learning

GALE
CENGAGE Learning

Farmington Hills, Mich • San Francisco • New York • Waterville, Maine
Meriden, Conn • Mason, Ohio • Chicago

GALE
CENGAGE Learning®

Copyright © 2017 by Hometown Girl Makes Good, Inc.
The Carsons of Mustang Creek #3.
Wheeler Publishing, a part of Gale, Cengage Learning.

Wheeler Publishing Large Print Hardcover.
The text of this Large Print edition is unabridged.
Other aspects of the book may vary from the original edition.
Set in 16 pt. Plantin.

LIBRARY OF CONGRESS CATALOGING-IN-PUBLICATION DATA

Names: Miller, Linda Lael, author.
Title: Forever a hero / Linda Lael Miller.
Description: Waterville, Maine : Wheeler Publishing Large Print, 2017. | Series: The Carsons of Mustang Creek ; 3 | Series: Wheeler Publishing Large Print hardcover
Identifiers: LCCN 2017001729 | ISBN 9781410493705 (hardback) | ISBN 1410493709 (hardcover)
Subjects: LCSH: Large type books. | BISAC: FICTION / Romance / Western. | GSAFD: Love stories. | Western stories.
Classification: LCC PS3563.I41373 F667 2017 | DDC 813/.54—dc23
LC record available at https://lccn.loc.gov/2017001729

Published in 2017 by arrangement with Harlequin Books S. A.

Printed in the United States of America
1 2 3 4 5 6 7 21 20 19 18 17

Dear Reader,

Welcome back to Mustang Creek, Wyoming, home of hot cowboys and the smart, beautiful women who love them.

Forever a Hero is the story of Mace, the youngest of the three Carson brothers. A cowboy-turned-vintner, he's focused on taking his successful winery to new heights — and though he has no interest in selling it to corporate executive Kelly Wright, the woman he rescued from trouble once upon a time, he's got more than a little interest in her.

Mace might be the hero Kelly never forgot, but she's determined not to mix business with pleasure. She's returned to Mustang Creek to make him an offer he can't refuse, and she intends to get her way. But when her attacker returns for vengeance, Kelly might find that Mace's arms are the safest place of all.

If you read the previous two books in this trilogy, *Once a Rancher* and *Always a Cowboy,* you'll recognize a lot of the characters, and I hope you'll enjoy reuniting with them.

Ranch life runs deep with me. I live on my

own modest little spread called the Triple L, and we've got critters aplenty: five horses, two dogs and two cats. And those are just the official ones — we share the land with wild turkeys, deer and the occasional moose, and I wouldn't live any other way.

My love of animals shows in my stories, and I never miss a chance to speak for the silent furry ones who have no voices and no choices. So please support your local animal shelters, have your pets spayed and neutered, and if you're feeling a mite lonely, why not rescue a four-legged somebody waiting to love you with the purest of devotion.

Thank you for bending an ear my way, and enjoy the story.

With all best,
Paula Lael Miller

CHAPTER ONE

It all happened in a matter of seconds.

And every one of those seconds felt like a year.

Mace Carson had been cruising along behind the unfamiliar car up ahead ever since he'd cleared the city limits of Mustang Creek a few minutes before, when the other rig suddenly fishtailed on the rain-slick pavement and spun a full 360. The slow-motion spin, weirdly graceful, and at the same time potentially deadly, was sickening to watch.

He eased his truck to the side of the road, jammed down the emergency brake pedal, then groped for his cell phone and muttered an expletive, watching the situation unfold, helpless to intervene as the vehicle shot toward the steep slope on the opposite shoulder, where there were no guardrails. The drop was nearly fifty feet, by his calculations, with no trees or boulders to break the fall.

Not that either would have been ideal, anyway you looked at it.

With a second curse, he was out of the truck and running to do what he could, heedless of the pounding rain, phone in hand, thumb on the button that would speed-dial 911.

Meanwhile, the car came to a precarious stop at the edge, teetered and then slipped again, winding up at a precarious angle, half on the road, half off, passenger-side down. The mud, a few inches deep and slick as snot, offered the briefest purchase.

Mace didn't rattle easily, but in those moments, his heart zoomed into his throat. He was close enough now to glimpse the driver, a woman, pale and wide-eyed with shock, leaning hard into the car door, as if she hoped to waft right through the metal to the safety of solid ground.

"Don't move!" he said, never knowing if he'd shouted the words or simply mouthed them, dropping the phone to the ground because he was going to need both hands to get her out before the mud gave way and sent her *and* the car tumbling downhill, ass over teakettle.

He saw her nod. Stiffen.

He gripped the door handle, never taking his eyes off her face, realized instantly that the locks were still engaged.

"Shift into Park," he told the woman, giving silent thanks that the air bags hadn't deployed. The mechanisms were sensitive; in some cars, especially newer models, no collision was required. An abrupt change of direction could trigger them. "And then unfasten your seat belt. Slow and easy, now — no sudden moves."

Another nod from her. He was either yelling or she could read lips, because she did what he'd told her to do. With a flash of relief, he heard the locks release.

The car slid a few inches farther down the hill.

Bracing his feet, Mace pulled at the door. Gravity worked against him, but he'd bucked a lot of bales in his time, dug a lot of postholes and like any man who did hard physical work, he was strong.

A wedge of space opened between them.

"You're gonna have to get out on your own," he told the woman, who was trembling so badly her teeth chattered. His voice sounded strangely calm, at least to him, considering the circumstances. "For obvious reasons, I can't let go of this door long

9

enough to give you a hand."

She slithered through the gap as if boneless, landing on her hands and knees at Mace's feet.

When he let go of the handle a heartbeat later, the door slammed shut with an impact that set the rig in motion. As he helped the woman up from the ground, the car lurched violently, tipped onto its side and rolled over, then over again and again, gaining momentum with every flip, finally landing with an echoing crash on its top, square in the middle of the creek below.

Still gripping the shuddering stranger by both arms, Mace closed his eyes briefly, comparing what might have happened with what actually had. This was one lucky lady, whoever she was.

In the aftermath of the adrenaline rush, Mace felt a little shaky himself, but he quickly recovered. He needed to focus on what, if anything, still needed to be done; while the woman appeared to be in one piece, she could be in shock, or she might have hit her head at some point and gotten a concussion. Or suffered internal injuries of some kind.

Growing up rough-and-tumble, like any ranch kid, and competing in his share of rodeos, he knew some injuries didn't show on the outside, the way cuts and bruises did. Not immediately, anyhow.

That made his fight-or-flight response spike again, and he took a moment to breathe his way through, line up his thoughts.

Satisfied that the lady was still upright and her eyes hadn't rolled back or anything, he looked down the hillside.

He'd half expected the car to explode into flames when it hit bottom, rain or no rain, but it just lay there, so coated in mud that its color, rental-beige as he recalled, was indiscernible now. With all four wheels turning slowly, the rig reminded Mace of a turtle on its back, kicking in an effort to right itself.

"Holy shit," he said, exhaling the words.

The woman looked up at him, rain-soaked, still pale, but with a quiver of amusement playing at the corners of her mouth. "You can say that again," she replied. "But please don't."

He gave a short, hoarse burst of laughter at that. She was shaking, and he wasn't entirely sure she wouldn't buckle to the ground if he loosened his grip, but she had grit, no doubt about it. Considering what she'd just been through, he wouldn't have considered hysterical sobs, a good old-fashioned fainting spell or a spate of violent retching out of line.

"Are you hurt?" He wished he'd asked the obvious question sooner, instead of just thinking about it.

She shook her head. Her hair, hanging in dripping tendrils, not quite long enough to touch her shoulders, was some shade of blond. Her eyes, still huge, were a remarkable shade of green, flecked with gold. "I'll be fine," she assured him, raising her voice to be heard over the continuing downpour. "Thanks to you."

"Any pain? Numbness?" Mace asked, unconvinced.

"I have a few bumps and bruises," she answered, "but nothing hurts, and there's no numbness, either. I guess I'm shaken up, is all — that was a close one." She bit her lower lip before going on. "If you hadn't been here —" She stopped, shook her head again and wiped her eyes with the back of one hand.

"I was, though," he said gently. "We'll get you checked out, just to be on the safe side."

Her response was a disjointed jumble of words, partial sentences. "The car — it's a rental — I'm not sure I signed up for the extra insurance."

"Let's worry about that later," he told her.

"Right now, we're headed for the hospital."

"I really don't think I'm injured —"

He held on to her arm with one hand while he bent to retrieve his phone from the asphalt. It looked a little the worse for wear, although it probably still worked just fine. "If it's all the same to you," he said lightly, "I'd rather hear that from a licensed medical professional."

She sighed.

"Plus, this rain isn't helping," he added, squiring her carefully toward his truck. It would've been faster to pick her up and carry her, but if she *was* hurt, it wouldn't do to jostle her around like a sack of feed.

They reached the truck, and he opened the passenger door, but before he could offer any assistance, she'd climbed onto the running board under her own power and then settled herself in the seat. For the briefest of moments, looking into her face, Mace had the impression that he knew this woman from somewhere.

"If I thought it would do me any good to argue," she said with a hint of a smile, "I'd repeat what I've been saying all along. I don't need to see a doctor. Besides, you've done enough already."

"You're at least partly right," Mace responded. "Arguing won't do a damn bit of good, and I only did what anybody else would have done, under the circumstances. As for not needing to see a doctor, well, that's debatable."

"Seriously. I'm absolutely certain that all I need is a hot bath, a couple of aspirin and some sleep. So if you'd just drop me off at my hotel —"

"Sure thing," Mace agreed amiably. "I'll do that — after the doc looks you over and says you're good to go."

"I'm fine." She was certainly persistent, not to say stubborn, but this time, she'd met her match. He was as bullheaded as they came.

Mace shut the truck door without answering. Maybe she was right, and she really was okay, but he didn't intend to take the chance, and he was tired of standing there in the rain, yammering.

As soon as he was behind the wheel and under cover, the rain slowed to a drizzle.

It figured.

She was shivering, arms wrapped around her ribs, and staring bleakly through the rain-speckled windshield.

Mace cranked up the heat, glad he'd left the engine running earlier, and looked over at her. Tried for a grin and fell short. "Hey," he said gruffly, switching on the wipers to

14

clear the windshield. "You're safe with me, if that's what you're worried about. I might be a stranger, but I'm also one of the good guys."

She glanced at him curiously. "But you're *not* a stranger."

So, he'd been right. This wasn't their first encounter.

Damned if he could recall where and when they'd crossed paths before, though. And that was odd, because even wet and bedraggled and more rattled than she probably thought she was, she wasn't the kind of woman a man forgot.

"I'm not?" he asked, checking the mirrors before making a wide turn and heading back toward Mustang Creek.

She sighed, rested her head against the side window. She sounded almost wistful when she responded. "You don't remember?"

"I know we've met someplace," he replied. "But that's all I've got at the moment."

There was a long, slightly forlorn pause. Another sigh. "Maybe we could talk about old times another day," she said at last, seeming to shrink into herself. "I'm so tired."

Normally, Mace wasn't the type to put things off, but he wasn't going to press for

15

particulars. Not yet, anyhow.

"Just don't fall asleep," he said.

"Why not?" she asked with another sigh and a small yawn. "I've had a long, hard day."

"Because you might've hit your head."

She opened her mouth, obviously intending to protest, but then she must have thought better of it. Or maybe she was too exhausted to put up an argument.

"Thanks," she said. "For everything."

Mace acknowledged her words with a slight inclination of his head, keeping his eyes on the road. Several minutes passed before he broke the silence. "What happened back there?"

"I'm not sure," she replied, and her voice was slow, sleepy. "One minute, I was cruising along, looking for the turnoff to the resort. The next, I was hydroplaning. Maybe I blew a tire or something."

"You were speeding," he commented blandly.

She frowned. "Are you going to lecture me on road safety? Because I'm really not up for that just now."

He grinned. "Unfamiliar roads, heavy rain —"

"I was in a hurry."

"To do what?"

16

"To get to my hotel. As I said, I was ready for this day to be over."

The outskirts of Mustang Creek were in sight by then; the small regional hospital was on the far side of town, about ten minutes away. He wasn't given to cop fantasies, but at that moment he wished for a light bar and a siren.

"Another few seconds and your *life* might have been over."

"Thanks for that," she retorted with a new briskness Mace found reassuring, despite the tartness of her tone. "I might not have figured that out on my own — how I could've been killed, I mean."

Keep her talking, he thought. *If she's pissed off, oh, well. At least she's awake.*

Although she'd been slouching before, she suddenly sat bolt upright, making patting motions with her hands. "My purse," she said, her voice fretful. "It's still in the car."

Mace was always astonished by how dependent women were on their handbags, as if the things were a necessary part of their anatomy rather than an obvious burden. Something else to keep track of. "It isn't going anywhere," he said quietly and with a note of prudent caution.

Her eyes were big with alarm when she turned to look at him, and patches of pink

17

pulsed impatiently in her cheeks. "My entire *life* is in that bag!" she cried. "And it's a Michael Kors, too."

A purse with a name, he thought, but he wasn't stupid enough to offer up the quip when she was clearly riled. Keeping her awake was one thing; causing her to blow a brain-gasket was another.

"I'll make sure you get it back."

"Suppose it's underwater? My phone — my wallet — do you *know* how much a designer bag costs? And what about my laptop? My clothes?"

"I guess that's a possibility," Mace observed casually, "given the laws of gravity and everything."

"How can you be so calm?" she asked, fuming. Then she answered her own question. "I'll *tell* you how. It isn't *your* purse!"

"You have me there," he admitted, not unsympathetically. "I don't own one, as it happens. Reckon if I did, though, I'd keep that fact to myself."

Her cheeks flared brighter, but a giggle escaped. "This is serious," she said.

Mace shook his head. "No, ma'am," he said, navigating the familiar streets of his hometown. "Car wrecks are serious. Concussions and busted spleens are serious. But a bag named Michael winding up in a creek? Not so much."

"I should call the car rental company," she said, apparently not one for segues.

Mace got his cell from his shirt pocket and handed it over. "If that'll make you feel better, have at it," he said.

She took the phone, then simply stared down at the screen, blinking. "I don't know their number. The contract is in the glove compartment, possibly submerged."

"Plenty of time to get in touch with them," Mace said. They were almost through Mustang Creek; the turn for the hospital would be coming up in a minute or so. "Might be a good idea to call your family, however." When she didn't answer right away, he offered suggestions — with an agenda. "Your folks? Husband? Boyfriend?"

She huffed out a frustrated breath. "My parents are on a cruise through the Greek Islands," she said. He caught the sidelong look she threw his way, although he was still gazing straight ahead, slowing for the turn-off. "And I don't have a husband *or* a boyfriend, for your information." A few seconds passed. "Do you?"

He laughed, swinging onto the paved stretch leading to the hospital. "Do I have a husband or a boyfriend?"

She worked up a good glare, but it fizzled

19

into a wobbly smile before they reached the parking lot near the entrance to the emergency room. "I was joking," she said.

"I laughed, didn't I?" Mace parked the truck, shut off the engine, then came around to her side to open the door and help her down. This time, she let him, and as soon as her feet touched the ground, she swayed and put a hand to her forehead.

Mace slipped an arm around her waist, supporting her. Once again, he considered carrying her; once again, he dismissed the idea as too risky.

"I'm just a little dizzy," she murmured as they entered the well-lit reception area. "No big deal."

Ellie Simmons was behind the desk, and she stood immediately. She and Mace had gone to school together.

"I don't have my ID or my insurance card," said the woman whose name Mace suddenly realized he didn't know.

"She was in an accident," he told Ellie, relieved by his friend's affable competence. "South of town."

Ellie rounded the long desk and conjured up a wheelchair, eased the patient into the seat. "What about you, Mace?" she asked. "You hurting anywhere?"

Mace shoved a hand through his wet hair.

Wet as he and his companion were, he figured they might have passed for shipwreck survivors if there'd been an ocean within a thousand miles. "I just happened along," he said.

"I do have insurance," the wheelchair occupant piped up.

"We'll get to the paperwork in good time," Ellie said, already wheeling the new arrival away from Mace toward an examination room. She bent her head, addressing the patient. "What's your name, honey?"

The passenger hesitated long enough to prompt an exchange of glances between Ellie and Mace. Ellie raised an eyebrow at him in silent question.

Mace shrugged. "I have no idea."

"Kelly," the woman in the wheelchair said in the tone of someone experiencing a revelation. "Kelly Wright."

"Well, Kelly Wright," Ellie said as they disappeared into the ER, "you're in luck. Dr. Draper is on duty tonight, and she's the best."

Mace watched until they were gone, suppressing an urge to follow, ask a lot of questions, make damn sure Sheila Draper ran all the right tests.

Whatever the right tests happened to be.

Since Ms. Wright still had his cell, he went

21

to the pay phone, a near relic in this day and age, dug in his jeans pocket for coins and called his friend Spence Hogan, Mustang Creek's chief of police.

Spence took a while getting to the phone. When he did, he spoke in his usual brusque manner. "Hey, Mace," he said. "What's going on?"

Mace explained, none too succinctly.

"Sam Helgeson called it in five minutes ago," Spence said. "I've already got a squad car and a wrecker on the way." He paused. "You okay, buddy?"

"I'm fine," Mace said. Where had he heard *that* before?

"You sure? You sound pretty jumpy to me."

Mace gave a long sigh. "I'm sure," he said.

"Hold on a second," Spence muttered. "Deputy Brenner's on the radio. He's at the scene."

Mace waited. He heard some back-and-forth on Spence's end, although he couldn't make out what was said. He was too busy wondering what was going on with Kelly Wright back there in the exam room and, at the same time, rifling through his mental files, which — when it came to women, were considerable — in search of a connection.

He came up dry.

He'd probably known half a dozen Kellys in his time, gone to school with a few of them, dated one or two on the rodeo circuit, but the name Wright didn't ring a single bell.

Spence came back on the line. "You said there was only one woman in the car before it went over the bank, right? No other passengers?"

"Just her," Mace replied. "Doc Draper's checking her out now."

Spence released an audible breath.

"What?" Mace prompted, worried by Spence's hesitation.

"According to my deputy," Spence said, "he and the tow truck driver were taking some personal items out of the car when they smelled gas. They hightailed it uphill with whatever they'd managed to gather, and it's a good thing, because the rig burst into flames and then blew sky-high. Fire department's on the way, to make sure it doesn't spread. Thank God for this rain."

Mace squeezed his eyes shut, opened them again. "Christ," he breathed, the blaze as vivid in his mind as if he'd witnessed it. He thought how close he'd come to stopping by his favorite bar for a beer after his afternoon meeting with the guy who maintained his website, how he'd have lingered there awhile, shooting the shit with friends and neighbors, maybe playing a round or two of pool. If he hadn't remembered that Harry, the family's longtime cook and housekeeper, was serving her legendary sloppy joes for supper that night, if he'd thought there'd be leftovers once his two older brothers, Slater and Drake, ate their fill —

If.

Most likely, the Wright woman — Kelly — would've been trapped, unable to push open the driver's door, with the rig on a slant like that. She would have gone over the cliff along with her car and, if by some miracle she'd survived the rollovers without losing consciousness, burned to death.

He swore under his breath.

"Reckon this makes you a hero," Spence put in, gravely wry.

"I was there, that's all," Mace said. "Right time, right place. You would have done the same thing if you'd been there, and so would just about everybody else around here."

"Just about everybody," Spence noted with a very slight emphasis on the middle word.

Mace made no comment. Every town had its lightweights, and Mustang Creek was no exception, but that was beside the point. All that mattered now was that the Wright woman hadn't gone rolling down that hillside with the car. She'd walked away, still breathing, possibly in need of some patching up, but alive.

A shudder went through Mace, reminding him that his clothes were soaked through, clinging to his hide, clammy and cold. He was hungry, he was tired to the marrow of his bones and he was damn grateful that fate, so often fickle, had dealt Kelly Wright a decent hand.

"Mace?" Spence asked. "You still with me?"

"I'm here," he replied.

"I'm guessing there isn't a whole lot more you can do tonight. Might be best if you go on home."

"Soon as I know Kelly's all right, I'll do just that. She'll probably need a ride to the resort. That's where she's staying."

"Fair enough," Spence agreed diplomatically. "I'm thinking the lady will be admitted for observation, though, and the kind of tests they'll want to run can take hours. You really want to cool your heels in the waiting room for that long?"

Mace sighed. "She's from out of town. Seems like somebody ought to hang around until they decide whether to keep her overnight or turn her loose."

"Fine," Spence conceded. "We'll do what we can on our end."

Mace found himself nodding, then realized his friend couldn't see him. "Her name's Kelly Wright, and the car was a rental, but she couldn't say which company she used. That's about all I can tell you, as of now."

"Not to worry," Spence said. "Mustang Creek PD works in mysterious ways its wonders to perform. Ask Ms. Wright to call me when she feels up to it, will you? There'll be some paperwork, of course."

"I'll do that," Mace answered. Goodbyes were exchanged, and the call ended.

Mace was pacing the floor when a young couple hurried through the main doors, looking anxious. The man carried a toddler, bundled in a blanket and whimpering.

Ellie appeared immediately, her smile wide and white and reassuring. She greeted the new arrivals, handed the woman a clipboard and led the trio to an exam room.

When she returned to the reception area, she returned Mace's cell phone. "Kelly asked me to give you this."

"Thanks," he said. "Any news?"

Ellie shook her head. "Not yet," she said,

gently noncommittal. "Want some coffee?"

"No, thanks." He was hyped up enough, he figured, without a caffeine buzz.

"How's your night going?" he asked. He wasn't a talker under normal circumstances, but the waiting was driving him crazy.

"Better than yours, I'd say," Ellie replied with an understanding smile. By then, she was back at her station behind the reception desk. "So far, business has been pretty slow. Which, of course, is a good thing."

Mace realized he was fresh out of sparkling conversation. He sat down in an orange plastic chair, opened an outdated copy of *Field & Stream,* read one paragraph of an article about trout fishing in Montana and gave up.

Another hour passed, during which an elderly woman was brought in with respiratory problems, and the young couple returned with a prescription and their child, now sound asleep, head resting on the man's shoulder. Mace nodded in greeting, and the man nodded back.

Soon afterward, Sheila Draper came out, spotted Mace and smiled as she approached. She was a good-looking redhead with a figure that did great things for the blue scrubs she was wearing.

"Hey, Doc," Mace said. Sheila had grown

27

up on a neighboring ranch, and the two families were longtime friends.

"Hey, yourself," Sheila responded. She carried an electronic tablet but didn't consult it, and there was a twinkle in her bright green eyes. "You can rest easy, Sir Galahad," she said. "Kelly isn't seriously injured, just shaken up and a little dehydrated. I'm admitting her overnight, for observation and the appropriate fluids."

Something unclenched inside Mace. He heaved a deep sigh. And even as the question took shape in his mind, he wondered why he needed to ask it. He'd done what he could for Kelly, and he knew she was in good hands, had been from the moment he'd brought her in.

He asked, anyway. "Could I see her?"

Sheila shook her head regretfully, touched his arm. "Not tonight, Mace. I gave Kelly a sedative, and she's on her way upstairs. I'm guessing she'll be zonked before she gets to her room." The rest went without saying — Kelly needed sleep, not visitors.

He nodded again, sighed again.

Then he thanked Sheila, said goodbye to Ellie and left for home.

Mace Carson didn't remember her. Not quite, anyway.

That was okay for now, Kelly decided, rummy from the sedative she'd been given minutes before. She remembered well enough for both of them.

She closed her eyes against the bright overhead lights and the dizziness as she was wheeled, lying on a gurney, into an elevator, then down a long hallway. She flashed back, momentarily, to another hospital, another night, over a decade before.

The recollection made her want to curl into a fetal ball, but the medication and the IV needle lodged in her arm rendered any such movement impossible. Too much effort.

Another memory flooded her mind, soothed her. Mace had been with her that other time, too. He'd accompanied her to the hospital, holding her hand. He'd told her everything would be all right, that she was safe now, that nobody was going to hurt her. He'd promised to be there when the police came to question her, and he was as good as his word when she was discharged the following morning. He'd driven her to the police station, sat with her while two SVU detectives questioned her about the events of the night before, when, walking to her dorm, she'd been assaulted and nearly raped.

Mace, a student at the same California college, had heard the scuffle, hauled the man off Kelly and restrained him until the police arrived.

How could Mace have forgotten all that? Perhaps he made a habit of saving people. Did it happen so often that one incident blended into the next until it was all a blur?

She giggled at the thought.

Tomorrow, or maybe the next day, she would see Mace again. If he still didn't recall their first meeting, she'd just have to refresh his memory, though that wasn't her first priority.

She'd come to Mustang Creek to do business with the man, after all, not to renew their old — and brief — acquaintance. Great Grapes International, the company she worked for, wanted to establish a partnership with Mountain Winery, something they'd done successfully with other vintners.

Big of them, Kelly thought. As far as she could tell, the board members had zero doubt that everything would go their way; their confidence bordered on outright arrogance, in her opinion. She didn't know much about Mace Carson as a person, after one dramatic encounter and a few brief meetings during her attacker's trial, but recent online research had filled in a lot of gaps.

Carson wasn't likely to be swayed by the money GGI was prepared to offer, as the Carsons were among the wealthiest families in Wyoming. Mace's company appeared to be a labor of love, rather than a source of income; the winery was debt-free, and the net profits went to various charities.

Kelly had explained these things to upper management, of course, or tried to, anyway. And she had gotten exactly nowhere.

Failure wasn't an option, her boss, Dina, had informed her cheerfully. If GGI had a motto, it would be Rah-rah-rah.

Thinking about it, Kelly sighed. She knew the power of a positive mind-set, especially after years of company-sponsored "you can do this!" seminars, ranging from standard motivational talks and "trust exercises," like depending on someone to catch her when she fell backward, to trekking barefoot over beds of red-hot coals.

She'd done all those things and, yes, it was true — the experience of walking on burning embers *did* cast a new light on what was possible.

It was *also* true, however, that no amount of positivity or fearlessness or persistence was going to sway someone who didn't want to be swayed. Mace Carson, she was all but certain, fell into this category. He liked his independence far too much . . .

Kelly was in over her head this time, and she knew it, but she had too much riding on this deal to give up without even trying. She was up for a promotion of life-changing proportions, with some heavy-duty perks, such as profit sharing and stock options, access to company jets, opportunities to work overseas, six-figure bonuses and more than double her present salary.

The equation was a simple one: no deal, no promotion.

Lasso the moon, or crash and burn.

Bruised and scraped, dazed by pain meds and good old-fashioned exhaustion now that the adrenaline rush had subsided, Kelly closed her eyes. Sighed again.

She could worry, or she could sleep.

She chose the latter.

CHAPTER TWO

When Kelly opened her eyes again, morning was in full swing, and bright sunshine had replaced yesterday's rain. She took a few minutes to orient herself — she was in a hospital room in Mustang Creek, Wyoming. There were three other beds, all empty.

She performed a brief mental scan of her body.

A mild headache.

A few aches and pains.

In other words, nothing major.

A nurse's aide appeared, carrying a breakfast tray and sporting a cheery smile. Her name tag read Millie.

"If I were you," Millie began, deftly maneuvering the bed table into place and setting down the tray, "I'd go out and buy myself a lottery ticket. Considering what could have happened, you're a lucky woman."

Kelly smiled. "Maybe I'll do that."

"How do you feel?" Millie asked, lifting a metal lid to reveal a plate of runny scrambled eggs, limp toast and two strips of transparent bacon.

"Much better," Kelly answered, eyeing her breakfast with a wariness she hoped wasn't too obvious. Until about five seconds ago, she'd been hungry.

Millie chuckled, evidently the perceptive type. "First we patch people up," she joked, "and then we confront them with hospital food. Ironic, isn't it?"

Kelly grinned, picked up a slice of toast and nibbled at the edge. Her headache was already beginning to subside; this woman's mere presence was a tonic. "I don't suppose you know when I'll be discharged?" she ventured.

Millie sighed, though her smile didn't waver. She removed the plastic lid covering a cup of coffee. "Can't say," she replied. "The doctors are making their morning rounds, though, and I'm sure one of them will have an answer."

With that, she headed for the door, nearly colliding with a tall, dark-haired man in jeans, a long-sleeve white shirt, boots — and a badge. He smiled down at Millie, took off his hat and stepped aside to let her pass before entering the room.

"Ms. Wright?" he asked.

Kelly nodded, set down her coffee cup.

"My name's Spence Hogan," the man said, "and I'm the chief of police. Mind if I come in?"

Kelly was only half kidding when she answered. "Not at all. Unless you're here to arrest me for leaving the scene of an accident, that is."

His smile was the kind that probably caused a seismic shift every time it flashed across that tanned, rugged face. "You're in the clear, Ms. Wright," he said, crossing the room to stand a few feet from her bedside. "I'm here to take a statement, that's all. And, unfortunately, to tell you that your rental car is a total loss."

"I figured it would be," Kelly said, wondering why he'd come to the hospital personally rather than sending a deputy or someone from the office.

Clearly, he'd guessed what she was thinking, because there was a spark of amusement in his eyes. "I came by to look in on a friend who's recovering from an emergency appendectomy. It made sense to kill two birds with one stone, so to speak, and pay you a visit, too."

"Oh," Kelly said.

He took a smartphone from his shirt pocket and tapped an icon. "I just need a few details about what happened," he told her. His voice, deep and laconic, reminded her of Mace's, a fact that both jangled and soothed her nerves. His eyes were clear and direct as he met her gaze. "First, though, I have some news. The rental car people have been notified, and they're sending a replacement from Jackson. Should be here by the end of the day."

"That's good." Kelly hesitated, almost afraid to ask. "My things — my handbag and laptop and suitcases — were any of them recovered?"

"The purse and the laptop came through all right — evidently, they were thrown from the car while it was rolling down the hill, because my deputy found them on the bank." Spence Hogan paused, winced humorously. "I'm afraid everything else went up in smoke when the rig exploded."

Kelly gulped. "The car *exploded*?"

"Yes," Hogan answered, solemn now. He was probably thinking how easily Kelly herself might have been blown to flaming pieces; *she* certainly was.

"But it wasn't burning when Mace — Mr. Carson and I left. And the rain was really coming down hard."

Hogan raised one shoulder slightly, lowered it again. "Must've been some kind of delayed reaction. It happens."

A shudder ran through Kelly. She felt herself go pale and, for one awful moment, she thought she might throw up.

Concern furrowed the chief's brow, and he slipped the smartphone back into his pocket. "We'll talk about the accident later," he decided. "Do you want me to call a nurse or a doctor?"

Kelly swallowed hard, shook her head, attempted to smile. "I'm okay," she said.

And she was. Thanks to Mace Carson.

Talk about déjà vu.

She'd come to Mustang Creek to see Mace again — but not for *personal* reasons; she was on an important mission for GGI, and he was a vintner with a flair for innovation. She was here on business, in other words.

The opportunity to reiterate her gratitude for his help ten years ago was a bonus.

Chief Hogan took a business card from the same pocket housing his phone and laid it on the bedside table. "When you're feeling better, give me a call."

Kelly, busy breathing her way through the what-might-have-been scenario splashing across the screen of her mind, promised she'd be in touch. Hogan excused himself and left.

Five minutes later, Dr. Draper, a titian beauty with shadows of fatigue under her eyes, arrived. "Hello, Kelly. Remember me?"

Kelly smiled. "Yes. You were on duty in the ER last night, when I came in." She paused. "Was that a test?"

Dr. Draper laughed quietly. "It wasn't, actually, but I would've been pretty concerned if you'd said no." She came to stand beside the bed, took Kelly's pulse. "How are you feeling today? Any double vision? Pain?"

"No double vision," Kelly replied, as Dr. Draper put the earpieces of her stethoscope in place and listened to her patient's chest. "I had a slight headache when I woke up, but it's gone now."

Dr. Draper nodded, tugged the stethoscope free of her ears and let it dangle from her neck like a strand of pearls. "Any dizziness?"

"No," Kelly answered.

"I'm going to release you, then," the doctor said. "I strongly suggest you see your own physician in a week or so, and obviously, if there are symptoms in the meantime, you need to seek medical assistance right away."

"Okay," Kelly agreed. This woman wasn't much older than she was. What was it about doctors, whatever their age, that made a successful, confident adult feel like a five-year-old?

"Is there someone who can pick you up?" Dr. Draper asked. "I'd rather you didn't drive for a day or two." When Kelly didn't answer, the doctor went on. "Some of the local hotels provide car service, or we could arrange for a cab."

"That won't be necessary," a familiar voice said from the doorway.

Kelly's heartbeat quickened when she saw Mace standing there, looking fabulous to the infinite power in an ordinary cotton shirt, jeans and boots. His dark blond hair was still damp from a recent shower, and a fashionable stubble accented his strong chin. Like Chief Hogan, he held a Stetson hat in one hand.

Dr. Draper turned toward him. "Mace Carson," she said wryly. "What a surprise."

He smiled guilelessly. "Just being neighborly," he said. "I figured the lady would need a ride to her hotel."

The doctor looked back at Kelly. "Does that arrangement work for you?" she asked.

Kelly blushed like a teenager. "Yes," she answered.

Dr. Draper nodded. "All right, then," she said. "I'll sign you out, but you'll need to stop by the business office before you leave."

Mace saluted the doctor as she approached, and she gave him a shoulder bump as she passed, which made him laugh.

A brief silence fell.

Kelly broke it a minute or so later. "I have to get dressed," she said, and immediately felt lame for stating the obvious.

"I'll be at the nurses' station." Mace started to turn away, then turned back, a question dancing in his eyes. "You need any help?"

"No," Kelly said too quickly.

Mace grinned. "I'm sure one of the nurses would be glad to lend a hand."

"Go away," Kelly snapped, her cheeks burning again.

The grin broadened. "Give me a shout when you're ready," he said.

And then he was gone.

Half an hour later, after dealing with her insurance company online, she was riding in Mace Carson's truck again, headed for the resort.

Kelly still didn't have her purse — which contained her phone — or her laptop, and the clothes she'd packed so carefully for the trip had been reduced to the particle level.

After a moment's mourning for her Armani pantsuit, which had set her back a month's salary, she shifted her focus to what really mattered. She was alive and in one piece.

When Mace spoke, he caught her off guard. "You were Kelly Allbright, not Kelly Wright, when I knew you," he said without looking her way.

"You remembered," she said quietly.

"Yeah," Mace responded. "I didn't make the connection until I checked my schedule this morning and saw that my assistant had penciled you in — without mentioning it to me. Wanda is part-time, and she tends to be forgetful. Anyway, when I realized we had an appointment, I went online for some background info."

Kelly smiled, somewhat dreamily. She was okay, she really was, but she was still drifting from last night's drugs. There'd been a series of tests, she thought, but she couldn't be sure. "Sorry I missed the meeting," she said.

"No problem. I'm pretty flexible."

"Impressive, for a superhero."

"I'm just a man, Kelly. I did what anybody else would do, ten years ago on campus, and last night."

Memories of her near-rape, a decade before, circled Kelly like wolves. She'd been walking back to her dorm after a night class when, out of nowhere, she was attacked. She'd screamed and struggled, certain she was going to die. And then, suddenly, Mace was there.

He'd hauled her assailant off her, flung him aside. Called the police while keeping one booted foot on the guy's throat.

She'd scooted backward, a low, continuous moan shredding her throat.

"It's over," Mace had said. "You're safe now."

You're safe now.

"Did I ever thank you?" Kelly asked, as they made the turn onto the road leading to the resort.

"About ten thousand times," Mace said, not unkindly.

"I wasn't sure. I was so scared that night."

"I know," he told her sadly.

"You disappeared."

"I graduated," Mace stated. "Went to Napa to work with my grandfather. He owns a vineyard there."

She nodded. "Yeah, you told me about your family back then. When you were in LA for the trial." She paused. "Did you ever wonder what became of me? Afterward, I mean?"

He didn't reply, merely shrugged.

42

"I was married for a while," Kelly told him, aware that her end of the conversation was a bit disjointed. "After I graduated, I mean. It didn't work out."

"I'm sorry to hear that." The resort came into view, sprawling and elegant.

"Did you get married?"

"No," Mace answered.

"Why not?"

"I was busy," he said.

"I appreciate what you did, Mace. Both times."

"I know about a hundred guys who would have done the same thing."

"I don't," Kelly told him. "Thank you again."

"You're welcome," he said gravely.

They'd reached the portico in front of the resort. Mace brought the truck to a stop, and an attendant trotted over, smiling.

"Welcome," he said.

"Thanks," Kelly responded, strangely dazed.

"Ms. Wright has a reservation," Mace explained to the young man.

The attendant nodded. "Yes, Mr. Carson," he said.

"Mr. Carson?" Mace shot back, softening his brisk tone with a grin. "Chill, Jason. I've known you since you were in diapers, re-

43

member?"

Jason smiled. "I remember," he confirmed. "But we're supposed to call everybody either 'sir' or 'ma'am,' no matter who they are. It's in the manual."

Mace shook his head as if disgusted, but Kelly noticed the slight twitch at one corner of his mouth. "Fine," he said, opening his door. "I'll be out of here as soon as the lady's settled in. Mind if I leave the truck with you for a few minutes?"

"No, sir," Jason said. "I'll keep an eye on your ride until you get back." As he spoke, he opened Kelly's door, helping her out.

"I can take it from here," she said.

Mace didn't listen.

Neither did Jason.

She allowed Mace to escort her inside.

Her purse and laptop were waiting for her at the main desk.

"Ms. Wright," the receptionist said, tapping away at her computer keyboard. "Here you are. We expected you last night."

Kelly reached for her damp, mud-streaked purse, rummaged for her wallet, extracted her company credit card. "Something came up," she said.

Oddly, the clerk, a college-aged blonde, glanced questioningly at Mace before accepting the card.

"Just give the lady a room," he said.

Kelly was confused, but she didn't ask any questions and continued to hold out her credit card.

The clerk accepted it, swiped, handed it back. "How many key cards would you like?" she asked Kelly, with another look at Mace.

Kelly was mildly annoyed. *"One,"* she said pointedly.

"Certainly," the clerk said, beaming. She handed over the key card. "Enjoy your stay."

"Thank you," Kelly said, realizing she sounded ungrateful.

"Do you have luggage?" the young woman asked.

"No," Kelly answered, holding the other woman's gaze. "It blew up."

Beside her, Mace chuckled.

"Oh," the clerk said, looking baffled. Then she brightened. "We have several good shops right here on the premises. Clothing, makeup, toiletries — whatever you need."

"I'm glad," Kelly said, not sounding glad at all. What was the matter with her? This poor woman was trying so hard to be helpful. There was no reason to be testy.

And yet she was.

She felt unsettled, out of her element in this place, with this man.

Which was crazy on two counts. One, she'd stayed in fine hotels and resorts all over the world and fit right in, thank you very much. And, two, she couldn't think why she found her reactions to Mace Carson mildly disturbing. He was attractive, sure. He'd saved her life, not once, but twice.

And she was grateful, of course.

Then what was bothering her so much?

She didn't know.

She stepped away from the reception desk, key card in hand. She craved a hot shower and a room-service meal, but first, like it or not, she'd have to visit one or more of the resort shops, find something to wear, buy basic grooming supplies. Her linen pantsuit, the outfit she'd traveled in the day before, was wrinkled, and there were stains on the knees from crawling out of the rental car while Mace held the door, and landing on the wet, muddy pavement.

Caught up in practicality, Kelly was startled when Mace gently took her elbow.

"Let me know if you need anything," he said.

"What about our meeting —"

"We can reschedule," he replied. "I'll be in touch."

With that, he turned and walked away.

Kelly was relieved — she needed to think, and that was difficult to do with Mace Carson around — but part of her wanted to call out to him, even run after him, get him to stay, cling to him.

Cling to him. Like a drowning swimmer or some fragile, needy creature, afraid to be on her own.

Well, Kelly reminded herself, she was none of those things. She was smart, sophisticated, successful. She was *strong*. Thanks to therapy, a loving family, good friends and a lot of hard work, she'd long since put the trauma of the attack behind her. She'd made mistakes along the way, marrying Alan Wright — among other, lesser poor choices — but so what? Everybody screwed up once in a while, didn't they?

She turned resolutely and headed for the first of a series of small, eclectic-looking shops.

Twenty minutes later, she was in her room, a spacious minisuite with a balcony and a spectacular view of the Grand Tetons, looming snowcapped in the distance. They were a comforting reminder, those mountains, that the world was a solid place.

She tossed the bags containing her purchases onto the bed, scrounged in her soggy purse for her cell phone and peered at the screen. The familiar icons were there, although the battery was nearly dead.

She thumbed Contacts, found her boss's name, pressed Call.

Dina answered on the first ring. "Kelly? Oh, my God, *where have you been?* I've been trying to reach you since yesterday afternoon — I must've left a dozen messages!"

Kelly drew a deep breath and filled Dina in as succinctly as possible, feeling more exhausted with every word.

"You were in a *hospital*?" Dina broke in midway through the tale. "The car actually *blew up*?"

"Yes," Kelly replied with a sigh. She brought the remainder of the story home with the mention that she'd lost every stitch of clothing she'd chosen and packed so carefully before leaving her California condo the morning before. "Someone retrieved my laptop, which may or may not be in working order — I haven't checked yet. My phone survived, too, but it's in the red zone, so if the call drops, you'll know why."

"Do you want to come back to LA and regroup? We could reschedule your meeting with Mace Carson for next month, or whenever you feel ready."

"No. I'm here, and I'm fine, really. If you could ask Laura to stop by my place, gather up some of my clothes and overnight them to me at the resort, I'd be set."

Laura was Kelly's assistant, and she had keys to the condo. She would know which outfits would work best on a business trip.

"You're sure about this?" Dina sounded uncertain.

"I'm sure, Dina," Kelly confirmed, smiling. "I've come this far, and you know me, I'm all about follow-through."

"You're a real trouper," Dina said. Then, with a note of pleased resignation in her voice, she added, "Okay, then. I'll tell Laura, she'll know what you want her to do. In the meantime, charge your phone, have something to eat and don't worry about your laptop. If it won't boot up, order a replacement —"

Just then, Kelly's cell phone went dark and silent.

She set it down on the nightstand, found the charger and cord in the bottom of her purse and plugged it in.

After that, she followed the mental to-do list that had taken shape in her brain while she was talking with Dina.

Shower.

Put on one of the two wispy sundresses

she'd bought downstairs.

Brush her hair and her teeth.

Order room service. Something substantial, and to hell with worrying about carbs and fat grams. A cheeseburger, for instance. Or a thick steak and baked potato, loaded with sour cream, chives, grated cheddar.

Finally, boot up her laptop, fingers crossed.

If the sleek computer was ruined, her company would provide another, just as Dina had promised, but restoring her notes, contacts and a variety of templates for forms and contracts and the like would take up valuable time.

An hour later, scrubbed and dressed and fed, Kelly sat in the chair in front of the small writing desk, laptop open and ready, rubbed her hands together, murmured a prayer and hit the power button.

The screen lit up instantly.

"Yes," Kelly whispered. She clicked on icon after icon, periodically reminding herself to breathe.

Everything was there. It was a cyber-miracle.

The hotel phone gave a jangly ring, and she picked up the receiver. "Kelly Wright," she said, distracted.

The call was from the main desk. Her

replacement rental car had just been delivered, and was waiting for her in valet parking. Would she like the keys brought up?

Kelly thanked the caller and replied in the affirmative, before turning back to her computer, opening the mailbox and drafting a brief email to Dina, letting her know the laptop was working fine, for the moment at least. She ended the note quickly, opened a new window and flashed a message to her assistant, Laura, who responded almost immediately, brimming with OMGs and emoticons and thank-God-you're-all-rights.

Kelly was smiling to herself when someone knocked on her door and announced, "Valet service."

A city girl, as well as a frequent traveler, Kelly crossed the room, looked through the peephole and saw a young man in a staff uniform, grinning and holding up a set of keys.

She was back in action.

CHAPTER THREE

Mace was not a man given to obsessive thoughts; he was too busy for that, as a general rule. But at day's end, with the landscape he loved surrounding him, cloaked in the purplish-pink haze of dusk, he couldn't get Kelly Wright out of his mind.

He did the things he always did — checking the equipment in the winery, locking up his small, cluttered office an hour or two after he should have, walking between the long rows of vines, acres of them, looking for any sign of disease or blight. All the while, he was soaking in the singular energy of good dirt and growing things.

He'd probably missed supper — again — but he was used to that, and so was Harry, the Carson family's longtime cook and housekeeper. She usually left a plate in the fridge or warming in a slow oven, the food foil-covered, with his name scrawled atop it in black marker, invariably followed by a series of exclamation points.

Mace smiled, aware that the emphatic punctuation was meant for his two older brothers. Slater and Drake were active men with normal appetites, and as nourishing as Harry's meals were, neither of them was above foraging for leftovers in the search for a late-night snack. The labeling was her way of warning them off, should they be tempted to help themselves to Mace's supper, and it was effective — most of the time.

Both Slater and Drake were forceful types; like Mace, they'd been raised to go after what they wanted. But they usually knew better than to purloin grub Harry had posted as off-limits.

He was about to leave the vineyard and head for the house when his phone signaled an incoming text. He took it from his shirt pocket and squinted at the message, expecting to hear from a buyer, or one of his salespeople, or maybe his mother, reminding him, as she sometimes did, that even wine moguls had to eat and sleep.

Mace stopped, everything inside him quickening as he read the text. It was from Kelly, and it was brisk. Intriguing, too, on a personal level.

If you're free, let's have lunch tomorrow, here at the resort. I'm eager to give you a preliminary overview of what our company has to offer in terms of worldwide distribution. If you're agreeable, we can meet in the lobby at noon. I've made reservations at Stefano's.

Mace had been to more lunch and dinner meetings than he could count since the first viable crop of grapes had been ready to ferment, and not a single one of those meetings had ruffled him in the least. *This* one, however, turned his breath shallow and practically doubled his heart rate.

Why was that?

He scrolled back to the top of the text and read it again, wondering at his mixed reaction. The message was crisply phrased and to the point, all business, and he respected that; it was the way he did things, too. Time was money, and all that.

Still, something about this message, the cool professionalism, maybe, scraped at a tender place inside him and made him feel like a stranger.

Which was reasonable because, like it or not, he *was* a stranger to Kelly, as she was to him.

He'd happened to be in the right place at the right time to lend a hand when it was needed, ten years ago and again last night, but Kelly had thanked him on both occasions, and that was that, as far as he was concerned.

The first time around, it had been enough to know the assailant was in custody and, with his extensive rap sheet, on his way to the state prison for a long stretch.

Mace had been dating someone else back then, and there'd never been a romantic attachment between him and Kelly. He'd held Kelly's hand in the emergency room, been with her when the police took her statement, then come back to testify at the trial months later. They'd been acquaintances, not lovers or even friends, really.

He'd graduated within weeks of the incident and gone straight to his grandfather's vineyard in the Napa Valley for some hands-on training in the art of fine winemaking. He'd put in months of eighteen-hour days under the old man's tutelage, followed by the rigors of starting an operation of his own once he returned to Wyoming and the ranch.

The truth? He'd been too focused on his work to think about Kelly and that night on campus or the trial, except on rare occasions when some news report triggered the memory. Even his then-girlfriend, Sarah, as undemanding a woman as he'd ever known, had finally gotten tired of waiting for him to surface from the grind and pay her some attention. She'd sent him the modern version of a Dear John letter in the form of a text, something along the lines of, "Have a nice life." He'd been hurt, although he'd known, even then, that the relationship between him and Sarah was going nowhere.

It made sense that Sarah's message had rattled him, but *this* one?

Kelly had suggested a business lunch, period. Most likely, he'd imagined the standoffish tone, and that was troublesome, too. It was one thing to be concerned; the woman could easily have been seriously injured or killed if she hadn't gotten out of that car when she did.

The problem was, he'd been *more* than concerned.

He'd *hovered.* Even now, he was hyperaware of Kelly. Reading *nuances,* for God's sake, like some obsessive fool.

He had to step back, he decided. Get his bearings.

Stop thinking like a stalker.

That idea was ludicrous enough to bring on a grin as he walked toward the main house, looking forward to a hot shower, a warmed-up supper and a good night's sleep.

By morning, he'd be his old, levelheaded, roll-with-the-punches self.

He paused on the side porch, in a shaft of light from the hallway leading to the kitchen, took out his phone and thumbed a response to Kelly's text. It was short and sweet.

See you tomorrow at high noon.

True to her word, Laura had overnighted a packed suitcase to Kelly, and it must have arrived while she was having breakfast in the resort's small, busy bistro, because when she returned to her room, there it was on the luggage stand. When she opened it, she blessed her youthful assistant for making all the right choices.

Inside were:

Two tailored pantsuits and two silk camisoles.

A simple black cocktail dress and a strand of pearls, just in case there was a dinner meeting or an unexpected social event.

Shoes and bags for each outfit.

Laura had thought of everything; she had a talent for that. She'd also included plenty of lacy bras and panties, three pairs of jeans, several long-sleeve T-shirts, socks and sneakers. There was a soft cotton nightgown, as well. Plus a bathing suit and cover-up.

Finally, Laura had tucked in a zippered bag containing basic cosmetics and toiletries. Ordinarily, Kelly wore a minimum of makeup, only lip gloss, mascara, a tinted moisturizer and a little blusher.

Everything she needed was there.

She chose the day's clothing carefully, selecting the black pantsuit, a favorite of hers, with a short jacket fitted at the waist, and a beige camisole with plenty of lace at the neckline to soften the look.

It was the perfect outfit, the female version of the classic power suit, flattering but strictly in a no-nonsense, keep-your-distance-please kind of way.

Except for the lace, maybe.

Would that send Mace the wrong message? Make him think she wanted more than a handshake and a signed contract?

Seduction was definitely *not* her style. She was a serious, committed professional, and she never, but *never,* mixed business with pleasure.

Admittedly, she'd been shaken up after the accident that had wiped out rental car number one the day before. She'd probably come off as a little needy. Well, if she *had* given Mace that impression, she was determined to set things straight, ASAP.

No matter how sexy he was, with his loose-hipped cowboy walk and his broad shoulders and his brown-blond hair brushing the back of his collar, she would keep everything in perspective. She was grateful for his help, naturally, but she was no fairy-tale heroine, swooning and sighing in her prince's strong arms after the most recent encounter with a fire-breathing dragon.

No, sir. She would conduct their meetings, make her final presentation, complete with graphs and figures and flashy photos of jet-setters enjoying fine wine in exotic places, and then she'd return to LA and the satisfying, if somewhat lonely, life she'd made for herself there. She had a great job, a nice place to live, fine clothes. She had friends.

Well, actually, she had business colleagues rather than friends, but with her schedule, who had time for girls' nights out, weekend spa visits and gossip?

She certainly didn't. They simply didn't fit into her schedule.

And *forget* romance, much as she missed the benefits. She'd gone on exactly six dates in the three years since her divorce, and every one of them had been disastrous for one reason or another.

Feeling her hard-core commitment to her

career slip just slightly, Kelly squared her shoulders and silently reminded herself that, yes, she'd once dreamed of a happy marriage and children. She'd totally missed the boat, but nobody had it all. In her own experience, jobs like hers took up too much space and energy to coexist with a spouse in a satisfying way. Her own divorce, and those of a good many of her associates, proved the theory.

She'd seen a few couples make it work, of course, but they were exceptions to the rule, and, in her circles, incredibly rare. Plus, there was no telling how much of their alleged happiness was an act, a mere facade, a cover-up for secret shouting matches and God knew what other kinds of dysfunction.

It wasn't for her; she was sure of that.

Mace Carson wasn't the first attractive man she'd encountered, and he wouldn't be the last, so she'd better keep her perspective. Looking the way he did, Mace surely had his choice of women eager to share his bed, and even if he *did* want to settle down, which she doubted, he was country, through and through. He was probably interested in an old-fashioned girl, content to stay at home instead of working toward goals of her own. A wife who'd prepare his meals, iron his shirts, bear and raise his children, vote as he voted, the whole bit.

Although she knew she wasn't being fair, Kelly shuddered at the images unfolding in her mind.

She wanted no part of such a life.

Not that he'd shown any signs of offering.

Strangely deflated all of a sudden, Kelly went on about her business. With renewed purpose.

For all his private resolutions to take a step back and stay cool, the sight of Kelly standing in the resort lobby, looking sharp in a black pantsuit with a splash of beige lace in the V of her fitted one-button jacket, struck Mace like a punch to the solar plexus.

Hot damn, he thought. *Hello, square one.*

He'd spent half the night trying to untangle the complicated emotions Kelly Wright stirred in him, things he'd never felt before with any of the women he'd dated, including his college girlfriend, Sarah. And he'd expected to *marry* her.

After Sarah, and his return to the ranch following the apprenticeship with his grandfather, he'd dated a lot, going out with local women — Mustang Creek had its share of smart, sexy females — but the majority were visitors, come to ski in winter or explore nearby Yellowstone Park in summer, or just to relax at the resort.

In other words, they were merely passing through. They'd had lives and careers in other places, and that had been fine with Mace. It was when the talk turned to settling down, as it inevitably did at some point, that he started backpedaling like crazy.

Now, here was a whole different Kelly from the damp, shaken one he'd driven to the hospital the night before. This was the real her, no doubt — strong, independent, ready to sell him on some kind of partnership with her company.

It was a brand-new rodeo.

But the lace . . .

Did he want to take her to bed?

Hell, yes. He was a normal human being, and Kelly was sexy as all get-out. He even suspected she might be receptive to a little down-home country charm, followed by some sheet-tangling.

The problem was, Kelly was vulnerable in some way the others hadn't been. If and when he made love to her, he wanted it to be for the right reasons.

Not because she was grateful for his help, then *or* now. And not because she was bruised and far from home and in need of some comfort.

She owed him nothing, in his opinion, and he certainly didn't expect a sexual payback. No. Unless Kelly came to him willingly, with a clear head, he wouldn't lay a hand on her, no matter how badly he wanted her.

All these thoughts tumbled through his mind as he stood, hat in hand, watching her watch him.

Maybe their gazes held too long, because after a moment, Kelly's air of confidence seemed to slip just a little. She looked a mite uncertain as she eyed Mace's crisp white Western shirt, jeans and polished boots. A pink blush blossomed in her cheeks.

Fortunately, she recovered quickly, approaching him with a let's-do-business smile and a hand extended for a shake.

"Hello, Mr. Carson," she said.

The formality of her greeting both saddened and amused him, but he tried not to let either response show as he took a firm grasp of the extended hand and shook it. "Mr. Carson, is it?" he asked mildly. "How about calling me Mace?"

"Mace," she repeated, looking nervous again. As before, she reined that in quickly — though not quite quickly enough. "I'm Kelly," she said, and then seemed embarrassed.

He grinned. "Yes, I know."

"Right," she said, and swallowed visibly.

"You mentioned lunch?" Mace prompted with gentle humor. "In that text you sent me last night, I mean?"

"Yes," she said, still off her game. "Lunch. I made a reservation at Stefano's."

"Good choice," Mace said. He gestured with his hat, indicating the restaurant's entrance on the far side of the lobby. "Shall we? I'm hungry."

Again, that fetching blush colored Kelly's cheeks. "Absolutely," she said after drawing a breath so deep it raised and lowered her slender shoulders.

He imagined those shoulders bared, smooth and sun-kissed, along with her perfect breasts.

Mace shook off the image. Thought about offering his arm, then decided against it. Kelly was clearly on edge, and he didn't want to make things any more difficult for her — or for himself — than they already were.

"Relax," he said in a husky whisper. "This is business, remember?"

Her smile was on the wobbly side, but it was a smile, at least, and it was beautiful. "I guess I'm still a bit jumpy after the other night. Sorry."

They were moving by then, approaching

64

the restaurant. "You're feeling okay, though?" he asked. "Nothing hurts?"

She shook her head. Her honey-colored hair was done up in a fashionably sloppy bun, exposing her long, elegant neck, and Mace suppressed a powerful urge to take her shoulders in his hands, trace the length of that silken flesh with his mouth.

"I'm in great shape," she said.

You can say that again, Mace thought wryly. But all he said was, "Good."

They reached the podium in front of Stefano's, and Kelly took charge, giving her name to the hostess on duty and saying she had a lunch reservation for twelve o'clock.

Cindy Henderson, the kid sister of one of Mace's closest friends, beamed a smile at Kelly and nodded, taking two menus from the shelf under the podium. "Yes, Ms. Wright. Your table is ready." Cindy turned twinkling eyes on Mace. "Hey, Mace," she added. "It's been a while. How've you been?"

"Same as usual," Mace replied easily. "You?"

"I landed that full-ride scholarship I was after," Cindy answered proudly, looking over one shoulder as she led the way to a window-side table. "I'm majoring in agriculture." A pause. "Maybe you'll give me a job

65

at Mountain Winery after I graduate?"

Mace chuckled. "Maybe," he said. "Depends on your grades."

Kelly, he noted, was taking in the exchange with amused interest as she walked beside him, though she said nothing.

"My *grades*?" Cindy asked. "Mace Carson, you know darn well I've had a 4.0 average for the last four years."

"That was high school," Mace teased. "College is harder."

Cindy was cheerfully scornful. "I can *handle* college," she said, keeping her voice down as they wove between tables, each one occupied by locals or resort guests or some combination of the two. "And I'm serious about working at the winery after I get my degree."

"Fine and dandy," Mace said. "But graduation is a ways off, isn't it? A lot of things could happen between now and then. You might decide working at a winery isn't for you, once you've seen how many other options there are. And you'll meet plenty of guys, too — a lot more than you have here in the old hometown. Suppose you run into Mr. Right, and he has plans that don't mesh with yours?"

"No way that's going to happen," Cindy said with the unshakable optimism of a sheltered kid raised in a small town. "I'm coming back here after college and marrying Jimmy Trent."

Jimmy Trent was Cindy's high-school boyfriend; he was a couple of years older than she was, and he'd joined the air force on his eighteenth birthday. Last Mace had heard, he was in flight school. Once his enlistment was up, he hoped to work for one of the major airlines and, after he'd racked up enough hours, open a small charter operation.

Out of the corner of his eye, Mace saw Kelly smile again, although she still kept whatever she was thinking to herself. She didn't know Jimmy was in the service and might be deployed to a war zone as soon as he finished his training.

"All I'm saying," Mace persisted mildly, "is that things can change."

Not surprisingly, Cindy wasn't convinced. "Not for Jimmy and me," she said. "We have goals and we know how to reach them. Plus, we're meant to be."

"I hope you're right," Mace said. And he meant it.

He should've realized his friend's kid sister thought she and Jimmy had their future locked in; she was too young and, after her solid upbringing, too innocent to understand how tricky life could be.

Cindy rolled her eyes, smiling that sweet smile of hers. "You sound just like Mom and Dad *and* Mike," she said. Mike was her brother, more than a dozen years her senior. Mike worked for Fish and Wildlife, and he and Mace went way back.

"Yes," Mace agreed, sitting down. "And maybe you ought to listen to our advice."

Fat chance. He'd been Cindy's age once and, back then, he'd known everything there was to know, and then some.

Cindy handed Kelly a menu and gave one to Mace. "Next, you're going to say Jimmy and I ought to let things unfold," she said with more than a hint of sarcasm, "instead of mapping out our whole lives in advance, because we're both going to have a lot of new experiences and meet a lot of new people."

"That's about the size of it," Mace said with a grin and a shake of his head. Might as well change the subject, since he was getting nowhere with this kid. "What's the special today?"

"Mushroom risotto with baked chicken breast," Cindy answered, waiting. "Aren't you going to warn me about fast-talking college boys with only one thing on their minds?"

Kelly's eyes sparkled as she watched him over the top of her menu, and he could see she was trying not to laugh.

"Would it do any good?"

"It would be a waste of breath," Cindy responded briskly. "I'm not interested in any guy but Jimmy."

"Right," Mace said with, he hoped, the appropriate note of cheerful skepticism.

Cindy's smile didn't falter, but then it rarely did. "*You* dated the same person all through college," she said. "Her name was Sarah, wasn't it? She came back to Mustang Creek with you a couple of times, during Christmas break."

Mace stole a glance at Kelly and saw that she was leaning forward slightly, a tiny smile curving her mouth, one eyebrow raised.

"And look how well *that* turned out," he said.

"Oh." For once, Cindy was taken aback.

"Yes," Mace said matter-of-factly. "Oh. Any chance of getting something to eat in the near future?"

Cindy had the grace to look embarrassed, but although her smile wobbled a little, it held. "Would you like a drink while you're looking at the menu?" she asked, finally remembering, evidently, that she had a job to do.

Mace met Kelly's gaze and raised his eyebrows questioningly.

"We'll definitely want wine," Kelly said, speaking for the first time since they'd stepped up to the podium at the restaurant's entrance. "Something with the Mountain Winery label, of course. In the meantime, I'll have a glass of unsweetened iced tea, please, with lemon and lots of ice. Later, when we know what we're having to eat, we'll decide on the wine."

"Coffee for me, thanks," Mace added, relieved at the change of subject.

Cindy bustled away.

"What's good here?" Kelly asked, studying the menu. "I love risotto, but I'm not in the mood."

Mace grinned. "*Everything* is good," he replied.

Kelly smiled. "That really narrows it down," she said, meeting his eyes and then revisiting the choices listed. "The lobster salad sounds tasty." A slight frown creased her otherwise smooth forehead. "Of course, we're a long way from the ocean, so seafood might be risky."

"Not here," Mace said. "Stefano has his lobsters flown in from Maine, alive and kicking — so to speak."

Kelly winced briefly, probably imagining

the cooking process. "There really is a Stefano?" she asked. "It's not just the name of the restaurant?"

"There is most definitely a Stefano. He's a master chef and he happens to own this place." He paused. "The restaurant, which is a five-star establishment, by the way. Not the resort."

"And he wound up in Mustang Creek, Wyoming?" Kelly asked with a teasing note in her voice.

Mace leaned closer. "Yep," he drawled, smiling. "Strange as it might appear, he prefers snowcapped mountains and wide-open spaces to concrete and skyscrapers."

"I'm going with the lobster salad, then," Kelly said. "What about you?"

"I'm a sucker for Stefano's prime rib. It's excellent."

"Then we'll order red wine *and* white," she said. "You choose, since you're the expert."

Cindy returned with the iced tea and coffee. "I'll bring over a basket of rolls in a minute or two," she said, her smile as bright and genuine as ever. "One of the guys in the kitchen is taking a fresh batch out of the oven."

"Yum," Kelly said, the tip of her tongue slipping out to moisten her lips.

Mace shifted in his chair, cleared his throat. Just like that, he'd gone as hard as a railroad spike.

"Do you need more time?" Cindy asked. "Or shall I take your orders now?"

"May I?" Mace asked Kelly, glad the lower half of his body was hidden by the tabletop and its pristine white cloth.

Kelly nodded, almost shyly. "Please," she said.

He ordered the lobster salad for Kelly, prime rib with all the trimmings for himself, along with glasses of his best cabernet and the award-winning pinot grigio he was so proud of. At his recommendation, both were among a group of popular house wines available by the glass as well as the bottle.

"Now," he said, when Cindy had moved away, "let's hear your proposal."

Kelly looked alarmed for a moment, a reaction Mace enjoyed while it lasted. "Oh," she said. "Yes."

"Or," Mace went on smoothly, before she had a chance to launch into whatever pitch she planned to make, "we could enjoy our lunch, get to know each other a little and talk business later. I'd like to show you the winery this afternoon, if you're up to it. That way, you can experience the place firsthand."

Kelly glanced down at her expensive, take-no-prisoners outfit with uncertainty. It was perfect for a boardroom, no argument there, but a working winery and acres of dusty vineyards? Not exactly.

"You'll want to check out the grapes," he added when she said nothing.

The hesitation was over. "I'd like that," she said quietly.

Mace smiled, as pleased as if she'd agreed to go skinny-dipping in a sun-dappled creek. He let his gaze rest on the lace peeking from beneath her jacket, then looked quickly away. "You ought to swap out those clothes first, though. We're talking behind the scenes here, not just the tasting room. Comfortable shoes will save you a few blisters, too."

He fell silent. For a long interval, they simply stared at each other, something invisible and yet entirely real arcing between them.

Mace couldn't have said what was going through Kelly's mind, but *he* was picturing her upstairs in her room, with the shades drawn, slipping out of that perfectly fitted pantsuit, taking off the slacks, the jacket, the lace-trimmed top, slowly revealing her shapely legs and arms. He put the image in freeze-frame before she got to her bra and panties, which were probably skimpy enough to be sexy as hell, because his groin, already giving him trouble, had turned to granite.

At this rate, they'd be at their table for the rest of the day, just so he wouldn't have to stand up and let Kelly see how much he wanted her. If it came to that, he decided, he'd "accidentally" spill a glass of ice water into his lap, or maybe a whole pitcherful.

He drew a series of deep breaths.

Kelly, still looking directly into his face, fiddled with her napkin.

Cindy broke the spell by delivering the promised bread basket and, soon after that, two glasses of wine.

Kelly's hand trembled almost imperceptibly as she helped herself to a roll. "Still warm," she said, somehow combining a sigh and a croon as she spoke. She split the bun between her fingers, and steam escaped, along with the familiar yeasty aroma. Then she reached for a butter knife.

It was such an ordinary, everyday thing to do, buttering a dinner roll, and yet there was an erotic element to her movements that struck Mace like a body blow, forcing him to look away. Again. Just as he recovered his equilibrium and turned to face her again, she took a bite.

"Mmm," Kelly murmured, eyes closed. "Delicious."

Barely suppressing a groan, Mace shut his eyes, too. *Get a grip, Carson,* he told himself.

"Is something wrong?" Kelly asked after a second or two, with a note of genuine concern. Clearly, she was unaware of the effect she was having on her potential business partner.

"I'm fine," Mace said. The lie came out sounding hoarse, but if Kelly noticed, she didn't let on.

"I love fresh bread," she added with a blissful sigh.

Cindy returned, bringing Kelly's lobster salad and his prime rib. Mace was relieved by the interruption, and although he'd lost his appetite somewhere along the line, he picked up his knife and fork.

Kelly smiled with a hint of sadness as she watched the girl walk away, resuming her duties. "I was like that once," she said softly. An instant later, her expression made it obvious that she regretted the remark.

Mace forgot his own concerns as he studied Kelly's face. "You were like what once?" he asked, reaching for his cabernet.

She lowered her eyes for a moment, raised them again. Their gazes connected.

The charge reminded him of the business

end of a cattle prod.

Kelly's spine was straight as she raised her shoulders on an indrawn breath and then looked down again. "Full of plans, I guess," she answered reluctantly. "You know. Convinced that things would turn out the way I expected."

Mace gave a slight, rueful smile. "I can relate," he said.

She paused, a forkful of lobster salad halfway to her mouth. "You can?" She seemed surprised. "Are you telling me you're disappointed in your life?"

Mace shook his head. "It's not that. I love what I do. Love living on the ranch — it might sound corny, but the place is literally in my blood." He paused, then went on. "There isn't much I would change."

"But there is . . . something?"

He sighed. He'd opened himself up to that question, he supposed. "I always figured I'd have a wife and kids by now," he admitted.

She took that in, quietly chewing the food she'd just put in her mouth.

"What about you?" he asked. *What dimmed your light, Kelly? Was it the attack, that night on campus? Or something that happened afterward?* "You said you were 'full of plans' once."

Kelly looked uncomfortable as she swallowed the bite of food, then took a sip from her wineglass. She smiled with an effort, a kind of fragility that tugged at Mace's insides. "The usual things. Life in general, I guess."

"Can you be more specific?" he asked.

She dodged his words neatly. "You wanted to be married, start a family?"

Mace smiled. "Nice try," he said. "But the conversational ball is still in your court, isn't it?"

Kelly sighed, put down her knife and fork. Pondered her reply. "I guess so," she said, speaking so softly that Mace had to strain to hear. She went on, after more consideration. "Like I told you, I was married for a little while. My husband was a decent guy — he never cheated or anything like that. It was just that we wanted . . . different things, Alan and I."

"Such as?"

"I wanted a few more years to build my career. Alan wanted children right away."

"You didn't want kids?"

"I did," Kelly said. "But we were so young, just getting started. I thought we should wait until we were on solid financial ground, with a house and a bank account and everything." She fixed her gaze on something beyond the window beside their table. "That was the agreement from the beginning," she added. "I wasn't asking Alan to wait forever, just until we were ready."

"Sounds reasonable," Mace told her.

Kelly nodded. Her eyes were somber, even a little misty. "I thought so," she agreed, dropping her gaze to her salad. Picking up her knife and fork once more. When she looked at Mace again, she'd rustled up a flimsy smile. "Your turn."

Mace ached for her, but he returned her smile. "Fair enough," he said. "But there isn't a whole lot to tell."

"Sarah," Kelly prompted gently. Thanks to Cindy, that much of his personal history was out in the open, anyway.

"Sarah," he confirmed. "We dated in college."

Kelly waited, saying nothing.

Mace had always kept his own counsel, especially where his love life was concerned, but for some reason, with this woman he hardly knew, he found himself talking.

"We were in some of the same classes, freshman year, and we just sort of gravitated toward each other as time went by. Maybe it was because we had some things in common — Sarah grew up on a farm, I was raised on a ranch — and I think we both

78

felt a little out of our element at the beginning, a couple of country kids on a crowded campus in a major city, a long way from home."

"Did you love her?"

Mace weighed his answer. "I thought so at the time," he told her. "I was pretty torn up when she called it off, but looking back, I know she was right. I have two older brothers, and they're both married to incredible women. Seeing Slater with Grace and Drake with Luce — short for Lucinda — completely happy, sharing everything and starting families . . . Well, that got me wondering if I'd ever actually known what real love was like."

Kelly smiled a soft, sad smile. "My parents are crazy about each other," she said. "I used to think every marriage was like theirs."

Mace wanted to take Kelly's hand, but something stopped him. "Mine were pretty tight, too, as I recall," he told her. "But our dad died when my brothers and I were young, and our mother never remarried. She's a great mom, and she certainly taught us to admire and respect women, but when it came to love between a man and a woman, we didn't have a whole lot to go on."

Kelly nodded and her eyes misted over, although she was quick to blink the moisture away. "Sorry," she said.

Mace knew she'd run into some kind of emotional roadblock, and he wasn't going to push her past it. After all, this was supposed to be a business meeting, if an informal one.

True, Kelly had been the one to get the conversational ball rolling, but she probably hadn't expected things to get so heavy, so soon. It was time to lighten up, get outside, soak up some sunshine and breathe some fresh air.

He pushed his plate away. "I'm about finished here," he said. "How about you?"

Kelly surveyed her half-eaten salad with a combination of relief and regret. "I'm definitely full."

"In that case, why don't you head on upstairs and change your clothes? I'll sign the check and meet you in the lobby in a few minutes."

Kelly's eyes, tearful a minute before, glinted with a sort of mischievous triumph. "I've already taken care of it," she said.

Mace laughed and spread his hands in good-natured surrender. "So much for my reputation as a macho cowboy," he said. "By nightfall, everybody in Mustang Creek will know I let a woman pick up the lunch check. For all practical intents and purposes, I'm ruined."

Kelly made a face, retrieving her handbag from the floor beside her chair. "Oh, well," she teased. "I'm sure you'll reestablish your alpha-male status in no time."

Exactly what, Mace wondered, as he rose to pull back her chair, did *that* mean?

Had it been a gibe — or an invitation?

Most likely neither, he decided. He was doing that nuance thing again.

As he and Kelly walked toward the exit, and the lobby beyond, Cindy hurried to catch up.

"Was something wrong with the food?" she asked in an anxious whisper.

Mace waited for the ever-present smile to slip from Cindy's face, but it didn't.

"Everything was great," Kelly said, quick to reassure her. "Really. I guess we just got too caught up in . . . talking business."

Cindy seemed pleased. And reassured. Stefano, the chef–restaurant owner, was notoriously sensitive about his creations, and when plates came back to his kitchen with leftovers on them, he tended to fret. In fact, he'd been known to confront retreating diners in the lobby or even the parking

lot, offering free meals, wanting explana-
tions.

Mace waited until they'd reached the
lobby to call Kelly on the fib. "That was
'talking business'?" he asked with a grin.

Kelly didn't miss a beat. "No," she admitted brightly. "But I did enjoy the wine."

With that, she turned and made for the
elevators.

CHAPTER FOUR

The moment the elevator doors closed, Kelly sighed, thankful to be the only passenger, and punched the button for her floor with a little more force than strictly necessary. Then she leaned back against the wall, her cheeks flaming, her heart beating too fast.

What or *who* had possessed her, back there in the restaurant?

She certainly hadn't been herself, Kelly Wright, the ultimate professional, a top executive with one of the most innovative corporations in the country, if not the world, and on the fast track to a vice presidency.

She'd planned to get things back on course, dispel any impression Mace might have, after the accident, that she was weak, needy, perhaps even desperate for a big, strong man to protect little ol' helpless Kelly from a dangerous world.

Instead, she'd behaved like a ninny, asking personal questions about girlfriends and parents, revealing the fault lines in her brief marriage and the resulting disappointment she'd hardly admitted to *herself,* let alone the owner of a winery meant for great things. If she'd blown this deal, Dina would kill her when she got back to LA, and she could flat out forget the promotion to VP of Sales.

Goodbye profit sharing. Farewell, stock options and private jets.

The doors opened, and Kelly stepped out of the elevator, rummaging in her purse for her key card, still mentally kicking herself. She'd hosted dozens of semi-casual lunches in the course of her career, and she knew the drill — stay in charge of the situation, but smile a lot and encourage the standard harmless small talk. Listen to stories about golf tournaments, fishing trips, that recent vacation. Scroll through endless snapshots and videos on the other person's smartphone. Remember every name mentioned — not only those of the significant other and any children they might have, but those of dogs, cats and parakeets, as well.

Today, she'd broken all her own rules. Or most of them, anyway.

How was she going to get this project back

on track?

She had no idea.

Maybe Dina had a point, Kelly thought, when she'd suggested postponing the pitch until some later date. She could go back to LA, regroup, return to Mustang Creek in a few weeks or a month, and try again.

But whether her boss was right or wrong, Kelly knew it wasn't in her to chicken out that way; she'd lose respect for herself if she waved the white flag, made excuses and beat a hasty retreat — and Mace would know exactly why she was running away.

She stopped in front of the door to her room, shoved the key card in the slot at a crooked angle, got the blinking red light that meant the lock was still engaged and withdrew the card in frustrated disgust.

After drawing a deep breath, holding it for a count of six, and letting it out slowly, she tried again. This time, the lock clicked, and she pushed open the door.

Inside, she kicked off her shoes, not caring where they landed.

"This is ridiculous," she said aloud. "Get it together, Kelly. *Now.*"

Maybe she got it together and maybe she didn't, but she found a pair of jeans and a pretty T-shirt, pink with white stripes, and laid them on the bed while she let her hair down and shook it out. Moving purposefully, she took off the pantsuit, hanging the jacket and slacks neatly in the closet, pulled on the jeans and T-shirt, then her socks and sneakers.

She was still nervous, which was not only unprofessional but silly . . . and yet she was excited, too. Not just because she was spending the afternoon with Mace, either. Her interest in the winemaking process, from growing and tending to the grapes to bottling, labeling and marketing the finished product, was genuine.

No matter how many vineyards she visited — and she'd visited plenty of them, from the sunny slopes of France and Italy to California, Arizona and central Washington State — she learned something new every time.

After giving her hair a quick brushing in front of the bathroom mirror and reapplying her lip gloss, Kelly placed a call to the valet desk and asked to have her rental car brought around to the front of the hotel.

And then she waited five minutes, so she wouldn't seem too eager to meet up with Mace in the lobby.

It was sweet agony, that little sliver of time. Part of her wanted to crawl under the bed and refuse to come out until Mace gave up and left, while another part urged her to get back to him as fast as she could, taking the stairways between floors rather than waiting for an elevator.

Instead, she watched the minutes blink by on the bedside clock, but it wasn't easy.

It was a huge relief to pick up her handbag, make sure her key card was inside, and leave her room. She walked sedately along the hallway toward the elevator, pushed the button and waited, glad there was no one around to see how hard she was working to stay calm.

Moments later the elevator arrived. There was a family inside, a husband, a wife, a girl of five or six and a boy no older than four. They were wearing swimsuits, the woman sporting a striped cover-up, as well, all clutching beach towels and smiling with anticipation.

"We're going to the pool!" the little boy informed Kelly, practically jumping up and down in excitement. "I'm gonna swim!"

Kelly smiled, momentarily distracted from her own misgivings about the afternoon ahead by a pang of envy. If her marriage had worked out, she might've had children of her own by now. "That's great," she said, meaning it.

The little girl, wearing flip-flops on her

tiny feet, gave her brother a tolerant look. "Where else would we be going in swimsuits?" she asked.

The woman placed a hand on her daughter's blond head, smiled at Kelly and said, "She's six, going on thirteen."

The man laughed. "God help us," he said.

Kelly made a mental note to reassess her ideas about the nonexistence of happy families in today's warp-speed world, but that would have to wait. She needed to stay focused on her next goal — convincing Mace Carson she knew her stuff when it came to marketing fine wine.

They reached the lobby, and the doors opened.

She stepped out, turning to the picture-perfect family. The pool was another floor down. "Have fun swimming," she told them.

"We will!" the boy cried as the doors closed again.

She was still looking back, smiling, when she collided with a hard and distinctly masculine body.

Mace immediately gripped her shoulders, steadying her.

He grinned when Kelly faced him, all too aware that she was blushing again.

"Oops," she said. "Sorry."

"I was about to say the same when you

88

beat me to it," Mace said, dropping his hands to his sides now that she was in no danger of ricocheting off all that man-muscle. "Except, maybe, for the 'oops.' "

Perhaps it was the smile in Mace's eyes, or his easy manner, or the prospect of an afternoon visiting the winery and walking through the vineyard, but Kelly felt a subtle shift. She finally relaxed, let go of the self-doubt she'd been feeling for nearly twenty-four hours.

In short, she was herself again. No less attracted to Mace Carson, admittedly, but *herself,* focused and positive and brimming with creative ideas.

"The truck's out front," Mace said, gesturing for her to precede him. "And, by the way, you look great in those jeans."

She sent him a sidelong look as they headed in that direction. "I'll be taking my own car," she said. Yes, the doctor had advised her to wait a few days before driving, but she felt fine. "The last time I drove, I almost went over a cliff. I guess this is the automotive version of getting back on the horse after being thrown."

"Makes sense," Mace said. "Think you can keep it on the road between here and the ranch?"

Kelly laughed. "We're about to find out,"

she said.

Outside, under the huge portico in front of the hotel, Mace's truck awaited. A blue compact was parked behind it, and Kelly supposed it was her rental car, since there were no other vehicles around.

Sure enough, one of the parking attendants, a pretty young girl about the same age as Cindy, who'd served their lunch, hurried forward.

"Ms. Wright?"

"That's me," Kelly said, pulling out the tip she'd tucked into her jeans pocket during the five-minute wait upstairs in her room. The girl smiled, walked over to the driver's side of the blue car, Kelly following, and opened the door for her.

Kelly slipped behind the wheel, took a single deep breath and handed over the gratuity. "Thanks . . ." she said, squinting at the valet's name tag, "Maggie."

"Thank *you,*" Maggie replied, accepting the tip. About to close Kelly's door, she turned her smile on Mace, who was standing beside his truck, an expectant grin on his sexy, unshaven face.

Maggie laughed. "You can open your *own* darned door, Mace Carson — sir."

Mace shook his head, as if to lament the state of today's youth.

Then he climbed into his late-model truck, with its extended cab and outsize tires. It was black — Kelly hadn't noticed many details the night before — and would've looked fancy if it weren't for the mud splatters left over from yesterday's bad weather.

Maggie turned back to Kelly and smiled. "You have a nice day, Ms. Wright," she said, shutting the car door.

Kelly's palms were moist where she gripped the wheel and, for a moment, she was almost queasy as muscle-memory reminded her, in no uncertain terms, of the terrifying sensations she'd felt when she'd lost control of the *other* rental car on that slippery country road.

That was then, she reminded herself firmly, and this was now. The sky was clear and achingly blue, the sun was bright, the mountains majestic in the near distance.

Kelly kept her eyes on the road, following Mace's lead. Her brief trepidation was gone, and good riddance. She was a California native, after all, and she'd lived in the LA area since college. If she could handle those infamous freeways, the 405 included, she could certainly manage the highways and byways around Mustang Creek, Wyoming.

She was back on the proverbial horse and

ready to ride like the wind.

Ten minutes later, Kelly found herself in an alternate dimension, surrounded by open spaces and dazzled by breathtaking scenery. She took in the ranch house, which looked more like a midsize hotel, the stables Mace would probably describe as a "barn," the rail fences and windswept pastures populated by cattle and a variety of horses.

She'd visited many vineyards in connection with her job, but this place was more than that.

She parked at the top of the long gravel driveway, alongside Mace's truck. Shut off the rental car and climbed out.

Kelly was a city mouse; she liked shopping malls, upscale boutiques and trendy bars. She enjoyed attending corporate meetings, flying first class, staying in fine hotels, although, for all that, she wasn't particularly status conscious. She was responsible; she had an impressive investment portfolio, owned her condo outright and paid the balances on her credit cards in full every month.

Her wardrobe was carefully coordinated and yes, expensive, and her handbags cost more than the car she'd driven in college — no knockoffs for *this* girl.

As the cliché had it, clothes didn't make

the woman, but there was something to that idea about dressing for success.

All of which meant she was out of her element on a cattle ranch.

And fascinated by the differences.

As she and Mace met up between their vehicles, she felt that same dizzying sensation, but instead of questioning the reaction, she simply enjoyed it.

Was Mace her type?

The men she'd dated, although there weren't many of them, had been smooth and sophisticated, wearing tailored suits and driving sleek foreign cars, but Mace was off that grid. Sure, he was intelligent and articulate; he was also an enigma, wealthy in his own right, even without the wine operation, yet comfortable in jeans, boots and shirts that probably came from a modest Western store.

The man had nothing to prove to anyone, and he knew it.

While Kelly, her undeniable success notwithstanding, had to shift mental gears in every new place or unfamiliar situation, Mace seemed comfortable in his own skin, as that other old saying went. He was flexible, certainly — his innovative wines proved that — but deep down, he was as solid as the mountains of Wyoming.

He loved this land, this ranch; he'd said the place was in his blood, and being there, Kelly knew it hadn't been an idle statement. Intuitively, she understood that Mace was one of those rare people who carried the essence of their home within themselves. They *belonged,* no matter where they happened to be.

It was an enviable quality.

"Ready for a look around?" Mace asked, bringing Kelly back from her meandering thoughts.

"Absolutely," she said, landing in the present moment with a thump. "Where do we start?"

Mace grinned, shoved a hand through his hair. "With the winery, I guess," he replied after a glance in the direction of the grand house. "Harry will kill me in my sleep if I don't introduce you to her, but that can wait."

"Harry is a 'her'?"

He nodded. "She's the family housekeeper, and the best cook this side of the Mississippi, though if you quote me to Stefano on that, I'll have to deny everything."

Kelly laughed. "If I happen to run into Stefano the Great, I'll lie like crazy," she promised.

"Oh, you'll run into him, all right," Mace said, feigning concern. "He's likely to track you down and ask why you didn't finish that lobster salad at lunch today."

Amused, Kelly rested her hands on her hips. "If I remember correctly, you left plenty of food on *your* plate, mister. Won't Stefano be after you for an explanation, as well?"

Mace sighed. "Yeah," he said with humorous resignation. He was leading Kelly toward his truck as he spoke. "But I plan to put all the blame on you."

Kelly laughed again and slugged Mace lightly in the arm. "And people say you're a hero?"

Suddenly he stopped, and his expression turned serious. "I'm no hero, Kelly. Just a man."

She didn't argue, although she could've made an airtight case that he *was* a hero. As for being "just a man," well, Mace Carson wasn't *just* anything, but she respected his humility.

Knowing it would be all too easy to slip back into rescued-princess mode, Kelly decided it was time to change the subject. "Are we going far?" she asked, inclining her head toward the truck.

Mace's face changed again; the grin returned. "The winery is that way," he said, jabbing a thumb in the direction of the pastures she'd admired on the drive in. "It's about five miles from here, and there are ruts in the cattle trail we call a road that are deep enough to swallow your rental car." He shrugged casually. "If you'd rather hike or ride a horse, we can do that."

Kelly let him know she hadn't been on horseback since summer camp, when she was twelve, and though she worked out regularly at home, she wasn't up for a five-mile walk. "You win," she said. "Let's take the truck."

"I was kind of hoping you'd choose the horse," he teased, opening the truck's passenger door for her.

"It's tempting," Kelly said, and it was. "I'm a greenhorn, and I haven't ridden in a long time, but I'd like to try again — eventually."

"That can definitely be arranged," Mace said, helping her into the truck.

Her seat belt fastened, Kelly looked down at her sneakers, then at Mace's boots. She'd be needing a pair of those, she decided. Not the fancy showboat kind she could have found so easily in LA or the pricey boutiques at the resort, but the real deal.

They wouldn't be hard to find in a place

like Mustang Creek, where cowboy boots were practically part of the landscape.

"You seem to be feeling good," Mace ventured, starting the truck and steering toward an open gate on the other side of the stable. An ancient, weathered man waited at one side, ready to close the gap after they drove through.

"Just like new," Kelly confirmed. The truck jostled and jolted through the gate.

"That's Red, by the way," Mace said, raising a hand to the old man as they passed. "He's been working for the Carson outfit for so long, he doesn't recall when he signed on."

Kelly watched in the rearview as Red closed and latched the gate behind them. "That's loyalty," she said. "But shouldn't he have retired, say, thirty years ago?"

Mace chuckled. "Don't let Red hear you say that," he answered. "That old coot is still spry, and he knows more about cattle and the cowboy trade in general than any man alive."

"He plans to die with his boots on?" Kelly asked. She might not be a cowgirl, but she'd seen her share of Western movies.

"That he does," Mace replied, tossing her another of those devastating grins of his. "I'm impressed, Ms. Wright. I wouldn't expect a city slicker to know the vernacular."

Kelly smiled. "My dad and I are big John Wayne fans," she said. "Mind if I roll down the window?" She wanted to feel the wind ruffling her hair.

"The Duke," Mace said with reverence. "They don't make 'em like that anymore." He glanced at her, and there was a twinkle in his eyes. "And, no, I don't mind if you open the window."

The truck bumped overland, reminding Kelly of a mechanical bull she'd ridden once, somewhere in Texas. She'd gone to a cowboy bar with half a dozen business associates after an intense meeting, and she'd probably had a little too much to drink.

"You did say there was a road here somewhere?" she asked. The breeze coming in through the window smelled of sweet grass, wildflowers and, alas, manure.

"I said it was more of a cattle trail," Mace corrected. "We haven't gotten to it yet."

"And this is the only way to reach the vineyards and the winery?"

He laughed. "I didn't say that," he replied.

Kelly gave him a mock glare. "There's an actual road?" she demanded. "Besides the route we're taking now?"

"Sure is," Mace replied, clearly enjoying the exchange. "We have a retail shop and a tasting room, and we run tours a couple of times a week."

"Not to mention trucks coming and going," Kelly said wryly, as the one they were riding in bucked along over rough ground.

"This is a shortcut," Mace told her.

Kelly rolled her eyes, trying hard not to laugh. *"Or,"* she said, "it's a kind of initiation. Something along the lines of snipe hunting."

"Never," Mace lied. She saw the corner of his mouth twitch.

"You just like doing things the hard way?"

"I do appreciate a challenge," he admitted.

Suddenly catching on to the subtext, Kelly didn't respond. She just held on tight and relished the soft breeze, thinking of pioneer women, traveling overland in covered wagons for months on end, fording creeks and rivers, rattling up and down mountainsides.

Eventually they bumped onto the aforementioned cattle trail, but it wasn't much better than the rocky terrain they'd already covered.

Mace finally broke the silence. "You all right over there?" he asked, his voice subdued.

Kelly was moved by his concern, knowing he'd remembered her overnight stay in the hospital. "I'm just fine," she told him with a smile. "Really."

He seemed uncertain. "You were banged up —"

"No," Kelly pointed out. "I was fine. You were the one who insisted I visit the ER."

Mace remained thoughtful.

"Hey," Kelly persisted, determined to keep the mood light. "This is nothing. I'll have you know I once rode a mechanical bull."

Mace turned her way, obviously confused. "What?"

She gave an exaggerated sigh even as a smile formed on her lips. "I said —"

"I heard what you said," Mace answered, and the expression on his face was priceless, part amusement, part skepticism. "I'm not sure I believe you, though."

Kelly tried to look offended. "I can prove it," she said. "I have video." Maybe two seconds' worth, but she *had* ridden the robot bull.

Mace tilted his head to one side, as if confounded, though the gleam in his eyes told another story. "Okay," he allowed. "Mind telling me what that has to do with spending the night in a hospital?"

"I'm trying to make a point here," Kelly informed him loftily.

"Which is?"

"*Which is,* I might be a city girl, but I'm tough."

"Did I say you weren't?"

"Not directly," Kelly replied airily, folding her arms. "But you wanted to see my reaction to a rocky ride across the open range." She paused for effect. "How'd I do, cowboy?"

Mace gave a husky shout of laughter. "You did all right," he said as the roof of a long building came into view. "For a greenhorn."

"Don't forget the mechanical bull," she said, pretending to be miffed.

From his expression, Kelly guessed he was enjoying the image.

"Did you stay on for the full eight seconds?" he asked.

She frowned. "Huh?"

"That's rodeo-speak," Mace told her. "During the bull-riding event — in which, by the way, they use real bulls — the main objective is to stay on the critter's back until the buzzer sounds. In eight seconds."

"Oh," Kelly said.

"How many seconds?"

Kelly bit her lip, murmured her reply.

Mace leaned in her direction. "I didn't quite hear that," he said.

"Three, I think," Kelly answered, throwing in an extra second for the sake of her dignity.

Mace's whistle sounded like an exclamation — a rude one.

"What?" Kelly nudged him, feeling a little indignant, although she teetered on the verge of laughter.

Mace flashed her another grin. "I'm impressed, that's what. Three seconds isn't a bad ride, even on a motorized barrel with a hide and a couple of horns glued on for effect."

Just then, they crested a hill, and the vineyard came into view, acres and acres of it, set in tidy rows. The winery occupied the long building she'd glimpsed before, standing on a low rise, overlooking the crop.

Kelly spotted a paved drive, winding its way up from a dirt road and opening onto a spacious parking lot, empty at the moment except for a vintage roadster out front and a truck backed up to a loading dock in the rear.

"Is that car —" she began.

"An MG?" Mace finished for her. "Yep, '54, all original parts." He pulled up beside the gleaming green roadster and shut off the truck's engine. "It belongs to my mother. My grandfather gave it to her a few years ago, and she recently had it restored."

Mace got out of the truck, came around to her side and opened the door. She climbed down on her own because she wanted to prove she was able-bodied, her recent brush with disaster and brief hospitalization notwithstanding.

Mace didn't comment; he simply shut the truck door behind her and headed for the main entrance. The double doors were made of thick glass, and a closed sign dangled in one of them.

Mace punched a series of numbers into a pad on the outside wall, and the locks gave way with an audible buzz.

He pushed one of the doors open and held it for Kelly.

Inside, the silence was complete.

"Where is everybody?" she asked, stepping past Mace into a reception area furnished with comfy chairs and sofas. The art on the walls was quality stuff, with a distinctly Western theme, and the floors were wide-planked hardwood, held in place by pegs instead of nails.

"We just shipped a major order. I gave everybody except the field crew a few days off."

"Generous of you," Kelly commented, feeling slightly disconcerted. Mountain Winery was a small venture in comparison to other wineries. If her company couldn't count on a steady supply of the product, Dina and the board of directors would lose interest in an alliance, fast.

Before Mace could respond, a beautiful woman, around sixty, appeared in a nearby doorway. She was fit, and she wore jeans, a tank top, boots, along with a knowing smile. "My son is definitely generous," she said affectionately. "But he's also a hardheaded businessman. Once harvest rolls around, the whole outfit will be working overtime."

"Mrs. Carson?" Kelly asked, extending a hand as she approached.

The woman's grip was firm as they shook hands. "Blythe," she corrected. "You must be Kelly Wright. May I call you Kelly?"

"Um, sure," Kelly said. She'd read up on Blythe Carson before she left LA, a routine part of her preparations, but there was precious little information about her online, and the few pictures she'd seen fell far short of the reality. It was hard to believe this woman was the mother of three grown sons and the legal owner of a ranch valued at many millions of dollars.

Blythe smiled. "Well, Kelly, are you feeling better? According to Mace, you've had a rough time since you arrived in Wyoming."

Kelly looked back over one shoulder,

meeting Mace's eyes, then turned to face his mother again. "I had a close call," she said, "but I was lucky. Your son came along just in time."

Mace said nothing. There it was again, that reticence. Did the man even *have* an ego?

"None the worse for wear, then?" Blythe asked. Her voice was like music, though it had a husky quality, too. Considering her beauty, her charm, her kindness — considering everything about her — it seemed incredible that she hadn't remarried after her first husband's death.

Blythe must have loved Mace's father very much.

"None the worse for wear," Kelly confirmed.

Blythe looked past Kelly to Mace. "I'm out of here," she said. "It's been a long day."

"See you at home," Mace said.

"If you know what's good for you," Blythe went on, "you'll invite Kelly to stay for supper. Harry's counting on it. She's been cooking most of the day."

"I guess that depends on Kelly's plans for the evening," Mace told her, his tone so noncommittal that Kelly didn't know whether he wanted her to accept or refuse.

Her plans, such as they were, included

room service, a bubble bath and reading in bed.

Compared to a family dinner, the prospect seemed not merely dull, but lonely, too.

Blythe didn't press for a decision. She simply told Kelly she'd enjoyed meeting her, gathered her belongings and left the winery. Outside, the MG purred to life.

Kelly turned back to Mace. According to her extensive research prior to the trip, Mace was the sole owner of Mountain Winery, but as she'd learned from experience, the internet wasn't always reliable when it came to cold hard facts. If Blythe was a partner in the business, that would complicate negotiations — and Mace had used the word "we" several times in reference to the enterprise.

Mace seemed to be reading Kelly's mind. "Mom helps out when she can. Since her father's a vintner, she knows a lot about winemaking." He paused. "I'd like her to be present at one of our meetings. Maybe the day after tomorrow?"

"Of course." Kelly had come to Wyoming to talk business, but at that moment, she was strangely reluctant to do so. She'd liked the easy banter, enjoyed feeling like a friend instead of a glorified sales rep with a bullet-point agenda.

She immediately bristled at the thought. *A glorified sales rep?* Where had *that* come from?

"Come on," Mace said. "I'll show you where the magic happens."

As he spoke, he put out a hand, and Kelly took it. His fingers and palm were callused; here was a man who did hard physical labor, despite his net worth — which had to be considerable.

Mace gave her fingers a gentle squeeze, then led her through the same doorway Blythe had come through minutes before, into a long corridor. There were offices on both sides, Kelly noticed, a total of four.

Three of the doors were closed, but the last stood ajar, revealing a desk, a couple of computers and stacks of file folders and printouts piled everywhere.

Mace caught Kelly sneaking a peek and grinned. "It looks like the aftermath of the Johnstown Flood in there," he said, "but I know where everything is."

Kelly hoped the low lighting in the corridor hid her blush of embarrassment. She wasn't a snoop, she wanted to insist, but she bit her lip to hold back the declaration. "That," she retorted, "is what they all say."

"Nevertheless," he said, "it's true."

They moved on to another set of doors

and, once again, Mace held one open, gesturing for Kelly to go inside.

The room was massive, the walls lined with gleaming equipment and, in contrast, row upon row of wooden barrels. The space was climate controlled, and the machinery gave a low, continuous hum.

The loading bay was visible from where they stood, and two men were working there, stowing the last few crates of wine in the truck Kelly had seen earlier.

"Hey, boss," one of the men called with a wave.

"Hey back at you," Mace responded.

The second man closed the doors on the back of the truck, slid a metal bolt into place. "Gotta get on the road," he said. "Nice to see you again, Mace."

Mace nodded cordially and the man jumped to the ground, climbing into the driver's seat and starting the truck. The other man rolled down the door of the loading bay and walked toward Mace and Kelly, rubbing his hands down his blue-jeaned thighs as he did.

"Who's the pretty lady?" he asked good-naturedly.

Mace made the introductions. "Kelly Wright, meet Tom Harper."

Kelly and Tom shook hands. The man had

a thick head of dark hair, bright brown eyes and a great smile.

"Tom is the proverbial jack-of-all-trades," Mace told Kelly. "As you've just seen, he isn't above loading trucks, but his official title is wine master."

Tom acknowledged Mace's remarks with a slight nod. "Kelly Wright," he said musingly, making a light-hearted pretense of trying to place her. Then his eyes flashed with a smile. "That's right," he said, all but snapping his fingers in that now-I-remember way. "You're the damsel in distress."

Mace glowered at him. "Hardly," he said.

Kelly smiled, amused at Mace's reaction. "That would be me," she told Tom, "though, as you can see, I escaped the dragon unharmed." She turned and batted her eyelashes at Mace. "Thanks to the prince here."

Tom chuckled. "In case you're wondering, my boss — aka, the prince — didn't say a word about what happened the other night. My wife's a nurse, and she was on duty when Mace brought you to the hospital."

Kelly vaguely remembered telling Dr. Draper all about what had happened while she was being examined in the emergency room. A nurse had been present, as well — Mrs. Tom Harper, no doubt.

Mace gave Tom a benign but pointed look. "Must be about quitting time," he said.

Tom ignored Mace's annoyance, although he must have noticed. "Good to meet you, Ms. Wright," he said. "And I'm glad you're okay."

"Thanks." Kelly smiled, liking the guy more with every passing moment. "And it's Kelly, not Ms. Wright."

"Guess I'd better run," Tom said.

"Best idea you've had yet," Mace grumbled.

Tom laughed, said his goodbyes and left the winery through a side door.

"Nice guy," Kelly said when she and Mace were alone again.

"Yeah," Mace agreed, finally lightening up a little. "Except for his big mouth."

Kelly laughed. "Relax. I know you didn't brag all over town about saving the poor, silly California woman from certain disaster."

Even though you did save me, like it or not. Twice.

Mace glanced away, sighed, muttered something to himself.

"Why are you so sensitive about this?" Kelly asked, serious now.

He turned his head, met her eyes. "It was no big deal," he said.

"It was to me," Kelly told him, still solemn. And when Mace didn't reply, she spoke again. "What's really going on here, Mace? Why are you so touchy about taking any credit for what you did?"

He was silent for a long time, although he never looked away from her face. Then, after another sigh, deeper than the last and more exasperated, he said, "Because I don't want you thinking you owe me anything in return. You said thanks and that was enough."

Kelly was at once intrigued and frustrated. "Are you afraid I'm going to follow you around from now on, adoringly, babbling words of gratitude?"

Mace seemed taken aback. *"No,"* he said.

She wasn't letting him off the hook. "What, then?"

He rested his hands on her shoulders, his touch light, even tentative. "All right," he muttered. "It's just that I think something might be . . . starting. Between us, I mean. And I'm not talking about any business deal here." He drew a long breath, released it. "Maybe it's just my imagination and I'm making a damn fool of myself, but if we have a chance, the two of us, we need to be equal partners from the start."

Kelly stared at him, momentarily speechless.

When she finally found her voice, it was barely more than a whisper. "It's not your imagination," she murmured.

That was when he kissed her.

CHAPTER FIVE

The touch of Mace's mouth was gentle, warm, more promise than demand.

More question than answer.

It never occurred to Kelly to push him away, or turn her head. No, she rose onto the balls of her feet, became neither giver nor recipient, but part of the kiss itself, part of Mace, as he was part of her.

He didn't use his tongue, though she would have welcomed that — and a lot more. She felt charged in every cell, as if she were dancing on an arc of lightning.

When Mace broke the connection, Kelly plunged from the heights like a skydiver without a parachute, half expecting to strike hard ground and shatter into pieces.

Mace cupped her right cheek in his hand, thumbed away a tear she hadn't known was there.

Kelly couldn't speak. The ordinary world felt thick around her, as though she'd been caught in a mudslide, or quicksand, and might be sucked under at any moment.

Reflex made her grasp Mace's shoulders, hold on for dear life.

He covered her hands with his own.

"Are you okay?"

"Um, I think so," Kelly murmured, loosening her grasp on Mace by degrees as she settled back into herself. There were so many questions she wanted to ask — had he felt the power of that kiss, the way she had, or was it just another flirtation to him, soon to be forgotten? And if he *had* felt it, what did it mean?

"If that was too much, too soon . . ."

"No," Kelly said so quickly that heat stained her cheeks. Then, again, more slowly, "No."

Mace drew Kelly close, kissed the top of her head. "This might be a good time to show you the vineyard," he said.

Kelly allowed herself to lean into him, just a little. To rest against the hard width of his chest, listen to the steady thud-thud-thud of his heart.

It had been so long since she'd taken shelter in a man's arms, felt safe there.

"This would be a *very* good time to see the vineyard," she said with laugh.

They left the winery then, neither one saying a word, and after Mace had punched in another code to lock the doors, they headed for the leafy rows, the vines rimmed in the last fierce light of the day.

Mace didn't hold her hand as he had before, but their arms brushed against each other at intervals.

Kelly had that strange, otherworldly feeling again, although it wasn't urgent, like before, when Mace had kissed her. She wondered if she'd bumped her head, after all, when her rental car went off the road, and done something to her brain, something the scans hadn't picked up.

They walked along the rows in comfortable silence, and Kelly reveled in the scents of leaves and fertile dirt and ripening fruit. She'd visited so many other vineyards, in so many other places, but, strangely, this one seemed all new.

Maybe, she thought, it wasn't the vineyard that made her want to put down roots right here in this rich soil and simply grow, like the plants all around her, to blossom in spring, flourish in the summer heat, bear fruit in the fall, stand leafless and vulnerable in the winter snow.

It was a crazy, whimsical idea, completely unlike her.

If this strange mood continued, she decided, she'd follow Dr. Draper's advice and seek medical help.

In the meantime, though, she intended to savor the experience.

"Stay for supper?" Mace asked when he and Kelly got back to the main house. This time, he'd taken the road instead of the cattle trail. Twilight was settling over the countryside by then, and the inside lights shone in that way that always made him feel a strange, soft mixture of joy and sorrow, as if he were homesick for a place he'd never really left.

He'd half expected Kelly to make a dash for her car the instant he'd parked the truck, but she didn't move. Neither did he; he just sat behind the wheel, listening to the engine tick as it cooled, and waited.

"Why not?" she replied quietly.

Okay, so it wasn't wild enthusiasm. But she'd agreed to stay, and that was enough.

For now.

"Let's go inside, then," he said. "Before Harry comes out and *drags* us to the table."

"You're sure I won't be imposing?"

"Imposing? You heard my mother — Harry's been cooking for hours."

She smiled at him, opened her door before he could open it for her.

116

She looked down at her jeans and T-shirt, then up at the house, and seemed to withdraw slightly, as though reconsidering. "Please tell me your family doesn't dress up for dinner," she said.

Mace felt a brief ache behind his breastbone, but he smiled. "Are you serious? This is a *ranch.*"

Kelly eyed the house again. "Some ranch," she remarked. "That house looks like something out of *Gone with the Wind.*"

"It's home," Mace said casually. "You expected the Ponderosa?"

She laughed softly. "Maybe I did," she said. "It's not exactly what you'd call rustic, this place. On the other hand, it seems to belong here."

Mace nodded, resting one hand on the small of Kelly's back, glad she didn't pull away. The gesture was automatic, bred into him, like opening doors and pulling out chairs and taking off his hat in the presence of a lady.

"There's a story," he said as they mounted the steps to the porch.

Her face was eager in the glow of the outside light. "Tell me."

"When my great-great-grandfather — I forget how many greats — settled this ranch and made himself a little money running cattle and mining, he went back East to find a wife. He found her in Savannah, living in what remained of her family's old plantation house, after Sherman and his men left half the state of Georgia in ashes. She wasn't in love with him, not at first, anyway, and he didn't figure he had a chance with her, poor though she was, given that she was a true lady and he was a cowpoke from someplace west of nowhere. He proposed, thinking she'd refuse, and she hauled off and said yes. They got married and headed over here, by railroad, then stagecoach, then covered wagon. Legend has it she never complained, either along the way or once she got a look at the ranch and his cabin. By the end of that first winter, as the story goes, they were in love. They roughed it for a few years, started a family, and when he began to make real money, they drew up the plans together and gradually expanded this place, made it as much like the house she'd left behind as they could."

Kelly's eyes shone. "*That* is the most romantic thing I've ever heard."

Mace gave a reasonable facsimile of a courtly bow as he opened the door. "Welcome to the Mustang Creek version of Tara," he said.

The inside of the Carson house, it turned

out, was even more impressive than the outside. The furnishings were an eclectic blend of old and new, everything fitting together to make a home, gracious but somehow rustic, too.

Kelly heard laughter somewhere nearby as Mace showed her to a powder room off the massive kitchen, where she could wash up. When she'd finished, he was waiting for her, looking freshly scrubbed.

He offered her his arm and must have sensed that she was nervous, despite her effort to hide the fact. "Nobody bites," he whispered.

Kelly had been in grand houses before, of course, attended elegant affairs, exchanged small talk with the rich and famous. This, like the vineyard, was different. Mainly, she supposed, because Mace Carson lived here.

He escorted her into a spacious dining room, into the boisterous heart of his family.

Much to Kelly's relief, Mace had been telling the truth when he said the others wouldn't be dressed up. Blythe had changed clothes since leaving the winery, but she'd chosen black jeans, a blue cotton blouse and sandals, and she looked elegant as well as casual.

Mace introduced her to his eldest brother,

Slater, a successful documentary filmmaker, and his wife, Grace, who managed the resort where Kelly was staying. Then she met Drake, another brother, and his wife, Luce. Both couples had young children, already in bed.

Finally, she met Harry, a tall, angular woman with kind gray eyes. She was the only woman in the room wearing a dress; Grace and Luce, like their mother-in-law, sported jeans and blouses. Luce was barefoot.

"Now that you're all here," Harry said with all the authority of a judge calling a courtroom to order, "sit yourselves down so I can get supper on the table."

"I'm starving," Kelly confided, once she was seated at the long dining table, next to Mace. "I'll probably eat way too much."

"Just make sure Stefano doesn't get wind of it," Mace said.

The meal was beyond delicious — chicken, breaded and fried to golden crispness, mashed potatoes and gravy, green beans boiled with bacon and onions, just-baked biscuits and soft butter. Mace's own wines added to the taste extravaganza and, for dessert, there were three kinds of pie.

The talk around that big table was lively, and there was a lot of laughter. Mace's brothers were handsome, like him, and although there was a family resemblance, both Slater and Drake were distinct individuals with very different opinions, which they expressed without hesitation.

Mace stated up front that Kelly was in town for a series of meetings about a joint marketing effort, but his brothers clearly believed there was more to the story. And his mother happily agreed to join them for one of those meetings.

It didn't take Kelly long to realize that, although they minded their manners that evening, Blythe Carson's sons were a rowdy bunch and generally made a sport of ribbing each other. She knew that as soon as she wasn't around to overhear, Mace would be in for some razzing about the woman who came to dinner.

She also knew he'd be able to hold his own with no trouble at all.

Grace and Luce, both beautiful women, made Kelly feel completely comfortable, asking intelligent questions about her end of the wine business, her impressions of Mustang Creek, whether she was comfortable at the resort.

Kelly thoroughly enjoyed the evening, the company and the food, and she was grateful that no one asked about the accident, or how she was feeling. While she appreciated all the kindness and concern she'd been shown since then, she didn't want to be remembered, once she returned to LA, as the woman who went off the road.

She wasn't embarrassed by the incident; anyone could run into trouble on a rain-slick road. It was just that should she come to anyone's mind after she'd gone, she hoped it would be because she had been a nice person, a good businesswoman, someone they'd enjoyed being around.

After dessert and coffee, she and Grace and Luce tried to help clear the table, but Harry was having none of that. Kelly thanked everyone for a lovely time and said she'd call it a night.

Mace walked her to her car.

The night sky was blanketed with stars from horizon to horizon, and their brilliance made Kelly's throat catch. Love LA though she did, between the smog and the ambient light, she'd forgotten what it was like to look up and see the universe on display, wild and fiery and incomprehensibly ancient.

"It's so beautiful here," she whispered, awed.

When she met his gaze, she saw that Mace was looking at her, not at the sky. "That it is," he said, his voice almost gruff.

Kelly wanted him to kiss her again.

And *not* to kiss her again.

Everything was moving too fast and, at the same time, not nearly fast enough. She felt breathless, wonderfully confused, hopeful and scared.

"I guess if I offer to drive you back to the resort," Mace said quietly, with a hint of a smile in his eyes, "you'll say no."

"I will, absolutely," she confirmed. "I'll need my car in the morning and, furthermore, I'm fully capable of getting myself there safely — despite my reputation for reckless driving."

Mace grinned. "Well," he said, "there is that."

Kelly laughed and gave him a playful shove in the chest. "Anyway, I need my rest. I plan to get up early, get some work done."

"Such as?"

"*Such as* proving to a certain winemaker that my company can triple his business," Kelly said on a light note. "That's what a partnership with us can do."

Mace's frown was nearly imperceptible, but it still worried her a little. In fact, she might have panicked if it hadn't been for the gleam in his eyes. "Suppose this winemaker is happy with his business the way it is?"

Kelly couldn't allow herself to think how much was riding on this one deal, and she regretted tipping her hand a moment before. "If he's willing to hear me out," she said carefully, "I believe I can convince him."

Mace tilted his head back, studied the stars, and his gaze was steady when he looked at her face again. "Fair enough," he said. "He'll listen. No promises beyond that, though."

"No promises," Kelly agreed.

A silence fell, brief and oddly comfortable, given the directness of Mace's statement. But then, would she want him to be anything *but* direct? He clearly didn't play games, and that was refreshing.

Mace spoke first. "I don't think you've mentioned how long you'll be in Mustang Creek," he said cautiously.

Kelly didn't hesitate. "As long as it takes," she said. "I can always change my flight back to LA, and the rental car deal is open-ended."

That made him smile, a bit wickedly. "Well, now," he answered, rubbing his chin thoughtfully. "That might inspire some foot-dragging. On the winemaker's part, I mean."

Kelly laughed, filled with a strange, vibrant joy that she was standing under that canopy of gleaming stars, facing this man, within touching distance. "Good *night,* Mr. Carson," she told him.

He opened the rental car's door for her, bowed ever so slightly. "Good night," he replied.

She didn't want the moment to end, but prudence won out. If she stayed too long, she knew, the charge of anticipation between them might spark a blaze she couldn't extinguish.

Wouldn't even *want* to extinguish.

"Can you fit in a meeting tomorrow?" she asked.

"I can work it into my schedule," Mace responded. "As long as it's on horseback."

Kelly swallowed. "Horseback?"

"That winemaker you were talking about convincing?" Mace said. "He's three parts cowboy."

A sweet, scary thrill raced through Kelly's bloodstream at those words, and she bent her head, rummaging through her purse for the car keys — and a minute to collect herself, let the pink in her cheeks subside a little. "Then it's settled," she said when she managed to look at him again. He was still holding the car door, and starlight sparkled in his hair. "What time?"

"Whatever works for you." It was an easy drawl, a gentle challenge.

"Afternoon," Kelly decided. "I have some things to do in the morning." Like buying a pair of boots and doing some stretches, so she wouldn't have sore thighs when the ride was over.

"One o'clock?" Mace asked.

"One o'clock," Kelly agreed.

He closed the door, then stepped back, lifting a hand in farewell as she started the engine and shifted into Drive. She made a three-point turn and headed down the long driveway.

She drove carefully through the deep and quiet country night, alert but oddly jumbled inside, too, full of contradictory emotions and wild thoughts.

She was crazy, thinking the things she was thinking.

She'd never felt so sane as she did right now.

She was falling in love.

She was determined *not* to fall in love.

She'd worked hard to build a life in LA, and she cherished her independence.

She was, as hard as it was to admit, lonely.

No matter what, she needed to make some changes; she knew that much, anyway.

What changes?

That was the question.

■ ■ ■ ■

Dina called the next morning, while Kelly was finishing a light breakfast in the resort's bistro, her laptop on the table beside her — usually a no-no, like watching TV during a meal. She answered with a cheerful, "Hello, Boss Lady."

Dina cleared her throat. There was something tentative, even reluctant, in the sound. "So," she began, after a deep and audible breath. "How's everything? Any more near-disasters?"

Kelly might have been alarmed by what she heard — or sensed — in Dina's voice, but that morning, with the glorious panorama of the Wyoming countryside beckoning from just beyond the restaurant windows, she was simply happy.

She smiled as Grace Carson waved, passing by the doorway. Waved back. "No more disasters, near or otherwise," she replied. "As for the business aspect, Mace and I will be getting together again this afternoon." No need to mention that the meeting room would be the wide-open spaces, and the chairs would be saddles. For some reason, she wanted that tidbit of information to belong to her and no one else. "I think we're making progress."

"Okay," Dina said, drawing the word out.

Kelly tapped a few keys on the laptop, then closed it with a snap. "Dina, what's going on?" she asked. "I can tell something's up. What is it?"

Dina heaved a sigh. If Kelly's job was high-pressure, Dina's was doubly so. She had a board of directors to report to, dozens of employees to oversee, numbers to crunch.

Strangely, Kelly was briefly transported back to the peaceful vineyard where she'd walked with Mace and once again found herself wanting to be a part of the vines and the earth that nurtured them.

Dina's reply brought her back with a mild jolt. "I've been offered a new job, Kelly," she said. "In London."

"Oh," Kelly said, absorbing the news, struggling to grasp the implications. Obviously, from Dina's tone and mood, there were some. "Are you taking it?"

Rhetorical question. Dina had seemed restless for at least a year, and she visited the UK whenever the opportunity presented itself. Although there'd been no mention of a man, Kelly had long suspected there was more to those trips than meeting with high-level wine merchants and visiting castles.

"Yes," Dina confirmed, still sounding reluctant.

"Congratulations," Kelly said. "I'm happy for you." Then she waited for the rest.

"Thanks." A sigh. "The board's already selected my replacement," Dina went on after an excruciating pause, and immediately bogged down again.

By then, Kelly could guess what was coming. She wasn't the replacement. Did Dina expect her to be surprised or angry by this development? If so, she was way off base, because Kelly knew she didn't have the experience the job required; her focus was on the next rung of the ladder, VP of Sales.

Dina had always been her strongest supporter when it came to that goal, but Kelly knew she deserved the promotion, that her merit spoke for itself.

"Dina?" she prompted, frowning a little.

"They're hiring Alan," Dina said, as if flinging herself over some invisible finish line. "*Your* Alan."

The announcement struck Kelly like a physical blow. "What?"

Dina said nothing.

"He's not *my* Alan," Kelly blurted out.

Having dropped the bomb, Dina tried to strike a conciliatory note. "I don't think he'll want to cause you any problems," she said, rushing the words as if she couldn't wait to get rid of them. "And he's highly qualified, Kelly. His background in investment banking speaks for itself, as you probably know. He's remarried — of course that isn't news to you, either — with a couple of children, and, well, he *does* have a reputation for effective leadership —"

"Isn't this a conflict of interest or something?"

"No," Dina said. "It's true that the board frowns on married couples working for the company, but you and Alan are divorced. That's different."

And if she forced the board to make a choice, Kelly knew, they would go with Alan, despite her excellent performance.

"I need to think about this," Kelly said when the gap in the conversation grew too wide.

"Of course you do," Dina agreed quietly.

Alan Wright. Her ex-husband. Her boss?

Their divorce had been amicable enough. Kelly didn't hate Alan, and he didn't hate her. And while she hadn't exactly followed his career, she'd run into him at various business functions over the years, known about the second wife and the children and his meteoric rise in the corporate world. She'd even been happy for him.

130

Sort of.

All of which was beside the point, unfortunately.

She couldn't imagine working with him, not the way she'd worked with Dina. No matter how civilized she and Alan might try to be, there would still be an awkwardness, a lack of objectivity.

"Call me when you're ready to talk," Dina said. "You have time to decide what you want to do. The transition is going to take a while."

How long? Kelly wanted to ask, but she didn't. She was still reeling, still trying to regain her balance.

"Okay," she said, hating the weakness she heard in her own voice.

Let this conversation be over.

It wasn't. "Kelly?"

"Yes?"

"Are you all right?"

"Sure." *Sure. Except for the bottom falling out, leaving me flailing in midair. Other than that, I'm just peachy.*

"You have a lot of vacation time coming. You could take a few weeks off —"

"I'll get back to you," Kelly broke in.

"Right," Dina answered, deflated.

Kelly sat there, unmoving, the phone still pressed to her ear, the last of her breakfast cooling on her plate, long after Dina said goodbye.

Mace knew something was wrong — very wrong — the moment Kelly got out of her rental car, in front of the barn. She was putting on a good front, in her well-fitting jeans, T-shirt and honest-to-God Western boots, but even before she spoke, the message was clear. *Don't ask.*

He would respect that, of course. Whatever was bothering the dazzling Ms. Wright, and whether or not to talk about it, was strictly her call.

"Nice boots," he said with a smile. He'd already saddled their horses, having chosen his paint gelding, Splash, and a gentle bay mare, Coco, for her.

Kelly paused, looked down at her feet, apparently surprised by the reminder that she was wearing boots. When she raised her eyes again, she was smiling, too, although the expression didn't quite reach her eyes.

"The salesperson at the Western store swore they were greenhorn-friendly," she said, her gaze slipping sideways, to the horses. "Round toes, solid heels, sturdy shafts for ankle support."

Mace suppressed an urge to walk over to her, smooth her hair, tell her that everything would be okay.

"Good," he said, not moving. Not wanting to rush her or enter her space if she wanted elbow room. "Pointed toes and fancy stitching are for rodeo queens and movie stars, not serious riders."

"So I'm told," she said with a nod, still keeping her distance.

"Ready to mount up?" Mace asked when she didn't make a move, either to advance or retreat. "Coco here is an easygoing horse. She probably doesn't even remember how to run or buck."

Kelly laughed nervously and brought one hand to the base of her throat. "I'm as ready as I'll ever be," she said with cheery bravado.

He wondered if she wanted to back out, but was too proud to say so. "If you're scared, that's okay," he ventured.

She shook her head, then laughed again, this time with a little more conviction. "I'm definitely scared," she said. "But I'm not about to let that stop me."

Mace liked that answer. It was honest, and it was as gutsy as hell.

"You won't get hurt," he said. "I promise."

Normally, he wouldn't have given his word, because bad things happened in the real world and even the most experienced rider could be thrown. But this was Coco, who was so mellow-natured she was practically inert, and he meant to take it slow and stay close by.

"I believe you," Kelly said, and the way she spoke made something inside him struggle to break free and soar against the bright summer sky.

He gave a nod and waited, two sets of reins resting loosely across his palm, because no matter how long it took, the first move had to be Kelly's.

Finally, after a deep breath, she approached. He helped her into the saddle, handed her the reins, adjusted the stirrups and made sure her feet were set just right.

Coco, true to form, swished her tail and stood there like a sawhorse in a wood shop, her eyes closed for a brief snooze.

Mace swung up onto Splash's back and showed Kelly how to hold the reins, one in each hand, light against her palms. Not knowing how much she remembered from summer camp, he warned her never to wrap them around her hands, or saw on them when she wanted the horse to stop.

She listened, paying close attention.

"A horse's mouth is tender, and even the best bit will hurt if you pull too hard," he said.

She nodded, concentrating, biting her

lower lip. The woman was scared shitless, but she meant to see this through, come what may, and Mace knew he'd always recall that this was the moment he'd fallen in love with her. He'd been sliding in that direction by degrees ever since she'd run her rental car off the road, but that was when *he* went over the edge.

Still, his focus right now was to reassure Kelly, keep her safe, let her feel her way into what was, for her, a new experience.

When she released another long breath and said she was ready, he nudged Splash into motion. Coco woke up from her nap and plodded alongside.

When a delighted smile blossomed on Kelly's face, Mace felt a rush of emotion that tightened his throat and made his eyes sting.

"This is fun," she said, surprised.

"We'll take it easy, just the same," he told her quietly.

They rode through the same pasture gate, once again held open by a grinning Red, onto the range. The grass blew in the gentle breeze like a green banner, and the sky arched overhead, spacious and so blue it hurt to look at it.

Kelly eyed a cluster of grazing cattle about a hundred yards away, and her nerves kicked up again. "They won't chase those cows or anything, will they? The horses, I mean?"

Mace might have chuckled if he hadn't been so taken with this woman and her courage. "You've seen too many Westerns," he said with a grin. "Splash has done some cattle driving, all right, but he takes his orders from me. As for Coco, well, she probably wouldn't run if her tail caught fire."

Kelly's eyes were wide, bright with cautious joy. "Good," she murmured. "That's good."

They ambled along in companionable silence for some time, although Splash made it obvious that he wanted to pick up the pace. He was a cutting horse, used to working for a living, but he cooperated with the subtle signals he knew so well.

Finally, when Mace could see that the tension in Kelly's shoulders had eased, and she wasn't sitting bolt upright waiting for all hell to break loose, he spoke.

"Where is it?" he asked.

Kelly looked at him, clearly puzzled. Her cheeks were flushed, but it was pleasure this time, not embarrassment. He knew that from the shine in her eyes. "Where is what?"

"The hard sell," Mace said. "Isn't that why we're here?"

She blinked, then recovered from her confusion. "Oh," she said. "That."

"Yeah," Mace responded. "That."

Kelly hesitated and, for a moment, he thought she might spill whatever had been troubling her when she drove up to the barn a while ago, but she didn't.

She started reeling off facts and figures, plans and potentials.

Mace was glad he had a head for numbers, because once Kelly started, they came tumbling out, one after another, along with market forecasts, the potential for international sales, the success of American wines competing with European varieties. She spoke of profit margins, trade shows, websites and expansion, expansion, expansion.

Listening, Mace felt both fascinated and slightly guilty. He was proud of his wines, and he'd put them up against anything out there, but he liked the operation the way it was, too. Liked knowing all his people and their families. Most of all, he liked the physical aspect of cultivating the vineyard, working hard under a hot sun, shoulder to shoulder with the seasonal folks, college kids, migrants and older men and women looking to feel useful and make a few bucks in the process.

His sales force was small, mostly part-

137

time, and the bulk of his business was done online, anyway.

The sort of growth Kelly was talking about would mean going to conferences all over the country, if not the world, wearing three-piece suits and pandering to the kinds of people he made a point of avoiding.

He should have told Kelly all this up front, he supposed, but the fact was, he made a policy of listening to just about every pitch that came his way, since he always learned something from the encounter. So when she'd contacted him a few weeks before, he'd agreed to her request for a meeting.

Of course, he hadn't known who she was at the time, hadn't a clue that she'd show up and toss his whole life into a cement mixer, figuratively speaking. And he probably wouldn't have done things differently even if he had. Something was happening between him and this woman, and whatever it was, he intended to let it play out.

Kelly must have seen some emotion in his face. She stopped the selling barrage long enough to study him. "Too much, too soon?" she asked, bouncing along on Coco's wide back.

"It's an interesting concept," Mace said, reluctant to throw cold water on the presentation, which had obviously been well rehearsed. He was tempted to buy into the plan, if only because he knew how much it meant to her, but he had his employees to consider, as well as his own preferences where the winery was concerned. It was a case of *if it ain't broke, don't fix it,* and however hackneyed that policy might be, he knew it was valid.

"But?" Kelly asked, concerned.

"Sounds like there'd be a lot of changes involved."

"And a great deal of money," Kelly said.

He *had* money, and plenty of it, though he wasn't about to say so. "Some things," he said, "are more important than money."

He braced himself for the inevitable "Like what?" and the disappointment that would have come with it.

Instead, Kelly said, "Of course. But your wines are special, Mace. Don't you want to see how they'd fare on a worldwide basis?"

"There are plenty of excellent wines out there," he said carefully. He could've strung her along, kept her around for a while, but it wasn't in him to do things that way. If she left town, that would be an answer in its own right. "And I know ours is as good as we can make it at present, and getting better. For me, that's enough."

Kelly took that in, looking solemn. "You're sure?"

"It would take a lot to change my mind."

"Do you mind if I try?"

He bit back a grin. "Not at all," he answered, staring straight ahead so she wouldn't see how pleased he was. "As long as you remember what I said. I'm not the corporate type, and my people are happy with the status quo. Like as not, you'll be wasting your time trying to talk me into the plan you've outlined."

"But you're not saying no?"

"I *am* saying no," Mace replied. "And it's only fair to tell you, I'm damned single-minded."

She was quiet again, pondering. The wheels were definitely grinding inside that pretty head.

Just when Mace thought she'd rein Coco around and head back to the barn, scared or not, she took him by surprise. Again.

"I have some vacation time coming," she said. "And I like a challenge."

CHAPTER SIX

After the ride, Kelly needed time to think. Without distractions.

She helped Mace put the horses in their stalls and brush them down — with a lot of instruction — and then she left, driving back to the resort. Stretches or not, her thighs ached, so she ran a hot bath, swallowed two aspirin, stripped off her clothes and soaked.

Mace Carson was as likely to change his mind about the deal as the Grand Tetons were to pick up and move to Boise; that much was clear. So why wasn't she packing, calling the airlines, letting Dina know the mission was a bust?

There was no single answer to that, of course. For one thing, she didn't want to leave Wyoming, not just yet, anyway.

For another, her job was essentially history, with her ex-husband taking over the company in a matter of weeks. She could ask for a transfer, maybe follow Dina to London, or spend a few years in Europe. Given her track record, she could probably work in the field, or even telecommute.

Trouble was, while she definitely enjoyed traveling abroad, she didn't want to live there on a long-term basis. And even if she didn't actually work in the corporate offices in LA, she would still be accountable to Alan. There would be memos, emails, staff meetings.

Could she deal with that?

Unequivocally, no, she couldn't.

Was it plain old ego? Pride?

It did nettle her a bit that Alan, even without experience specific to the wine industry, could step into a top spot so easily. She might have suspected gender bias, if Dina hadn't held the position first.

Then again, maybe Dina's plum job in London wasn't a step up. Maybe it was lateral, or even a demotion. Kelly would likely never know and, anyway, what did it matter? From an occupational perspective, she was totally screwed.

Moreover, what were the odds? Of all the corporations looking for a boy genius to spearhead their operations, Alan had to wind up in *her* company?

Talk about your crappy coincidence.

And Kelly knew it *was* a coincidence. Alan probably didn't give a damn where she worked, and even if he did, he wouldn't have gone to so much trouble just to mess with her head. He had a lovely family now and, besides, he wasn't the vindictive type. Most likely, he'd go out of his way to show her there were no hard feelings, invite her over to meet his wife and kids.

She wished him well, but she had no desire to socialize.

Kelly sank deeper into the bathwater until her chin was submerged.

Everything about this sucked.

Didn't it?

Wasn't there the tiniest part of her that wanted to whoop for joy? To explore other options?

She wasn't going to starve or end up sleeping on a sidewalk. She wasn't rich, but she'd socked away some serious money over the last few years — one of the benefits of not having a life — and, thanks to several generous if well-earned bonuses, she owned her condo free and clear. It was in a desirable location by LA standards, and even in a slow real-estate market, she'd have no trouble selling it.

Okay, good. No reason to freak out and move into her parents' basement.

Next question — what *did* she want to do?

She had no idea, beyond sticking around Mustang Creek for a week or two, selling Mace Carson on the modern idea of progress. Better to go out with a major success to her credit, right? A deal with Mountain Winery would look terrific on her résumé, and she wouldn't feel like a poor sport or, worse, a loser.

Kelly began to relax, although her thighs still hurt like crazy.

She got out of the bathtub, dried off with a fluffy resort towel and put on clean jeans, another T-shirt and her trusty sneakers. Looking around the luxurious minisuite, she pondered the ethics of her situation.

Should she move to a cheaper place, one she could pay for herself, without getting the heebie-jeebies about her credit card balance?

Maybe, she decided. But not yet. Not while she was still an employee, trying to make a major deal.

Her cell phone rang, and she expected to hear Dina's voice when she answered.

Or Mace.

The caller, it turned out, was Spence Hogan, the chief of police.

Yikes. She'd forgotten all about her promise to get in touch with him, fill out an accident report.

"Chief Hogan," she said with a little too much emphasis.

"Ms. Wright?"

"Yes," she answered, still overeager. What was the matter with her? It wasn't as if he'd be sending out a SWAT team to bring her in. "Please, call me Kelly."

She rolled her eyes at her own words.

"Only if you'll call me Spence."

"I'm sorry I haven't called about the accident report. I completely forgot."

"No problem," Spence said pleasantly. "I can bring it by the resort, if that would be easier for you."

Kelly felt strangely restless at the prospect of waiting around in the hotel. Besides, as chief of police, Spence surely had other things to do, while she was at loose ends just now. "I don't mind coming to the station," she said. She glanced at the bedside clock. "It's almost four-thirty. Is that too late?"

Spence chuckled. "We're open 24/7," he answered. "Come on over. The report won't take long. It's routine, but the law requires it."

"Of course," Kelly said. "I'll be on my way as soon as we hang up."

"See you soon," Spence told her. "You

know how to find the station? It's on Second Street, behind the post office."

"I'll figure it out," Kelly assured him. It was crazy, but she was glad to have somewhere to go, even if it was the police station to fill out a form. She wasn't ready to call it a day — order room service, catch up on her email and other long-distance office work, then climb into bed with a book.

Thanks to the GPS feature on her phone, Kelly found her destination easily. It was a one-story brick building, with a paved parking lot, a flagpole out front, flying both the state and national flags.

Kelly parked well away from the two official vehicles in the lot; she felt silly doing that, but she was still a little worried about her driving karma. It wouldn't do to dent a cop car. One accident report was enough. *More* than enough.

As she approached the heavy glass doors, wondering if they were bulletproof, Spence appeared on the other side and opened one for her.

"I appreciate this," he said.

Was the man always this polite? She'd been the forgetful one, after all, not him.

"So do I," Kelly answered lightly. "Mea culpa."

Spence grinned. He was dressed as before,

in jeans, a starched Western shirt, boots — and a badge. "Come on in. There's coffee but, fair warning, it's been sitting in the pot for a while."

A pretty, big-haired woman was hauling a huge, rhinestone-studded handbag from her desk as they entered the small reception area. "I see the chief's complaining about the coffee again," she said pleasantly. "I plead innocent. Deputy Baker made the last batch."

Kelly laughed. "I was going to refuse, anyhow."

The other woman smiled. She was petite, full-busted, and she glittered like a 1970s country singer onstage, but the look worked on her.

"I'm Junie," she said. "And I run this place. Don't let Spence's badge and service revolver fool you — he's just a front man."

Spence sighed. "All too true," he said with amused resignation. "Junie, this is Kelly Wright."

Junie's improbably long, thick eyelashes fluttered with recognition. "From what I've heard, you almost made the news the other night. And not in a good way."

"Almost," Kelly agreed.

"Welcome to Mustang Creek," Junie said, smiling again. "It's a great town, full of nice folks. Hope you won't write us off because one of our roads just about killed you."

Kelly liked this woman, wondered what it would be like to have her as a friend. No doubt it would be a whole new experience, visiting cowboy bars, dancing to the juke-box, playing pool. "I haven't seen much of Mustang Creek yet," she said, as Junie hung the heavy handbag over one shoulder and rounded the desk. "But I promise I'll give the place an honest chance."

"Good enough for me," Junie said. Then she turned her attention to Spence. "I'd stay and chat for a while, but I've got a pedicure booked and if I don't show up on time, Doris will make me wait till next week."

"Can't have that," Spence said drily. "Much as I'd love for you to stay and 'chat.'"

Junie laughed and waggled her fingers at both of them. "I'm gone," she said. And, a moment later, she was.

Spence shook his head, watching the other woman depart. Kelly couldn't help noticing the sparkles affixed to the pockets of her trim jeans as she sashayed toward a small pickup truck parked near the entrance. "Thank God Doris is a demon for punctuality," he told Kelly. "Junie's idea of a chat is an exchange of personal histories, starting at birth."

"Phew!" Kelly joked, dragging the back of one hand across her forehead in exaggerated relief. "*My* life story is pretty darn boring," she added, "but I'll bet Junie's would hold my interest."

"Everybody has a story," Spence said. "Junie's is a lively one, all right. Talking to her is like skimming the first few pages of an exciting book when you were planning to get a good night's sleep. All bets are off."

"I'll remember that." Kelly followed Spence as he led the way toward an office door in the back of the reception area. In truth, she was hoping she'd get the chance to see Junie again, hear whatever the other woman wanted to tell her.

It was bound to be entertaining.

Spence's office was neat; there was nothing on his desk besides a computer monitor, a telephone and an old-fashioned calendar with flip pages. His cowboy hat rested on its crown on the surface of a well-stocked bookshelf against a nearby wall. "Have a seat," he said, indicating a chair opposite his own.

He stood until she'd sat down, then took a clipboard from a drawer and handed it across, along with a pen.

"Junie filled in what details we had," he

said. "Mainly, you just need to sign it."

Kelly took the clipboard, scanned the form, clicked open the ballpoint pen. "Seems right," she said, adding her signature to the appropriate line with a flourish and handing the clipboard back. "What happens now?"

"Not much," Spence said. "The report will be filed, because even in the age of computers, paperwork is still the darling of bureaucrats everywhere. The rental car people will want a copy, too."

Kelly sighed, moved to rise from her chair. "Well," she said, "that was easy."

Spence was already on his feet. "Are you going to be in town for a while?" he asked.

The question gave Kelly pause. She knew she hadn't broken any laws, but didn't the police always ask that or a similar question when a person was under investigation?

Damn. She was being paranoid.

Spence smiled; clearly he'd caught her reaction. "My motive for asking is strictly social," he said. "My wife wants to meet you, and so do her friends. She's planning on throwing some kind of females-only get-together in a couple of weeks. Blythe, Luce and Grace will be there, too."

"Oh," Kelly said, with a little burst of delight. Of course she'd had lunch with girlfriends over the years, but not often, and not for the purpose of getting acquainted. The talk had mostly been superficial, more about networking and subtle one-upmanship than the simple pleasure of being together. "Yes. I'll be here for a week or ten days. And I'd love to meet your wife."

Spence nodded. Cordial. At ease. "Good. Her name is Melody. If it's okay with you, I'll give her your number."

"Great," Kelly said. Was it pathetic, her eagerness to spend time with Melody Hogan and her friends? "Will Junie be there, too?"

Spence chuckled, walking her to the exit. "Couldn't keep her away even if they wanted to," he said. "You'll be hearing from Melody soon."

It occurred to Kelly as she made her way to her car that she'd had more pleasant surprises since her arrival in Mustang Creek than she'd had in years — Mace himself, the boisterous family meal at the Carson ranch, the breathtaking spill of stars in the night sky, the rough-and-tumble ride overland in Mace's truck, the meeting on horseback.

And now this gesture of friendship, of welcome.

She sat for a moment behind the wheel of

the car, her eyes misted with tears.

She had sisters, four of them, all older, and she'd had plenty of friends, especially in high school and college. She was fond of her family, but her contact with them took place primarily during family events and holidays. And most of her school friends had fallen away, moving to distant cities, building careers, starting families, and although she still kept in touch with some via social media, it wasn't the same.

Maybe she was making too much of a prospective invitation, a call she hadn't received yet, but even the prospect was a gift. How on earth had she managed in the last ten or so years without close friends to confide in, to laugh and cry with?

She sat up a little straighter, started the car, checked the mirrors before backing out of her parking space. She was going to make some changes, beginning right here, right now. Never again would she let her work take over her life; ambition was fine, but hers had become all consuming.

Still not ready to go back to the resort, Kelly drove around Mustang Creek, driving up and down practically every street. She watched children playing in front yards, running through sprinklers and spraying each other with hoses. She saw dogs chasing balls and Frisbees in the town park, cruised past the local library and considered marching in and getting a card, checking out a stack of books. Had she even set foot in a library since college?

Once or twice, with her mother, when she was visiting her parents in Bakersfield, her hometown. On those occasions, she'd reveled in the smell of old books, promised herself she'd find a branch near her condo in LA, become an active patron, read something besides business journals, sales reports and the financial pages in ever-dwindling newspapers.

She would haunt bookstores, too, the way she once had, before she got so busy.

The moment she returned home, however, she was immediately caught up in the constant demands of her job, swamped by phone calls and emails and projects that had to be done yesterday, no matter what. There was always another pitch to be made, another plane to be boarded, another business dinner to get through.

Now she asked herself why she hadn't just yelled "Stop" one fine day. Accepted a few invitations to have coffee with people who went to her gym, lived in her building, had their hair and nails done at the same salon she frequented.

What exactly had she been chasing so hard all that time? Or, more to the point, what had she been running from? Why was she so afraid to slow down a little?

Remarkably, intelligent as she was, she'd never asked herself those questions. She'd always been able to justify her pursuit of success, success and more success, the next promotion, the next "atta girl" from Dina and the board, the next comma between the numbers in her investment and bank statements.

Still, how much was enough? Where was the finish line?

Mace's simple statement earlier that afternoon, on their horseback ride, came back to her. *Some things are more important than money.*

She'd come perilously close to countering, "Like what?"

That impulse alone, in her opinion, was an indication that she needed to rethink a few of her ideas.

It would've been easy enough, she supposed, to blow off what Mace had said. He probably had more money than he could spend, so naturally making more of it wasn't high on his to-do list.

And it wasn't as if the remark had been original or profound.

Nonetheless, it was true.

Kelly continued to drive, mulling over all those things in her beleaguered brain, staying well within the speed limit, doing her best not to annoy people in other cars by slowing down to gawk at this building or that. She admired century-old churches, followed the narrow roads winding through the pioneer cemetery, considered the hotels serving the tourist trade, ranging from sad little motels with cracked parking lots to the ultramodern and truly grand.

Something for everybody, she thought with a smile.

Smack in the middle, she spotted an all-suites place and, without thinking about it, she turned into the lot.

Twenty minutes later, after a brief tour, she emerged from the lobby with a key card in hand. If she was taking vacation time, then it was going to be on her own dime, even if she *was* still planning to sell Mace Carson on bringing his winery into the twenty-first century.

Her chances, she figured, were almost nonexistent.

Still, win or lose, she'd have a lot of fun trying.

"You're doing what?" Mace asked when he

got a call from Kelly shortly after supper that night.

"Moving," she replied. "I'll be at the Mountain View Suites in town."

Sitting on the screened-in side porch with his feet up, Mace smiled. "Why?"

"None of your business," came the nearly instant answer. "But I'll tell you, anyway. Like I said, I'm taking some vacation days — booked them today — and it wouldn't be right to bill the company for that."

Vacation days? Yeah, she'd mentioned it, but now she'd really done it! Mace resisted an urge to let out a celebratory whoop, mainly because it would spark too damn many questions from his nosy family.

"So, no more hard sell?"

"You wish. If you let this opportunity pass you by, you're not as smart as I think."

He laughed. "Some people just don't know when to quit," he told her, although he was delighted that Kelly wouldn't be hightailing it back to LA in the immediate future.

"As if you know anything about giving up, cowboy."

She had him there, but he didn't have to admit it. "So why the Mountain View?"

"Reasonable prices. Full kitchens. Free

Wi-Fi. Insuite washers and driers. Shall I go on?"

"Grace would probably comp you at the resort if it's putting a strain on your budget."

"Unnecessary," she said. "I love the resort, but I don't want to live on restaurant meals, good as they are. I'm a little out of practice, but I used to be a decent cook."

Mace paused, considering his next words carefully. Finally, he settled on, "Makes sense."

"Shall I prove it to you?"

"Prove what?"

"That I can cook. I'm moving first thing in the morning, and I'll be busy most of the day, but the evening is wide-open. If you're brave enough, I'll make supper."

Again he waited, not because he was uncertain — *hell,* yes, he wanted to say — but he didn't think he should come on too strong.

"Hello?" Kelly prompted, when some thirty seconds must have gone by. "Are you still there? Or did the thought of my cooking send you running for the hills?"

He grinned, rubbing his jaw, rough with a day's growth of beard. "I guess I'll risk it," he said. "What shall I bring?"

"Wine, of course. Red and white, since I haven't settled on the menu just yet, and it could go either way."

"You got it. Are you going to tell me what was bothering you when you got here this afternoon?"

"Who says anything was bothering me?"

"I do. It was obvious there's something on your mind."

"You're a perceptive man."

"I try, but you might be the first woman who ever said so."

Her laughter was followed by, "I can believe that."

"Are we going to talk business tomorrow night?" he asked.

"Probably. Is that a deal breaker?"

"No way. I love it when beautiful women try to change my mind."

This time the pause was on her end. Finally, she said, "Be here at six. And don't forget the wine."

"What's your room number?"

"It's 702. See you then?"

"Yep. If I listen to your pitch, will you tell me what that solemn expression on your face was all about?"

"No guarantees."

Wasn't that *his* line? How many times had he said some version of that to a woman? He smiled to himself. "Okay," he responded, "but I'm a persistent man."

"And I'm a persistent woman. Ought to be an interesting evening."

"Agreed. Is this a formal affair, or can I wear jeans?"

"It's not formal and it's not an affair."

Not formal. Excellent.

Not an affair?

That remained to be seen.

"Okay, see you tomorrow," he said. And with that, the conversation was over.

Mace was still looking at his phone when the inside door squeaked open and Drake came out.

He leaned against the wall and folded his arms, grinning at Mace. "Am I interrupting something, little brother?" he asked.

"Sorry to disappoint you," Mace replied, returning the grin and dropping his phone into his shirt pocket, "but you're not. In fact, you missed the whole show."

"Kelly?"

"Kelly," Mace confirmed. Both his brothers knew him well, and fooling either one of them would require more effort than he wanted to make.

"More 'business'?"

"Maybe."

"*Maybe*," Drake repeated. "Mysterious."

"She's in town to sell me on some fancy plan to triple my business and get my wines on the tables of the rich and famous the world over."

"I trust you've told her you don't give a rat's ass which wines the rich and famous drink?"

"Not in precisely those words, but yeah, I told her I'm not interested in rapid expansion."

"And she's still in town? Interesting."

"She lives in LA. Maybe she just wants a break from crowded freeways and smog."

"Maybe." Drake's grin was almost a smirk. "You know what I think?"

"No, and I don't give a damn, but you're probably going to tell me, anyway."

"Absolutely. Kelly is a beautiful woman with a passion for the wine trade. Last night at supper, we all figured you were avoiding each other's eyes because you were both afraid you'd fall in if you looked too long."

"Poetic. I didn't know you had it in you, Drake."

"I'm a romantic devil. Just ask Luce."

Mace laughed. "She's not objective where you're concerned."

"True," Drake said. "You remember when Luce first came here, searching for wild horses? You and Slater knew we were in love before we did."

"I remember," Mace said carefully. "But —"

"But this is different? Is that what you were going to say? Well, take it from me, it *isn't* different. I've never seen you look at a woman the way you looked at Kelly last night. You're done for, little brother."

"Maybe I just want to sleep with her," Mace ventured; he didn't want to have this conversation, but he wasn't going to get out of it before it ran its course. "Did you ever think of that?"

Drake's mouth twitched at the corners. "That's a given," he said. "She's gorgeous, and she's sexy as hell, if a little on the prim side. But I think you want more than a roll in the hay with this one."

"And if that's what you think, it must be true?"

Drake shook his head. "Stop trying to throw me off, Mace. By now, you ought to know it isn't going to work."

"Is there a point to this discussion?"

"Yes," Drake said, and he looked serious now. He moved away from the wall, came to sit in the chair facing his brother's. "Kelly talked quite a bit about her life in LA at supper last night. She's got a good job, opportunities to travel. A lot could go wrong here, in a situation like this."

"A lot can go wrong *anywhere*," Mace pointed out tersely.

Drake ignored the remark. "Could you live in LA, Mace?"

"No." He liked the City of Angels well enough, but it was, after all, a *city*. A little concrete under his feet once in a while was fine, but without the strength he drew from standing on fertile soil and grassland, right up through the soles of his boots, he would become a person he had no idea how to be.

"Could she live here?" Drake pressed quietly. Mace didn't ask why his answers were so important to his brother; he already knew.

It was because Drake cared. Because he didn't want to see Mace get hurt or fall into a trap that would be hard to escape. Divorce was rare in the Carson clan; once you threw in with somebody and said "I do," you *did*, come hell or high water.

When Luce first arrived on the scene, and it was clear that, for Drake, the earth and the sky had changed places, Mace had asked similar questions. Same with Slater, as he and Grace alternated between powerful attraction and all-out warfare before they finally settled their differences and got married. The brothers were close and, at least with each other, they never hesitated to say what they thought, whether the listener wanted to hear it or not.

Mace's answer was honest, the only one he could have made, but it still wasn't easy.

"I don't know."

"Don't move too fast," Drake said gruffly. "That's all I'm saying. You've been sowing the proverbial wild oats for a long time, brother — since you and that gal, Sarah, you used to bring home at Christmas broke up, and that was years ago. You know all about women in general, but when it comes to the specifics, you might be a little rusty."

Mace had to laugh. "I suppose I deserve this, after all the lectures I gave you about Luce," he said. "Is Slate waiting in the wings to share *his* opinion of my emotional IQ?"

Drake's grin was back. "Probably. And you're right. You've got this coming — what goes around, comes around, as Red always says," he replied. He stood, then rested a hand on Mace's shoulder. "Take your time, little brother. Get to know Kelly, and make sure what she wants is what *you* want, too. It's possible that she's as committed to LA as you are to the ranch and the vineyard, and while compromise is inevitable in any relationship, that one might be tough. If one of you goes in feeling you've given up too much, you'll both be in trouble."

There was nothing original in Drake's brother-speech; Mace knew it backward and forward, would have made it himself if the situation had been reversed. *Had* made it himself. Why, then, did the reminder come as a relief as well as an irritation?

Drake was at the door, about to go inside. "Drake?"

His brother stopped, didn't turn around. Waited, his back to Mace, his head tilted to one side.

"Thanks," Mace said. "Not so much for the lecture, which I could have done without, but for the intention behind it."

Drake gave a low chuckle and returned to the house.

For a moment, Mace felt a sting of envy, knowing Drake would spend tonight and however many more tonights fate might allow, each one followed by another tomorrow, with Luce. They had one child already, and they were getting ready to add to their family.

Slater had Grace, a teenage stepson and a little boy.

He, on the other hand, would be going to bed alone, getting up alone. He was tired of cold sheets, tired of the hollowness that usually settled into his belly at sunset — going-home time, supper time, being the odd man out all the time. And he wanted to be somebody's dad, a situation he'd done everything he could to avoid over the years.

The flash of envy was just that, a flash, gone as quickly as it came. Mace loved his brothers and their wives and their kids, and their happiness meant as much to him as his own — possibly more. He didn't always agree with Slater and Drake, any more than they always agreed with each other, or with him. When they were younger, they'd tangled often, gone beyond heated words to flying fists, as fierce as three junkyard dogs after the same bone.

And even then, if challenged by an outsider, they would've stood back-to-back, bloody-knuckled and fiery-eyed, and fought as long and as hard as they had to, not for themselves, but for each other.

It was complicated, having brothers.

Mace uttered a gusty sigh and thrust himself to his feet, ready for a hot shower and a deep, sound sleep. Sure, he'd be alone, but there were worse things, obviously, like bedding down with the wrong woman, night after night, and waking up wishing you were still single.

Kelly might be the wrong woman, or the right one, forever or for a while.

No telling how things would shake out,

since life seldom gave advance notice of the next major — or minor — development. Even when the trail ahead promised easy traveling, there was always that sudden bend, that steep hill to climb or that deep chasm to fall into.

For now, given the lack of crystal balls and heavenly messengers, it was enough, *had* to be enough, to know he'd see Kelly again in less than twenty-four hours. She was making supper for the two of them, her own idea, and apparently wasn't planning to rush back to LA first chance she got. She was moving to another hotel, still a temporary arrangement, of course, but, from her description, more like a home than the resort could ever be, for all its luxury.

Beyond that, he didn't dare draw conclusions.

He'd knock at her door at six sharp, bearing two bottles of his best wines, and see where things went from there, if they went anywhere at all.

With his head about as clear as it was likely to get, for tonight, anyway, Mace went into the house. He climbed the back stairs, walked along the familiar corridor to his room — or rooms.

As boys, he and Slater and Drake had slept in much smaller quarters on the first floor of the house, each of their spaces adjoining the next, the doors open when they wanted to talk or argue or engage in a spur-of-the-moment pillow fight, friendly or otherwise. They'd shared a bathroom, an arrangement that worked well enough until they hit their teens.

Now, as adults, two of them with growing families, they had private apartments, complete with small kitchens, spacious living rooms with fireplaces, and modern bathrooms. Drake and Luce were building a house of their own on the ranch property, while Slater and Grace had decided to stay on at the home place, planning to expand their living space to include Drake's, once he and Luce and their family had moved out.

Showering, feeling tense muscles relax as multiple jets blasted hot water, Mace smiled to himself, wondering what his great-great-grandfather would have thought of all these modern renovations to the house he'd patterned after his bride's venerable mansion outside Savannah.

He was sure about one thing, anyhow. It would have pleased the canny old pioneer to know his sons and daughters had stayed on this land, loved and protected it, brought up their children here, seen their children's children carry on the legacy, their roots strong and deep and as permanent as ordinary mortals could reach.

CHAPTER SEVEN

Kelly was in the process of checking out of the resort, her belongings already stowed in the waiting rental car, when a man in a chef's striped pants and white tunic suddenly burst through the restaurant and steamrolled straight toward her.

"Was it the food?" the balding, slightly paunchy man demanded, not angrily but with a sort of miffed desperation. "Is that why you're leaving early, Ms. Wright?"

How did he know her name?

Mystified, Kelly simply stared at him.

"Uh-oh," murmured the receptionist she'd dealt with.

The man stopped a few feet from Kelly, fists knotting and unknotting at his sides in obvious agitation. Mercifully, upset as he was, he didn't seem like the violent type.

Of course, she thought. He's the chef, and he probably makes a point of remembering customer's names, especially if he thinks they're dissatisfied.

"Stefano, I presume," she said with a genuine smile and an extended hand.

He nodded.

"You didn't enjoy your lobster salad?" Stefano asked, sounding more hurt than angry. He looked, in fact, as though he might burst into tears of frustration, though he did shake her hand, albeit tentatively. "Is that it?"

Remembering Mace's description of the famous and clearly passionate chef, Kelly was hard put not to laugh. She'd thought Mace was kidding when he warned that Stefano might confront her, wanting an explanation for her slacker's appetite.

"It was absolutely delicious," she said. The situation was certainly colorful, and God knew she understood how important Stefano's work was to him, and why. She'd often wanted to chase down some client and behave in exactly this way, although she'd never actually done it.

The man wasn't just a cook or even a master chef. He was an artist.

And something of an egotist, it seemed.

Stefano dropped Kelly's hand and gaped at her. "Then why didn't you *eat* it?" he blustered finally.

"I wasn't very hungry," Kelly said reasonably, her manner kind but not apologetic.

"Then why —"

Kelly raised a palm. "There isn't any more, Mr. — Stefano. I don't eat when I'm not hungry, no matter how good the food is. And yours, believe me, is fantastic."

Stefano opened his mouth, closed it again, obviously stymied.

"Especially the dinner rolls," Kelly added, afraid the man might hyperventilate or blow a blood vessel if she didn't throw him a solid compliment to hold on to. "They were even better than my grandmother's, and that's saying something."

Stefano blinked, swallowed visibly and found his voice again. "You must come back," he said. "When you intend to eat." A pause. "As my guest, of course. You can even bring Mace Carson with you. He used to enjoy my prime rib."

"I'd love to come back," Kelly said. "But not gratis. Our meals were perfectly fine, and I insist on paying full price. If they hadn't been, I might have accepted your generous offer."

Once again, Stefano blinked. His bushy eyebrows drew together. "When?" he asked.

"Soon," Kelly replied. She wanted to get on with her day, without hurting this man's feelings.

"Tonight?" Stefano pressed.

Just then, Grace appeared, breezing across the lobby. "For heaven's sake, Stefano," she said. "Not *again*. We've discussed this unfortunate habit of chasing down our guests and giving them the third degree, haven't we?"

Stefano reddened. Then he gathered his impressive countenance and jutted his chin. "Yes, madam, we have," he told Grace with affronted dignity. "But I remain a perfectionist."

With that, he turned and strode away, toward the restaurant.

"No shit, Sherlock," Grace said under her breath, watching the genius as he stormed off to his own domain. Then she turned a questioning gaze on Kelly, who laughed.

"Not you, too," Kelly said. "Please tell me you're not offended because I've checked out early."

Grace smiled, her eyes dancing. "I think you've had enough hassle for one morning," she said. "But if you're dissatisfied with your room or the service or anything else, I hope you'll tell me."

"Everything was great," Kelly said. "Now that I plan to stay in Mustang Creek awhile longer, I need more space, that's all. And there's the little matter of integrity. My company has been footing the bill for my stay here in spa heaven, but I'm taking some personal time, so I want to cover personal expenses myself."

Grace pondered that, nodded. "I could arrange for a reduced rate," she said, "since you're a friend of the family and all."

A friend of the family. Kelly liked the sound of that.

But she shook her head. Half an hour before, she'd gotten the call from Melody Hogan and accepted her invitation to a "small gathering" at her and Spence's place, Saturday at noon. Knowing Grace would be there, along with Luce, as Spence had said, Kelly didn't feel a wrench at leaving the resort, where they often ran into each other.

"Thank you, but I've already made other arrangements, and I'll see you again on Saturday at the Hogans' place?"

Grace's eyes lit up. "I wouldn't miss it," she said. "Luce and Blythe are coming, too, of course."

"Good," Kelly said happily. "I'll see you then."

Fifteen minutes later, she was in her modest but well-equipped suite at the Mountain View. The lone bellman on duty, who probably doubled as desk clerk and security officer in a pinch, carried in her things.

She thanked him and handed over a tip. No doubt she'd gone a little overboard where the amount was concerned, but the man was seventy if he was a day, and most likely worked at the hotel to supplement his Social Security and whatever he'd managed to save.

He beamed. "Thank you, Ms. Wright," he said, holding the bill in one palm and glancing down at it intermittently, as though he thought it might change to some smaller denomination.

"Kelly," she said, pretending to squint at his oversize name tag. "Walter," she read aloud.

"You need anything, anything at all, Ms. — er, Kelly — you just call the desk and ask for Walter. I'll be Johnny-on-the-spot."

"I'll do that," Kelly confirmed.

Walter asked if she wanted ice.

She thanked him and said she wouldn't be needing any right away.

Finally he left, closing the door softly behind him.

Kelly stood in the middle of her living room, with its open kitchen and sliding doors leading onto a small yet adequate balcony. It wasn't her professionally decorated LA condo, but it wasn't crowded with *stuff,* either, however expensive and tasteful that stuff might be. There was no history here, and she liked that — no memories of all-night bouts of drawing up proposals or going over reports or justifying expense accounts, no memories of lonely Sunday afternoons and rushed weekday mornings when she barely had time for coffee, let alone a decent breakfast. No sleepless nights to look back on, spent going over and over every aspect of her life, wondering what she should have done differently. Or planning some dreadfully important meeting. Or unable to relax because she had to catch an early flight to this city or that, this *country* or that, all too aware that she'd have to hit the ground running when the plane landed, regardless of jet lag. She needed to be fresh and perky, ready to shine and sell, sell, sell.

It seemed fitting that her cell phone came alive just then, deep inside her ruined handbag. Michael, the purse with a name, she thought with a smile, remembering Mace's comment that first night.

The custom ringtone meant the caller was her boss.

"Hello, Dina," Kelly said cheerfully, having found the phone seconds before voice mail would've kicked in.

Dina didn't bother with a responding "hello." "What have you decided? About the job, I mean. Tell me you're past all that business about reporting to your ex-husband. You're *millimeters* from being made VP, you know."

Kelly laughed softly. "Dina," she said. "Breathe."

"It's just that —"

"*Breathe.* I'm taking some of that vacation time you mentioned. Except for the Carson deal, I'm not thinking about work."

A puzzled silence ensued. "Really?"

"Really."

"So why do I get the distinct feeling that you're planning to resign?"

"Because you're a very perceptive person, I guess," Kelly replied. "I'm just about sure I'll do exactly that."

Dina groaned. "But you've worked so hard —"

"Maybe *too* hard. I need to think things through, Dina, before I make a final decision."

"This wouldn't be happening if the board hadn't hired Alan," Dina said, her tone almost accusing.

"No, it probably wouldn't. But let's face it, Dina. This isn't a tragedy, even by first-world standards. It might even turn out to be a blessing."

"Don't go spouting a bunch of positive,

keep-your-chin-up nonsense," Dina ordered. "I know what this job meant to you." A pause. "What happened, Kelly? And please don't tell me this is about Alan taking over my slot, because it isn't — not all of it, at least. You're a class act, and if you really wanted to stay on, you would. You'd figure out a way to deal with the Alan situation, rise above your misgivings and go right on racking up stellar successes. So, I repeat, *what happened?*"

"I'm not entirely sure," Kelly admitted, struck by Dina's assertion that working with her ex wouldn't have sent her rushing for the door if she really, truly wanted to keep this particular job. It was a point she hadn't considered before then.

"Well, then," Dina blurted, misreading Kelly's hesitation for second thoughts and switching her tone from near-wheedling to smug certainty. "Take all the time you need. Eventually you'll come to your senses."

"Or not," Kelly said. She might never "come to her senses," but explaining that to Dina was too daunting a task to undertake, especially now, when her mind was on supper with Mace, and on recipes and a grocery list. Maybe a bouquet of fresh flowers to add a homey touch . . .

"There's a man!" Dina cried with the

exuberance of a sinner who's just seen the light, startling Kelly so much she flinched. "This is all about *a man*!"

Kelly said nothing. Yes, there was Mace, and the attraction between them was strong, but the fact remained that, even though he'd saved her life twice, they barely knew each other. And "this" was about so much more than Mace; it was about her entire way of living her life.

"I'm right!" Dina crowed. "Who is he? No, wait. Educated guess — has to be our potential client, Mace Carson!"

"Dina," Kelly said quietly, "please. I like Mace, and I think he likes me, but it's much too early to speculate."

"Not for me, it isn't," Dina insisted. "Spill it. Tell me *everything.*"

"Did I ask you, even once, about your recent fascination with the UK?" Kelly asked mildly. "Or why you'd suddenly give up a job you've always claimed to love and move to London?"

A short, rather bruised silence fell, and Kelly regretted being so blunt. She and Dina liked each other, but they certainly weren't confidantes, not when it came to personal matters.

She was about to apologize when Dina spoke. "If you *had* asked," she said somewhat sadly, "I would have told you. I've been secretly married for nearly a year. His name is Ian, he's wonderful and he absolutely refuses to 'move house,' as he puts it, and join me in the States."

Something soft and sweet and a little sorrowful moved in Kelly's heart. Her boss, the thrice-divorced, semimilitant feminist, married and plainly in love?

Would wonders never cease.

"Oh, Dina," she said. "That's marvelous."

Dina gave a dreamy sigh. "Yes, it is."

"I'm so happy for you." That was true. Dina was successful for a reason, but she was sometimes hard-edged, snappish, even bitter, not the sort of person you questioned about her personal life, unless you wanted your head bitten off. Kelly had given her a wide berth at those times, assuming Dina's moods were prompted by glass-ceiling frustrations, profit margins and the ups and downs of the global economy.

No doubt these things had been factors, but now Kelly knew there'd been more to the other woman's dissatisfaction. Most likely, she'd been lonely, overstressed, caught up in the grind with no exit in sight.

"I wish we'd talked about something besides sales goals," Dina said quietly. "Why didn't we, Kelly? Why didn't we go out to lunch once in a while, or order in and tell each other about our lives?"

"Chain of command?" Kelly ventured. "You were — are — my boss, Dina. I couldn't have told you about my life — if indeed I'd had one — outside my job."

"And you believed I'd think less of you if you said you were worried about your parents aging, or that you still grieved for the family dog, even after years and years? If you'd said something like, 'damn it, I want it *all,* a career *and* a family, and why the *hell* is that fine for a man and criminal for a woman'?"

Tears burned in Kelly's eyes. "Yes, probably. Is that what you would've said to me if we'd bared our souls over lunch or after-hours drinks?"

"That and a lot more," Dina said.

"So, Mr. Wonderful aside, is the London job what you want?"

"Technically, it's a step down," Dina replied, without apparent resentment. "And I don't mind telling you, Alan is starting out at twice the salary I'm earning after ten years of hard work and healthy balance sheets, which really, truly and completely pisses me off. Still, I've realized I can let that go, that and a bunch of other things. I have plenty of money of my own, thanks to a decade of busting my backside with few opportunities to go on spending sprees, and I'll be fine financially, job or no job. Fact is, I'm tempted to apply at one of the bookstores on Charing Cross Road and stay as far away from the corporate world as humanly possible."

Kelly smiled. "How does Ian feel about that?" she asked. It felt daring, asking such a question, even after Dina's remarks about the friendship they might have enjoyed if they'd taken a few small risks, and her plain regret that neither of them had reached out.

"Ian," Dina said with a laugh. "He's a major stockholder in BP, among other megamoney machines. He's a lawyer — make that a 'solicitor' — but that's a hobby, really. All his cases are pro bono."

"So he won't be fretting over your contribution to the family finances?"

Dina laughed again. "God, no. He says I'll put him in a higher tax bracket if I draw a big salary. I could spend my days running up charges at Harvey Nicols and Harrods, lunching with Lady This and Lady That, or wandering around home sweet ancestral home, which happens to be a country monstrosity surrounded by statues and all the rest, and he'd be perfectly happy."

"Wow," Kelly said, because no other word

seemed to fit.

"All this, and the man loves me like I've never been loved before," Dina said. "I even like his ex-wife and his kids. He has two teenage sons, both in boarding school, so we don't see them all that much, but when they visit us in London, they're *actually polite.* And friendly."

"Sounds lovely," Kelly commented. "In fact, it sounds like something out of a fairy tale." Not her cup of tea, but still a dream life, by anybody's measure.

Dina gave a wry chuckle. "Well, Ian and I do butt heads once in a while, and it sometimes bothers me that he won't spend even *part* of the year in LA. He's up for an occasional visit, that's all. He's kind of a snob, calls the US 'the colonies,' and he can be pompous, too. Very, very British. We're both stubborn, of course, but . . . well, there's something deeper running beneath all the small differences, like this underground river of everything that's good."

Kelly sank into an easy chair, facing the balcony. "It doesn't sound as though you're going to miss the company all that much," she observed.

"I'll miss some of the people. You, for instance. You'll come over and visit, won't you? I'll show you the sights."

"That would be nice," Kelly said. A pleasure trip might be good for her, especially after years of traveling mostly for business.

"I may be having an insight here," Dina confessed with a smile in her voice, after a moment of comfortable silence. "Sharing these things is probably healthy, but it's also tiring. I'd better get off this phone before I lay my head down on my desk and take a nap. As of today, I still have a job."

Kelly laughed again, astonished at how great it felt and realizing she'd fallen out of the habit somewhere along the line. Except for the occasional rueful chuckle, usually accompanied by a shake of the head, she'd been much too serious for much too long.

"So do I, sort of," she said.

"I'm going to ignore that 'sort of,'" Dina answered cheerily. "Enjoy your vacation, Kelly. Climb a mountain or play golf or go parasailing — whatever blows your hair back." A pause. "And speaking as one workaholic to another, remember that life is short, and it won't be what you did that causes you regret, when your time comes. It'll be what you intended to do and didn't."

"True," Kelly said. "And Dina? Thank you."

"Back at you, kiddo."

After that, they exchanged goodbyes and

the call was over.

Kelly had about a million things to do — choosing a recipe for the supper she'd be sharing with Mace that evening, making sure she had the kitchen equipment she'd need, shopping for the ingredients — but she sat perfectly still for several minutes, assimilating everything she and Dina had said to each other.

For the rest of that day, as he worked, cultivating and pruning the vineyard, wading through invoices and communicating with salespeople, helping to clean and sterilize equipment in the winery, Mace felt like a high-school kid looking forward to a hot date with a pretty girl. The grin that kept coming to his face, unrelated to whatever he happened to be thinking about or doing at the time, brought a pang of sweetness deep in his heart.

More than once he caught himself whistling some tuneless ditty, and he wasn't a whistler.

Damn good thing neither of his brothers was around; they'd have picked up on his mood right away, guessed the reason for it in no time flat and ribbed him unmercifully.

Around two in the afternoon, his mother stopped by his office, dressed for town and bearing gifts.

Mace pushed back his chair and stood, a little startled, when she came through the door.

Blythe smiled. "Sit down," she said. "I'm only staying for a moment."

He didn't sit.

"Feels good to stretch my legs," he said.

Blythe shook her head. "Either I trained you right, or you're just bone stubborn," she said when he remained standing. "Both, I imagine." She plunked a paper bag on his cluttered desk. "Lunch was served an hour and a half ago, and Harry is beside herself, convinced you'll die of starvation any second now."

Mace chuckled. "I might have lasted a while yet," he replied, instantly ravenous. Because they both worked on the ranch, he and Drake usually went back to the main house for the midday meal, much to the housekeeper's delight. Harry loved to feed and just generally fuss over anybody she could round up, man, woman or child.

"It sure is quiet around here," Blythe commented, already back at the threshold and halfway gone.

"Yep, sure is." Mace opened the paper sack and peered inside, extracted a thick roast beef sandwich, oozing horseradish

185

sauce against the plastic wrapping that enclosed it, a clear container of fruit salad mixed with whipped cream, and a home-made doughnut the size of a tractor tire. His mouth watered. "If you see Harry before I do, tell her thanks for the grub."

Blythe waggled her fingers in farewell. "I will," she promised.

Mace was busy unwrapping the sandwich. "Thanks for the delivery service, too," he added.

"Don't get used to it," his mom replied sunnily, vanishing from sight, off to do whatever was next on her agenda.

Mace laughed and sat down to eat his lunch.

What did cowboy types eat?

Kelly asked herself that question, silently of course, as she stood in the supermarket, perusing a cooking site on her smartphone.

Steak, with some kind of sauce or marinade?

Redundant. The Carsons raised beef on their ranch, after all.

Chicken, then?

The site offered as many versions as there were stars in the night sky over Wyoming.

Suddenly, Kelly felt overwhelmed. Maybe she ought to call Stefano, ask him to whip up one of his specialties, something complicated and elegant and inevitably delicious.

No. That would be a cop-out. Besides, she'd told Mace she could cook.

A woman maneuvered her shopping cart around Kelly's.

"Sorry," Kelly told her, realizing she'd been blocking the way to the cereal aisle. She backed her own cart into an open space.

The woman smiled. "No problem," she said.

Still flummoxed by the wealth of choices on the recipe site, Kelly switched to her personal calendar and felt a surge of hope when she saw the notation for her parents' return from their cruise.

They'd been home in Bakersfield for two full days.

She speed-dialed their landline.

"Hello, sweetheart," her mother sang out after the third ring. Just another benefit of modern technology — caller ID. "How are you? More to the point, *where* are you? There was no answer when we called your place, and we didn't want to bother you at work."

Kelly smiled. Neither of her parents carried a cell phone, so they probably hadn't considered calling hers. "I'm fine, Mom. And I'm in Wyoming at the moment."

"Wyoming," Beth Allbright repeated, as though the state was some distant and exotic place. "Well, at least you're on the North American continent for once."

Kelly watched as more shoppers passed, wheeling their carts, and moved back a little more. "How was the cruise?" she asked. "Did you and Dad enjoy it?"

Her parents had both retired young after selling the thriving dry-cleaning business they'd operated for years. Thankfully, they were healthy, with plenty of shared interests. They were close to their daughters and grandchildren, all of whom lived in the LA area. Beth and Frank usually traveled in their well-equipped RV with their aging beagles, Charlie and Fred, but now and again they left the dogs with a neighbor and boarded a cruise ship for a change of pace.

This time, they'd gone to Hawaii, making both legs of the journey aboard an ocean liner.

Kelly's dad, always on the lookout for a deal, had outdone himself, booking an ocean-view minisuite with a balcony at half price.

"We had a wonderful time," her mother replied. "Your father danced the hula at a luau, and I have video to prove it."

Kelly laughed at the image of her dad in a

grass skirt, although he probably hadn't taken the experience quite that far. "That I have to see," she said. "Bet Charlie and Fred were glad to see you when you got back."

As if on cue, the beagles barked in the background.

"Oh, they were," Beth said fondly. Then, to the dogs, she added, "You boys quiet down. I'm talking to your sister."

Kelly's heart warmed, and her eyes misted over briefly. Charlie and Fred, like all their predecessors, were members of the family.

Beth refocused her attention. "When are you coming back from Wyoming, sweetie?" she asked. "Your dad and I would love a visit, and so would your sisters, not to mention the boys."

"I'll be back home in a couple of weeks," Kelly said, hoping there wouldn't be any questions about the unusual length of her stay. Most of her business trips were relatively short.

She wasn't ready to talk about Mace, or the fact that, even though she'd never been here before, Mustang Creek seemed to be welcoming her back after a long and difficult journey. As for the accident with the rental car on the first day of her visit, well, it would be better to describe that in person, so her parents could see for themselves that

189

she hadn't been injured.

"My goodness," Beth said. "A couple of weeks?"

"This client is a particularly tough sell," Kelly hastened to explain. "I'll arrange a weekend visit after I get back to LA."

"Good!" Beth's delight was obvious. "Frank!" she called to Kelly's dad, who must have been nearby. "Kelly's coming for a visit soon."

She heard her dad's voice, if not his words, heard the pleased excitement in his tone. As if caught up in the celebratory mood, Fred and Charlie began to bay.

"Hush!" Beth told them. "Frank, take the boys out back if you don't mind. I can't hear myself think with them carrying on that way!"

Again, Kelly laughed. "Mom," she said. "Mom?"

"I'm sorry, dear," Beth said sweetly. In the background, the screen door creaked open and closed with a familiar thump. "Those silly dogs are so excitable."

"I need a recipe, Mom," Kelly said after giving her mother a chance to catch her breath.

Beth's voice revealed her pleasure at the request. "You're going to *cook*?" she teased. "You, the queen of frozen diet food and take-out salads?"

Kelly waited, half expecting her mother to turn from the phone and convey the news to her husband and the family pets. *Frank! Kelly asked for a recipe!*

It didn't happen.

With a smile, Kelly answered, "Yes, Mom. I'm staying in a suites hotel with a kitchen, and I'm having someone over for supper tonight, so I need an idea. Something quick and foolproof and absolutely delicious."

This time, it was Beth who laughed. "That's a tall order," she remarked, "but anything for you, sweetheart. Your grandmother's baked chicken spaghetti comes to mind."

Kelly's mouth watered at the mention of that savory casserole, a family favorite, and one she'd helped her mother make dozens of times. She ran through the remembered ingredients, the dish being a thrown-together affair, no measurements required.

"That's it," Beth confirmed when she'd finished. "Bake it at 350 for about forty-five minutes, and don't forget to sprinkle the top with lots of Parmesan toward the end and let that brown."

"Thanks, Mom," Kelly said.

"Who's the 'someone' you want to impress?" Beth asked as Kelly joined the other shoppers.

Kelly wasn't irritated by the question — it was natural, especially for a mother — but she *had* been hoping it wouldn't come up. "A client," she said, trying not to sound evasive. After all, there were some things a woman didn't want to say to her mother, not in a crowded supermarket, anyway. "I'll fill you in later, okay? I'm in kind of a hurry right now."

"I'll be expecting an email," Beth responded knowingly, "if not another phone call."

A rush of affection for her mom, her dad and the rest of her family, including, yes, her canine "brothers," swept through Kelly like a warm summer breeze. She missed them all with a poignancy she hadn't felt — hadn't *taken the time* to feel — in years.

Kelly promised to be in touch again soon, and I-love-yous were exchanged, followed by goodbyes.

She made quick work of her shopping, picking up staples for her own use, along with the ingredients for tonight's main dish and an accompanying green salad. Her last stop was the floral corner, where she passed over the cut flowers for potted ones, choosing mums so yellow they seemed to radiate color and brightness, like little suns sending out rays.

Back at the Mountain View, Walter greeted her in the parking lot and insisted on carrying in her groceries. When Kelly tried to tip the older man, he shook his head and feigned a dour expression.

"Thank you for offering," he said, "but no, ma'am." Then, probably to show he hadn't taken offense, he smiled broadly. "What you gave me this morning was too much and, besides, this is Mustang Creek, not the big city, and we're in the Mountain View Suites, not the Ritz. I don't mind a gratuity now and then, mind you, but the tourists keep me supplied with greenbacks." He paused, regarding her with the benevolence of a doting grandfather. "Anyway, I'd like to think we're friends."

Touched, Kelly held out a hand, and the old man took it, almost shyly. "Thank you, Walter," she told him, choking up. Their grip tightened simultaneously before parting. "Friends," she said.

Kelly made a mental note to invite Walter back for coffee sometime soon, when he was off duty, so they could chat.

Maybe, she decided, after seeing him out, she was beginning to get the hang of this friendship thing.

And it was about time.

Happily, Kelly put the groceries away in the fridge and the cupboards, filled the kitchen sink with hot, soapy water and scrubbed the large glass baking dish she'd bought at the supermarket. The suite came with everything else she needed, for now, anyway — a colander, a large cooking pot, even a wooden salad bowl with matching tongs.

She hummed as she worked, cubing and browning the chicken breasts, boiling and draining the pasta, adding spices and tomato sauce and a splash of cooking wine. Finally she mixed everything together, poured it into the casserole dish and covered it with a clean dish towel, letting it cool on the counter before putting it in the fridge.

On a roll, she rinsed out the salad bowl, washed the tongs and the scarred wooden cutting board, and fetched a knife from the utensil drawer. If she was serious about bringing her cooking skills up to code, she thought, she'd need more specialized equipment, but for now, the supplies were adequate.

Her mood dimmed briefly. She was thinking long-term, as though she'd moved into a permanent home, not a temporary space. Whatever happened with her job, she'd be going back to LA at some point, back to her condo and her silver sports car and — and what?

Or whom?

Besides her family, and possibly her eager young assistant, Laura, no one was waiting for her. Her condo was one of several dozen in the complex and, except for brief smiles and perfunctory nods in the lobby, the elevator or the corridors, she didn't know her neighbors.

She'd lived there for several years, but if she left for good, she wouldn't leave so much as a ripple behind. The doorman might notice her absence when Christmas came around and she didn't show up to hand him her annual check, but that was the sad extent of her influence.

To be fair, she hadn't gone out of her way, either. In fact, she wouldn't have remembered what name to scrawl on the envelope of the doorman's holiday card if she hadn't made a note of it on her cell phone.

How was it, then, that she and Walter were already on a first-name basis?

Then there was Dina. Granted, the woman was her boss, but still. Before today's phone conversation, she'd been a virtual stranger to Kelly, and vice versa.

She'd changed in the few days since she'd come to Mustang Creek and gotten a crash course in making friends, but there was more to it than that, of course.

The whole process had begun alongside a rainy road when, teetering on the edge of a cliff, scared and in shock, she'd looked through the driver's window of her doomed rental car and locked eyes, for the first time in a decade, with Mace Carson.

CHAPTER EIGHT

When Kelly opened the door of her suite at six o'clock that night, the sight of her nearly knocked Mace back on the heels of his boots. Every time he saw this woman, it seemed, something about her came as a surprise.

She wore jeans and a simple T-shirt, and her hair was up, loosely pinned, with a few tendrils escaping here and there. Her skin glowed and so did her eyes, and the smile on her lips all but stopped his heart.

Looking at her, he wished he'd gone to the florist's on his way over, or maybe stolen a few blossoms from his mother's flower beds.

At least he'd remembered the wine.

"Come in," Kelly said, holding the door open wide.

For a moment, Mace just stood where he was, aware that he was a man at a cross-roads. If he stepped over that threshold, he realized, with sudden and blinding clarity, the whole course of his life would change, never be the same again.

He could bolt, he supposed.

Make some lame excuse and beat a trail back to the ranch, back to the world he knew so well, back to the work he did, the people he'd always known and those who'd joined the family more recently — his sisters-in-law, his little nephews, young Ryder, who wasn't blood kin but might as well have been. Fourteen and a royal pain at the time, ignored by his birth mother, shunted aside by his father, who happened to be Grace's ex-husband, the boy had come as part of the deal when Slater and Grace got married. Slater loved the kid like his own, and so did Grace.

Kelly looked up at Mace, still holding the door, and her welcoming smile had given way to an expression of puzzled concern.

"Is something wrong?" she asked.

Mace felt like three kinds of idiot, standing there with his tongue in a tangle and his heart thundering fit to bust through his chest. "Um, no," he managed, fairly shoving the two bottles of wine at her, then raising his free hand to take off his hat before remembering he'd left it in the truck.

Her smile was back, tentative and soft.

The wine bottles rested in the curve of her arm.

"Are we going to have supper in the hallway?" she asked with a twinkle.

Mace finally recovered enough to sustain forward momentum, although he hadn't collected his scattered wits. He stepped inside, knowing full well he'd left some version of himself behind for good.

"For a moment there," Kelly commented, "I thought I'd be dining alone tonight."

His laugh was hoarse, awkward. "It's just, well —"

She touched his arm as she closed the door. "Take it easy, cowboy," she said, her voice gentle, her eyes dancing. "It's just supper."

"Whatever it is," Mace said, "it sure smells good."

Heading toward the kitchen counter, she looked back over one shoulder and raised an eyebrow. "You doubted my cooking talents?"

He couldn't tell her about his temporary meltdown, so he told a white lie. "Not for a second," he said.

She put down the wine bottles, opened a drawer, took out a corkscrew. "Do the honors?"

"White or red?" he asked, grateful for the

task, since it gave him something to do with his hands.

"Both," she said. "Either one works with what we're having."

"And that would be?" he asked, picking up the corkscrew.

"My grandmother's famous baked chicken spaghetti." She spoke with her back to him, searching the cupboards, then reached for a pair of wineglasses on a high shelf.

Mace, turning the corkscrew in the red, took advantage of the moment, admiring her perfect backside and her narrow waist.

As she rinsed the glasses at the sink and dried them with a kitchen towel, he regretted the decision he'd made to move slowly, since every caveman instinct urged him to sweep Kelly Wright into his arms, carry her to the first soft surface available and make love to her until the sun came up tomorrow morning. Or maybe the morning after that.

Sure thing, cowboy, argued the voice of reason. *Make a move on the lady before she's ready and see where that gets you.*

He left the white corked and put the bottle in the fridge to chill.

Kelly brought the wineglasses over, set them down. Mace poured the rich, spicy red his winery was best known for.

They clinked their glasses together, holding each other's gaze.

"To your grandmother's spaghetti," Mace said.

"To telling the truth," Kelly replied with a wry note in her voice.

They both took a sip, savored it before swallowing.

As soon as he'd placed his glass on the counter, Mace asked, "So what's up with that toast?"

She smiled that slightly mysterious smile that made him bat-shit crazy, but in a good way. "You looked downright terrified when I opened my door a few minutes ago," she said. "Why?"

Mace had relaxed considerably. "First of all," he said, "I *wasn't* 'terrified.' And *second,* I'm not telling you anything until you fill me in on whatever had you in a twist before our horseback ride yesterday."

Kelly averted her gaze. Took another sip of wine. When she'd swallowed, she set the glass down again and sighed. "It's no big deal," she said with a reluctance that indicated otherwise. "There's a . . . complication, with my job."

"What kind of complication?"

She raised her shoulders, lowered them again. "I guess you'd call it a difference of opinion," she said. "They've hired someone to replace my boss — she's moving to London, to join her husband — and I don't think I can work with this person."

"Okay," Mace said, wondering if he had the right to ask for more details. Kelly didn't strike him as the temperamental type, and she was too professional to engage in petty politics, the preserve of the small-minded and insecure.

The next moment, Kelly surprised Mace, as she so often did. It was one of the many things that intrigued him about her, this way she had of catching him off guard. "I used to be married to him," she said.

Mace didn't know what to say to that, so he kept his mouth shut and waited.

"It isn't that there's any bad blood between Alan and me," she said, turning away. She picked up a pair of pot holders and reached for the handle on the oven door.

Mace took the pot holders from her while she opened the oven, then lifted the casserole from the rack, setting it on the stove top. The stuff smelled so good his stomach rumbled audibly, but the top was still bubbling, as hot as lava about to pour from the mouth of a volcano.

"Do you really want to hear this?" Kelly asked.

He did. But he wasn't going to press her

if she didn't feel like elaborating.

"If you want to tell me," he replied, watching her face.

She nodded, trying to smile but not quite getting there. She took a bowl of salad from the fridge, shut the door with her elbow. "Let's eat while we talk," she said. "I'm starving."

He grinned, wanting to touch her cheek or cup her chin in his hand, but doing neither. "Me, too," he said.

They sat at the small table set against a nearby wall, starting with the salad, giving the spaghetti concoction time to cool down. Drinking more wine.

"I told you a little about Alan before, I think," Kelly began after a few bites of greenery and colorful vegetables.

Mace nodded. "You said he wanted kids right away, and you didn't," he recalled, being careful with his wording. The story was Kelly's to tell or keep to herself, as she chose.

"Yes," Kelly said, distracted again. Looking away briefly, as though watching a memory unfold on the screen of her mind. When she looked at him again, she seemed more relaxed. "I thought I wasn't angry," she went on, "but now I know I was, deep down. We'd talked about having children a lot before we were married, and we'd agreed to wait a few years to start our family — or, at least, I *thought* we'd agreed. When Alan suddenly changed his mind six months in, I felt cheated. Deceived."

"Understandable." There was more Mace wanted to say, and there were questions he wanted to ask, but he suspected that Kelly had been holding these things inside for a long, long time.

"We tried," she said. "To save the marriage, I mean. We talked and cried. We got counseling." She pushed away her salad plate, stared into the deep burgundy remains of her wine, but didn't pick up the glass. Heaved a sigh. "Nothing really changed, though. I wanted to wait, Alan was suddenly desperate to be a father. There was no middle ground."

Mace nodded again.

Kelly rose and went to retrieve the casserole dish from the stove top and get a serving spoon from a drawer. She set the whole works in the center of the table.

When Mace didn't move, she reached for his dinner plate.

He took it out from under his salad bowl and handed it over.

A smile wobbled on Kelly's mouth, and the look in her eyes made him want to hold her, offer what comfort she would accept, anything from circling his fingers around her hand to taking her straight to bed.

He remained still, like a man standing in the middle of a frozen river, thin ice cracking around his boots.

She scooped baked spaghetti onto his plate and gave it back, then helped herself to a considerably smaller portion.

Although his appetite had declined considerably, Mace began to eat.

Kelly nibbled, looking down at her food. Saying nothing.

Her cheeks were a shade of apricot-pink that reminded Mace of a summer sunrise.

The food was good, but he had difficulty swallowing.

He got up from the table without a word and went to the kitchen sink. After finding two plain drinking glasses in the cupboard, he filled them both with water and brought them back.

Kelly reached for hers immediately, drank thirstily.

"Thank you," she said.

"You're welcome," Mace replied, his voice low and gruff.

She glanced pointedly at his plate. "You don't like my cooking?"

"It's good," he said. Sometimes, he reflected, being the proverbial man of few words really and truly sucked. If he'd been a talker, he might've known what to say to make her feel better, but maybe this time it was kinder to listen.

Ironically, questions pounded at the back of his throat. Did she still love her ex-husband? Did she regret standing her ground, going through with the divorce? Did she wish she'd gone ahead and started a family, or had she convinced herself that motherhood wasn't for her?

He wasn't about to ask, and he certainly respected Kelly's right to decide when and if she wanted children, especially since she and her ex had discussed the subject before their wedding and come to terms, but he wasn't without sympathy for Alan's position, either.

He wanted kids of his own as surely as he wanted to live on Carson land for the rest of his life, and no matter how much he might love a woman, those two factors were deal breakers.

Yes, he would be willing to compromise on just about anything else. Every marriage required some giving in on both sides if it was going to last.

Kelly brightened. "Okay," she said, and he recognized the word as a turning point. As far as she was concerned, it was his move. "So. Why did you freeze on my doorstep when you arrived? I wasn't kidding earlier when I said I expected you to run for your life."

Mace gave a raspy chuckle at the image and shook his head, more than a little embarrassed. He liked to think he was the type to run *toward* a challenge, not away from it, but she had him cold. He *had* been scared shitless by the sudden realization that he was about to step out of one world and into another.

"I guess I *was* a bit unnerved," he told her. "I'm attracted to you, Kelly — I haven't exactly made a secret of that. I've been with a lot of women in my time, and if I've had a personal motto, it was 'free and easy.' " He paused when she raised her eyebrows slightly, getting the message. "There was sex, and plenty of it, but it was *safe* sex, I made sure of that, and so did my partners."

She blushed again, and her mouth twitched. "I'm glad," she said. Evidently the conversational tables had turned; now *Kelly* was the one listening, wary of stemming the flow.

"Anyway, when you opened the door, looking as delicious as ice cream on a hot day, I had this overwhelming sense that I'd come to a real fork in the road. If I turned around and went the other way, things would stay the same for the most part — not perfect, certainly, but pretty damn good, anyhow."

Kelly regarded him patiently, waiting, as he had waited.

He'd have given a lot to know what was going on inside that beautiful head of hers. There was something happening between them, for sure, but when he told her the rest, she might pull back, which would be all right if their connection was temporary. But what if it was permanent?

He drew a breath, puffed out his cheeks, exhaled in a rush. Life was nothing if not risky, and there was a lot at stake here. It was a case of win, lose or draw, and two of those potential outcomes were dangerous territory.

"On the other hand, I knew that coming inside, spending the evening with you — well, that would change everything. I'd be all in, as they say in poker. No turning back."

He waited again.

Kelly kept him in suspense for several minutes; her expression gave nothing away.

A thought strayed into his mind. The woman must be one hell of a negotiator, and she was probably a born poker player, too.

Finally she smiled. "And you decided to take a chance," she said.

Mace wasn't exactly relieved, but some of the incipient panic had subsided. "You could put it that way," he said, overcoming an urge to sit back in his chair and fold his arms across his chest. He was no expert on body language, but he knew those moves might send the wrong signal.

Kelly gave up all pretense of finishing her supper. She rested her hands lightly on either side of her plate, fingers uncurled. "I'm glad you stayed," she said quietly.

Every muscle in his body eased; the sensation was strange, dizzying, the exact opposite of an adrenaline rush. "What happens next?" It was a dangerous question, but he couldn't have held it back any more than a rodeo cowboy could hold back a bull or a bucking bronco when the chute gate swung open.

"I guess that depends," she replied.

He frowned. *Here it comes.* "On what?"

"On what we both want, I suppose," Kelly said, fiddling with her fork now, watching him thoughtfully. "A fling would be nice. I've been so busy for so long that I kind of like that idea. Something — how did you put it? — free and easy. No promises, no expectations, nobody saying the word *forever.*"

It was a deal he'd offered many times in the past, with lots of other women, and he'd always been happy when it was accepted.

This time, like everything else about his association with Kelly, was different. He was on the receiving end, getting his comeuppance, some people would say.

And he didn't care for the feeling, not one bit.

"Why the frown?" Kelly asked. Her expression was soft, but her eyes were fierce with intelligence.

Mace cleared his throat, shifted in his chair, folded his arms, then unfolded them again. "I don't have any objection to a fling," he said, hearing the uncertainty in his tone. "Right now, I can't think of a damn thing I'd rather do than take you to bed. It's just that flings tend to be finite. It's assumed from the first that they'll fizzle out at some point."

"Like a lot of marriages," Kelly said mildly. She was speaking from experience; he couldn't refute that, and God knew statistics backed her up.

"Like a lot of marriages," he confirmed, momentarily defeated.

"You want something more . . . open-ended? Than a summer affair, I mean?"

He sighed. "I want the *option* of something more," he said. "But if what you mean by 'open-ended' is one or both of us dating other people, I can tell you that won't work for me."

Kelly widened her eyes, and she grinned slightly. "You are a very unusual man, Mace Carson."

"How so?"

"Oh, come on," she countered. "Surely you know that most men are *not* naturally monogamous. It's instinctive, old-brain stuff, all about continuing the species."

He laughed, without expecting to, and it felt good, provided a sort of inner release. "Thanks for the science lecture," he teased, "and I'll admit there's some truth to that theory, but there *have* been a few evolutionary leaps along the way. We have bigger brains than our distant ancestors did, and the capacity to reason, although some folks do make you wonder if everybody got the genetic memo. The ability to think things through, choose one option over another and all the rest of it, comes with a degree of responsibility."

Kelly placed one elbow on the table and held her chin in her palm, watching him.

"I'm impressed," she said. "You believe in holding yourself accountable for your own actions. It's a rare trait, in case you haven't noticed. In today's world, people seem to feel entitled to whatever they want, and if getting it hurts someone else, so be it."

"That's a pretty cynical attitude," Mace said.

"Maybe," she allowed sadly, "but look at the news. Kids killing other kids for a pair of shoes or a cell phone, or just because they want to know what it feels like. Bullying some classmate, online and off. Adults joining terrorist cells. And don't even get me started on war. It's as if everybody thinks the whole world is virtual, like the games they play on their phones and computers."

Mace leaned forward when he saw a hint of tears in her lovely eyes. "Kelly," he said, "those people represent a fraction of the human race. They make the news *because* they're an aberration, a rarity. How many times have you seen a headline that celebrates the good things that happen all day, every day, all over the world?"

Kelly was quiet, and her eyes were still suspiciously moist. Then she said, "I want to believe that, I really do. That there's more kindness than crime, I mean. But sometimes it's hard."

Mace pushed back his chair. "Come here," he said. It was an invitation, not an order.

She hesitated, then stood, looking uncertain, drying her tears with the back of her right hand.

He took her left, pulled her gently onto his lap, wrapped his arms around her. She gave one small, choked sob and rested her head against his shoulder.

"Tighter," she whispered.

Mace drew her closer still. Kissed the top of her head.

"I'm not weak," she insisted, her voice muffled by the fabric of his shirt. "This is *not* about weakness."

He smiled against the silky softness of her hair. "I know," he whispered.

"Is it about sex?"

The smile gave way to a chuckle. "Only if you want it to be," he assured her. "Suppose I just hold you for now? We can decide the sex question later."

This time, it was Kelly who chuckled. "There's only one Mace Carson," she murmured without lifting her head.

"My brothers would tell you one is plenty," he said. "And they're not alone in that opinion."

She laughed again, a mixture of amusement and sorrow. She slipped her arms around his neck, snuggled against him.

"As long as you understand that I'm not the clingy type."

Mace grinned, enjoying the scent of her hair and skin. He'd gone hard to the point of pain, but there wasn't much he could do about that. "I hear you, Kelly," he said. "You're one tough cookie, and I admire that, along with a number of your other qualities. Still, even the strongest woman needs to be held once in a while. Nothing wrong with that."

She squirmed a little, either in all innocence or because she enjoyed getting a reaction.

"This is nice," she said. Her lips brushed the curve of his neck.

He groaned. "Nice," he said, "is a relative term."

She giggled.

So it *was* deliberate.

"Am I bothering you?" she asked.

"It's agony."

She sat up straight, studying his face. "It is?"

He grinned. "My favorite kind of pain," he said.

She slapped both palms against his chest, laughing. "You *like* pain?"

"Only certain varieties," he replied.

And then, because their lips were almost touching, and because it was the natural thing to do, he kissed her.

Unlike their first kiss, which had been more about testing the emotional waters, this one was fierce and deep, rushing through Mace's blood like fire.

Kelly responded with equal heat, opening for him, her tongue sparring with his.

Mace ran his hands up along her sides, cupped the fullness of her breasts, felt her nipples go hard even through two layers of cloth.

She moaned and turned her head to one side, breaking off the kiss, her breathing as quick and shallow as his own. Her hair was coming down from its pins; her eyes were bright and full of heat.

"What you said before, about responsible sex —"

Damn, Mace thought. He'd brought condoms, then left them in the truck, hidden in the glove compartment.

He could only manage a grim nod.

Kelly rested the tip of one index finger against his mouth. "You forgot," she said with a mischievous smile.

"Sort of," he said. "I have condoms in the truck."

She raised both eyebrows. "Do you make a habit of that?"

"No. It was intentional." He groaned. "I'll go get them." He didn't like the idea of walking out in public looking as if he were trying to smuggle a stolen fence post in his pants. Besides, he wasn't sure his knees would hold up long enough to get down to the parking lot and back.

Kelly smiled. "No need," she said, brushing his lips with hers. "I happen to have some on hand. So to speak."

Yes, Mace thought.

The opportunity to throw her question back at her was too good to miss. "Do you make a habit of that?" he asked.

She grinned, between nibbles at his lower lip. "No," she murmured. "It was intentional."

He stood, lifting Kelly as he rose, carrying her.

"If you're going to change your mind," he said, "now would be a good time to say so."

"I won't be changing my mind," she replied.

And she didn't.

Kelly had been intimate with exactly three men in her life — two boyfriends, one in high school and one in college, and Alan,

216

her ex-husband, which meant she was practically celibate.

And therefore unprepared.

Now, as Mace carried her into her nondescript hotel bedroom, as he set her down with a combination of gentleness and strength that made every pulse-point thrum, she realized that none of her previous experiences could have prepared her for this one.

Her thoughts were strangely clear, considering the tumult rocking her body in waves; she knew exactly what she was doing, knew she was taking emotional risks, that there might be pitfalls ahead, regrets. Oh, yes. Hindsight was indeed 20/20; clichés *became* clichés, after all, because they were true.

Knowing all that changed nothing.

She wanted Mace Carson, *needed* him as she had never needed a man before, even in her marriage bed. She craved the hard heat of him, flesh against flesh, and every fiber and tissue, every cell, cried out to take him inside her, to enclose him, to conquer and be conquered.

She kicked off her shoes, frantic to bare some part of herself. She watched as Mace removed his shirt, braced himself on one knee, looking down at her as though she were a riddle of some kind, challenging but not impossible. Then he smiled.

"Condoms?" he asked, his voice gruff.

"Drawer," Kelly said, directing him to the bedside stand with a nod.

He immediately opened the drawer, found the small packet and peeled away the box's wrapper.

The delay, brief though it was, almost drove her mad.

She started to get out of her clothes, not just remove them, but claw at the fabric, rip them away, anything to be free of them. Mace, his chest bare and totally masculine, stopped her, taking a gentle hold of her wrists. He didn't speak, didn't need words — his message was clear in the silence, heightened by it.

Let me.

Slowly, garment by garment, he *unwrapped* her, as though she were a gift, long-anticipated and far too precious for haste.

When he'd stripped away the last barrier, Kelly was wild, driven by primal instincts, reveling, for the first time in her life, in the simple yet complicated, frustrating and glorious *gift* of being a woman.

The rest of Mace's clothing might have dissolved into thin air, for all Kelly knew, because when he stretched out beside her, he was wonderfully naked, his flesh warm and — hard, everywhere.

He caressed her, his hands at once callused and tender, moving over her breasts, stroking her nipples, exploring her belly, parting her thighs.

Suddenly, her pulse was pounding against his fingers as they teased her, prepared her.

She whimpered, her back arching to follow the movements of his hand. "Not yet," she murmured. "Not yet."

He ignored the plea, kissing her deeply, bringing her to that first, shattering orgasm, her cries of release captured by the warmth of his mouth.

When she settled down, gasping, feeling as though every part of her had melted into the bedspread, he kissed the tip of her nose, the space between her eyebrows, her chin and, finally, her mouth.

"Damn it," she said, only half in jest. "It's over."

He nibbled the length of her neck. "Think so?" he asked.

She blinked. "There's more?"

Mace lifted his head, and his eyes smiled, sultry and surprised. "If I didn't know you'd been married," he told her, "I'd think this was your first time. Not that it wasn't great, because it was."

Her cheeks blazed. In some ways, he was

right — it *was* her first time. She'd seldom come to climax with Alan, and always softly, remotely, an echo but never the sound itself.

This one had been a thunderclap — a thunder*storm.*

"Well," she said, slightly miffed at being caught out, "it isn't."

Mace laughed, a throaty sound, wholly masculine. "Shall we stop and discuss it?" he joked.

"God, no," Kelly replied.

Again, he laughed.

She'd expected, frankly, that the best had already happened; now it would be a matter of letting Mace have his turn, receiving him graciously, stroking his back and murmuring to him.

Boy, was she in for a shock.

The orgasm to end all orgasms, as she'd thought of it, proved to be only the beginning, the first in an escalating series of pinnacles, each one fiercer than the one before, each one preceded by another round of delicious foreplay.

By the time Mace actually took her, after a brief pause to put on a condom, Kelly was frenzied, every part of her moist with exertion, aching for more and then still more.

The final release was simultaneous, cataclysmic for both of them.

When it was truly over, when the last echo of the last cry had faded away, when Mace collapsed beside Kelly, his body half sprawled over hers, she wept.

Mace felt her tears against his temple, met her gaze, held her chin when she would have turned away.

"What is it?" he asked, his breathing still ragged, but slowing.

"Nothing," Kelly choked out. "Everything!"

He smiled, smoothed her cheek with one thumb. "Want to tell me about it?"

"No," Kelly managed to say. "Not now."

"Okay," he agreed huskily.

She sniffled. She might have told him she was crying because their lovemaking had been so powerful, so far beyond anything she'd imagined it could be, that she was in awe, but that would have meant explaining, too, that she was mourning all the things she'd missed on the way to now.

Finally, because she had to say something, she cupped his beard-bristled cheeks in her hands, looked into his eyes and whispered, "I never knew it could be like this."

Once again, Mace surprised her. "Neither did I," he said very quietly. "Neither did I."

After that, they slept, arms and legs entwined, foreheads touching.

CHAPTER NINE

On the drive home, his older brother, Drake, had called him. "I'm feeding the horses."

That was Carson-speak for *This is where I am and I want a word.*

So Mace parked the truck in his usual spot by the house and walked to the stable, which had recently gotten a face-lift of new paint and a new roof.

"Okay, what's up?" Drake dropped a saddle on a peg and dusted off his hands.

"Meaning?"

"Any reason you missed dinner, and oh, wait, didn't come home at all last night?"

"I called Harry to let her know."

"About dinner. Your bedroom was empty."

"What are you, some kind of night watchman? I sleep in the office at the winery all the time."

"Right." His brother's dark blond brows drew together. "I hate to break it to you that your ability to be anything other than transparent exists only in your mind. Your truck wasn't here. Is she the woman I think it is?"

His older brother was always blunt, but he was also usually on the mark. Mace defended himself. "I never said there was a she."

"Oh, yeah, there's a she. And I know who it is. You have that starry-eyed, heifer-hit-between-the-eyes look. Grab a bag of feed and make yourself useful while you tell me the truth. I also happen to know you didn't sleep in your office last night. Grace noticed because she called the winery office with an order — and didn't get an answer. You do realize you can't keep secrets around these parts, don't you?"

Oh, he did. Mace hefted a bag and took it toward the stalls. "I figured I had the option of having a personal life. Maybe I'm wrong."

"Yeah, you are. And," he added, "you can trust me and Slate with anything."

Mace could tell his brothers anything in confidence; he did know that. He shrugged and shut the door. Stroking the silky nose of the inquisitive horse who'd poked his head over the top of the stall, he elaborated. "Kelly invited me to dinner last night."

"Good." Drake smiled broadly.

As he filled a bucket with water, Drake said over his shoulder, "We all like Kelly, but you do know that mixing business with pleasure is a piss-poor idea, right?"

"I never said —"

"So, is she *the one*?"

Drake really was the most direct person he knew. Maybe he dealt with far too many cattle and horses and saw no need for subtlety. Mace shrugged. "I realize you have a theory that when a man meets the right woman, a bolt of lightning comes down and strikes some sense into him. But you might recall that you weren't too fond of your wife when she first showed up at the ranch."

Drake, of course, thought that over. He thought everything over. Mace found it annoying, but then, they had a legendary habit of annoying each other. He finally said, "That's true enough. I still *knew.*"

Mace said succinctly, "I'm not you."

"Yeah, not as smart as me."

Now they were back in a comfortable place, taking a few digs at each other as usual. "Really? Says who?"

"I'm pretty sure everyone. When did you get so damned nosy, anyway?"

"I think you're both adolescent fools. *Bickering* adolescent fools." Red came in and dumped a load of coiled rope on the floor.

"Now give me a heads-up on the current Carson brother dispute."

Drake smirked and launched into a deliberate twang. "He's got a girl, but he's being closemouthed about whether it's the real thing or just another fling."

"Cut the hokey Western talk," Mace snapped. "And you know very well that she isn't a girl, and she isn't mine."

"Didn't play your cards right, son?" Red cocked a bushy eyebrow and tipped back his hat. Mace had always maintained that the ranch foreman went to the store each year and bought seven of the same flannel shirts and wore a different one every day of the week. This year it seemed to be a yellow-and-navy theme. The hat stayed the same.

"Didn't get a royal flush," Drake observed with a grin.

The fun they were having at his expense didn't bother him. Mace was in a good mood. "Please excuse me from this conversation."

"Sure, but that north herd needs to be moved," Red told him. "Any chance you can help?"

"Will do. Just give me a second."

"We'll saddle the horses. Meet us there."

"Deal."

He went to the house, changed his clothes,

and wasn't surprised to find his mother doing the books for the vineyard office in the dining room, ledgers all around her and the computer screen showing a spreadsheet. He met her with a kiss on the cheek and the words, "I'm thirty-one."

"Trust me, I know how old you are." She met his eyes. "Your relationships are your own business."

Today she wore her hair, the same color as his, in a simple twist. Silver bracelet, long denim skirt, short-sleeve white blouse. She looked elegant and about twenty years younger than sixty-one. "By the way, I do appreciate that you called so the entire household wouldn't worry about you."

He'd considered more than once how living at the family home was a mixed blessing. It made no sense to get his own place and then have to drive to the ranch every single day. The same was true for Drake, who actually ran the operation. They had a lot of livestock and if there was an emergency, Mace was on hand to help out. Slater often went on location, which entailed traveling, so living here, Grace didn't have to be a single parent when he was away. Not with an entire household to pitch in. As well, the house was huge, built over a hundred years ago when having a big family was the norm. Leaving his mother and Harry to rattle around in it alone didn't appeal to any of them.

But privacy was a bit of a problem.

Mace said evenly, "If I didn't know you'd already figured out I was with Kelly, I'd think I was about to get the third degree. I don't want to sound like I took Trite Talk 101 in college or anything, but she's . . . special. I'll admit that, but I can't tell you where this going. If it goes anywhere at all."

"I wasn't judging."

"You weren't?" He folded his arms and leaned against the desk.

"No." She tucked her hair behind one ear. "Slater has a child with a woman he never married. Grace was married before and her stepson from her ex's first marriage lives with us. All relationships are complicated. As you pointed out when you walked in here, you're more than old enough to make your own decisions. Now then, I have the figures ready for our meeting with Kelly — Ms. Wright — so let's do a recap and make sure we can talk reasonably about what kind of sales they anticipate, what they expect from us and so on."

He glanced at it. "Looks good to me. But nothing's going to change the fact that we're producing as much as we can right now.

Unless we expand, I'm afraid Kelly's company is of no use to us — and vice versa. Besides, I really don't want to expand. I want to make wines, not manage a lot of people."

His mother tilted her head in the thoughtful way he'd known since childhood. "I see your point. Let's hear what she has to say when we talk to her this afternoon. Oh, and keep in mind that you could always hire a manager to oversee the day-to-day operations."

"Then I'd have to manage the manager." Her vision was clear to her, of course, since the vineyard had originally been her idea, but it wasn't as clear to him.

"Anyway," he went on. "Drake and Red need me to give them a hand. I'll be back as soon as possible."

Kelly had a fair idea of what she was walking into.

A hornet's nest.

It remained to be seen whether she could pull this off. She'd received an urgent email this morning, followed by a conversation with Dina; the company was "changing its business model" — which turned out to mean that they wanted to *buy* rather than partner with the various wineries they had in their sights. She wondered if Alan's pending control of the company had anything to do with it. In any case, it meant that her offer was going to change. And if Mace had problems with the previous deal, wait till he heard this new version!

Mace Carson was polite, considerate in bed — and out of it — but she sensed that he went his own way.

She'd carefully picked out a short black skirt and ivory top, plus two-inch heels. A spritz of body spray was the only perfume she wore. Her makeup was polished but minimal. She reminded herself that he'd seen her first thing in the morning. Tousled hair, sleepy eyes, naked . . .

Don't go there.

She realized again how gorgeous the house was. She bumped up the driveway in her rental car, past grazing cattle on either side. Originally she'd expected antlers on the front porch, but instead she'd found a sprawling antebellum structure with blooming pots of flowers on the veranda. Suddenly she noticed several horsemen coming in at a gallop, kicking up dust.

As they came closer, she saw that Mace was one of them. He was riding a different horse this time, not Splash, the paint gelding he'd ridden before, during their first "meeting."

She waited, shading her eyes with one hand.

"Almost late," he said as he pulled up, his mount dancing sideways, "is still on time, right? Sorry. We'll ride over to the winery for our meeting. Faster that way."

Ride? On his horse? She was wearing a Dior black pencil skirt. He must be joking.

"Hey, Kelly," Drake said. "Good to see you again. And my brother's right — it really is faster. Oh, your car will be perfectly safe here, so don't worry about that."

"Look how I'm dressed! I can't possibly —"

"Sure you can." Drake swung off his horse, picked her up without any warning and hefted her sideways onto Mace's horse, draping her across his lap so his arm could curve securely around her. Her audible gasp didn't faze Drake one bit.

"My apologies if I delayed your meeting. We were moving cows, and the new bull broke out of his pasture. Ever tried catching a young bull? Not a one-man job." He tipped his hat and walked away with his lanky cowboy stride. The horse followed him, trailing the reins. The two dogs she'd met earlier came along, too.

"As you can see," Mace said drily, "Drake

believes that talking too much is a waste of time if action can solve the problem. The rest of my family's not quite so direct, as you no doubt discovered."

"I have," she muttered, trying to keep her briefcase from bumping the horse's shoulder. Mace had the high hand and he knew it. "I bought this skirt and blouse on Rodeo Drive in Los Angeles, by the way — and the boutique didn't offer any Western wear."

He nudged the horse to a path around the house. He laughed, his blue eyes alight. "Yeah, but you did buy yourself those cowboy boots the other day. Too bad you didn't wear them. Riding really is more practical, makes it easier to get around. You can't grade roads everywhere and still graze cattle. Besides, who wants to drive a car when you can ride a horse? Meet Stormy." He patted the horse's glossy black neck. "The night he was born, a front came through that made us all wonder if the house would be standing in the morning. He earned the name."

"He's beautiful." She meant it, even if sitting on the lap of a man she'd spent a steamy night with hadn't been on her agenda for this trip — much less being perched on a horse while wearing heels and a skirt.

"He sure is," Mace agreed, balancing her easily, the well-mannered horse walking along. "He's eight now. I had to train him myself. Luckily I had Red. He can talk to horses like no one else I've ever seen. He just looks them in the eye, tells them straight up what he expects, and they tend to do it."

She loved how he talked about people and animals as if they were family. "I'm looking forward to seeing him again," Kelly said softly.

"Red's the father I no longer have."

He said it so matter-of-factly she didn't know how to respond. Finally she just asked. "What happened? I remember you told me he died when you were young."

"Riding accident. A fluke," he explained briefly. "He didn't land well when he was thrown."

He sounded stoic about his father's tragic accident, but she knew he wasn't. "I'm so sorry."

"Thanks. Me, too."

She might've pointed out that she wished she hadn't heard that particular story while she was sitting on a horse, but his arm was firmly around her, keeping her safe. And the last thing she wanted to do was trivialize his grief with a remark like that. Besides, she drove a car every day and that was more dangerous, as recent events proved. "I still can't believe this view."

He nodded. "This is why I don't live in a city."

"Even though you went to school in LA, I can't really picture you in a city."

"Yeah, the big city sounded good at the time, a lot more exciting than a place like this. I found out it was just too noisy and crowded for me. In fact, I knew I hated it the very first day. That was probably the most valuable lesson I learned."

"But you stayed."

"Of course. I'd signed up for it, hadn't I?"

She was getting the strong impression that if a Carson made a promise, there was no more to be said. Good information to have. "Many college freshmen have changed their minds and gone home."

They were approaching the winery. She'd noticed the Mountain Winery logo when she'd come here earlier; this time she studied it more carefully. Whoever created it had perfectly captured the Tetons in the background and the picturesque old building that also appeared on the labels. One of the distinct selling features of the wines was the way each different kind had a label with a wild animal — like a mountain goat for the merlot, or an osprey for the chardonnay.

They suited the Wyoming setting exquisitely. Her favorite was the wolf in the snow for the full-bodied cabernet; that was the wine that had initially captured her attention when it was awarded first place at a vintners' festival. She'd been one of the judges.

Great marketing and great wine was a magical combination.

She just hoped she could convince him — even though he'd already told her it wouldn't be an easy sell.

Kelly suspected there wasn't much enthusiasm for her presence when it came to the business side of their relationship.

Well, she had news for him. She'd try her damnedest to get her way.

Chapter Ten

Maybe he should've reminded his mother that he was all grown up.

Blythe had met other women he'd dated — slept with — but Kelly was different. Special, as he'd told his mom earlier that day. He'd never been this . . . serious, if that was the word, about a woman before. And the business relationship only complicated things.

"Uh, Mom. Here we are. Kelly's ready for our meeting."

All sophistication seemed to wave goodbye and fly out the window. He should've added, *Aw shucks, I'm taking her to the freshman sock hop.* To make it worse, he was fairly sure he'd tracked in either mud or manure across the polished wood floor of the office. He really hoped it wasn't the latter, but he wouldn't be surprised if it was.

After helping Drake recover that damn bull yet again, he was dusty and disheveled,

235

and a faint whiff told him that he *had* forgotten to scrape the manure off his boots.

Dead sexy, right?

On the other hand, Kelly looked killer in that black skirt with her shining blond hair brushing her shoulders, totally professional and collected even if he and Drake had made her ride over on a horse. She stretched out a slim hand. "Wonderful to see you again, Mrs. Carson."

"You, too, Kelly. And it's Blythe, remember?"

A moment later, he realized his mother was looking at him expectantly.

A chair. He grabbed a spare one so they could all sit together at the long table he used as a desk and for staff meetings, and held it so Kelly could sit down. She thanked him politely, opened her briefcase and said succinctly, "I've had the tour, and I'd love another one, but should we first discuss why I'm here?"

She addressed his mother. He didn't mind that at all. He liked, even loved, what he did, or at least most aspects of it, but Blythe Carson was from a famous winemaking family, and she had certain ideas about how things should be done.

"We'd like to buy Mountain Winery."

Buy? Maybe his hearing was going.

Until Kelly opened her mouth and said that, he'd been fairly sure he'd let his mother handle it, since he'd already made his feelings on the subject crystal clear.

That decision followed his sophistication in full flight.

Kelly took a sheaf of papers from her briefcase. "I know we're a major distributor of boutique wines from small producers, but there's been a very recent change in our business model. What we'd like to do is buy your company. Here's our offer. Please ask me any questions you need answered."

Whatever he'd expected, it wasn't *that*. "Come again?" he said.

His mother, however, didn't look surprised. She just said evenly to Kelly, "I talked to my father this morning. He told me he heard — via the grapevine, so to speak — that your company has been acquiring a number of small wineries."

The two women regarded each other as if he wasn't even there.

"No." Mace said it more emphatically than he'd intended, and then with some effort modified his tone. "Sell? No."

They continued to ignore him. Kelly tapped the papers with a manicured nail. "Once you read that, you'll see that the operation will basically remain under your control. We aren't going for change. We just want more of the same — quality wines and a unique Western slant to the brand, because there aren't many wineries in this state. The liquors, of course, are part of the deal. That's a different market, and we know how to reach it, as well."

He'd only begun to experiment in that area, making a couple of different brandies and one coffee-based liqueur; Harry swore it added a new dimension to her award-winning pie when she took home the blue ribbon from the county fair yet again.

All fine and good, but . . . no.

"We aren't selling," he said firmly, even though his mother was at that moment glancing over the papers, brow furrowed; she'd obviously guessed this was exactly what would happen.

Kelly finally looked over at him, her gaze direct. "Do you have any idea what we could contribute to the success of Mountain Winery? All the heavy lifting, so to speak. Marketing, payroll, inventory, all the things you don't like to do."

"How do you know what I like to do?"

The minute those words came out of his mouth he felt like an idiot — again. He almost added something about *making wine,* but fortunately stopped himself. Why embarrass himself even more? "I told her you don't enjoy any part except the creative process. Evidently you weren't listening." His mother raised her brows. "I hope you do realize the reason you and Drake clash so much is that you're so similar. He'd rather rope a stray calf in a blizzard than balance a spreadsheet."

"There's a clause saying you need to continue to be in charge for a specific number of years." Kelly provided the information helpfully, her smile serene. "The wines are good because of you, after all."

He could tell that she sensed victory in the air. He only smelled the manure. "Flattery isn't moving you down the pike. No."

"Maybe you need to think about it." The traitor, his mother, sounded sincere, her hands resting on the polished table.

He turned to her in consternation. "You aren't *really* considering this."

She shrugged. "I feel we should. At least we need to talk about it."

He grew up on a ranch his family had owned for decades. His father had worked for himself, Drake worked for himself, Slater ran his own production company . . . He wasn't going to sell out and work for someone else.

No way.

But he did respect his mother's opinion. It was just that he saw a conflict between her desire to follow a family tradition and *his* desire not to conform to a corporate standard. She wanted a successful brand and vineyard; he wanted the same thing, but maybe not on the same scale or by the same methods.

"You haven't even looked at the offer, Mr. Carson," Kelly said calmly.

"*Mr.* Carson? Really? I seem to recall that you and I are on a first-name basis." He could've added that he'd heard her moan his first name more than once when they made love, but he didn't want to embarrass her just to make a point. This unexpected twist had thrown him.

She flushed at that. "I'm trying to stay as professional as possible on a business level."

"I like our personal level better."

For someone with such a soft, tempting mouth, she sure could set her lips in a stubborn line. "I repeat, you haven't even looked at the offer."

"You'll find I'm not all about money. I want to do what I do the way *I* want to do it."

Her responding smile had a challenging quality. "What a coincidence. The company I work for wants you to do just that."

"For them. Not for me."

"I see you're catching on." She held his gaze. "Yes, for them, but nothing would really change in the day-to-day operation except that you could offer your employees more benefits, like paid vacations and expanded health care, not to mention a nice 401(k) plan. To some extent, this *isn't* all about you."

That was a low blow, but he had to admire her ability to touch a nerve. Although he paid well, the business wasn't big enough for any of those benefits. He did employ several full-time people to do the bottling, put on labels and load the wine into boxes for shipping; if they needed a day off, he simply gave it to them, with pay, and did the work himself.

He stuck to his guns. "No way we'd sell anyone part of this ranch."

"We don't want that. It's the label we're after, and, of course, the formulas. Keep the land, the building, the whole works. Essentially, you'll be selling us the name. You can even continue to develop your exceptional wines and, if you wish, we'll distribute and market them. Under another brand name, of course. It's a win-win."

Now she was hitting the edge of sassy. She might look like the pretty college girl she'd

241

once been, with her stylish clothes and smooth blond hair, but she knew what she was doing and what she wanted.

His mother, who served as an adviser but didn't actually own any part of the winery, let their argument go on without stepping in — without smoothing the troubled waters in her usual diplomatic way. *That* he didn't like. There was a sensation of being outnumbered, especially since she'd more or less admitted that this particular offer wasn't a complete surprise to her, thanks to his grandfather.

It would be nice if someone had kept *him* in the loop.

What he needed was to talk to his brothers. Slate would have a good perspective on this situation, and no one was more grounded than Drake.

Blythe Carson broke into his thoughts just then. "Mace is used to running the show and as you pointed out, he does a great job of it," she told Kelly. "I'm sure he'll consider the offer very carefully." A long pause. "On a different note, would you care to stay for dinner again? As Kelly this time, not Ms. Wright?"

That meeting had been more — and less — successful than Kelly had expected. She'd assumed there'd be pushback from Blythe Carson and had been pleasantly surprised. Mace's reaction was exactly what she'd thought it would be, with a firmness that evoked images of a difficult battle ahead.

But dinner with him held an appeal she didn't care to analyze. She also realized that the better she understood the dynamics of this family, the better her chance of success on the business end. Hey, she could rationalize as well as anyone else.

Above all, she *wanted* to spend another evening with Mace.

"I'd love to stay. Thank you."

"I don't have to warn you that it's not usually a peaceful meal, with children of various ages, dogs underfoot, three brothers, two wives, sometimes even an ex-girlfriend. I think Slater's business partner and investor is in town, so he'll be there, too. But Harry's take on Italian food is not to be missed. She calls it 'Wyoming Italian' and uses bison for the meatballs and makes a sauce using veggies from my garden. Speaking of which, I'm supposed to collect garlic for the bread. Make sure Mace gives you a glass of his new concoction. It's a take on white burgundy, something I've only had in French wines. I think it's my new favorite for watching the sunset from the front porch."

With that she rose in a graceful swirl of long skirts and left the office.

Kelly tried a conciliatory smile. Mace didn't smile back, sitting there sprawled in his chair, long legs extended. "I can see now why you chose to make last night a no-business-talk affair," he muttered. "How did you know how I'd feel about this?"

"I'm very well aware that people who run family-based wineries tend to be passionate about what they do."

His expression was sardonic. "Or just passionate? Why do I get the feeling now that I was being played?" He frowned at her. "Did you *really* just find out that GGI wants to buy Mountain Winery?"

The question stung, because it was entirely unfounded. "Yes!" she snapped. "I really just found out." She felt hurt but knew she had to tell him that the company would settle for a partnership if he refused their new offer. Her only real leverage, if she had any, was going to be convincing him that the sale would give him more time to experiment, create new blends, since that was his true genius. He had the palate, the vision and, beyond a doubt, the willingness to work hard, all traits of a truly innovative winemaker.

Could they keep their attraction, their growing personal connection, separate from the business proposal she had to pitch? Would he even give her the *chance* to explain the company's offer? Did he believe that she truly hadn't known about it? And could she forgive him for thinking she had?

She decided she could. She also decided to take the direct approach. "Before we go any further," she said, "I think we need to come to an understanding. If you think I'd ever sleep with you to make a deal, you're so far off base you might as well be on another planet. I'm not the calculating type, Mace. And I had no idea the offer was going to change! As I explained, I just learned that the company's undergoing a major re-organization."

Thankfully, he didn't argue. Instead, he apologized. "That comment was inappropriate and — I agree — illogical. I'm sorry. It's just that I haven't figured out how to feel about all this, so cut me some slack, okay? If I'd been asked, and I wasn't, I would've made book that my mother would turn you down flat."

A man who could apologize? That was in his favor. "I'm out of my element, too," she said evenly, "and once again I'm not talking business. Why do I get the impression your mother knows what happened last night?"

"If she does, she didn't hear it. Call it intuition."

She believed him.

"You did warn me," she admitted, gazing out the window at the beautiful view. There was a bird of prey perched on a branch in her direct line of vision — she guessed a golden eagle judging by the size and coloring, but she was hardly an expert in ornithology — and it lifted off and flew gracefully away as she watched. "Your sister-in-law runs the resort, the waitress knew you when we had lunch there, and you spoke to the police dispatcher on a first-name basis . . . I'm from LA. I'm not used to that."

"I'm not used to anything else really. On that note, let's go take another look at the winery. My feelings on the offer aside, I'm happy to share."

He could switch on the facile charm when he chose, and she wasn't immune to it, which was disconcerting. It was clear to her that they understood each other on some level, but that could be both good and bad. They might be evenly matched in the stubborn department. Except that he was playing on his home turf and she was the visiting team.

She sat back in her chair and regarded him from his boots to the width of his shoulders in the denim shirt to his nicely disheveled blond hair. "Just to give you fair warning, I have an interesting slant on our marketing strategy. I was wondering if your older brother's production company might be willing to do a television commercial for the winery. I know it isn't his usual thing, but it would help advertise his upcoming film on the area, too. I saw that documentary he did on the cliff dwellings in Arizona and New Mexico and loved it. He knows what he's doing and he knows Mountain Winery. That would be such a win all around. The company would pay for it, and he'd get free publicity."

Mace didn't even glance at the paperwork his mother had left on the desk; Kelly already knew that he wouldn't, not in front of her. "That's a diabolical move," he murmured."

"I'm a cunning sort of person," she said, since they were openly flirting now, despite being at odds with each other. "I drove my car off the road just to get your attention."

"No, you didn't." He sighed. "I wish I wasn't so attracted to you. Or that we'd met again in a completely different situation — something with no business attached. Why the hell couldn't they have sent a paunchy, balding middle-aged man?" Another sigh. "You're articulate and persuasive enough that my mother took you seriously. But I'll tell you once more. I'm *not* interested."

"I could swear you were."

"I mean not interested in the deal," he amended with a laugh. "Okay, you win that one. As an olive branch I'll give you a glass of the white my mother mentioned. I got the idea from an industry magazine article about white wines with true complexity. It isn't easy to create something unique, and just like champagne, it has to be called by a different name if it's not from that particular region in France. So I decided to use a varietal grape from Oregon. I grafted it to some of our vines. Let's go."

She let his enthusiasm wash over her as he rose and offered his hand. This, his skill as a winemaker, was exactly why she'd come to Wyoming.

The building was as perfect as she remembered. This was her chance to explore the tasting room, with its old polished bar rescued from a historic hotel, racks of different wines for sampling, antique glasses — she suspected Blythe had acquired those — and an array of old guns displayed on the rough wooden walls.

The promised wine was everything Blythe had promised. Not too dry, but certainly not sweet, with overtones of apple and smooth honey, it still managed to be refreshing. Perched on a stool at the old bar, she was an instant fan.

"This is fabulous. Have you settled on a name for it yet?"

Mace, sitting next to her, shook his head and then looked wary. "No. Oh, no, don't tell me. You'd love to come up with one."

"I would." She considered, savoring the aftertaste. He was a gifted alchemist in cowboy boots and dusty jeans. "Bliss River Blend? No, too simple. We need to capture the character. Give me a minute."

"We've got lots of time. I had enough grapes to produce a few bottles, that's all."

"But there'll be more. This is absolutely delicious. We can really sell it in high-end restaurants and liquor stores that cater to customers with discerning palates. It has a delicate balance, perfect acidity and a very smooth finish."

His gaze held amusement, however reluctant it might be. "You *are* confident, aren't you?"

"I'm hopeful you'll see the big picture here. That would be a better way to put it." She thought, with a trace of guilt, about her tentative plan to quit her job.

"Could we talk about last night? I thought it was good for both of us, but I can only speak for myself. Though I could swear —"

She interrupted. "No, we can't talk about last night, not now, anyway. Focus." She had a glimmer of inspiration. "What about Mad Scientist Elegant White? Eclectic labels really catch the eye of the buyer."

He slapped his forehead theatrically. "Why didn't I think of that? Oh, maybe because I'm not fond of being called by that nickname. It's always been a favorite of my brothers."

"Okay, let me suggest this one — Wild Cowboy Elegant White. Or Rugged Cowboy Elegant White, or —"

"Annoyed Winemaker Elegant White." He held out a hand. "I saw that gleam in my mother's eyes. It wouldn't surprise me if a campaign's been launched to ensure that I'm no longer the only single Carson brother. Just giving you fair warning. Any chance you'll go out and get a big tattoo of a flying pig or something similar that'll deflect her? You exude wholesome *and* intellectual. Maybe you can take up chewing tobacco. That might do the trick." He didn't have to worry about marriage pressure. Kelly had rushed in the first time, and regrets were a dime a dozen, but *older and wiser* was a saying for a reason. If she ever did get married again, she told herself, she'd take things slowly, make sure she and her prospective husband were on the same page when it came to the most important issues, like having children.

And she'd never pictured herself with a cowboy. Instead, she'd imagined someone who loved the symphony, enjoyed taking quiet walks and talking for hours in out-of-the-way coffee shops. They'd visit the great capitals of Europe on their vacations, visit museums, collect art, read poetry to each other.

Her ideal man, she figured, would be an intellectual, a college professor, perhaps. Someone sensitive and caring.

In other words, she wanted someone romantic and giving, not as stubborn as a corralled mule. Not someone who rode in like a cyclone and had her slung onto a horse for a business meeting. Mace Carson was incredibly attractive, and sexy as hell, but was he marriage material?

She liked him — a lot — but what they had together was all sizzle. A fling.

She'd decided that this morning after he'd left. She was pretty sure she wasn't his type, either. Regardless of what he'd said about how being with her had changed his life, she was convinced that he wanted a sweet, spunky cowgirl, not an uptight career woman.

"I'm going to skip both of those suggestions — pig tattoo *and* chewing tobacco — if you don't mind, but I'm not looking to get hitched, so don't worry about it." She put her hand in his and let him pull her to her feet. "*Are* we friends?"

"If you'll forgive me for turning you down, I'm talking about the offer, not you personally." He tugged her closer. He smelled like fresh air — with more than a hint of . . . manure?

"If you'll forgive me if I talk you into a decision that makes good fiscal and practical sense." She read the expression on his face even as he lowered his head. "Mace, what are you doing?"

"You can't guess? Just having a flashback from last night. I'm going to kiss you."

He did. Long and slow.

Oh, he's an indulgence, all right.

"I'm happy to keep our relationship strictly personal," he said against her mouth.

"When we negotiate this deal, I warn you, it'll be professional." She frowned. "*Strictly* professional."

"There will be no negotiations." He

smoothed his hands down her arms. "I wasn't all that enthusiastic about greater distribution. Selling the winery? That's not going to happen."

His dark blond hair evoked images of apple cider or fall leaves, she decided — rich and warm. "I'll change your mind," she taunted him.

"You can't."

"I can."

"I don't believe you."

"Just wait."

CHAPTER ELEVEN

There were a lot of fires to put out that day, and every time Mace dealt with one blaze, another one sprang up.

First, a bull had gotten loose while he and Drake were moving cattle from one pasture to another, then his horse came up lame, and that was just the start. By the time Kelly blindsided him with the offer to purchase the winery, he'd definitely been on edge.

Now, this phone call. Mace sighed in exasperation, but a sense of humor surfaced. "Sure, of course, I can help out. I'm headed there right now."

He pushed a button on his cell and looked at his guest as she bent over to grab another bottle and examine the label. They were in the temperature-controlled room where he kept the bottles that were ready to be shipped; it featured custom racks made by a local carpenter from fallen timber, and Kelly was studying each vintage in turn.

"Feel free to stay and look around some more," he said, "but there's a dirty diaper with my name on it. I need to go back to the house."

Obviously mystified, she put the chardonnay back and straightened, which was too bad. He'd really been enjoying the view of her backside in that tailored skirt. "What?"

He pointed at his phone. "That was Red. Apparently my mother went to town, Drake's out, Grace had to go to the resort to handle payroll, Slate's off filming something and Harry had errands to do. Long story short, they nabbed that old cowboy to watch my nephew during his nap, and he's perfectly capable of roping a mountain lion, but changing a diaper is not in his skill set. He said Will woke up unhappy and he can tell — or maybe smell — why, but he doesn't know what to do about it. He's panicking. In his own words, he'd rather grab a pissed-off rattlesnake by the tail than try to figure out how to deal with this situation. I'm not sure I'll do any better, but I'll give it a try."

Kelly glanced around. "Between our earlier tour and today, I've seen enough, anyway. I might be able to get GGI to up their offer, now that I've got a better idea of the potential."

"I haven't even looked at the *first* offer." He said it flatly. "Did I happen to mention that I don't have a cash flow problem, so no amount of money is going to convince me?" He paused. "Have another glass of wine. I'll be back after I handle the diaper crisis."

"I'll go with you. I've got a whole bunch of nieces and nephews, so I've changed quite a few diapers in my life. As the kid sister, I was the go-to babysitter, which means I'm a pro. I can take care of a dirty diaper with my eyes closed."

That sounded promising. "Are you trying to bribe me?"

"Is it working?"

He laughed, eyed her footwear. It wasn't as if she could walk to the house in those fancy heels, and while he was willing to do his duty as an uncle, he sympathized with Red. Messy diapers weren't his forte, either. "Probably not the way you're hoping it will. And I hope you don't mind, but we're going to ride back."

She had a beguiling smile. "I don't mind, since the baby obviously needs to be changed ASAP."

"Let's go, then."

He'd left Stormy tied to the old hitching post next to the antique water trough, just loosening the saddle cinch when they'd arrived, a habit ingrained in him since childhood. He tightened it and lifted Kelly up before swinging into the saddle behind her. Her pose with that fashionable skirt pulled down, slender legs together, impractical shoes dangling as she perched on top of a horse, sidesaddle, made him laugh again. They were certainly a mismatched pair.

"We could call the wine The Cowboy Meets the Lady. Then below that in smaller letters add Wyoming Elegant White Blend."

Kelly turned to smile up at him. "Not bad. I like that. I'd almost say you're in the wrong business, but I've tasted your product. Don't quit making wine to go into advertising."

He slipped an arm around her waist and nudged Stormy with his heel. "I have no intention of doing that." He breathed in the fresh scent of her skin and hair. "I hope you're okay with riding fast. It takes a lot to rattle Red, and he's beside himself."

"Go for it."

The gelding was in the mood for a good run, so he responded with enthusiasm. Their swift arrival at the house found Red pacing the porch with a squalling infant, and Kelly immediately took charge. When Mace eased her down, she didn't hesitate to hurry up the wide steps.

"Hi, it's great to see the legendary Red again." Kelly smiled. "He's so cute. Can I take him?"

Red looked grateful. "Young lady, I'd be mighty obliged if you did."

"Okay. Where's the diaper stash?" She reached for Will and the baby quieted at once, wide blue eyes staring up at her.

That was one relieved old cowboy. "I got a bag full of baby stuff right here handy. All kinds of lotions and tissues and stuff in there I've never seen before." Red was practically babbling. "How I got railroaded into this is a mystery to me. There's this changing thing on the couch inside, but I didn't think I'd have to use it. I'm gonna stick to cattle from now on."

Kelly cuddled the baby and headed for the door. "My pleasure. This should be a quick fix." The way she handled the infant told Mace she knew exactly what she was doing. "Hi, Will," she whispered. "How about some new pants?"

Red came over to take Stormy's reins once Mace had dismounted. "I'll ride him back to the stable and brush him down. Least I can do, considering that pretty little gal just saved me from diaper duty." The old man paused, staring after Kelly as she disappeared into the house. "That's one fine-looking woman, son."

"I've noticed, all right. And you damn well know it."

"A few people around here have remarked on your interest," Red admitted, his grin so wide it threatened to split his weather-beaten face in two. "Your mother took to her right away, along with Grace and Luce. Drake and Slater, too."

"As usual, everybody around here seems to be minding my business instead of their own."

Red regarded him with twinkling eyes. "That's the way close families operate, I reckon," he said. "Now that I'm off the hook where the baby is concerned, I think I'll just mosey along and get some real work done."

Amused, Mace watched Red beat a hasty retreat, then went into the house.

He found Kelly standing in the kitchen, the baby nestled happily in the crook of one arm. With her free hand, she extended a plastic bag. "I would dispose of this outside, if I were you," she said. "I believe it qualifies as hazardous material."

Making a big deal of holding his breath, Mace carried the evidence to the trash bins next to the garage.

When he came back, Will was in his high

chair, next to the kitchen table, cheerfully flinging bits of dry cereal in all directions. Kelly was firing up Harry's space-age coffeemaker.

"Men," she said rather smugly. "You're all wimps when it comes to poopy diapers."

"Guilty," Mace replied, holding one hand up as though swearing an oath. "You can't really fault us for seeking out an expert when things go south, though."

Kelly crossed the kitchen and gently stroked Will's cheek, her eyes sparkling. "I'm hardly an expert," she replied lightly. "My sisters are a fertile bunch, so I've had a lot of practice, especially since we gather at my parents' place for every major holiday. Six of the kids are under two years old, which means we all get a turn at changing diapers — among other things."

"That explains it," he said. "No wonder you're a natural."

"Comes with the territory," she said.

He wondered if her feelings about having kids of her own had changed in the years since her divorce. Then he wondered why he was wondering.

He went over and smoothed Will's hair, his touch light. "Babies are hard work," he said. "If you're the parent, anyway. On the other hand, being an uncle is perfect. I can hold Will until he makes a peep, then I just hand him over to his mom or dad. Seems like the older they get, the more complicated they are — Slater's daughter, Daisy, is about to hit puberty, and I can tell you I don't envy him *that.*"

Kelly smiled and nodded. "My oldest sister's daughter is fifteen. The ongoing arguments about wearing makeup, having slumber parties every weekend, and the fact that she desperately wants a horse, make *me* tired and I'm not even part of it. Lacey would love it here. If that child could move to a ranch tomorrow, she would."

"Horses we've got. And dogs, kittens and up until recently, wild horses and a really audacious young mountain lion that had to be relocated. Still have wolves and coyotes, different birds of prey, and plenty of other critters. Great place to grow up, but other than chores, there's not a lot to do except ride, camp, fish and argue a lot. My brothers and I were a handful." He poured two cups of coffee and carried them to the kitchen table. "Have a seat," he said.

Will yawned, and his head lolled to one side.

"Nap time," Kelly said, smiling. She sat down, ignoring her coffee, and hoisted the sleepy toddler out of his high chair, set him on her lap.

"There's a crib around here somewhere," Mace interjected, not so helpfully.

Will rested his curly head against Kelly's breasts. Lucky kid.

"He's fine for now," Kelly said.

They made a fine picture, the two of them, Mace thought, strangely choked up by the scene.

For a long time, neither he nor Kelly said a word.

Mace sipped his coffee, while Kelly's grew cold, though she didn't seem to mind.

When Will opened his eyes and let out a wail, Mace was on his feet in an instant. "He wants his blanket," he said. "I'll go upstairs and get it."

Kelly got to her feet, bouncing the baby boy gently and walking him back and forth across the kitchen. While Mace was gone, she looked around, taking in details she'd missed on her first visit.

The sunny, spacious room was well equipped, with state-of-the-art appliances, all in brushed steel, including a gleaming six-burner stove, and the countertops were granite, bluish gray, shot through with colors only nature could have created. The hand-hewn cabinets, in charming contrast to all these modern touches, glowed with a soft golden patina, the wood nicked here and there.

On the far side of the space stood an antique hutch full of old china, the treasure, no doubt, of some long-ago Carson bride, but the best part was the fieldstone fireplace, towering next to a set of French doors with delicately etched glass. Kelly peered through, saw a large patio and, beyond it, a swimming pool; the turquoise surface of the water sparked with dancing sunlight.

Remembering the brother-talk about skinny-dipping that first night, Kelly had to smile.

Still holding Will, she moved to stand in front of the cold fireplace, imagining how cozy the kitchen would be on chilly days, a blaze crackling on the hearth, warming the occupants. The mantel was broad and heavy, its front piece beautifully carved in a motif of running horses. Small but sturdy iron hooks at the bottom suggested generations of children hanging their Christmas stockings there, perhaps beneath sprays of pine or spruce, or an heirloom nativity scene . . .

Kelly's throat thickened a little, and, for a few moments, she missed her mom and dad, her sisters and brothers-in-law, her nieces and nephews.

Will interrupted her bout of homey nostalgia by grabbing a handful of Kelly's hair and tugging slightly.

She laughed and kissed his warm, plump cheek. "Pretty nice spread you've got here, little cowboy," she said.

He gurgled happily, and Kelly felt her heart swell with a strange, happy ache.

A few minutes later, Mace reappeared with a well-loved yellow blanket in hand. "Sorry it took me so long," he said, grinning as his nephew stretched one chubby arm in his direction, fingers opening and closing. He handed it over, and Will clutched the soft bundle, burying his face in it. "I had to do some searching."

"Just how big *is* this house?"

Mace leaned against one of the counters. "Real big," he answered. "Around fifteen thousand square feet, I guess. When my great-great-granddad and his homesick bride first moved in, this room was the whole place, but it was fancy, even then. More than a simple cabin, that's for sure."

"So they turned it into a version of her family home, right?"

"Yeah. Over the years, they added on, duplicating the mansion in Savannah as best they could, and subsequent generations expanded on their original design." He paused. "It's comfortable."

"Comfortable" was an understatement — this was a mansion, after all — but, as vast as it was, it had an air of casual welcome. Remarkably, for all its fine furnishings, it wasn't at all pretentious.

Kelly sighed appreciatively. "It's lovely, Mace."

"Thank you." Another pause, a shrug. "It's home."

Now that he had his favorite blanket, Will was sleepy again. He was heavy, but Kelly didn't want to let him go, so she cuddled him closer. "Men are so different from women," she mused.

"Where did that come from?" Mace asked, steering her to one of the upholstered chairs facing the fireplace, taking the one beside it. "Not that I would object to the statement. I see it as a damn good thing."

She smiled. "I don't always do segues," she admitted. "I was just thinking how men tend to think in straight lines, while women think — well — sideways. What I'm trying to say is, if there's a problem, men go ahead and try to solve it right away. A woman will consider why it happened in the first place, what it means."

Mace's expression was one of wry confusion. "This discussion is pretty convoluted, and I'm still not sure where it's going, but I might need a glass of wine to navigate. Luckily I have resources."

She made a face at him, over Will's head, which rested on her shoulder by then. Judging by the baby's slow, deep breathing, he was about to fall asleep. "I wouldn't mind a glass myself," she admitted.

"At your service," Mace said with a slight grin, rising from his chair.

He disappeared into another room and came back, minutes later, with two glasses of red. He handed one to Kelly, clinked his own glass against hers before sitting down again. "Did you find your way out of the conversational maze while I was gone?" he teased. "Something about men and women thinking differently?"

She laughed. "There *is* a point to my little speech," she said. She took a sip of wine, set the glass aside, stroked Will's little back. "You, being a man, are direct, sometimes to the point of being arbitrary. Women — such as your very smart mother and I — are usually more flexible."

"Okay," Mace said with wary amusement. "I guess I follow — so far. Not that I'm admitting I'm 'arbitrary.' "

"Right," Kelly said. "What I meant was,

while your mother is curious about GGI, and how your operation happened to pop up on its radar, she's reserving judgment, looking at the facts. Whatever she recommends in the end, she's at least open to discussion. You, on the other hand, barely listened to what I had to say. You just said no, right out of the gate."

"I don't want to sell, Kelly. I love what I do. And it seems to me you're the one who isn't listening." There was no anger in his voice, no frustration or impatience. He cleared his throat, and his gaze was steady on her face when he went on. "Is it just me, or is this conversation about more than GGI and its designs on my winery?"

What was he, Kelly wondered, a psychologist in dusty boots and denim? Was it that obvious how much she enjoyed holding Will? How she might even be fantasizing, just a wee bit, about holding a child of her own?

If so, they were on dangerous ground. She hadn't forgotten what happened with Alan, how he'd suddenly changed his mind about their previous agreement to wait awhile before starting a family. He'd become more and more insistent with every passing day, and Kelly had been hurt, bewildered, felt cornered and, yes, betrayed. Inevitably, with no resolution in sight, they'd filed for divorce. In retrospect, Kelly knew she and Alan probably wouldn't have made it, anyway, but the whole experience had been painful, just the same.

Maybe things would have turned out differently if she'd given in to Alan's demands and gotten pregnant; she didn't know. She would have loved their child without reservation. There was no question about that, but she would've resented Alan on some level, too. *He* would have breezed right on with his career, after all, while she put her own on indefinite hold, falling further out of touch with her professional life with every day that passed.

It wasn't the sacrifices that galled her, though, she reflected, sitting there in someone else's house, holding someone else's little one. Her love for their baby would have more than compensated for a gap in her résumé. No, what had gotten under her hide, what chafed her still, was the *assumption* that Alan's career, *Alan's* education and hard work counted more than hers.

And why was that?

Because he was a man.

Kelly felt her face heat up, and she knew Mace was watching her, so she decided to give him a straight answer. "Maybe we are talking about more than the sale of the winery," she said quietly, pausing to plant a distracted kiss on the top of Will's head.

"Marriage and kids, for instance?" Mace prompted gently.

Kelly blushed even more deeply. "I have my reservations about both," she said.

"Ya think?" Mace teased, though his eyes were serious.

She sighed heavily, wondering how she could explain feelings she didn't fully understand herself. "I like the *idea* of marriage," she said carefully, groping from one thought to the next. "I've learned the hard way, though, that the reality can be an emotional minefield. The person you thought you knew turns out to be someone else altogether."

Mace didn't speak. He was listening.

What a concept.

Kelly knew she was spilling her guts, probably saying too much, but she couldn't stop. When was the last time she'd opened up like this and felt as though she was being heard? Not judged, not pitied, but simply listened to?

Certainly not recently.

Still unable to close the floodgates, she went on. "As for children," she said wistfully, "I adore them. I love their innocence and their sense of wonder and the way they belly laugh when some ordinary thing delights them —"

Suddenly, just like that, the deluge was over.

"But?" Mace prompted very gently after several moments had passed.

What a rare person he was, Kelly thought. He hadn't just been waiting for an opening so he could jump in and take over the conversation, the way most people did; he'd waited in case she had more to say. Held a space open for her to fill or leave alone, as she chose.

"But," she replied, "I'm not sure I'm brave enough, or strong enough, to open myself up to the magnitude of loving another person, especially a child of my own, in such a dangerous world. Just look at it. The environment's in trouble, and it might be too late to save the planet. When one war ends, another starts. Economies are collapsing. And that's just the global stuff — what about school shootings and gang violence and drugs?"

Again, Mace waited.

"You through?" he asked kindly.

Kelly swiped at a tear tickling its way down her cheek. "For now," she answered with a small, strangled laugh.

Mace stood up, took the sleeping baby from her arms and carefully laid him in a nearby playpen, which Kelly had either not noticed before or deliberately screened out so she could go on holding Will.

The little boy barely stirred, except to shove one thumb into his mouth, favorite blanket close at hand.

Watching that did something to Kelly, something primal.

Mace crossed to her then, holding out one hand. "Come here," he said.

Kelly got up from her chair, took his hand and let him pull her into his arms. It was about tenderness, and reassurance, and taking shelter in the presence of another human being.

Letting her head rest on Mace's shoulder, Kelly sniffled once. She'd worn herself right out, and probably made a fool of herself in the bargain, but there it was.

"Say something," she said.

He propped his chin on top of her head. "Okay," he told her. "Everything you said before is true. This planet and everybody on it is in a fix — but there's one flaw in your logic."

"Oh, yeah?" She didn't move, didn't want to move, ever.

Mace laughed quietly. "Yeah," he said.

"Seems to me if there's one hope of pulling this world out of the soup, well, that hope is love. Wide-open, hell-bent-for-election, take-no-prisoners *love.* Sure, it's risky, putting your heart out there, but if we don't take the chance, you and me and everybody else who gives a damn, then that's it. Game over, lights out. The dark side wins and everything gets a hell of a lot worse."

Kelly took in his words, weighing and measuring them and finally accepting that they were true. And, like most truths, they weren't easy ones — living them, going beyond lip service, would require everything a person had, every resource, every ounce of courage and persistence and faith. In short, love.

After a very long time, she looked up into Mace's eyes. "Well," she said, "I'm still scared to death, but we can't let the dark side win, can we?"

He kissed her then, not deeply, but lightly, and as a sort of affirmation. "*Hell,* no," he said with a grin.

Kelly eased herself back a little, not because she didn't enjoy being close to Mace, but because a part of her wanted to melt right into him, disappear into all that strength and certainty and courage. Become a part of him.

Was such a thing possible, without losing herself in the process?

She didn't know. And at the moment, she wasn't ready to find out.

"You really believe all those things, don't you?" she asked.

His arms slipped to her waist, rested loosely there. "I really do," he confirmed.

"And you're not even a little scared? Ever?"

He made a sound, low in his throat, something between a chortle and a groan. "Sometimes I'm a *lot* scared, but, as John Wayne used to say, I saddle up, anyhow."

"The cowboy way," Kelly said, smiling.

"Yep," Mace answered.

"And the cow*girl* way," a third voice interjected.

Without stepping apart, both Kelly and Mace turned to see Blythe Carson standing in the arched doorway leading to the dining room. She looked wonderfully Western in her well-fitting jeans, loose white shirt and boots. Her hands were on her slender hips, and her head was tilted a little to one side, her expression conveying both amusement and speculation.

"Well, now," she said.

"Well, now, what?" Mace retorted, sounding the slightest bit annoyed at the interruption.

Blythe smiled impishly. "Just 'well, now,' " she responded airily. Then she crossed to the playpen, reached in and gathered up her grandson, blanket and all. The baby snuggled against her and dropped off to sleep again, and Blythe kissed the crown of his head, closing her eyes for a moment.

For the second time in a few minutes, Kelly was heart-struck, as ordinary as it was.

"Grace just called," Blythe explained. "She's running late, so I'm going to get this little cowboy settled in his crib. In the meantime, you two might want to clear out of the kitchen. Harry's headed this way, bent on making supper, and once she gets here, she'll be all over the room like a tribe of dust devils."

Mace nodded in agreement. "*And* raising hell about us getting underfoot."

"What happened to all that talk about a cowboy standing his ground, no matter what?" Kelly asked with a grin and a poke at Mace's ribs.

"Guess I left out the part about how we like to choose our battles," Mace said cheerfully.

CHAPTER TWELVE

That night at supper, Mace's brothers were in rare form, mainly because Kelly was there, he supposed. They'd all gathered around the kitchen table, instead of the one in the dining room: Slater and Grace, Drake and Luce, Blythe and Red and Harry, plus young Ryder, Grace's ex-husband's boy, and three of his friends. Raine, Slater's ex-girlfriend and the mother of his first child, Daisy, had joined them for dinner, although Daisy herself was at a friend's place. Will was there, too, strapped into his high chair and gleefully plastering himself with mashed potatoes.

As usual, Slater and Drake brought up just about every dumb-ass thing Mace had ever done in his life, but he didn't mind. Let them have their fun; he'd have plenty of chances to get back at them.

"So Mace here decides," Drake said, "if he can't have a pinto pony like the one he's seen Little Joe Cartwright ride in all those reruns of *Bonanza* he used to watch, then he'll improvise. So he got some house paint from one of the sheds and splattered a bunch of spots on Red's old white mule, Jethro."

"Took me the better part of a day to clean up poor ol' Jethro," Red lamented, but there was a twinkle in his eye.

"I was seven at the time," Mace pointed out mildly.

Nobody remarked on this statement. Instead, Slater jumped in with, "How old were you when you tried to join the circus?"

Mace leveled a look at his brother. "That," he said, "was Drake."

Blythe broke in good-naturedly. "That's enough," she decreed. "Believe me, when it comes to telling embarrassing stories — about *all* of you — I'll take the prize every time."

Drake and Slater instantly subsided.

Mace grinned.

Kelly did, too. She was concentrating on Harry's incomparable pasta, but he knew she'd taken in every word.

Eventually, the teenagers disappeared into the family room to watch a game on TV.

Will fell asleep in his mashed potatoes, and Slater lifted him from the high chair while Grace wiped the baby's face and hands with a damp paper towel.

Once he'd been put to bed and the adults had gathered around the table once again, Drake resumed the conversation. "Speaking of embarrassing stories, I got a tongue-lashing from Dad after you broke his golf club because *you* thought it would make a great rudder for the sled so we could go down that slope he told us was too steep."

"Yeah, but it worked pretty well," Mace said defensively, since everyone at the table was laughing, even him. "I just needed to get the hang of it. I even let you sit in front."

"So I could die first?" Drake said. "I appreciate your consideration. But let's face it, Dad was right, we were wrong, and no one should ever have gone down that slope." He grinned. "But you have to admit it was damned fun."

Slater snorted in disgust. "I can't believe you didn't invite me."

"Mr. Responsibility?" Mace said. "I don't think so. You would've talked us out of it."

"The hell I would." Slater grinned. "I would've sat in the back — and I wouldn't have broken the golf club as I guided us safely down."

Grace elbowed her husband in the ribs.

"The three of you are a dangerous combination."

"You don't know the half of it," their mother said, rising. "I've earned these gray hairs. Does anyone want coffee?"

"I'll help you." Kelly got up, looking a little out of place in her designer clothes, but since she was comfortable with it, so was everyone else.

The Carson family was like that, Mace thought philosophically. Accepting, easygoing, unconventional. For instance Raine, Slater's ex-girlfriend, was chatting comfortably with Grace, his wife.

Kelly brought him his coffee, and he truly had to resist the urge to pull her onto his lap, especially when she leaned over to set down the cup.

She brushed her hair across his cheek on purpose, he was sure of it. And she wore some sort of lacy bra under her blouse, and he knew she'd deliberately let him catch a glimpse.

"Thank you."

He suspected no one else at the table missed it, either. "You're welcome." She took a seat, and he wished he could see her legs.

His expression must have made his feelings obvious, since Drake choked on a mouthful of cake.

Okay, fine, he was hooked. No, more than simply "hooked." He was on the verge of a decision that might change his life — but it changed nothing about their business deal. If there *was* a business deal . . . He didn't believe she was using his attraction to her to try to persuade him; still, he'd be a fool not to consider it possible.

He was about to be a fool again.

"I'll take you back to your hotel whenever you're ready," Mace said in a for-your-ears-only tone. What he didn't say was that he'd gladly stay there with her as long as she liked.

Kelly didn't misunderstand him. "I'm uncomfortable with you driving back in the dark. Because I've heard about stray moose on the main street."

At least in that respect they were thinking along the same lines. He grinned. "It is kind of dangerous this time of year."

"They're migrating," Drake provided helpfully.

His brother must have supersonic hearing. They weren't whispering because that would've been rude, not to mention conspicuous, but they were speaking in low tones and sitting beside each other, while he was across the table.

"What are migrating?" Slater asked, his coffee cup halfway to his mouth.

"The moose," Drake said with a straight face. "Herds of them. Kelly is worried about Mace driving home after he drops her off."

"I wasn't aware that moose migrated at all, much less in August," Grace remarked with just a hint of sarcasm.

Slater wasn't about to be left out. "You'd be surprised. They're all over the place and a real menace. He'd better stay with Kelly."

Grace and Luce shook their heads. "Hey, you should win a best supporting actor award," Luce said with a grin. She turned to Kelly. "Carson men do grow on you, I promise."

Raine, who was stunning even without Grace's vivid beauty or Luce's delicate prettiness, added, "Yeah. Kind of like brown lichen on a rock."

"Hey!" All three of the males in question said it at the same time.

Daisy, Slater's young daughter, gawky in that preadolescent stage, told Kelly sincerely, "I've never seen a moose on Main Street."

When all the adults laughed, she looked around, mystified, and Blythe summarily put an end to that part of the conversation. "Ah, dinner at the Carson house. More coffee, anyone?"

The overt matchmaking was not unexpected because Mace had warned her, but she hadn't thought there'd be a team effort.

She was glad they liked her despite the winery offer. Still, it was hard to get a feel for how everything would go — their intense personal attraction *and* their uncomfortable business negotiation. Would one cancel out the other? She could only hope not . . . She assumed Blythe would be in favor of the sale, and yet she sensed that his mother — in fact, his whole family — would let Mace decide what he wanted to do about the offered deal.

About her, as well.

One thing she'd realized from their comments and their attitudes was that he wasn't involved with anyone else. Not at the moment, anyway. She'd already taken that for granted; Mace was an honorable man who wouldn't have slept with her if there was another woman in his life. But the confirmation was reassuring.

"Do I need to apologize? For my family, I mean." Mace climbed back in after shutting the main gate to the ranch. "They're quite the rodeo sometimes."

"Have to take your word for it. I've never

been to one."

"To a rodeo?" He seemed astonished as they pulled out. "Well, we'll have to rectify that. You can't come to Wyoming and not watch someone anxious to break a bone by climbing on an angry bull."

"Sounds interesting." She had to say, "I find your family dynamic not too different than mine. We don't get together often enough, but when we do we're quite the bunch."

"Try living in the same house with them." He shrugged comically. "Their opinions aside, I'm not lobbying to stay with you unless it's what *you* want."

"I'm lobbying for you to stay." She settled back against the seat after that bold move. She should buy a T-shirt with I Want to Sleep with You Again emblazoned across the front. "Original rules apply. No business talk."

"Done. You're Kelly and I'm Mace."

"I like your brothers."

"I do, too. Most of the time."

"That's how I feel about my nosy sisters, too. I like Raine, and Daisy's sweet and very polite, although I think your apprehension about puberty is dead-on. She's going to be one very pretty teenage girl."

They reached the outskirts of Mustang

Creek, and he slowed for the decreased speed limit as he nodded gloomily. "No more bikes and dollhouses. Being an uncle is going to take on an unknown slant. Maybe I can consult with you and your family on what to get a girl her age for birthdays and Christmas. Drake and I always competed trying to pick out something she'd really love and invariably got her the same thing." He briefly looked up as if petitioning a higher power. "Please tell me I don't think like him. That's all I ask in this life."

Kelly laughed as he quickly refocused on the road. "If you want an outside opinion, I'm guessing you do think alike, but I also want to say that it isn't bad. He's the smart, strong, mostly silent type."

"And me?"

She pretended to ponder, rubbing her chin. "I'd say you're a unique combination of the two — at home on horseback, so you're definitely a cowboy, like Drake. You're also creative, like Slater."

"So, I'm like both my brothers, but 'unique'? I don't follow your logic."

"You're deeper and more private, I think. More reserved, certainly. And you're a man of the soil. You like to see things grow, especially if you can aid in the process. You see cycles and patterns everywhere, but especially in the natural world, and you love the changing seasons, which is probably why you don't want to live anywhere but here."

"Pretty good," he informed her. "Want *your* analysis from a strictly amateur point of view?"

"Can't wait."

"Well, I hate to point this out, but you need to cut down on being so motivated and intelligent. Men hate that. Just rely on being beautiful. Way easier for us to process. More cleavage is advised, too. Attractive *and* smart is too much for our simple minds."

She glanced down. "I don't think more cleavage is available."

"With your permission, I'll check that out firsthand and let you know."

"Generous of you."

"That's how I am."

Was this why they liked each other? The sassy humor, the easy dialogue, the potent attraction?

"You're . . . irreverent," she said. "I like it."

"What the hell does that word mean?"

"See?" He had her laughing again. "You know precisely what it means. That was the worst attempt at stupid I've ever seen."

He inclined his head. "Oh, great. If only

Red was here to make fun of me, too. Yeah, I know it means I don't take anything seriously, but I actually do. Lots of things — and people."

"Am I included in that category?"

"I don't know if you even *want* me to take you seriously."

"Let's say we both know what we want for tonight and leave it at that."

"I can understand why you'd be cautious. I am, too, for that matter. You were burned once. And my ill-fated relationship, the one I thought might be serious enough to last, didn't. Sarah rode off into the sunset, too. Like Alan. At one time Slater thought he had it with Raine. At one time Drake thought he had it with Danielle. We're all allowed a free pass for the first big failure."

He was right, but then, he wasn't divorced, either.

"I have to admit," he went on, "that I've had a number of, uh, relationships since then. All short-term and ultimately not very serious."

Kelly nodded; in that respect they were very different . . . She'd had *no* boyfriends, serious or otherwise, since the end of her marriage.

"To my mind," he said, "if you have the sense God gave a goat — that's Red talking

285

— life's too short to be unhappy. Accept the failure. Just let it go."

But that had become a lot harder now that her ex had moved into *her* territory. Now that he'd encroached on her career, whether he knew it or not.

CHAPTER THIRTEEN

Mace parked at the Mountain View Suites and got out to open Kelly's door. She was independent enough that he found it unsurprising that all he had to do was shut it.

He wanted to kiss her right there in the parking lot. Had two young men in business suits not come out the front entrance just then, he might've done it and been the envy of both as they gave her a discreet but admiring glance.

It didn't even tick him off. He didn't blame them one bit; after all, he was on the lucky side of the equation. "That skirt is dangerous. Actually, you're dangerous."

"Luckily, you're around to save me from myself."

"Uh-uh. Not from yourself. *I'm* the one in danger there."

She didn't address that; instead she watched a group of canoes go by in the twilight on the Bliss, their lanterns hanging, laughter echoing above the gentle rush of the river. "What a beautiful night. It can't always be like this here, can it?"

"Oh, no," he answered truthfully. "In winter the river ices over, and the wind howls. I've seen Drake tie a rope from the house to the stable so he could make his way there to feed the horses without getting lost. We've all grown up pitching in to feed the cattle when the snow gets really deep. Horses first, though, or there'd be no cattle."

"That's the rule, huh? The things I don't know." She let him escort her to the entrance. "It's fascinating, and I'm not being flippant about that. I could use the GPS on my cell phone to get from here to New York City, but a rope to the stable?"

"In a blinding blizzard, people in other places have the option to stay inside. We don't."

"But you could freeze to death!"

His grin was wicked. "We have our ways of keeping warm."

She blushed.

When they entered the Mountain View lobby, Walter, the elderly and very proper bellman, wasn't at his station.

Just as well, Mace thought. When they reached her room, he didn't waste any time.

He immediately tumbled her to the bed and kissed her thoroughly, then indulged himself by running his fingers through her silky hair. "That's a fantasy that's been going through my mind all day long." His smile was rueful. "Pretty much everyone knew it, too."

She touched the corner of his mouth with a fingertip. "I think I might've been kind of transparent myself."

"You're so beautiful, Kelly," he murmured. *And smart. And kind.*

"And you're so handsome, Mace," she whispered back. "In that cowboy way . . ."

"Maybe we should continue our mutual admiration society discussion with less clothing on. I seem to be wrinkling your fancy skirt."

"Well, we can't have that." She went to work on the buttons of his shirt. "I need it to look good for the next time I ride a horse."

"My thought exactly. Let me help you out of it."

"Be my guest."

In minutes they were skin to skin, mouth to mouth. She whispered his name again and urgently pressed the small of his back. He didn't need the encouragement, his arousal firmly in evidence, unmistakable. She helped him slide on the condom, and her combustible reaction to his entry taxed his control. His muscles tightened as he tried to give her more time, but it turned out she didn't need any.

She wasn't shy about how much she enjoyed it, and neither was he. But things were going way too fast — and he wasn't talking about the fantastic sex.

Damn Drake with his view that when "the right one" came along, a man would know it. Instantly.

Was Kelly the woman he'd been looking for, waiting for, all his adult life?

He still thought so. And yet . . . he couldn't help a small niggling fear that rose up from time to time — that she was pretending to feel more than she did. That it was part of some plan to get what she wanted. His winery.

As if to confirm his suspicions, she asked, "This is just sex, right?"

He kissed her lightly, already in too deep to back off, even if that would've been the smart thing to do. "If that's how you choose to see it," he finally said.

"Good." She clasped his shoulders and closed her eyes. "I'm not ready for anything else."

"So you keep telling me," he murmured. She was already responding.

"Because it's — true —" A soft gasp.

He nuzzled her ear. "Maybe."

She gasped again, but she was still trying to make her case. "I'm no good at relationships. We've . . . established that."

Her body held him like a perfectly fitted glove. "Wrong," he said. "We've established that you were bad at it *one* time. And it wasn't even that simple. Your ex changed his mind about what he wanted, and you didn't." He slid one finger along her cheek, her jaw, her throat. "Hey, I tried ice-skating once to please a girl. That was a true bust. Both my pride and my posterior were never the same. Your failure pales in comparison."

She smiled. "Hmm, I like you."

"Darlin', we're in bed together. You're *supposed* to like me."

"You're using that slow cowboy drawl to try to charm me."

"And here I thought I just used something else to charm you."

Laughing, she gazed into his eyes. "That is the most shameless thing I've ever heard anyone say."

The curve of her mouth, the slender grace of her arms, the way she touched him, kissed him with artless passion . . .

Yes, he was falling in love with her. He was starting to understand Slater's attraction to Grace and Drake's almost immediate vulnerability to Luce. He was happy for them all, but . . .

This wasn't what he needed. Was it?

No, the situation was more complicated than that. Kelly might want him — as much as he wanted her — but Ms. Wright wanted something else from him, something he wasn't willing to give. He acknowledged that it was a personal flaw; he tended to become too absorbed in projects. And her "analysis" of him was right. He liked doing it all himself, being in total control.

He was still legendary for his garden experiments when he was just a kid. He'd discovered he had a knack for growing things, no doubt inherited from his mother. He grew a green bean plant that could've given Jack the Giant Killer's a run for its money. Slater swore he couldn't look at another green bean for about five years after that summer, he'd eaten so many.

He wasn't going to hand over control of the winery to someone else. Period.

So he chose to be his usual *irreverent* self. "The most shameless thing you've ever heard? Give me time. I can do better than that."

She couldn't sleep, which seemed odd, since

she was pleasantly tired, both physically and mentally.

Mace slept comfortably, his breathing measured, sprawled next to her in a larger-than-life manner, taking up more than his share of the bed.

The intimacy both drew her in and frightened her half to death. With Alan, she hadn't felt anything like it. That accounted for the fear. He'd typically fallen asleep after sex, which was often perfunctory, then she'd fallen asleep, and that was the end of it. There'd never been contemplation of the shape of his nose in the moonlight that spilled through the window, or the length of his eyelashes against his cheekbones, or the definition of his muscular biceps with his arms flung above his head.

Watching Mace sleep invited speculation. She rose up on one elbow and thought it all over. He was handsome, but she could deal with that; she'd been susceptible to Alan, but with maturity could make a clearer distinction between physical attraction and intellectual connection. Good-looking wasn't enough. A lesson she'd learned the hard way. A sense of humor counted more than she'd ever imagined, and, of course, self-confidence based on a solid ethical foundation. Thinking about Alan and their failed marriage brought back the career decision looming over her, but she resolved to put it aside for now, at least while she was with Mace.

Not that Mace Carson was without his challenges. She suspected he'd never settle into a pattern; he'd always be evolving, that inner drive just a part of him.

As she watched him, she realized he wasn't actually asleep. Without opening his eyes, he said, "I'd love to know what you're thinking about so earnestly while you're busy staring at me."

"You," she answered after a moment. "Wondering what it is about you that can make me do something so out of character."

"Not to scare you, but I'm wondering the same thing."

"You're the chemistry expert."

He tugged the sheet down. "Not the male-female type of chemistry. Not really."

"I think you know." She shivered at the touch of his fingers on the tips of her breasts.

His eyes were open now. "Okay," he conceded. "I might have a theory or two, but all I really know is that since you and I met up again, everything's different."

"I've changed your life?"

She shouldn't have asked it, but he'd

changed hers, to the extent that she knew he was erasing her past experience one brushstroke at a time. He didn't dissemble. "Come on. Do you think I do this every night?"

He was warm against her. "No," she said. And she sensed, *believed,* that they'd created the "something different" he'd been talking about.

Still, this was an infatuation, she told herself. She couldn't afford to think in more permanent terms.

He was obviously thinking along the same lines. "There's nothing wrong with being seriously in lust. I'm going to qualify that by saying you also have to like the person and enjoy spending time with her — or in your case, him — out of bed, too."

It was on the tip of her tongue to point out that he hadn't enjoyed their business meeting that afternoon, but she caught herself.

"I agree."

"We see eye to eye, then."

"Unless we're both standing up, since you're taller than me. I like this position even better by the way."

His laugh stirred her hair. "Taller by a little bit. Like a foot or so."

"Yup. A tall, delicious cowboy."

His mouth trailed teasingly over the curve of her cheek. "You say the nicest things."

"You *do* the nicest things."

His hands were working their magic, moving to strategic spots that made her sigh in open delight.

The second time, her climax was apocalyptic.

And the third time . . . There were no words.

CHAPTER FOURTEEN

Fog drifted through the valley. It floated in ghostly banks, filling the ravines. Good thing they knew this country.

They were looking for that damn bull again. The animal was like a magician, able to escape any kind of fenced enclosure without damaging it. He was young, true enough, but too darned big — or so you'd think — to jump over it like an Olympic athlete.

Riding next to him, Drake squinted through the mist. "He likes that little valley with the creek. So far, he's been heading straight there. Sorry to drag you out at dawn again, but Showbiz was already gone. He went out to catch shots of the old abandoned cemetery as the sun came, said this fog was perfect for ambiance. Not exactly how I'd like to start my day. Sounds macabre to me."

Mace didn't like the way his had started,

either. He hadn't wanted to leave Kelly, still sleeping, with nothing more than a note, but he decided to respond with a joke instead. "No, you'd rather go looking for an ornery, dangerous ton of beef on the hoof." He grinned as he said it. "Besides, I don't think you spook all that easily. And explain to me how a cemetery can be abandoned. Seems to me once you're there, you're there."

"I'm just pointing out that no one's been buried there for years. Bliss County keeps the grass mowed in the summer, but no one visits those graves anymore. How lonely is that?"

"Do you think the occupants care? You have too much imagination."

His brother looked comically affronted, then relaxed in the saddle. "Like hell I do."

"For your information, that isn't an insult." Mace just had to egg him on. "Not particularly, anyway. You're on the softie side. Let's just face it."

"Name one softie thing I've ever done," Drake demanded with a scowl.

Mace was afraid he was going to burst out laughing so hard he'd fall off his horse. "You've been slaving away on that cabin for Luce."

It was true. His brother's wife was a

student pursuing a graduate degree in ecological systems, and Drake wasn't comfortable with her being in a tent by herself, so with Red's help, he was building a small cabin. Mainly he wanted to make sure there was someplace Luce would be safe if she chose to stay up in the mountains for the night to do research, but the plan was that they could all use it. Mace, Slate and Red had been in favor of the idea, too; they preferred not to worry about her, either — and it happened to be their favorite camping spot. Sitting in a tent if the heavens decided to dump a rainstorm on you took the fun out of the whole experience. You might stay dry, and you might not. A cabin, on the other hand, offered both secure shelter and reliable heat.

Red was a born-and-raised ranch man . . . and he loved a challenge. Building that cabin provided it.

He'd insisted on the river rock fireplace. The old codger had handpicked each stone from the Bliss River, wading in knee-deep and selecting the stones, piling them in his truck and taking as many as he could carry at one time up on horseback. He was talking about an outdoor kitchen, too, maybe with a propane grill and a side burner, though how he was going to get *that* up to the ridge was a mystery to the rest of them. There was no road, just a narrow track for hiking or riding single file.

Knowing Red, he'd figure it out.

"That's being protective," Drake pointed out. "I think you remember that the mountain lion we tangled with once upon a time."

"Nice try," Mace countered, "but I still think you've softened considerably since the pre-Luce days. Turned downright romantic, in fact. You've gone all out, brother — had Melody Hogan make a clock featuring wild horses as a wedding gift for your wife and you got Hadleigh Galloway to do a quilt with the same theme for your bed. You also spend more at the flower shop in town than any man in this county. You're a legendary flower buyer. I hear they're thinking about opening a second location thanks to you." He was making that part up. "That has *softie* plastered all over it."

"Hey, just because you're funny-looking doesn't mean you are funny," Drake shot back, but his mouth was twitching with laughter.

A hawk swooped by, startlingly close, caught something in the grass and flew off into the fog.

"Since I look a whole lot like you," Mace

said mildly, "I think you just insulted your-self."

Drake ignored that. "Women love getting flowers. You might take note of that. Here we have a woman who's apparently capable of tolerating your obvious flaws, so trust me, you don't want her to slip away."

Sarcasm aside, buying her flowers actually wasn't a bad idea. He didn't want Kelly to assume that he was nonchalant about what was happening between them. Even if it was a temporary liaison, as he'd come to expect. "Suggestions from the flower expert?"

"She has those unusual sort of green-gold eyes. Something to match."

"There isn't a flower that color."

"I hate to talk to someone so naive, but they can tint white roses with just about any color."

Mace felt a twinge of amusement. Weren't they looking for a stray bull? Two cowhands ambling along, ready to go up against an extremely large, cantankerous animal while discussing tinted roses?

If they hadn't heard a snort nearby, he might've said more, but he drew the quick conclusion that they'd just found a loose bull in a haze of mist. "I take it you heard that, too."

"I think we hit pay dirt. I knew he'd be

here. He's pretty good once you get a rope on him, but that can be tricky." Drake had his loosely coiled lasso ready in his gloved hand. "All I need is a clear shot. The problem is, he's one smart son of a bitch. He can hear our voices, and he knows why we're here. Okay, you herd him and I'll throw."

No doubt about it, Drake was one of the best with a rope that Mace had ever seen. "Good luck to both of us," he muttered. "Even catching a bull his size is like searching for a penny on a snow-covered sidewalk. I hear him, but I sure as hell can't see him. Driving to the ranch, I can tell you visibility was about two inches."

"Red says it'll burn off by about nine . . . Hey, there he is!"

Peering into the fog, Mace caught a glimpse of a shadowy but undeniably huge silhouette, probably fifty feet away.

The resulting dance of horses, cowboys, bull and rope was at least successful, but not the smoothest. However, Drake knew his stuff and hit the mark, and once their target felt the rope around his neck, he settled down as predicted.

One mission accomplished, anyway.

Now Mace had another one.

■ ■ ■ ■

The discreet knock on her door almost didn't catch her attention.

The phone call informing her that the man who'd attacked her ten years ago had been released left her in a state of shock. Showing up in court and testifying against him had been one of the most difficult things she'd ever faced in her life. In the back of her mind, she'd known this day would come eventually, but she'd tried to not think about it. She refused to let him ruin her every waking moment.

Luckily it was Grace Carson on the other side of the door, her smile fading as she registered Kelly's expression. She was holding a bouquet in a vase. "These came for you — they were delivered to the resort by mistake. I was in the lobby talking to the desk staff when they came, so I thought I'd bring them over . . . They're from Mace. What did he do? I'll kill him if these are makeup flowers. No, I'll get Slater to do it."

The flowers were gorgeous. White roses with elegant gold accents. Kelly shook her head and stepped back. "Come on in. He didn't do anything. I just got some bad news. Those flowers are really beautiful.

Thank you."

"Thank my brother-in-law." Grace walked inside, beautiful in a gray skirt and matching silk blouse. "Apparently he told the clerk at the florist's that you were staying at the resort, which made sense to her because your boss sent flowers there after the accident. I guess he just wasn't thinking." She paused, obviously concerned. "I jumped to conclusions when I saw the look on your face. What bad news? *If* you want to talk about it."

Kelly sank onto the side of the bed, weak-kneed. "The man who attacked me back in college has been released. My sister just called to tell me. No one's happy about it, not the judge or the prosecutor's office, but that's the modern justice system for you."

Grace pulled out the desk chair and sat down, her expression sympathetic. "I didn't realize that had happened to you. How awful."

How much had Mace told his family about their first encounter, ten years ago? Was it possible that he hadn't mentioned the incident at all?

Kelly's smile was wan. "If it wasn't for your brother-in-law, I'm not sure how things would've gone for me. Luckily, he was walking across campus at the same time, and he saw the struggle and came out of the darkness like a superhero. All the police had to do was collect the bad guy. I'm happy to say I wasn't hurt at all, thanks to Mace, except for a few bruises around my throat. He read me the riot act every step of the way to my dorm, after we talked to the police. He knew how shaken I was, though, and checked my room. He looked under the bed and in the closet, even though the man — Lance Vreeman — was in custody by then, and what were the odds another stalker would be lurking there? Rationally, I understood that, but emotionally I was still off balance. It did make me feel better, as if I was a child who'd had a nightmare, and he knew it would. He used my phone to call my boyfriend at the time to explain what had happened, so he could come and stay with me."

Mace's help had restored some trust in the male of the species, but Kelly remembered the incident with vivid clarity. She recalled her terror when she'd realized she couldn't fight off her assailant, and her relief that there was someone who could — and did.

Grace's eyes held empathy. "I can vouch that the Carson men can be gallant. I had a vindictive ex-employee who came after me, but Slater was right there. I can also tell you that he's done Ryder a world of good. So have Drake and Mace. I used to be a police officer, and I can attest that there are some scary people in this world. Are you worried this man will come after you?"

A logical question, and she tried to think it over just as logically. "I felt a lot more comfortable when he was in prison, but my bigger worry is that he'll come after Mace. I was a convenient target, but Mace put Lance Vreeman in jail. What with the internet and social media, it's easy to find someone if you really want to."

Grace nodded. "Well, here's the good news. If he shows up in Bliss County, he's going to have a hard time keeping a low profile. People around here notice strangers. I can have Slater give Spence Hogan a heads-up. You met him, right?"

When Kelly nodded, Grace said, "So you know he's the chief of police. He's a good friend and an excellent cop."

That was helpful, anyway. She felt somewhat relieved, but not completely reassured. "Lance Vreeman is from a wealthy family, and they did everything they could to overturn his conviction. They never succeeded, but I can tell you he isn't quite sane. I had to sit in that courtroom, and those were the coldest eyes I've ever seen. No sign of remorse whatsoever. He had a prior arrest for assaulting a former girl-friend, but she dropped the charges."

"That sounds unfortunately familiar." Grace touched one of the roses, which sat on the desk in their vase. "She was probably just scared to death of him. Or . . . his family bought her off. Luckily, not all men are created equal. We haven't known each other very long, but if you'll take my word for it, Mace is one of the good guys."

"I agree." Kelly felt she had to explain her reluctance to get more deeply involved, despite her obvious regard for Mace — and her attraction to him. "The thing is, I was married before. I made a vow not to be a two-time loser. So I'm . . . cautious."

"I was married before, too. I made the same vow."

"I'm pretty sure this has to be just an interlude for both of us. But we're two consenting adults."

"It might be more complicated than you think. I know Mace."

What did *that* mean? "We haven't spent a lot of time together yet, and I'm including our business meetings."

"He wouldn't spend more than an hour with you if he wasn't really interested. I've tried to set him up with my assistant, Meg, who has the biggest crush on him. Raine's tried with a few of her friends. Even Bad Billy of Bad Billy's Biker Bar, has put in his two cents, and he's hard to ignore. When you meet Billy, you'll know what I'm saying. We've all batted zero. Mace doesn't tend to do anything halfway. He has the attitude that he isn't interested in wasting his time if the connection isn't quite there. He's had his share of relationships, but he's never dishonest about his intentions — or lack of them." She grinned. "Slater calls it the experimental approach. Observing and assessing . . . and then concluding a particular woman isn't right for him."

Even though she wasn't in what you'd call a joyful mood since talking to her sister, Kelly had to laugh. "That sounds like a Mad Scientist quote to me. Don't tell him I said that. I suggested a version of Mad Scientist as a name for one of his white blends, and he was far from enthusiastic."

"That's because Slater and Drake, and pretty much all the ranch hands, for that matter, learned he'd gotten that nickname in college for making his own beer. Apparently it packed a lethal punch, so they've been merciless, as older brothers will be. They even cajoled Raine into making a poster for his office, complete with a man in a long white coat standing over a bubbling caldron, with mason jars lined up on shelves behind him. It's a wonderful piece of art."

"I didn't see it."

"That's because Mace is being stubborn about putting it up. Gee, imagine that. Maybe you can change his mind." Grace rose. "I'd better get back to the resort."

When Grace left, Kelly tried to evaluate her current situation. If she was Lance Vreeman, she'd stay as far away from both her and Mace Carson as possible. She'd seen him watching her and Mace during his trial, though, and the level of animosity was off the charts. But Mace had been the one who'd stopped him, delivered those punches and restrained him. His testimony had sent him to prison because Kelly doubted she would've been able to clearly identify him if Mace hadn't intervened. Vreeman had been trying to choke her into unconsciousness.

She went cold all over when she remembered that terrifying moment.

And felt warm all over when she thought of Mace. She picked up her phone and called him. He answered with flattering speed. "We had a loose bull. No need to wake you up for that one."

"That is so romantic. The wayward-cow greeting always charms me. Good morning to you, too."

He laughed. "And good morning to you. It wasn't a cow, by the way. It was a bull. He'd be really insulted if he knew you called him a cow."

She couldn't stop herself. "There's a difference?"

"Hell, yes, there's a difference, city girl . . . oh, pulling my chain, I get it. Very funny."

"I try to be now and then. Listen, Mace, I got some news that might or might not be bad, but I think you should hear it. Oh, thanks for the roses — even if they did go to the wrong address."

"Sorry about that. I got a call from Grace. Kind of embarrassing, but I guess I've got too much on my mind. Besides you, I mean."

"It's understandable. Can we meet for lunch or is that not possible?"

He hesitated but then said, "Sure. There's this place, not exactly Beverly Hills ambiance, called Bad Billy's —"

"Biker Bar," she interrupted. "This probably won't shock you, but I've heard of it already. That sounds perfect. Grace assured me I need to meet Billy."

"Everyone on this planet needs to meet

Billy. He'd get rid of the bad seeds, kick them out and then feed the rest of us some of the best burgers in the world. How about one o'clock? I'll pick you up at the Mountain View."

"Thanks." She hesitated, then added, "I have a conference call with my boss scheduled in half an hour. I'm afraid I'll have to revert to Ms. Wright for a few minutes. Now that I've seen the operation, I definitely think I can get them to sweeten the deal." She ignored the fact that she was technically on vacation, that this would be one of her last meetings with Dina — and that she'd already insisted he wasn't interested.

"Kelly." His tone was exasperated. "It isn't about the money. I've mentioned that before."

"That's the very first thing you learn in my field. It's *always* about the money. We'll talk it over while I sample one of those famous burgers."

"Don't forget his killer Cajun sweet potato fries. You're a cynic, you know that? You look like the wide-eyed girl next door, but there's a bit of a shark in there."

"Killer fries always work for me. Guess I'll be having a salad for dinner."

"Forget the salad. I know the perfect exercise to burn off those calories."

"Very subtle, Carson." She couldn't help laughing. "See you at one."

CHAPTER FIFTEEN

The bar was crowded, but it always seemed to be like that, and the fog had dissipated, so there was a line of bikes parked out front. Apparently, this was perfect cruising weather.

Mace preferred horseback, but he could understand the appeal. Sunny day, blue skies, the wind whipping past you against a setting of majestic mountains and wide meadows . . . There were worse ways to spend your day than touring country like this.

Having lunch with a beautiful woman didn't hurt, either. Kelly looked fresh and eye-catching in a dark blue tunic and scarlet leggings, little gold sandals and some dangly earrings even he noticed, and he was typically oblivious to details like that. He'd caught hell from Daisy once when he'd asked if she'd cut her hair, and she gave a very grown-up female snort of derision and informed him that yes, she'd had it cut. Three weeks before. His mother had helpfully chimed in to say that on another occasion he'd complimented her on a dress she'd worn to various family events as if he'd never seen it before.

At least Drake had commiserated. *Glad you were the one to open your big mouth first. I swear I was about to say the same thing.*

So he stuck to safe ground, in case she'd worn the earrings in front of him already. "You're turning every head in the place, darlin'. Who can blame them? There's a table in the back, which is my favorite place to sit. I see Thelma's on duty today. She's an interesting experience. Maybe she'll even let us order. Sometimes she just decides for you."

Kelly allowed him to guide her through the maze of crowded tables, and he had to admit his hand rested possessively on the small of her back. When half a dozen people greeted him as they went by, she asked, "Do you know *everyone* in this town?"

"Pretty much." He pulled out her chair and sat down across from her with a grin. "That's how it is around here. It has its pros and cons. If you do something great, everyone knows it, and if you mess up, everyone's aware of that, too."

"Not exactly how I grew up."

"That's small-town America for you. Uh-oh, brace yourself, here comes Thelma and I see she has predetermined our beverage."

"You need a haircut," the woman said to Mace by way of greeting. With graying hair in ringlets, spectacles perpetually on the end of her nose, she was spunky and opinionated and a Bad Billy's institution.

"You always say that," he responded, but he kept his tone respectful. A man did himself no favors by ticking her off.

"I believe in self-improvement for those who need it." She turned to Kelly and gave her an assessing once-over. "I can tell what he sees in you. What the hell do you see in him is the real question. He's easy on the eyes, I guess, and makes good wine, so I suppose if you drink enough of it, he could be appealing." She plunked down two glasses. "Range Red Blend to go with your grub. I'll bring the food when Billy gets to it."

Kelly looked more than a little bemused as Thelma left, skirting several tables that seemed to want her attention. She waved at them with a brusqueness that said she already knew what they needed.

"Does she always insult you like that?"

"Don't think I'm special. She insults

everyone like that."

"I take it this is one of those days we don't get to order?"

"Looks like it." Mace picked up his glass and lightly swirled the liquid inside. "This is a nice wine to pair with burgers, so we could be in luck. Thelma's definitely a character, but you know what? I can't imagine this world without her kind of individuality. Maybe she's an acquired taste, but she's got a good heart."

"Don't take her advice about the hair. I like it. Just touches your collar." Kelly took a sip of her wine. "This is one my favorites. Now, we have a couple of things to discuss. Shall we talk business first? Want to do it now or after we eat?"

He considered for a moment. "Let's get it over with. Take your best shot."

"They upped the ante." Her fingers trailed the stem of the glass after she set it down. "Business as usual, except there'll be one corporate review every year. They'll pay a higher price to buy the company and to provide better distribution. Oh, and they really like the name Mountain Winery. They think it's atmospheric. And if we can convince Raine to do the labels, they're totally on board with that. The powers that be also loved the idea of Slater doing the commercial if he agrees. They'll pay for it all and allow him to use it in any of his films. It'll probably benefit the resort, shops in town, tourism in general."

She was canny; he'd give her that. It was no secret that he was opposed to selling the winery, since he'd made it abundantly clear. But she'd put pressure on all the right people. Raine and Slater were a particularly smart call.

There was no choice except to be candid. "That's all well and good, but *I* don't want to do this."

"Explain why."

He eyed her steadily. "Ms. Wright, I think you know exactly why. I'm currently my own boss. I can do what I want. There's no corporate review. I'm not interested in being influenced by certain sales figures and the input of others. I don't want to answer to someone who's got a different agenda when it comes to wine. For instance, I don't like light fruity blush wines such as white zinfandel, so I'll never make one. I realize they're popular, but guess what? Since I get to make all the decisions, that's not on my list. From a marketing point of view, you probably think that's poor business, but from my point of view, if I don't enjoy it, how do I know it's any good? How do I judge that? I'll bet you a million bucks your company would ask for projects like that because they'll be in it to make money. I'm in it because I make wine *I* want to drink."

"If the stipulation is that you have complete creative control, they're on board with that. As I've mentioned. You seem to be making all the right decisions with what you're doing now." She held up her glass and the liquid sparkled ruby red. "For instance, I really like this wine and I understand what you're saying. If you're a control freak, we can hammer out that issue in the contract. Uh, I believe I've already said that."

"*Freak?* Now, there's a romantic word."

Her gaze was reproving. "We aren't talking about us at the moment. We're discussing the winery sale."

"Is the business portion of our afternoon done?" He hoped so, but wasn't convinced he was off the hook yet.

She leveled a stern look in his direction. "Almost. Can I point out that if you don't like the business part of what you do, maybe it would be in your best interests to let someone else do it for you? In other words, let other people — who do this for a living — make decisions on the labels, figure out what the hot markets are, approach restaurants and boutique stores, hire shipping companies and in general give you more time to do what *you* like to do. You'd be paid not only the lump sum for the business, but also a salary."

Thelma returned, slapping down a dish, and he'd never been so glad to see her. "Billy's fooling around with a new appetizer. Stuffed mushrooms that aren't deep-fried. I don't know why he's bothering to try and fix what ain't broke, but there you go. He wants you to tell him what you think. These are on the house. For whatever reason, he trusts your judgment, Carson."

"He should." Mace attempted his most boyish smile. "I've been eating Harry's cooking for the past thirty years. I know good food."

"Hmph. Well, I'll admit that woman can cook." Thelma fixed Kelly with a steely stare over the rim of her cat's-eye glasses. "What about you? You one of those high-falutin' California foodies who put bean sprouts and avocado on everything?"

Kelly responded serenely. "Not on dessert. I draw the line at anything but ice cream on apple pie. The mushrooms smell fantastic."

They did. They were covered with melted cheese, and a hint of garlic came through, even over the ever-present smell of sizzling meat. That delicious smell — of burgers and fries — took Mace back to high school whenever he walked through the door. After track meets, the whole team would come to Billy's for a burger, a treat from their now-retired Coach Williams, and when they were done wolfing down their food, told to get right back on their training diet regimen. They'd had a winning season all four years Mace was on the team, which he remembered with nostalgia. He'd even thought about trying to join the team at UCLA, but that was a tough one, first of all, and second, he was taking some challenging classes. As a result, not only his mother but both of his brothers talked him out of it.

"If I had to predict, I'd say these are going to be fantastic." Kelly had helped herself to three of the mushrooms; she took a bite and closed her eyes. "Oh, yeah. And yes, my pitch is now over."

He was relieved by that — and she was right about the mushrooms. He devoured his portion in no time. "He scored a hit with this one."

"Lance Vreeman is out of jail." She said it matter-of-factly, with no prologue or preparation, but he strongly doubted she felt as detached as she sounded. The careful absence of any expression on her face suggested that much. "He served his sentence — and now he's out."

He'd never forget his own reaction when he realized what was happening that night ten years ago. He'd had to take a deep breath before he got carried away and seriously injured the guy who'd grabbed a slender young woman doing nothing more than walking alone across campus. When she'd looked back and started to run and Vreeman sprinted after her, Mace had probably broken his high-school record in the hundred-meter dash — a record that stood to this day. He didn't even know Kelly then, yet he'd been furious, not just on her behalf, but on behalf of all the decent men in the world.

He chose his response to her revelation carefully. "That's not good news, but I was surprised the judge came down on Vreeman with such a tough sentence in the first place. If it hadn't been for that prior charge, I doubt he would have. I take it this is what you needed to tell me?"

"I'm worried he might want revenge against you." She seemed adorably sincere.

"Let him try."

He sounded nonchalant, and the only concern Mace seemed to show was for her.

That was exactly what she'd been afraid of, and the way he lounged there, across the table from her, relaxed in what was obviously a familiar environment, was both reassuring and disquieting.

The arrival of Bad Billy himself kept her from replying. He was burly and middle-aged but looked like he could hold his own in a fight. He had a hilariously anxious expression on his face. "Well?" he demanded as he slid their plates in front of them with surprising finesse. "Thelma said you'd want bacon and your sweetheart wouldn't," he told Mace. "What did you think of the mushrooms? Don't pussyfoot around, either. Shoot straight from the hip. On the menu or not? You go first, young lady."

"On," she said decisively. "Yes. Hands down. Absolutely delicious."

He beamed. Then he fixed Mace with a fierce scowl. "How about you, Carson? Don't be shy. You never are."

Mace chose to live dangerously. "I might need another serving to decide."

"What?"

He quickly recanted, laughing. "Just kidding. Those are over-the-top terrific. On the menu for sure. Wait until I tell Harry. You know she's going to try to top them, don't you?"

Billy relaxed visibly and Kelly found it both funny and endearing. "I worked on that recipe for months," he said gruffly, "so tell her good luck. Enjoy your food. I need to get back to the kitchen."

He walked off, greeting people at various tables.

Mace picked up his burger. "At least Thelma got our order right."

"We *didn't* order." It did look and smell wonderful, though. Appropriately messy and those fries . . . She picked one up and took a bite. "Yum."

"Dip them in that." Mace pointed at two small bronze cups that had arrived with the fries. "I swear it's unforgettable. Don't let his black T-shirt with the motorcycle insignia fool you. It's white truffle butter. All these guys with tattoos and big bikes in the parking lot are eating truffle butter."

She took his advice and was glad she did. "I feel like I've traveled to another place and time. How did Thelma know I didn't want bacon?"

"I told you." He said it with a shake of his head. "She knows all and sees all. She's like Harry that way."

"She must." Kelly wasn't sure where to begin with the large, messy burger but she tackled it, although she wouldn't want to be immortalized on film trying to take that first bite. Still, it was worth the indignity.

There was no way she would finish the whole thing, and Mace was amused when she gave up.

"We're not all champion eaters," she announced as she set aside the last half of her lunch.

He raised one brow. "You've eaten at the Carson Casa. I have two brothers, which means eat fast or go hungry. Old habits die hard. I've seen Drake have third helpings and go to the kitchen after dinner to make a sandwich."

"I can't imagine your mother's grocery bills."

"Luckily we live on a ranch. Lots of beef available, and there's my mother's garden. Drake tried raising sheep in one of the far pastures for a while, but no one really likes mutton and he's couldn't bring himself to take in the lambs, so he sold them all off."

She pushed her plate toward him. "Help yourself. It'd be a shame to waste it."

He grinned. "Don't mind if I do. I usually eat a couple of these"

"You must be joking!" She was not feigning incredulity.

But he wasn't kidding; the plate was empty in no time. "I'm going to order one of Billy's famous brownies," he said. "You've got to have at least a taste."

"I'll try," she promised weakly.

He stood up and went in search of Thelma, having a brief conversation with her, then returning to his seat.

Seconds later, it seemed, Thelma was back, delivering the brownie. "Had this ready and waiting for you," she said smugly.

There was no denying the one nibble she had was heavenly, but Kelly absolutely could not take another bite. "Can we walk back to the ranch? What is it? Twenty miles or so? That might do the trick."

"I didn't know we were going back to the ranch." He looked understandably wary.

"I have a meeting with your mother."

Take the wariness and double it. His expression did not reflect enthusiasm. "About what?"

She inhaled a deep breath. "Your grandfather is seriously thinking of selling his winery to us, but he'd prefer that all negotiations go through her, since she was supposed to inherit it. You can't blame him. He's in his late eighties, after all."

Mace nodded slowly. "So I guess Mountain Winery isn't the top priority for your being here."

She wasn't too sure about that. "I think

one deal will be straightforward, and one's proving to be a challenge, thanks to you. Oh, and please don't point out that you didn't invite me to intrude on your life."

"I wouldn't dream of it. But why didn't you mention this before?"

"For one thing, I just learned about it in a conference call I had this morning with your grandfather, as well as my current boss and the head of Sales. After that, I spoke to your mother and emailed her the offer."

"Why didn't she —"

"Blythe's looking over the paperwork. She asked me not to say anything, so I didn't. She needed to get in touch with her attorney, as well."

Mace clenched his fingers on the old table and stared at her. "You've known since this morning and you're only telling me now?"

She chose her words carefully. "I kept my word. I'm sorry if that feels like a betrayal."

"I don't usually like people who keep secrets, but in this case, I think my mother was just working it all out. I *do* like people who can be trusted not to tell the secrets of others."

Kelly couldn't help feeling relieved by this. He certainly had the ability to surprise her! "Blythe told me I could tell you when she called me later this morning. She also asked for an afternoon meeting, as I said. There are some details that need to be adjusted, but she's decided we can move forward."

"Congratulations, Ms. Wright." He actually sounded as if he meant it. "A coup. I was worried about how my mother was going to run that operation from here without having to fly out at least once a month. Even then, my grandfather's always been so hands-on that probably wouldn't be enough. I was afraid I'd get roped into some of those trips. I have a hard time saying no if my mother asks me to do something."

Kelly smiled wryly. "But you have no problem saying no to me."

There was a wicked glint in his blue eyes. "Seems to me I've said my share of yeses, too. And I'm ready to say it again whenever you like."

"I'm not talking on a personal level."

"More's the pity then."

"You two going to sit here and make calf eyes at each other all day?" Thelma picked up the empty plate that had held the decadent brownie; only a few crumbs remained as evidence it had been there. "Go hold hands in the park or something. Another group on bikes just rolled in and they look hungry. I'm kicking you out."

Her purse was next to her, and Kelly

scrambled for her wallet and fished out the corporate card. "Here you go. That was the best burger I've ever had — even without bean sprouts."

Thelma put a hand on her hip and regarded the card. "Honey, are you addled in the head? I assume you've met the man you just had lunch with. It's already taken care of." Then she turned to Mace. "That tip'll come in handy 'cause I'm saving up for a new washing machine. The damn thing's clunking along like a freight train going up a mountain."

"Always willing to give to a worthy cause." Mace rose with alacrity and extended his hand to Kelly. "Shall we?"

She accepted it and let him tug her toward the doorway. True enough, there was a line of men and women in leathers and bandannas; she hoped they were good tippers. For the sake of that new washing machine . . .

He unlocked the truck and opened the door for her. "I know she's not your average waitress, but Thelma is lovable in her own way."

"She's memorable." Kelly got in the vehicle.

"She is that." Then he announced calmly, "Vacation or not, you're staying here in Wyoming for a while. No argument."

Chapter Sixteen

He might have crossed the line by giving Kelly an ultimatum to stay in Mustang Creek.

Well, that was too bad.

More importantly, he was deeply disturbed that Lance Vreeman was now on the loose. Maybe ten years in prison had given the man time to contemplate how stupid it would be to come after Kelly again. Or maybe it had given a psychopath time to fantasize about revenge.

Since he couldn't possibly understand how Vreeman's mind worked, he found it equally impossible to predict what path he might choose. The bottom line for Mace was that Kelly needed to be where he could keep an eye out for any potential threat.

There was no way he'd try to delude her into thinking he was really considering the sale of the winery because he wasn't, so he went in another direction.

He texted both of his sisters-in-law. If I needed to convince Kelly to stick around for a while, what would you recommend as the carrot? Granted, she'd said she was taking some vacation days, but he had to ensure she stayed in Mustang Creek to do that.

They both texted back the same thing. You.

Flattering, but still . . . I meant seriously.

Luce responded: We answered seriously. What's up?

Grace pitched in: I think I know.

Hey, Grace. Chat soon? That was Luce.

When women started to talk to each other, he bowed out. All the help I can get is great.

It took about three phone calls and close to an hour, but he was finally able to get hold of someone in the LA prosecutor's office who could give him the information he wanted.

"Yes, Mr. Carson, Lance Vreeman is a registered sex offender. Unfortunately, he's out of jail, and he only has to meet face-to-face with his parole officer on a quarterly basis. Our office handled the case as a felony because, frankly, there it gave us a chance to keep a dangerous man off the streets for a long time. It worked, too — he got a stiff sentence, even though we couldn't prove conclusively that he did anything except grab a young woman and start choking her. He went to prison for what we *speculated* he was going to do to Ms. Allbright, not what we what *know* he was going to do. I will say his expensive lawyers tried to get the charges down to a misdemeanor, but luckily the judge refused the motion." The prosecutor was silent for a moment. "Too bad the ex-girlfriend dropped the charges."

"Kelly had bruises. He was choking her." Mace was murderously angry every time he remembered that night.

"That's what sent him to prison for ten years," the man on the other end of the line pointed out. "I don't doubt for a minute that he's a criminal, but when I looked over the case file, I might have decided the same thing if I were a judge. Your eyewitness testimony proved that he had intent to potentially do her greater harm. I hope you noted the use of the word *potentially*. The judge stated in his ruling that we can't prove beyond a reasonable doubt what he was going to do next. He served his time. I'm not happy about this, either, but there's literally nothing we can do about it."

"It's . . . frustrating."

"To use a hackneyed phrase, you're preaching to the choir, Mr. Carson."

After they hung up, Mace brooded as he gazed out the window, for once not noticing the view. Realistically he knew Kelly wouldn't stop her life so he could babysit her, and he also didn't have the time to watch over her, day in and day out. Nights, however, were no problem at all.

He was a firm believer that for every problem in life there was a solution. He just needed to find this one. Since he thought with more clarity when he was busy, he went into the cooler working part of the winery, where different batches of wine were fermenting, all at different rates. They needed to be turned and, in some cases, stirred, before going through the rest of the process.

His grandfather had once told him it was like the cycle of life; the wines started out young and raw, and then they developed character, and eventually mellowed into maturity.

Cycle of life, indeed.

Aged too long, they started to fade and lose their vibrancy, just like people.

He thought about his grandfather, finally ending an era by selling his beloved winery — his vocation and his passion — retiring from the life he knew and loved. Mace experienced a pang of sadness, but then again, his grandfather was being practical.

Still, he understood why his mother had needed time and privacy to consider her decision. Relinquishing a family heritage shouldn't come easily.

All the more reason to keep Mountain Winery to himself, and that left him at odds with Kelly.

It wasn't as if he could even call her, although she was at the house with his mother, because Kelly was in negotiations with Blythe. None of that required his opinion.

If there was one thing — among many — he'd learned from Blythe Carson, it was that women could make their own perfectly valid, informed decisions without men weighing in. His mother hadn't asked any of them for their opinions, as far as he knew, although it wouldn't have surprised him if she'd sat down with a cup of tea and talked it over with Harry. They were as close as sisters.

He checked the inventory on the pinot noir, pleased it was selling so well, thought for maybe the fiftieth time about opening a boutique wine shop of his own in Mustang Creek. Then he rejected the idea once again. He didn't want to expand. Having to deal with rent and payroll, hiring and firing, obtaining a liquor license . . . The list went on. A wine shop would be lucrative, he thought, especially during the height of ski season and in the summer, when tourists came through to gawk at the scenery — and who could blame them? He'd lived here his whole life and never got tired of the vista of soaring peaks and grassy rangeland. It was a privilege to be able to grab his fly pole and head for the Bliss River on a whim. He and Drake did it often enough, keeping a running tally of who'd hooked the most trout that year. Slater used to join them, but if he wasn't busy with filming and production, he now spent every spare moment with his infant son.

What a cute little guy . . .

"I was told I'd find you here."

He glanced up from entering numbers into a spreadsheet to see Kelly walking toward him down the shadowed aisle, a faint smile on her mouth. She gestured at the bottles, neatly in their racks by type and vintage. "Your mother said you spend as little time as possible in your office."

He hit Save and looked at her searchingly. "How *is* my mother? I'm going to trust the famous 'women's intuition' on this one and your honesty. To my brothers and me, she's always calm and unruffled, but how much of that is for our benefit? She has to be feeling a sense of loss at the idea of selling her father's winery."

Kelly reached out to skim the top of a rack, her expression reflective. "I'd say yes, a little sad but that's tempered by relief. I think the fact that your grandfather was considering the deal himself before passing the baton to her absolved her of any guilt. As you said yourself, she can't run the business properly from here, and she knows it. Not only that, she isn't about to leave her home. As soon as a few of the stipulations are met, she's going to sign the amended contract. She mainly wanted to ensure jobs for a few loyal employees for a specific number of years."

That sounded like his mother. He nodded.

Kelly squared her shoulders. "There's a caveat. She also wants *you* to taste any new wines before they're bottled. I didn't disagree with that at all. The main objective is to make sure the quality and integrity of the product matches the brand your grandfather worked so hard to build. I'm supposed to persuade you to agree to that."

At last the leverage he needed, and he jumped on it. "If you agree to stay here until we find out just what Lance Vreeman's next move is, then, yes, I'll do it."

She would have stayed on in Mustang Creek for the time being, anyway, even without the stipulation, but if Mace wanted to believe he'd driven a hard bargain, let him.

His hair curled deliciously against the collar of his denim shirt, his eyes were that almost hypnotic shade of blue and she'd already learned that he was a determined individual. Imaginative, independent, capable of herding a recalcitrant bull and also making fine wines, not to mention being a talented, oh so sexy lover . . .

What had she gotten herself into, anyway?

This was all going way too fast. She'd hadn't even been in Wyoming a full week! She'd told Grace the truth — she was afraid that falling in love might be confused with sexual attraction. By her *or* by him. Or both.

Every girl deserved a fling with a smokin' hot cowboy, but real life was real life.

"I appreciate your wanting to protect me. It just isn't possible, not all the time. You're an intelligent man, so you know that."

Which sounded a lot braver than she felt.

He walked toward her. "Can't protect you? Like hell. I think we've established I'm taller than you."

"Well, yes." She retreated a step. "So?"

"Bigger." He took two more steps in

response and gripped her shoulders lightly.

"Can't deny that."

"I'm a crack shot. I'm not as good as Red, who claims he can shoot the warts off a toad — I have to admit I don't know why anyone would do that, but it's what he says. I'm up there, though."

She stifled a laugh. "I'm hoping that skill won't be necessary."

"Me, too, but I'm at your disposal if the need arises." His gaze dropped to her mouth. "I like kissing you."

"What does that have to do with anything?"

"It has to do with everything. Because if you leave, I can't do this." His mouth settled on hers, and Kelly figured she'd slide to the floor if his arms weren't holding her up.

"That would be a shame," she managed to say when the kiss was over, her voice barely a whisper. "And you accused *me* of using sexual manipulation."

"Hmm . . . didn't I already take that back?"

"I accept your retraction. Again." Laughing, she reluctantly detached herself from his embrace.

"Thank you." He bowed slightly, and she rolled her eyes.

"Now," he continued, "maybe we can start

to move on — with the personal aspect of our relationship."

Start to move on? They were talking the speed of light here! "I realize that technically we met a decade ago," she said carefully. "But we don't *know* each other."

He slid his hands in his pockets, standing a foot or so away. "Just intimately. No big deal — is that it?" His murmur held an ironic edge.

"I didn't say *that* at all."

"What's going on between us — it means something to me."

That should have brought her to her senses, but it didn't. She turned and walked away, looking bleakly at a rack of bottles. Chardonnay, with a mountain sheep on the label. "I'm divorced," she said painfully. "I put off having children for the sake of my career. Who knows? Maybe I can't anymore — and I live in a different state. Run away and run fast!"

"Way to sell yourself, marketing expert." He paused diplomatically. "The children thing . . . I hope you're not hung up on that, Kelly."

Was she? Maybe a little.

She'd seen him with his nephew and his niece, Daisy. He was part of the close-knit Carson family and, no doubt, he'd want children, too. She had to remind him that it wasn't something you could count on.

"Hmm, how about we go take another direction? You're beautiful, smart and have a sense of humor. My top three requirements, not necessarily in that order."

Nice of him to say, but there were some serious obstacles to anything except a few more nights spent together. They were both aware of it. She hadn't said anything he probably hadn't already considered.

"My return ticket to LA is open-ended, so we have time to resolve some issues, including this one." She indicated the room with a sweep of her hand. "I still think I can persuade you to sign that contract."

"I'm sure you can probably persuade me to do plenty of things, but not that." The infectious smile that was his alone surfaced. "However, mission accomplished when it comes to my grandfather's business, anyway. Let me guess. My mother invited you to dinner again."

She had. Blythe was a very gracious lady. "Yes, she did. And she promised some of your white burgundy to celebrate our deal, even though dinner's supposedly going to be very simple."

"Generous of her when I've made it clear I have a limited supply. But we'll bring a few bottles back to the house."

"She said you might be persuaded to part with one or two."

His lashes lowered a fraction, and he crossed his arms over his chest. "Yeah, I might. For you."

"Can I ask another favor? I'd love to see the artwork Raine did. The mad scientist poster?"

He looked hesitant, so she explained. "Grace told me about it. If nothing else comes of this, let me give you some marketing input as you start to distribute the liquors. That poster sounds like the inspiration for a perfect label. Besides, I'd just love to see it. She said it was strikingly well-done."

"Yeah, my brothers think they're funny calling me the 'mad scientist.' " Mace shook his head. "Everything Raine does is exceptional, but to spite them and their questionable sense of humor, I haven't hung it up yet. If I do, I surrender to the joke."

"Or win the battle by laughing at it."

"Okay, good point." It was a grudging acknowledgment. "I want the best for Raine, and I think you could open up a whole new world for her. She's very gifted. Of course I'll show it to you."

The fact that he was being so pleasant was

going to be the death of her. Kelly followed him to the winery office upstairs. The late-afternoon sun illuminated the mountains and warmed the room. She stared out the window. "Do you ever tire of this view? Is that even possible?"

"I was thinking earlier how I don't. I'll get Raine's picture — if *you* agree never to tell her I haven't hung it up yet."

"Deal."

He had it stowed behind the daybed, and when he tugged it out and displayed it, Kelly took a deep breath as she looked at the picture. The image was a clever, slightly caricatured version of Mace, accented by brilliant colors. "Do you have any idea how fabulous that picture would be for advertising purposes? I love it!"

"It's a picture of *me.* No, thanks. I don't, for your information, ever wear a white lab coat. That was her imagination at work."

No, he wore jeans and boots and denim shirts, usually unbuttoned at the neck — every woman's erotic Western dream.

Focus. She examined the picture more closely.

"You can tell she's a graphic artist. The colors are *so* good. We could have her change the hair to blond like Drake's. Or dark, like Slater's. That would be sweet revenge."

He considered it, laughing a little. "Okay, I like the way you think. Keep going."

No hardship there; her mind was already busy assessing the possibilities. "We could use it for the liquors. The coffee one could be Slater, the pear brandy would be Drake and —"

"The apple and cinnamon vodka me?" he said coolly. "There goes my revenge. I could swear I just kissed Kelly in the wine cellar, but Ms. Wright is the one in front of me now."

She stood her ground. "Ms. Wright came to Wyoming for business reasons. Kelly inspired her to do it."

"I'm glad." His voice was almost a whisper. "I'm starting to think Kelly and I might belong together, even if Ms. Wright and I never come to an agreement."

CHAPTER SEVENTEEN

Dinner was actually quiet.

Not a usual occurrence at the ranch. Drake was out for his weekly poker night. Slater, Ryder and the baby were at the resort to have dinner with Grace. Luce was in town, teaching an adult extension course in ecology. Harry had a church pitch-in and was naturally in high demand, so she was gone for the evening, but she'd left a plate of the same sandwiches she carted along to the event — thinly sliced roast beef and her homemade secret sauce on freshly baked bread. She'd also made cheese and broccoli soup, plus several varieties of cookies.

Harry had always made soup and sandwich night unforgettable.

Kelly seemed impressed, and as far as he was concerned, the wine was a perfect balance with the meal, which was obviously why his mother had suggested it. Born and bred in the one of the most famous wine areas in North America, and coming from a winemaking family, she knew what to pick to go with what meal. Some of her suggestions weren't what Mace would've expected, but she'd never failed to get it just right. Even the chef at the resort called her on occasion if he was featuring something unusual on the menu and needed advice on what wine his staff should recommend as a complement to the dish.

"I told myself I wasn't going to try to eat dinner tonight after Bad Billy's." Kelly sent him a lethal look across the table. "Here I am actually considering more soup. You, Carson, are a bad influence."

He reached for the tureen to pass it along. "Don't blame me, blame Billy and Harry. Just don't do it when I'm around. They'll be nice to *you*. I'm fair game."

His mother smiled, elbows comfortably on the table, a wineglass in her hand. "They both adore you, even though you went through that unfortunate phase with your hair in high school."

He'd done interesting things with sideburns and let some of his hair grow long but shaved off other parts, so it was hard to argue. "I was finding myself," he muttered.

Kelly grinned, and he loved the way her eyes tilted at the corners. "Can I see a

344

picture? Oh, and what did you find — when you found yourself?"

"I realized I wasn't an idiot, so why look like one."

His mother choked on a swallow of wine. She frowned at him reprovingly, but her eyes were alight with laughter. "Mason Carson, don't do that to me again." She confirmed his conclusion. "He did look ridiculous. I tried to not say anything. I figured it would pass. I'm happy to say it did."

"Thanks." He had to wonder why he felt so comfortable with Kelly. There was no urge to impress her, even though they'd known each other such a short time. "Mom might not have said anything, but Showbiz and Romeo had no mercy. Come to think of it, they still don't."

Kelly did take another ladle of soup. "I understand why you call Slater Showbiz. Why is Drake called Romeo?"

He had no problem telling that story. "On a romantic whim, which he would deny he has — although it's now recorded fact that he does — he took Luce to watch the moon rise over the mountains, with a waterfall in the background, starlit night, the whole package. What he didn't know was that Slater's crew had set up cameras so they could capture it for the Bliss County documentary, and they recorded that first kiss to be preserved for all to see."

"Drake is camera-shy," Blythe said. "Slater loved the accidental footage and somehow coerced both him and Luce to let him use it. Between the film crew and the gossip mill around here, people got wind of it and gave him the nickname. He wasn't any too happy about it."

"The mad scientist moniker stuck with me, and he's to blame. So it serves him right." Mace took what must have been his sixth cookie. This one was peanut butter with butterscotch and chocolate chips and tasted heavenly. "It's a beautiful place. That's why Slate had cameras put there." He tried to sound off hand. "I'll show it to you."

What he didn't say was how much their father had loved that spot; that was also why Drake had taken Luce there.

He was still brooding about how he'd said that he and Kelly belonged together. Maybe he was losing it. She'd said she wasn't ready for a relationship. She was right in that they had the necessary chemistry, but chemistry wasn't everything. There was still everyday life. She had hers, and he had his.

"I'd love to see it." Kelly's voice was soft. "I have to say California is a very beautiful state, but Wyoming has . . . I'm not sure how to put it. A breathtaking sense of place. It really isn't like anywhere else I've been."

"Good way to describe it," Mace said. "I have fond memories of California, both from childhood visits to see my grandparents and going to school there, once I adjusted to the sheer volume of noise and people in LA. But this is home."

"I can understand that."

"Then you should give it a try."

He couldn't explain why those words had come out of his mouth, but they had. No chance of sucking them back in. Kelly looked taken aback, and even the cool and poised Blythe Carson, hostess extraordinaire, seemed speechless.

He was on the speechless side himself. Two choices loomed now. He could gloss it over, or ride on down the trail he'd just chosen.

The latter was the more appealing, although as Red would say, it proved he was as loco as a bedbug in a rowboat out to sea. "I'm serious. Mustang Creek is a great place to live."

That observation made his mother jump up and declare that she was going to make a cup of coffee and check her email if they'd excuse her. They looked at each other as she left the room, and Mace smiled slowly. "I rarely see my mother rattled. I need to note this on a calendar somewhere."

"Better watch it, cowboy," Kelly said flippantly, "I might take what you just said as a real invitation."

"Be my guest." He was as much of a damn fool as Romeo. "Fine with me."

Kelly took a moment and then said carefully, "I just want to be sure we don't make any mistakes, that's all. Maybe I'm being overcautious, but I don't think I could stand it if everything fell apart again. So, if you have any doubts, you can retract that offer at any time, if it *is* an offer."

"Sure is. I like to take the direct approach."

"I've noticed that."

"So, do you want to take a chance?"

"Heaven help me, I think I do." Her smile resonated through his whole body. "But you're like a new-barrel merlot. Unpredictable and yet sometimes you're actually likable to the average palate."

"I'll take that comparison and raise you. You're anything but average. The moon's not full tonight so I can't outdo my brother, but if you'd like, we could take our wine and go sit on the veranda . . . and talk about this."

Talk about what, exactly?

As Kelly watched him pick up both their glasses and politely wait for her to precede him through the doorway, she wondered if she might just be outmatched. Since the divorce, she hadn't met anyone who really interested her. She'd always thought she would give marriage another try somewhere along the way, become a wife and mother, like her sisters.

Only it hadn't happened.

The night was beautiful, with wispy clouds passing overhead and insects chirping as dusk settled in. The breeze was fragrant with the scent of fresh grass.

Maybe it wasn't a moonlit mountain and a waterfall, but it was still quite the setting. She chose a wicker chair on the wide, gracious porch.

What to say next?

Let him go first. Mace was a quiet man, but when it counted, he was seldom at a loss for words.

And now was no exception. He sat in a chair opposite hers, extended his legs and handed over her wineglass. "I have an idea to propose, if you're remotely interested. You might call it a compromise."

She eyed him skeptically. "Oh, I'm dying to hear this one. Feel free to clarify."

"You have a business degree, don't you?"

"I do." *Where was this going?*

"I have an offer for you."

What?

He took a minute, contemplating his glass, and then lifted his gaze. "Make no mistake — I haven't changed my mind about selling the winery." He paused, considering his next words, whatever they might be. "I've decided, however, that I need a partner — a *full* partner. Fifty-fifty all the way. Has to be someone I can trust to handle marketing, plan advertising campaigns, employee incentives, all that. That way, I'd have the time I need to put in more vines, experiment with new formulas and processes. You really *could* move here, and run, market, manage, a shop featuring Mountain Winery wines and liquors." Again, he paused, quietly cleared his throat. "You could also handle the company's business matters, and I could do my thing. That way, we both win. What do you say, Kelly? Can you see yourself as half owner of a Wyoming winery?"

"Yes," Kelly replied. "But then GGI loses."

"They'll survive."

She smiled. "They will," she agreed. The company was well on its way to becoming a conglomerate. Mace's decision would come as a disappointment, but given their size and scope, it was merely a setback. "I'll call Dina — my boss — in a little while and break the news. She won't be pleased, but I can live with that."

A thrill went through her as she spoke. "I have to ask you something," she added. "When did you come up with this?"

"I've been thinking about it all along, on some level, but I guess it began to gel yesterday, when I realized how much I want you to stay — and not just for your own protection. But you're actually the one who put the idea in my head."

"How did I do that?"

"By pointing out, more than once, that I don't enjoy the business end of the operation all that much. That's *your* forte. I'll foot the investment and take the risk. I know this area, and I think we can make a go of it. Now that you've landed on my doorstep —"

"On your roadside," she interrupted. She could feel her pulse picking up as her heartbeat increased. She'd dreamed of starting her own business, a dream that had taken on new urgency with her changed career circumstances. Her tentative plan to quit was making even more sense. She knew a lot about marketing wine, thanks to her current job. She could translate that into retail and perhaps advise him on marketing and distribution for Mountain Winery.

"Roadside," he agreed. "Anyway, think about it. I'd never go into business with anyone my family didn't like and you've got that covered, so if you're interested . . ."

She felt an overwhelming rush of trepidation, a sense of exhilaration — and a very real urge to be sensible and back away. "If things don't work out between us on a personal level, you realize a business relationship would be awkward, to say the least."

"Good to know you're entertaining the possibility," he said quietly. "I think this could work."

He seemed to have ignored that she'd already pointed out the main reason *she* didn't think it would. "A personal relationship is different from a business one, anyway," he added. "I can be professional. Can't you?"

This wasn't a time to be less than honest. "I can be professional, but you're different."

Had she really just said that?

Mace wasn't about to let it go. "Have I been insulted? How am I *different*?"

"You're impulsive and artistic."

"You're a bit impulsive, too. Go with the flow, Ms. Wright."

She leaned back in her chair. "It's a great idea —"

"But?"

"We've been together less than a week, Mace."

"We've known each other for ten years," he countered easily.

"It's not the same thing, and you know it. We didn't meet at a party, or some college mixer, Mace. We met at a *crime scene,* remember?"

"I remember," he said.

She shivered involuntarily, and it wasn't from the breeze. "I don't think about it much, but when I do, usually after I've heard about something horrible happening somewhere in the world, or read about it online, and my faith in people is shaken, I think about *you.* I think about how you helped me, a total stranger, how you didn't hesitate or look the other way or simply decide not to get involved."

"I kind of lost it when I realized what was happening," he recalled. "Whatever was going on in my head, it wasn't very noble."

It was hard to believe she could laugh about anything related to that fateful evening, but she couldn't restrain a giggle. "You called that man names I'd never heard before. I wasn't tracking all that well, understandably, but I remember wondering what kind of place could produce someone like you."

He gestured at the mountains and deepening sky, as if to say, *This kind of place. Wyoming. The West.*

"It's so beautiful here," she said.

"I agree."

A brief silence fell between them.

Kelly was the one to break it. "About that partnership thing . . ."

Mace raised one eyebrow, ever so slightly, but otherwise, he didn't move. "What about it?"

"Well, you didn't say how much I'd have to invest. I mean, I have some money, but —"

"I said I'd take care of the investment." He laughed, startling her. "I don't want — or need — your money, Kelly. I'm interested in your expertise and your marketing savvy. Your ideas."

"But — you can't mean — it's just —"

Mace laughed again. "And you're articulate, too."

Kelly wasn't amused. She was stunned, she was confused, she was wary. But she *definitely* wasn't amused. "Your winery is worth a fortune, Mace. You can't just hand half of it over to someone you barely know."

"Can't I? It's mine, isn't it?"

"But that's crazy! I could turn out to be an embezzler or a complete incompetent. What then?"

"I'd be mighty surprised, that's what."

She could only shake her head. Things like this simply didn't *happen.*

"We might butt heads once in a while," Mace said, without particular concern. "That's natural. Partners disagree. Then they work out their differences and get on with it." He watched her for a moment, probably enjoying her reaction to the shock he'd given her, before adding, "What've you got to lose, Kelly? It's a sweet deal — no cash outlay, and you get to live here and eat Harry's cooking. If there's a downside, I'm not seeing it."

Fury jolted through her, hard. So *that* was to be her "investment"? Easy sex, anytime he wanted it?

"Live *here*? In your family's house? You can't be serious!"

He frowned. "Well," he said, puzzled. "Yeah."

That was when she realized she'd misread him — again. When it came to sex, she'd been a willing, even eager participant. He wanted her to stay on the ranch because she would be safer there. She felt like three kinds of a fool.

"Right," she said, even though it didn't entirely make sense.

"This can work, Kelly," he told her.

Could it?

"I agree. It could," she said. "I've always wanted to work for myself." She paused, blushed again. "Though in this case, it wouldn't be *just* for myself, of course."

Mace smiled. "Of course," he confirmed, letting her off the verbal hook. "And relax, will you? There's no need to watch your words. Like I said, this is a partnership."

"Do you suppose Raine would be willing to work on the labels and Slater would do a commercial?"

"Yep." He didn't miss a beat.

"You're so sure."

"If I asked them, yes, of course, they would. They'd walk on coals because they're family. I'd do the same for them, and they know it."

That was easy to believe, since she was just as sure her sisters would do anything for her, maybe even accept the idea that she might move to Wyoming.

It was something to think about as she contemplated this possible move. Sitting on a wide front porch with a handsome man, sipping wine, her life's dream in view — all of that might sway her more than a little.

"You sprang this on me." She was half joking, half accusatory.

"I sprang it on me, too." He wasn't even defensive. "But it isn't *always* stupid to have whatever you're thinking come out of your mouth. Sometimes it's better just to say it. Don't tell Drake that. Who knows what he might blurt out next?"

She had to laugh. "I think he's one of the nicest men I've ever met."

"I actually think that, too. Go figure. All we've ever done is argue, but he's a good guy."

"You argue in a brotherly way, and you both do it on purpose. Those are your mother's words, and I've seen the two of you in action."

"Talking about me behind my back, huh? I thought that was a business meeting you had."

"It was." In truth, Blythe Carson was a very efficient lady; by the time Kelly met with her that afternoon, she'd read over the contract, marked the specific changes she wanted, and spoken with her lawyer and the title company who'd handle the transfer. So the entire business part of the meeting took about fifteen minutes. The rest of it *was* spent talking about Mace and life on the ranch, and it included some gentle probing questions about Kelly's family and her career.

A horse nickered nearby, breaking the silence. This was such a peaceful place, she could imagine living here.

He was here. But Mace wasn't the reason she was considering it, she told herself. She failed to be convincing enough to pull it off.

It was time to face the inescapable reality that she'd fallen for him — and fallen hard.

CHAPTER EIGHTEEN

Hadleigh Galloway was in the back of her shop but came out at the tinkle of the bell, her hair in a ponytail, her lips curving in a smile. "Mace, I've never pictured you as a quilt man. More of a flannel blanket type. What brings you by?"

"I have a question, and if the answer is yes, I need your help." No formalities but none were needed. He'd known her since she was a toddler. His grandparents had been friends of her grandmother's and their families had frequently spent the Fourth of July together. She'd gotten even prettier as she hit adolescence, but it was no secret that Tripp Galloway had always been interested in her, and despite a few obstacles — including his first marriage and subsequent divorce — they eventually ended up together. Marriage, cute baby, the works.

"Like what?"

"I'm wondering if Bob and Martha might

sell the store. I know it's been for rent, but do you think they'd sell it? They've owned that building as long as I can remember."

He'd thought about it carefully, and purchasing the building rather than leasing appealed to him, had tax benefits according to his accountant, and — business aside — it featured a lot of the old Western charm that characterized Mustang Creek. Not only that, the place was originally a saloon, and Slater had unearthed photos of it while he was making the documentary set in Bliss County, which was to air later this month. Bob had once shown him the old sign that had been taken down when it became a dry goods store, before he and Martha turned it into a grocery. Mace hoped it was still there in the storage room. It would be great for the wine-tastings Grace had added to some of the packages the resort offered. He'd sweeten the deal by asking Kelly if she wanted to handle that part of marketing, as well.

It was Friday. The clock was ticking toward Monday, and he was counting on an answer from Bob *and* from Kelly before the next business day.

Hadleigh brightened. "You want to buy it? That would be *great*! I just talked to Martha on the phone the other day, and she mentioned that Bob wanted to get the kids interested in moving back and starting a business here, but he's finally given up. I think they'd all be in favor of selling, especially to you. Planning to open another wine shop, besides the one at the vineyard?"

He nodded, leaning against the counter that sported an antique sewing machine. "Yes. The shop we have now is pretty small, with limited hours, and it's a little off the beaten path, especially for the locals who want the wine but not necessarily the lectures and tours." He took a breath. "You run a business here in town. Based on your experience, what do you think? Will it work?"

"Oh, yeah." Hadleigh grinned enthusiastically. "*Please* tell me you'll carry some of that wine you gave Tripp and me for Christmas. Yuletide Snowfall? We had guests at the ranch, and they absolutely loved it. I did, too. Even Jim, who's strictly a beer man, drank some and then had a second glass, since Pauline was driving. I want to preorder a case of that right now."

That was good to hear. "You arrange for me to talk to Bob, and the wine's on the house, trust me. I know you're close because of your grandmother's friendship with both of them."

"He and Martha are like family to me." Hadleigh acknowledged that with a small fond smile. "They could use the money, too, since they're living on a fixed income. They've told me they want someone who appreciates the building's historical character to have it."

"I do."

"I know. So will they. I can't wait to see Slater's movie." She gestured at the front window. "Did you know your brother came by and filmed this whole street, including my shop? The store's in there too."

"Doesn't surprise me, but he's being damned close-mouthed about it until the final cut's done." Slater was a bit of a celebrity in these parts. "I heard he interviewed Jim, too." Her stepfather-in-law was definitely an old-style rancher, now retired and remarried.

"And he talked to Tripp, as well, to get a sampling of why successful young professionals would move back here. He also spoke with Charlotte and Jax Locke, and Tate Calder, since he was a corporate pilot but chose Mustang Creek as the place to raise his kids. And he interviewed Bex, because she created a successful business that blossomed into an entire chain. There'll be quite a few other people we both know in the documentary."

"We grew up here," he said drily. "It's kind of hard to find someone we *don't* know."

"What about you, Mace? Are you in the film?"

He nodded. "Drake, too."

Hadleigh's expression brightened from friendly to high-beam as she glanced toward the front window of her shop. "Uh-oh, here comes trouble."

The bell jingled again and her husband, Tripp, strolled in, carrying a squirming child and holding a sack. "You flirting with my wife, Mace?" he asked. "Hey, rumor has it you've got yourself a girl already."

"Mama." The baby reached out his arms for Hadleigh, who was laughing. "Mama, Mama, Mama."

Tripp handed him over. "Go for it, since Dada's worn out and could use that nap you refuse to take." He set the sack on the counter and said to his wife, "If I get the brilliant notion to keep that bundle of joy all on my own again, it's your duty as my loving wife to remind me that he just might blow out a diaper, require a bath and a change of clothes, and has more energy than a football team on game day. I brought you lunch, by the way. That brie-and-apple thing from the café. I tried to eat a sandwich while

I was feeding him and got up for two seconds to get him more carrots. The kid has a reach, I tell you. From his high chair he somehow grabbed my ham-and-cheese and tossed it on the floor. The dogs thoroughly enjoyed it."

By now Hadleigh was laughing so hard there were tears in her eyes. Mace couldn't conceal his amusement any more than she could. Hadleigh gasped out, "What can I say? He's his father's son. Not as easy as it looks, huh, Galloway?"

"I think it was revenge for the carrots. They didn't seem all that appealing to me, either." Tripp glanced at her suspiciously. "Did you set me up? I thought you said he liked carrots."

"I said I *hoped* he liked carrots." She was all wide-eyed innocence.

"So I was the first one to give them to him? You *did* set me up. News flash — he doesn't. He spit up half of them on my shirt. I had to get more carrots *and* change my clothes. At least I knew enough to keep my distance after that." Tripp turned to Mace. "If you haven't had lunch yet, I'm headed to Bad Billy's. Care to join me? I'll eat anything Thelma slaps down in front of me as long as it doesn't involve bright orange mush."

"Sounds good to me." Mace was still grinning when Hadleigh said serenely, "You two go on. I think someone's ready for his nap."

Sure enough, thumb in mouth, head nestled on his mother's shoulder, their son had already closed his eyes. Tripp muttered, "You've *got* to be kidding me. Do you have any idea how many times I tried —"

"Yes, I do. Now go eat lunch, and it looks like I'll get to enjoy mine, too. Mace, I'll text Bob and if the answer is yes, I'll tell him to call you."

He flashed her a smile as he followed Tripp out the door. "Thanks."

Tripp said with rueful humor as they walked down the street, "I swear women have a special magic. I stopped trying to understand it long ago. My son is apparently as susceptible as I am. All she has to do is be there, and I'm old news."

Mace couldn't help thinking about how much he missed his own father. "Don't sell yourself short. You're just as important, but in a different way."

Tripp nodded, his eyes suddenly distant. "True." He was silent for a moment. "You know, when I found out Jim had cancer, I couldn't have predicted the kind of impact that would have on me. I think I still rely on him more than I realize. If I need advice, guess where I turn."

"We're all fortunate to know him." Jim would give you the hat off his head, and Tripp had lucked out when his mother married him.

"We are." Tripp turned to him as they waited to cross the street.

They were both quiet for a few moments, then Mace changed the subject. "I'd like to buy the old store, if the price is reasonable, and knowing Bob it will be."

Tripp was as quick as Hadleigh. "You're opening another shop, here in town? Sounds like a great idea. Is this on the advice of the 'blonde bombshell'? I'm quoting Pauline, who heard from a friend that you two were involved in college and she came out here to see you."

Not quite accurate about the "involved" part, unless you counted putting Lance Vreeman behind bars. "Kelly works for a company that wanted to buy Mountain Winery. I'm hoping I can convince her to move here instead and help me manage the winery and the store."

The parking lot was jammed as usual. Billy waved at them when they walked into the restaurant, pointed to a corner booth and went back to work behind the busy counter. They slid in, waiting for Thelma to bring them whatever she'd decided they wanted to drink, and Tripp settled comfortably on the well-worn seat. "Damn, it always smells so good in here. So tell me, is another Carson male seriously involved with another California girl?"

Mace could point out that it was early days yet, and Kelly wasn't ready to make a decision like that. He tended to know what he wanted pretty fast, but not everyone did. "Serious? Hard to say. Kelly's been married before," he said neutrally. "She's mentioned it more than once. I can tell — and she's said this outright — that she's not rushing into anything."

"Remember, I was married before Hadleigh and I tied the knot. You know, that conversation with my ex isn't one I ever want to relive again. *Guess what, I think we made a mistake.*" He grimaced. "Hadleigh would've married that loser Oakley Smyth and been miserable until she decided to walk away, which would eventually have happened because he's a jerk and she would've figured it out."

"You put a stop to that, anyway," he said, recalling how Tripp had busted into the wedding and been the talk of the town.

"Damn straight. I'd promised Will I'd take care of her, and I did."

Will was Hadleigh's older brother, who'd been killed in Afghanistan. He and Tripp had been best friends and served in the military together. Tripp went on. "I'm just pointing out that perfectly reasonable people can make decisions that seem good at the time, but aren't. Caution is a reasonable stance in my book."

Mace listened to Hank Williams crooning from the jukebox. Bad Billy's never changed the selections. "I agree," he said finally. "But what better way to make a decision about living here than actually moving here? There's no law that says she has to stay."

"You really are that serious about her. Well, all you can do is give it your best shot."

"Look what the cat dragged in." Thelma set down two glasses. "It's only noon, and the two of you have things to do, so you're drinking iced tea. Tripp, that barbecue burger with coleslaw on the side will be here in five minutes, and Mace, you're having the same damn thing, get it?"

He got it.

When she left, he said under his breath, "How does she do that?"

Tripp picked up his iced tea. "I'm not sure I want to know. But she's right, it isn't beer-thirty for me yet, so this hits the spot."

■ ■ ■ ■

Lance Vreeman had sent her a text message. She knew it — knew it had to be him.

No one could be that stupid, and she didn't think he was stupid at all, but she didn't recognize the number.

How do you like Wyoming? I understand the town is nice. I'll have to check it out.

That was it.

At first glance she simply wondered who'd sent it, but that reaction was followed by dismay. It seeped in, at first resembling a trickle in a creek bed, until it turned into a tidal wave that could wash away an entire village.

What the heck?

Twelve nieces and nephews. Her sisters and their husbands. Her parents. There was no way she could protect them all. To make it worse, there was nothing overtly threatening about the message. She had no idea how he'd found her cell number, but she knew it was him.

She just *knew*.

She called Mace immediately, her hand

trembling. "Where are you?"

"My office . . . Kelly, what's the matter?"

"I really need to talk to you."

He didn't hesitate. "Fine, I'll pick you up right now instead of in an hour like we'd arranged. I'm walking out the door while I'm talking to you, headed for my truck."

"Thanks. I'll be in the lobby of the Mountain View." *Where there are lots of people.* Suddenly her suite no longer felt safe, which was probably ridiculous, since it had a perfectly secure door and only an acrobat could scale the walls to the balcony.

"I'll be there as soon as possible."

"Thanks. Don't break any laws or anything, I just . . ."

Need you. She'd almost said it. The very sound of his voice was reassuring. And when had she become such a wimp, anyway? She'd defined herself as a confident woman, good at her job, independent, levelheaded most of the time . . . except, as she'd recently discovered, when it came to Mace Carson.

"No problem," he said "See you soon."

She went into the bathroom and glanced in the mirror. Hair smooth, makeup understated, but maybe some lip gloss would help her look less pale. Earlier she'd changed into jeans, a soft pink silk shirt and slip-on flats, just in case she got tossed on a horse again.

Well, she was presentable, anyway. She took the stairs to the lobby and hovered by the tall doors until she saw him pull up.

He jumped out and came around to look searchingly at her face. "Everything okay?"

"I don't know. I want to be at the ranch for a while, that's all." There was an embarrassing quaver in her voice. "Let's go."

"Okay, that can be arranged. We'll talk on the drive?" He opened her door, his expression concerned. "Kelly, you seem shaken up and I —"

"You bet we'll talk." She climbed in, feeling better almost at once.

He got in, too, waiting for her to speak. She had to give him credit for his patience. In the end, she simply said, "I think he contacted me."

"He?" He caught on fast as he put the truck in gear. "You mean Vreeman? Are you serious?"

"I'll show you the text."

His expression tightened. "How the hell would he get your cell phone number?"

"Not from my family, I can tell you that much. So my answer is I have no idea."

Mace said something under his breath, and she thought it might have been "that bastard" with another colorful word inserted. "There's just too much information floating around these days."

"I agree. I'm trying not to panic about the fact that he also knows I'm in Wyoming." She added silently, *with you.*

His mouth was set in a thin line. "I think if it *is* him, he's putting himself in harm's way — and that harm would be me. You'll be staying at the ranch tonight. I'll forward the text to Spence Hogan."

Under other circumstances, she'd resent that presumptuous decree, but she was more shaken than she'd expected. On impulse, she'd grabbed her toothbrush and small cosmetic bag and stuck them in her purse. She was glad she'd had the foresight to do that.

"I don't like being afraid of him," she admitted. "And I wasn't until I heard he was released. It isn't just for my sake, either, or yours. I have family, you have family, and if he's got revenge in mind, we can't predict what he might do, who he might target. He was unstable before he went to prison. I doubt the experience improved his mental state."

"My thoughts exactly." Mace swung the vehicle in a smooth turn onto the county highway. "When his family wanted to sue me for assault, the detectives I talked to gave me the impression that Lance Vreeman had a juvenile record. It was sealed when he turned eighteen, so the prosecution couldn't use it in court."

"Suing *you* for assault! What nerve." She shook her head. "I was so horrified when I heard about that. It's preposterous!"

Mace took his eyes from the road just long enough to give her a wry glance. "Considering the situation, I doubt any judge would have heard the case. On the other hand, I *did* break that ass — er — Vreeman's nose, crack a few of his ribs and possibly limit his ability to reproduce." One shoulder moved in a shrug. "Sometimes bad things happen to bad people. I didn't lose any sleep over it."

"Neither did I, and feel free to call him an asshole in front of me."

"I wonder what Harry's fixing for dinner. I'm starving."

Kelly jabbed him in the ribs with her elbow but appreciated the reprieve from her distressing reality. "You Carson boys, I swear all you do is eat. Or think about eating. Poor Harry."

"Poor Harry? Who do you suppose introduced us to things like coq au vin and jambalaya? Between her and Red, with his inventive Wyoming dishes like that buffalo chili he swears by, we have no choice but to eat up. They'd be insulted if we didn't, and I don't want to hurt their feelings."

"Yeah," she said, "Or maybe you're just a bottomless pit."

"We also like a wee dram now and then," Mace supplied helpfully in the world's worst attempt at a Scottish accent, passing someone on the highway he obviously knew because they exchanged a wave. "And on that subject, I've come up with an idea."

"Wine or liquor?"

"The latter. A liqueur actually. Something on the order of limoncello, the Italian drink, but I'd add raspberries and call it Mountain Paintbrush. Can you imagine the label Raine could make for that?"

It wasn't subtle, but he was trying to distract her and she appreciated it. She couldn't help a suspicion that this inspiration had hit about two seconds ago; she went along with it, anyway. "I can. I'm a little surprised the marketing angle caught your attention, though."

"I'd leave that to you. I'm just saying it isn't a bad idea. Right?" His mouth curved in an audacious smile. "But I do occasionally have a marketing idea. We could have *you* on the label, bending over to pick some of that wildflower in a meadow. Show some tantalizing cleavage. Your blond hair would represent the lemon, and a red dress would be the raspberry. That'll sell it. There's my marketing angle. You're impressed, aren't you?"

He was doing this on purpose. She groaned. "You're going for the 'sex sells' approach, huh? Your problem is that men are unlikely to buy a lemon-raspberry liqueur, and the cleavage won't appeal to your buyers, who'd be mostly women."

He tried to look crestfallen. He failed. "And here I thought it would be a viable plan. You must admit that your breasts spilling out of a red dress would draw the male eye. Men everywhere would be drinking raspberry-lemon cocktails while watching football games and shouting at the screen about a bad call. I think I'm a genius. You're just jealous I came up with the idea first."

"Yeah, that's it. What I will admit is that the liqueur sounds pretty good, but your shameless exploitation of women is . . . well, shameless."

He was unrepentant in true Mace style. His brow furrowed. "I was kidding, but . . . what if? I'd want a drink that's not too potent, maybe something to mix with sparkling water or champagne for a fancy brunch or a wedding reception. Wheels are turning here."

The process of hearing him mull it over was interesting in itself. Her creativity took a different direction. "I bet the spa would be interested if you kept it light as far as the alcohol content goes. It's all about relaxation there. We could try places in California and Arizona, too, if it catches on here."

"*We?* Are you thinking about accepting my offer and working with me?"

"The real question is, are *you* thinking about it?"

He gave a sigh of exasperation. "Kelly, would I have brought up the subject otherwise? With any luck, I'll be signing on the dotted line to buy the building for the store soon."

That stunned her. "You're that confident I'll say yes?"

"I was raised by Blythe Carson. Her mantra is that if you want something, then you should go for it and always think positive."

"And you really want me for this project?"

"Oh, I want you." He said it without skipping a beat. "In more ways than you know."

CHAPTER NINETEEN

The horses grazed like ghosts in the meadow.

He walked to the fence, leaned his arms on the top rail and held out his hand. Mace loved this time of day, and there was no mistaking the eager response as the equine contingent recognized that he was distributing carrots and apples, crowding each other to get to him.

"Drake takes care of them. I'm just their sugar daddy," he joked, looking over at Kelly. "I spoil them, he gets to clean their hooves and call the vet if there's anything wrong. Ryder mucks out their stalls and grooms them. I like this arrangement, as you might've guessed, but my brother doesn't have to deal with spoiled grapes, a leaking barrel or something that comes out tasting like it could be mixed with olive oil and sprinkled on a salad. So there you go. It evens out."

Kelly had proved she wasn't afraid of horses and helped him out, plucking an apple from the bag. A young sorrel mare didn't hesitate, jostled her way in to take it. Kelly laughed delightedly and stroked the animal's neck. "She's gorgeous."

Her enthusiasm was a relief. She'd been visibly subdued during dinner, and while he understood to a certain extent, he realized he couldn't completely comprehend her sense of vulnerability. She was afraid of Lance Vreeman, and with due cause if he'd sent that message. Mace had the same fatalistic sense that Vreeman had done just that.

"I agree." He was looking directly at her. "The most unusual eyes. At the risk of sounding poetic, I'd say the color of a forest at sunrise."

She let the mare nuzzle her palm. "No, I'd say her eyes are brown."

"Oh, yeah, I guess I wasn't talking about the horse."

"I know I was panicking earlier, but there's no need to pour on the charm. I do feel better being here, mostly because I suspect Red carries around a six-shooter and could use it to . . . what was that, shoot the warts off a toad?"

"He'd face Vreeman with pistols at dawn

to defend a lady."

"I thought they did that sort of thing at high noon. I believe you're thinking of English gentlemen and their honor disputes." She leaned against the fence, her hair moving softly. He liked her in those formfitting skirts and high heels, but even more in jeans and a casual shirt. And her new boots, of course.

"Visibility is a lot better at noon. Cowboys are pretty practical even if we're susceptible to innocent maidens in distress."

"I think you're well qualified to vouch that I am *not* a maiden." Her eyes held a mischievous twinkle. "Or all that innocent."

"And I'm grateful for that. Always found them on the boring side. Ever been for a moonlit ride? Romantic as hell, and since we're going to be partners, we can talk about the store, along with our other plans for the company, as we ride off into the sunset, hand in hand. Mix business with pleasure."

She turned to face him, hands on hips. "If we ever got around to the business part, that is."

"We would — eventually. Anyway, things move more slowly around here than they do in LA. You'll have to get used to country pacing, if you're moving to Wyoming, that is."

"I haven't exactly decided to move here *or* go into business with you."

"But you will." He reached for her, tugging her into his arms. He nuzzled the sensitive spot right below her ear as the crowd of horses watched. "Think about it. You'll live in a place where you can hear wolves howl at night, see bighorn sheep in an open meadow and moose on Main Street, get a spittoon for Christmas —" He broke off, seeing her expression, and laughed quietly. "I swear Red gave me one when I was twelve. A spittoon, I mean. He probably found it at a flea market or something. Anyway, I thought it was way cool until I figured out no one had washed it in about a hundred years. The look on my mother's face was priceless — even before Red went on to say the thing had been salvaged from an old brothel."

Kelly's laugh was warm against his chest. "You do realize if I move here, it'll be because I'm falling in love with Red. I think between the toad warts and the spittoon, I've been swept off my feet."

Just hearing her say the word *love* made every muscle in his body tighten. His voice went lower. "Of course you are. That old codger gets all the pretty girls, damn him. His unique brand of charm can't be duplicated, although I've tried."

She ran her fingers through his hair, gazing into his eyes. "You do okay, Carson. I mean, you're no Red or anything, but let's face it, you're out of your league there. Who could possibly compare?"

"I agree he's one of a kind. I've always wondered if he and Thelma had gotten together, what their kids would be like."

Kelly dissolved into laughter, her arms around his neck. "I can't imagine."

"Maybe you could imagine that moonlit ride instead."

"You want to seduce me."

"It's a possibility." His smile was a mixture of feigned innocence and mischief. "What if I promise to be good?"

Her smile was wry. "You *are* good. That's the problem."

Those muscles turned into knots. "I meant I'll behave."

"Oh, that would be a first." She held him tighter for a moment and then relaxed. "I really don't mean to be high maintenance."

"You aren't," he reassured her. "That implies selfishness and drama, and I don't think either of those terms applies to you. It's common sense to be wary, but maybe there's a logical explanation for that text. It could happen if one of your friends had a problem with their phone, for instance, and borrowed one from someone else. Let's see what Spence can find out. In the meantime, want to saddle up and catch that ride?"

He did romantic all too well.

The sorrel mare's name was Bronze, and she followed Kelly along the fence to the gate. Drake saddled her, since he was in the stable, his two dogs as always his constant companions. He said in his easy way, "This sweetheart isn't a hard ride. No need to go heavy on the bit."

Kelly rubbed the mare's forelock. "Thanks. I'm sure we'll get along."

He nodded. "Nice night for a ride. I'd make my brother check fences with me, but for your sake, I'll let him off. It's just too pretty out not to take advantage. I predict he's going to give you the line about the air smelling like a fine merlot. Why he thinks that's clever, I don't have a clue."

"Hey," Mace said as he led out his horse, "I heard that."

"So?" Drake didn't even try to fake repentance. "Fess up, is there a possibility you might use that hokey line?"

"Not now and none of your business. And

Kelly and I will ride the north fence, so get rid of that long-suffering look."

"I *have* been long-suffering. It started thirty-one years ago, the day you were born. I believe there was a lunar eclipse that night. Coincidence? I think not. It was a sign."

"You were what? Two? Yeah, I'm sure you'd remember it clearly."

She could swear the dogs were grinning, both of them thumping their tails.

Kelly put one foot in the stirrup and swung into the saddle. "Not to interrupt your male sparring, since I know you two have made it a personal pastime, but Bronze and I want to take a ride." She'd become remarkably confident with horses in a very short time, Mace had noticed. Shades of summer camp?

He winked at her, and then nudged his brother. "Oh, no, she's being sarcastic!" Drake shook his head. "Better get rid of her right away. Nothing worse than an uppity female."

"I don't know. She's awfully cute."

"Can't argue with you there."

Mace mounted with true cowboy ease and moved forward, his big horse leading the way. "Oh, if you don't hear from us, there isn't a problem."

Drake's brows went up. "Staying the night

at the cabin?"

"We might."

That was the first she'd heard of it. Drake said off-handedly, "Good call. How about if Luce and I bring up breakfast?"

"That's actually a good idea. Thanks."

"See you in the morning, and make sure there's coffee," Drake added.

"Will do."

As soon as they were clear of stable yard and walking their horses abreast, Kelly said tartly, "Might've been handy to get a heads-up, Carson. I don't even have pajamas."

His glance was both wicked and derisive. "Like you'll need pajamas! Give me a break. Don't expect anything fancy, though. It's just roughed in, and there's no electricity, but there's an excellent selection of Mountain Winery wines, a battery-operated CD player for ambiance, and we have a water tank I'm glad I didn't have to cart up there. Lucky for me, Slate helped Drake do that. Plus we have a woodstove. I guarantee the cabin's way more comfortable than a tent on the ground. It's like camping, but with solid walls between you and all the critters."

In her childhood, camping hadn't been a family pastime. Her father had declared that once was enough after trying it with so many daughters, and he preferred a tropical beach and a private hammock rather than one giant slumber party in the next tent over that kept him awake half the night. So family vacations usually involved a condo by the ocean, Kelly and her sisters getting a summer tan under the supervision of their mother while he played golf. Then they'd have dinner out at someplace that played lively music and served the adults colorful drinks with fruit skewers.

This would be a different kind of experience. "Sounds better than the tent thing. I hope you realize I can't even roast a marshmallow on a stick."

"No problem. I really have no desire for a roasted marshmallow, and if I needed one, I wouldn't expect you to do it for me."

She did love that grin of his. "I'm just pointing out that this isn't my natural environment."

"You could've fooled me. You look great here. You fit right in."

"In these shoes?" Okay, she hadn't worn her Western boots, but there was nothing wrong with her sneakers, glittery though they were.

"Not everyone has to be a shitkicker to fit in. That's cowboy lingo, city girl."

"I get that, country boy."

"There's nothing much to do at the cabin.

Hope you're up for that. Maybe some elk will wander by. That's about the level of excitement."

"No moose?"

"Maybe I can give my famous moose call, and one will drop in for a glass of that white burgundy."

"Like I'd share that wine with just anyone, cowboy, even a moose! No way." The cabin sounded perfect. Isolated, quiet, the location remote. "This is the first I've heard of your famous moose call."

"All right, you caught me." Mace kept a straight face, but she could tell it took some effort. "*Famous* is an exaggeration. I try to keep my talent hidden so people won't be envious of me. I get enough of that already."

They walked along, side by side, and as Drake had said, Bronze was an easy ride. "Well, you're moderately good-looking, I suppose, you make fantastic wine, and you have a moose call nailed down, so no wonder. Wow, what every girl dreams of. The moose call is a game changer. I'd say Red has a contender for my affections."

"*Moderately* good-looking?" He tipped his hat back in feigned affront. "I think you just shook my self-confidence."

He was, hands down, the most attractive man she'd ever met, and she doubted anyone could shake him. "I meant good-looking in your own way."

"Oh, now I feel all warm and fuzzy. *In my own way.* What the heck does that mean?"

"Hey, it was a compliment."

"You might want to work on your technique." Then he said, "It's great to see you smile. We can handle this Vreeman mess, but can we make a deal? For tonight, let's forget everything — except us."

"I'd love to." She meant it. "Deal."

The ride was scenic and the landscape breathtaking, but the spot where the Carson brothers had built the cabin was ideal. A clearing on a ridge, trees and a vista of seemingly endless stars above . . . Who could possibly ask for more? There was an enclosure for the horses — a simple corral with a shelter — and while Mace took care of them, Kelly explored the cabin.

It didn't take long.

There was a single rustic table with a bench, and some sort of contraption she assumed was for the water tank had been attached to the wall above a couple of cabinets. A single antique hope chest sat against another wall. There was no bed, no sink and . . . what had she gotten herself into, anyway?

Correction. She hadn't gotten herself into

it; this was Mace's brilliant idea.

"Yeah, it's glorified camping," he said as he came in, plunked down a backpack and pointed. "But look at that."

He indicated the wine rack, which looked as though it had been made of antlers.

"Tell me you didn't —"

He shook his head instantly. "Of course not! The thing's made of resin or something like that. Have you *met* Drake?"

"Yes, I have. I think he saddled my horse for me not that long ago. Cut the sarcasm, cowboy. I take it he doesn't approve of hunting."

"To put it mildly. He's the same man who arranged a catch-and-release for a mountain lion poaching his calves. A mountain lion that also mauled his dog. No, that was molded from discarded antlers found here and there. Raine thought they'd make a great wine rack. She did the design, and Melody Hogan put it together."

She walked over to study it more closely. "It's really beautiful and suits this space. I wonder if we could commission one for the shop. Love how you can hang wineglasses from the top rack. It captures a sense of Wyoming. I bet if we could have some made on a smaller scale, we could sell them. And look at the wine charms! Did Melody make those? There's one to match each label. I see an owl, a hawk, a rattlesnake —" she sorted through the display hung from a hook in the rustic wall beside the wine rack and started laughing "— and a moose. Would she be willing to make more? I *know* we could sell these."

"Looks like I've created a monster, as they say. Grab two of those glasses and I'll get the wine. We can sit and talk it over. What do you think of the table? It came from the treasure trove Slate found in the resort basement, thanks to Grace, when he was researching the film. He brought it home, my mother refinished it, and Red made the benches out of reclaimed wood from the stable. There's an old bar down in that basement, too. I bet we could use it for a counter in the store and set the cash register there."

That sounded fabulous. Every one of her sisters would point out that she was crazy, but she'd already made up her mind. Kelly sat down on the hand-hewn bench and rested her elbows on the table. "Ply me with wine and we'll talk. Even though we said we wouldn't discuss business — or . . . or other concerns."

"I think you just love me for my wine." He deftly uncorked a bottle with an ornate opener attached to the wall. It looked antique and was topped with what looked like a miniature old wagon done in pewter, which had darkened with age.

"It doesn't hurt," she said as neutrally as possible. "But you do have a few other appealing qualities."

"Good to hear." He splashed pale gold liquid into the glass in front of her and settled down on the opposite bench, pouring one for himself, as well. "A few is better than none."

"And it's better than if I'd said *unappealing* qualities."

He waved that off. "I'm sure I do. Have some less than appealing qualities, I mean. My faults exist. I don't deny that. I try to ignore them. That's something else you aren't allowed to mention in front of Drake. We'd have to sit through an eight-hour lecture on what they are."

"And yet he'd probably jump into an active volcano if you fell in, just to save you."

"That would be downright stupid, so you could be right." He shrugged and laughed. "Oh, hell, it's no fun insulting him if he can't hear it. Can you repeat that in front of him, but leave out the heroic part and just say we agreed that he's stupid enough to jump into a lava flow?"

"Mace, you're impossible!"

He took a sip of wine and contemplated his glass. "You aren't that different from me. Driven, maybe more intense than the average person, definitely focused on what you do."

"What about the cliché that opposites attract?"

"Could be true, and it could be that it's different for everyone." He smoothly changed the subject. "So what do you think of the cabin?"

The setting was spectacular. "I'm anxious to see the sunrise. It's beautiful here, but it was already dark under the trees when we arrived. I can hear the stream, though. Is there a more soothing sound?"

She could hear the water bubbling over the rocks, splashing gently, part of the peaceful background.

"I can think of a few. I like hearing you breathing in the dark beside me."

"Don't do that to me."

"Fall in love with you? You're not giving me a lot of choice here." He went on as if this was an ordinary conversation, running a finger along the rim of his glass. "Is it going to make things worse if I point out that I was always sure that if it happened for me it'd be fast? Both of my brothers followed that path, too. Must be a family trait. I know that when Slate met Grace the night she stormed into his office with Ryder by the ear because he'd stolen a sign from Slate's truck, that was it. And when Luce arrived on the ranch, all starry-eyed over the wild horses that were driving Drake nuts, he couldn't have fallen faster than if he'd jumped off a cliff."

Her hand shook when she picked up her glass. "Jumping off a cliff sounds like an extremely risky proposition."

His gaze held hers. "The trouble is, once you're airborne, there's really no going back, is there? Red would probably say that even flapping your arms like a demented duck isn't going to save your sorry ass."

She almost spit out her wine. "Mace Carson," she said once she'd recovered. "Don't do that to me again!"

Her sisters were going to love him. All four of them had an irreverent sense of humor, not to mention they also liked wine. He was a sure thing, especially if you threw in that captivating bad-boy smile.

"Just enhancing the ambiance of the evening. We're in a remote cabin with a huge starlit sky . . . but I'll admit there might be bears roaming around. I'm trying to be like Red so you'll fall for me — You get the picture. I'm walking uphill here. Cut me some slack, okay?"

No, he wasn't walking uphill. At all. "Where are we going to . . . sleep? On the floor?" She eyed the rough planks. They looked rustic, yes. Comfortable, no.

"Do you see another option, city girl?" He lounged in his seat, clearly amused. "May I remind you this isn't a hotel in Beverly Hills?"

"You don't need to, thanks very much. There's no room service menu nearby for one thing, unless you count us as dinner for the bears. Wish you hadn't mentioned that."

He lifted a hand in supplication. "Okay, I'll take pity on your delicate sensibilities. There's actually an air mattress in that bench you're sitting on. It's quite comfortable. Ever made love in a sleeping bag?"

"Actually, no," she muttered, "and I'm *not* going to ask you the same question because I don't want to know the answer."

"Never did it with you. And I expect it's going to be something I'll remember for the rest of my life."

CHAPTER TWENTY

Slater had suggested the expensive foot pump because he'd slept out on film sites, mainly when he'd done the documentary on ghost towns. Mace had way too much imagination to enjoy that one, with its abandoned buildings and empty, dusty streets. The tumbleweeds rolling past lonely gaping doorways, loose shutters over broken windows — it was enough to give him pause, remind him of the vulnerability of human existence.

He inflated the air mattress and then got out the double sleeping bag, designed by some maniac who'd climbed Mount Everest, something Mace thought was a bad idea, since he'd had to deal with frigid temperatures his entire life but had never gone out looking for them.

"We should be warm enough." He gestured at the sleeping setup.

"I'm counting on that." Kelly's smile was

punctuated by the sexy way she started to unbutton his shirt. "It's really dark out there."

"I was planning on being right next to you all night." He had to admit it was hard to sound calm and cool when he was on fire. She'd be more than warm . . .

"Mmm." She rubbed his shoulders. "I like the sound of that."

"Kelly . . . aren't there a few things we ought to discuss?"

"No."

She rose up and kissed him, which was a good thing. Extremely good. He tugged her shirt out of her jeans and unfastened her bra, pushing it off her smooth shoulders.

She didn't want to talk. He thought he understood her reservations — and yet he probably didn't understand at all, since he'd never been married and then had to make the tough decision to divorce.

But the truth was, he'd made up his mind. About Kelly. About being with her.

In retrospect, that had probably happened ten years ago when he'd looked into her frightened eyes and helped her to her feet. If he hadn't been involved with someone else at the time — so was she — he might have pursued a relationship then. But he would never have taken advantage of her gratitude. He would've helped anyone in that situation, but she was . . . unforgettable.

"Discussion shelved." He clasped her chin so she had to look at him. "But not over."

"Granted." She ran her hand over his chest. "I'll just state that I'm really glad you're here, and I'm here, and that air mattress is a gift from heaven. That's all I'm capable of saying right now. You've thrown a lot at me in a very short time."

He muffled a laugh. "I guess I should be grateful you didn't give thanks for the air mattress first."

"It's high on the list, but you won. Now, I'm half-naked and you're half-naked, so could we get all naked?"

"You're asking *me* that?" His enthusiasm was no doubt obvious. He hoped he didn't injure himself trying to unzip.

"After the way you advertised the sleeping bag, I'm kind of intrigued." Her tone was saucy, and he followed the movement of her fingers as she smoothed back her hair.

If anything could be more satisfying than having her in his arms, he wasn't sure what that would be. "Let's try it out."

"Sex in a sleeping bag? Sounds like an eighties song." She wriggled free, unzipped her jeans with enviable ease, and when she bent over to step out of them, he admired the curve of her spine.

And her very perfect backside.

So true, and yet so wrong to point that out. *You have a great ass* was not what a man should say to a woman about to fall into his arms. Or his sleeping bag. Far too blunt.

But it wasn't as though he'd said *sex,* either. He'd said making love. Sex was great. Making love, as he'd recently discovered, was a whole lot better.

Naturally, she caught him in the act of shamelessly checking her out. He didn't even bother to defend himself. "Sorry, just enjoying the view. In fact, I believe I was ogling you. Before now, I thought *ogling* was a ridiculous word, but I think it applies. How would you define it? Eyeing with lascivious intent?"

"I must be ogling you then, too. We can look it up later, but I doubt there's a dictionary lying around here. Anyway, I'm headed over to that sleeping bag. How about you?"

He practically fell down trying to take off his left boot. His jeans came off in a flash, and when he slid in beside her, she was laughing. She was also soft, warm . . . and naked.

"I love you, Kelly," he said. And then he kissed her, with all the hunger he'd been holding back for so long.

And love her he did. He'd known for a while, whether he'd admitted it to himself or not. He'd been a total goner, ever since he'd first recognized her on that country road, that rainy night.

She kissed his shoulder, once she'd lifted her mouth from his. "Did you just say — ?"

"I said I love you."

She met his eyes, swallowed hard and replied, "Well, that's good, because I love you, too."

They were both silent for a long time, holding each other, together in this new truth, this shared understanding.

"I like being here, in the cabin," Kelly finally said.

"Just wait," he promised.

"Not interested in waiting," she murmured, then lightly bit his neck.

As if he needed more encouragement.

The sleeping bag was confining, but they managed with no trouble at all. His mouth found hers, his body found hers, and the pleasure was so intense that each time he thought it couldn't get any better, he was wrong.

Afterward she was very quiet, very still,

and as he drifted toward sleep, he was suddenly brought wide-awake by the realization that she was crying. Not loudly, not with any explanation, just crying against his bare chest.

"Sweetheart?"

She hiccuped. "I'm fine. I'm just glad you're you."

That was as clear as a flooded river full of floating debris.

"I'm glad I'm me right now, too. Kelly, what's wrong?" Another warm tear had dropped onto his chest as he peered at her in the darkness, the starlight giving only vague illumination through the window. "Talk to me."

"Mace, we didn't use — What if I'm pregnant?"

"If it happens, it happens," he said calmly. "I certainly wouldn't be unhappy about a baby. Hey, life is taking risks. Just this week I helped capture a loose bull in a pea-soup fog. Life throws stuff at you. That's how it works. Buck up, city girl."

She elbowed him, and pretty hard, too, but he was relieved to hear laughter in her voice. "Only country boys are reckless enough to go looking for a bull they can't even see. Don't use that as an example."

"Okay, my point is this — whatever comes

our way, we'll deal with it. Together."

She snuggled against him, relaxing as her panic subsided a little. "Like partners?"

"Like partners."

Part of her acknowledged that she'd come to Wyoming as much to see Mace Carson again, as to do her job. Work had given her a convenient reason, but what she really wanted was to see if the man measured up to the memory.

He did, and then some.

"I'm trying to work this all out. Some of us are logical, you know."

Said the woman sharing a sleeping bag with a handsome winemaker-cowboy somewhere in the wilds of Wyoming. A woman who suspected she'd just heard a wolf howl. Maybe she needed to reassess her capacity for levelheaded thinking.

She could imagine her conversation with her most inquisitive sister, Janice.

Janice: So how was the trip?

Kelly: I slept with the client almost every night and rode a horse while I was wearing that expensive skirt we shopped for, the one that cost more than a small car. I ate dinner with a cast of characters that included the client's older film-producer brother, his wife, his ex-girlfriend and their child, plus his wife's stepson whom she's raising even though she's divorced from his father. I met some real cowboys and learned some interesting phrases, and I believe there's a wolf slavering at the door of a cabin without a bathroom. Oh, yes, I'm quitting my job — *Alan's a factor there* — and moving to Mustang Creek to be a partner in a winery and run a little wine store. So, yeah, the trip's been uneventful by and large.

That might render even Janice speechless, which had been considered impossible at many family gatherings.

Mace didn't even seem to notice the howling. "What I said — that makes you cry?"

"No." She smacked his shoulder. "When I'm overwhelmed, sometimes I cry. My relationship with you falls into the over-whelmed category. You told me you love me. You want me to move here and to live with you. That's why I'm crying. Not sure it makes sense, but . . ."

He pulled her on top of him. "Is there a handbook I can read? I might need one. *Things That Make a Woman Cry and How Not to Do Them.* I swear every man in America would buy it."

401

She loved the solid feel of his body under hers. "I'll get to work on it. Please tell me that creature outside won't be out there, thirsting for our blood, all night long."

"What creature? Oh, that? He's at least a mile away."

"It sounds like he's on the front porch."

"There's no front porch, but we do plan to add one. Wait until you hear a mountain lion scream. It's like someone being murdered."

"Oh, lovely."

He chuckled. "Not when I was about six and up here camping for the first time. I freaked out. I'm positive my father was laughing, but he did a good job of hiding it. Slate and Drake did *not* do a good job of hiding it. If they could've paid that big cat to do it again, they'd have forked over the money. They made up some story about a legendary monster that roamed this part of the country, fangs dripping blood, you get the picture. I bought it, of course. Didn't sleep all night. My father intervened once he realized I believed them."

"My sisters once convinced me that Santa was going to bring me a puppy. I was about the same age. My mother got wind of it, and guess what I got for Christmas? But they had to walk and feed him. There *is* justice in this world. Samson was the cutest dog."

"Don't worry. I'll protect you from the big, bad wolf."

She knew he wasn't talking about the one who'd given that lonely cry. "Lance Vreeman is the stuff of my nightmares," she said with a shudder. "I'd rather run into that wolf out there."

"Neither of them will get near you. Not on my watch."

She did feel very safe at the moment, but she still threw him a derisive look. "I'm a perfectly capable person."

His hand smoothed her back. "I didn't imply you weren't, did I? I just stated that I'd stand between you and any danger. Without reservation."

"You *want* me to need you." There was both anger and despair in her voice. She dropped her forehead to his and sighed. Loudly.

Mace started laughing. "Sweetheart, is that a bad thing?"

"It can be," she muttered darkly. "I don't want to turn into one of those weak women who can't make the simplest decision without getting their husband's opinion first. If they wind up on their own, they're practically helpless. And have you looked at the divorce rates lately?"

"You know," he mused, as if she hadn't spoken. "I think we should get a dog."

"What?" She lifted her head and stared at him. "Were you even listening to me?"

"I heard every word you said." His strong shoulders rose under her hands. "You were spinning your wheels, that's all. Going over the same old ground. So I decided to throw in something positive and see what happened."

She blinked at him. "Seriously? We're about to risk everything, and you want to talk about *getting a pet*?"

"Not just any pet," Mace replied easily. "A dog." He looked thoughtful. "But, then, of course, that will be risky, too. It's easy to fall in love with the critters, but, like every other living thing, dogs can get sick or lost or hurt, or even die. Maybe it's safer to skip all that fun and unwavering devotion and canine comedy, so we don't get our hearts broken. Never mind that the dog loses out, too, since it doesn't get a home." A beat passed. "Yep, avoidance is the answer. I say we do absolutely nothing. *Feel* absolutely nothing."

She punched him in the shoulder. "That is so not fair. You're making me sound like the Cowardly Lion before he found his courage!"

He grinned. Then he roared.

And Kelly couldn't help laughing.

The man was insane — and it must have been contagious, since it seemed to be infecting her, too. "I've always loved dogs," she heard herself say.

Mace gave an exaggerated sigh. "If only they came with a guarantee against potential heartbreak."

She made a face at him. "Stop making fun of me, please. It just so happens that I'm all for getting a dog. The sooner, the better."

"Fine," Mace said. "Do we get a pup, or an older dog?"

"How about both?" *That* would show him.

"Good idea," he replied. "We could take Daisy and Ryder along when we visit the shelter."

"Why? Are you going for the Uncle of the Year award?"

"I've already got a lock on the title," he answered with a distinct lack of modesty. "Just don't quote me to Drake. He's under the illusion that *he's* the favorite."

"I see," Kelly said, teasing.

"Anyway, there's a method to my madness. Kids love dogs, and dogs love kids. This way, everybody wins."

With nieces and nephews of her own,

Kelly had to agree. She nodded, but there must have been some sign of reluctance in her face, because Mace's gaze narrowed slightly.

"Lost your courage already, cowardly lioness?"

"No," she said quickly. She had no misgivings, not about dogs, anyway. "What about your mother and Harry? How will they feel about a houseguest *and* two extra pets?"

He traced her lower lip with one finger. "My mother and Harry," he said, "will be delighted."

"Delighted? *That* seems a bit of a stretch."

Mace smiled. "It's a big house. There's room for togetherness — and privacy."

Kelly thought of her own family gatherings, noisy, happy affairs, with kids running everywhere and dogs chasing after them, barking joyfully. It was pure chaos — and completely wonderful.

Her eyes burned slightly.

"Yes, it's a big house," she agreed, picking up the conversational thread. "With lots of breakable treasures and imported rugs. Suppose there's a disaster, and some priceless vase bites the dust, or the carpets suddenly sport pee stains?"

Mace looked very serious. "I can't picture you staining the rugs or breaking the knickknacks," he said in a low voice.

She punched him again. "You never know when to stop, do you?" He didn't bother to deny the accusation, and they settled into a quiet time, thinking their own thoughts. For her part, Kelly was thinking about dogs. She'd wanted a pet when she was married, either a cat or a dog would have pleased her, but Alan had objected, for reasons she couldn't recall. Later, working long hours, living alone and traveling a great deal, there'd been no way she could give an animal a proper home.

Again, she was the one who broke the silence. "You're a little pushy, Mace Carson, but you're mostly okay."

"I'm just *okay*? Excuse me? I think that's a challenge."

A challenge he accepted . . . as he proceeded to prove he was a lot better than okay.

CHAPTER TWENTY-ONE

The phone conversation took about five minutes.

Bob told Mace he'd sell him the store, and at a very decent price.

Mace owed Hadleigh, so he called Tripp with a question. "I want to get your wife something special. The store sale is a go, thanks to her. How about a case of her favorite red and that Yuletide Snowflake she wants?"

"You mean the stuff she can't drink right now?" There was probably a smile he couldn't see.

"What do you mean she can't —" He interrupted himself. "Oh, wait. I get it . . . You don't waste any time, do you?"

"We want a big family."

"Doesn't sound like that'll be a problem." Mace was happy for them. "Congratulations. How about the wine for when the kids are driving her to distraction and she needs to sit on the couch and watch a movie with her feet up while you take care of them?"

"Oh, thanks." Tripp was laughing. "Throw me under the bus. I appreciate your solicitude for my wife at my expense."

"Not to crush your self-confidence, but she's a lot better-looking than you. I'm shallow enough to prefer her for that reason alone."

"I can't disagree there." Tripp laughed again. "The wine would be appreciated, I'm sure, but much as Hadleigh likes you, I think she's just as pleased about helping out Bob and Martha. They're living in a sixty-and-over trailer park, but have their eye on a condo on the golf course. This deal should make that possible."

"I'll drop off the red wine and the Snowflake when it's ready, and your lovely wife can look at them longingly until she's allowed to have a glass or two again." A good deal for everyone, he thought as they ended the call, smiling broadly.

"What's the cat that ate the canary smile for?" Harry asked, bustling into the kitchen, busy as ever but at least stopping to pour herself a cup of coffee. "Let me guess. It has something to do with a certain blonde."

He was at the kitchen table, having just inhaled two cinnamon rolls. "Yes and no.

Yes in that I've decided to buy the old store on Main and Bob wants to sell. Plan is, Kelly's going to set it up and work there. And no, because Hadleigh Galloway is expecting again. I just talked to Tripp."

"Is she really?" Harry looked pleased. "Her grandmother would've been so happy, bless her. As for the store, I always thought you should have a shop in town and that would be the perfect spot."

He was thinking about another roll. Whatever Harry put in her icing was so addictive he wondered if he'd need rehab to shake the craving. He gave in and grabbed a final roll. "And the reason you didn't say anything about a shop before now would be?" he asked her.

"I was waiting for you to figure it out."

He didn't respond and just ate his roll, then inelegantly licked his fingers. "Every time you make those, I think they're the best I've ever had."

"Mace, you do realize that if I put that frosting on shoe leather, you'd eat it, right?"

"Depends on who wore the shoes." He wiped his mouth with a napkin and stood. "Thanks, Harry."

"Hmph," Harry snorted. "Not so fast. When's our next new arrival going to get a bowl in my kitchen?" She took the empty plate from his hand, even though he had every intention of rinsing it and putting it in the dishwasher himself.

He stared at her, then shook his head. "How can you possibly know I convinced Kelly we ought to adopt a couple of dogs?"

Harry gave him a narrowed-eyed look. "A 'couple' of dogs, is it? As for your question, I make a point of knowing what's going on around here, out of self-preservation, and that's nothing new. For instance, if you three boys think I don't know you all cracked that antique bowl on the sideboard playing flag football in the dining room on a snowy day twenty-five years ago, you'd be mistaken."

"You weren't even home!"

He might as well have signed a confession. They'd admitted to breaking the bowl, but not the flag football part. There'd been a stubborn united front not to name the culprit.

"It was me."

She waved a hand airily. "Oh, Slater and Drake have both owned up to it, as well. Nice of you to take the blame, at this late date. Now then, how many guests do you think will be at the wedding?"

"What wedding?"

"Yours. For dessert I thought we should serve your favorite pie instead of cake. I've been thinking over the menu, too."

He was hopeless in this type of situation. "You have?"

"When are you going to ask her? I need a date."

"Harry, she hasn't been here a week. As she keeps pointing that out."

"And yet you've made up your mind." She didn't seem fazed at all. "Haven't you?"

Fine. She was a seer. There could be voodoo involved. He hastily tried to head her off. "Kelly's first marriage —"

"Was not to you. Back to the menu . . . What about that mustard-crusted ham I make on homemade biscuits, medium-rare roast beef and, of course, plenty of garlic mashed potatoes, with a couple of salad choices."

Maybe Kelly was right and this was racing out of control.

"I'm not positive where I fit into this discussion."

Harry shooed him off. "Me, neither. Run along."

That open door was a relief. He left the kitchen and hurried toward the stables, almost slamming into Slater at the bottom of the steps. His brother grabbed him by the arm. "Whoa, what's up? The house on fire?"

"No. Harry seems to be planning the menu for my wedding. Is it any wonder I took off?"

Slater looked amused. "No, gotcha. Man overboard on purpose. I'd jump ship myself. Grace likes Kelly, by the way. Hmm. I must've missed the family memo so I wasn't aware you'd proposed."

"Here's the interesting part. I haven't."

Well, not yet. He'd just asked her to move in with him, take a chance on a business venture that might work but might not, and impulsively suggested they get a pet together.

"So Harry's made up your mind for you, huh?" Slater folded his arms across his chest and propped himself against the railing. "You're toast, man."

"I'm getting that feeling. Next thing I know, they'll be picking out bridesmaid dresses for Kelly's four — yeah, you heard me, four — sisters. There's also a passel of nieces and nephews. Twelve, I think. And more than half of those are girls."

Slater whistled. "That's a lot of females. I'm feeling pretty lucky that Grace just has that one brother down in Texas."

Mace took in a lungful of fresh air. "Kelly had a bad experience before and rushing her seems wrong. As she keeps telling me,

413

she hasn't been in Wyoming long."

His brother met his eyes. "You fell in love with her ten years ago. I'm not a psychology expert or anything, but I think she fell for you, as well. You're the chemist. Wasn't there that magic formula from the beginning?"

There had been, but he'd been involved with someone else and so had she . . . And, of course, they hadn't seen each other since. Until they met again on that dark, rainy night.

Slater cracked up over his expression. "That's a *yes.* Let me point out that Jim Galloway, longtime widower, went on a cruise and came back a married man, and he's one of the happiest guys I know. Pauline is great. This assumption that marriage requires a particular timeline is a myth. It's your life and it's her life, and if you're both comfortable with it, go forward. How about carrot cake for the reception?"

"Not you, too," Mace muttered. "Jeez."

"I have a fondness for just about anything Harry chooses to make, but if I get a vote, that's one of my wife's favorites. Please make Grace happy."

"Isn't that your job?" Mace threw over his shoulder. "Besides, I suspect this whole wedding thing is going to be based on opinions that don't include mine. Harry said something about pie. You can enter into that argument with her, but I'm on my way to the winery right now."

"Ah, yes. Your safe haven."

Kelly needed to talk to someone older and wiser.

Her great-aunt, Edith Matilda, was a logical choice. Feisty and opinionated, she'd be completely honest, and it had been too long since Kelly had talked to her. Now was as good a time as any.

"Aunt Eddie. How are you?"

"Sharp as a tack. And you? How's Wyoming?"

She really was with it. "I can't believe you know where I am."

"I keep up with things."

"You must." Kelly couldn't suppress a laugh. "I need some advice. Why do you suppose I thought of you?"

"Because I'm full of it." Her great-aunt chortled. "I meant advice, by the way. I've been on this earth, learning from my own mistakes for a lot of years. This has to do with that handsome young cowboy, right? The same one who rescued you ten years ago. Your hero."

Kelly was standing on the sidewalk outside

the building proposed for the new store. It was a little dated, but it fit the small-town Western theme. Square facade, weathered siding of real wood, tall windows. They'd have to replace the rusted-out sign. She focused on only one of Edith's comments. "How do you know he's handsome?"

"Well, I have a vague memory of him at the trial. And I checked him out online. Mountain Winery. He's a good-looking young man, but so was Alan. That means nothing. What's he *like*?"

"Mace is focused, artistic, has a sense of humor. He probably works too hard. Loves the land here and loves his family."

She left out the part about how talented he was in bed, because her great-aunt didn't need to know that. Although shrewd as Aunt Eddie was, she'd no doubt come to that conclusion already. She might be in her eighties, but she wasn't unworldly.

Kelly blushed, even though no one could see it.

"He sounds as good as he looks," her great-aunt said diplomatically. "What advice do you need?"

"I think I'm going to move here and run a new enterprise featuring the wines he makes. I know it's crazy, but I'm standing in front of this charming old building he

416

just bought, and I'm *so* tempted to do it. Leave the career and the life I've worked so hard to build, lease the condo and change everything. I'll be starting from scratch for the second time. Just answer me this — *am I crazy?*"

"Crazy only if you don't do it." There was no equivocation. "Sweetie, I completely understand how badly Alan disappointed you, how he broke his half of the bargain. If you want my advice, here it is. You need to begin trusting yourself again."

"I'm trying."

"He's well-intentioned?"

Kelly sighed. "Too much so. He wants us to take his niece and stepnephew with us to pick out a puppy. He wants me to live with him, run his business and he's impossibly romantic. He bought me roses to match my eyes."

Edith laughed gleefully. "Oh, Lord help me, is that over the top or what?"

Some people waved at Kelly from a passing car, and she was sure she'd never seen them before in her life. Kelly waved back, anyway. "I'm not saying I'm being logical, I just don't want to rush into another mistake."

"You do realize you've already made up your mind?"

But there was another complication. "Alan's going to be the new CEO of my company," she said bluntly.

"Well, that actually makes your decision easier, doesn't it?"

"In some ways. But what if —"

"What if this man is all wrong for you? I suspect you'd rally. He sounds very different from Alan, though."

Mace *was* different. That much she knew. "He is. I'm more worried about him than I am about me. I don't think I was very good at marriage the first time around."

Her aunt said clearly, "Honey, that's called falling in love. If you were more worried about *you,* then that would be all wrong."

A valid point. Which, of course, was why she'd called. For good, solid guidance. "Thanks. I picked up the store keys from the realty agent a few minutes ago and I'm going to look around. So bottom line, I'm not crazy?"

"Not from my point of view. Love you, sweetie, and keep me posted."

Kelly rang off and switched into job mode. The keys stuck in the ancient brass lock; she'd been warned she might have to wiggle them a little, which proved to be true. With a certain amount of effort, she was able to get in the door.

Her first reactions were both positive and negative. The place was old. Really old. And beyond quaint.

A project she could sink her teeth into.

Nothing had been updated in years. Or more accurately, decades. It wasn't surprising that no one had leased or bought it, and the sheer challenge took her breath away. At the same time, as she looked at the sagging shelves, the old hardware, the aging, rusted freezers, she felt a sense of . . . fate.

She could make this work.

There was history buried here, and the store could be so beautiful. Rip out the metal shelving and expose the scarred hardwood floors. She knew a carpenter in California who could create custom wine racks, and she'd ask Melody Hogan to make one of those striking clocks in the image of the storefront. Kelly had already decided exactly where she'd hang it — behind where people would check out. The walls were all knotty pine and, refinished, they would be gorgeous.

The coolers weren't usable, but that wouldn't be a huge expense.

She went to explore the back, where Mace said the office was located. Ideas were flooding in as fast as she could process them. Maybe Bad Billy would agree to a daily delivery of his decadent brownies, because wine did pair well with chocolate. In turn, they could hand out menus to the tourists.

When she'd finished prowling around, she finally headed over to the office space.

Oh, she had to be dreaming!

The antique desk was probably Civil War-era. The walls were scattered with vintage maps of Wyoming before it became a state, and they looked original. Could be worth a fortune. She did notice a faint hint of dead mouse in the air, but that didn't deter her enthusiasm. Yes, she could definitely work with this place. The carriage lamp on the desk had once been oil, converted to electric, with a heavy glass shade that must be well over a century old.

She was already wondering how much the racks would cost to ship, what it would take to restore the floors and to buy new coolers.

Taking pictures with her phone as she assessed the space, she was interrupted when there was a knock on the glass front door.

She immediately recognized police chief Spence Hogan. Her heart plummeted, but he quickly reassured her, correctly reading her fear.

"There's nothing wrong, Ms. Wright. As you know, Mace is a friend of mine. Everyone in town is happy he bought this place and will put it to good use. He was at the Bliss County courthouse just now, applying for the licenses he needs, and we ran into each other. He said you were here and I wanted to drop by."

"He asked you to look in on me, didn't he?"

"You *are* alone in an empty building," he said with a slight smile.

"In the middle of the day in the middle of town," she protested.

"He told me about what happened in California." Spence turned and pointed down the street. "My office is right there. You already know Junie. The other dispatchers are equally efficient or I wouldn't employ them. Here's my card with my cell number. Lance Vreeman sounds like bad news, and that text was from a burner phone. You can call me, day or night."

She took the card from him, and the muscles in her shoulders loosened in a way that told her she was tenser than she'd realized. "Thank you so much."

"Of course. That's my job. Oh, my wife will be a customer here." His eyes twinkled as he glanced around. "She loves Mace Carson's wines. It'll be great to see this place take on new life."

It was a measure of the Carson influence to have the chief of police drop in to check on her. She appreciated it — and at the same time, she was reminded that she wasn't in California anymore.

She wouldn't miss the traffic, the noise, or any of the bustle, but this was certainly going to be a different kind of life.

"I'm glad you feel the shop's a good idea. Now, if I can get the same approval from Bad Billy and Thelma, I'll be able to relax and assume that we'll succeed at this."

"You're a local already if you know those two characters."

"We've met," she said, grinning. "I'm thinking of marrying Billy and asking Thelma to be my maid of honor."

"Don't forget to invite me. I'd love to see *that* ceremony. In fact, I'd pay to see it. Bad Billy in a tux and Thelma in a bridesmaid's dress? Could you insist on lime-green chiffon or taffeta or whatever that stuff is? And make sure there's a big satin bow in the back." He chuckled, then immediately sobered. "Listen, you need to be vigilant, and since I know Mace is concerned, I'm concerned, as well. Without that text I might've thought he was overreacting, but it bothers me, and when something bothers me, I listen to my gut. I don't like this."

She didn't, either. "I hate the idea of living my life looking over my shoulder."

"Then don't. Mustang Creek's a safe place, and people look out for each other. The last hysterical call that came in was when Mrs. Dahl went out to her garden and found a bear calmly sitting there eating her prize tomatoes. She was more upset about losing the tomatoes than she was facing down that bear."

"That would make me hysterical," Kelly said, leaning against the old counter. "The bear more than the tomatoes, but I'm a city girl."

"You'll get used to it here."

"The city *is* scarier," she murmured.

"I'll grant you that." Spence Hogan tipped his hat. "I hope you won't need to find me, but if you're at all worried, feel free to yell for help."

Mace pulled up about ten minutes later and strolled through the building with her, listening to her excited comments with a faint smile on his face. She ended up stopping abruptly. "I thought this was what you wanted. But you're laughing at me."

"I absolutely want this and I am laughing. I love your fire. You take everything so seriously. It's one hundred percent or zero for you, Kelly." He reached for her.

She scooted away. "Oh, listen to the man who waves his magic wand over vats of fermenting wine day and night."

"I didn't say being passionate about something is bad. Or passionate about *someone* . . ." He wouldn't let her evade him and caught her hand to draw her in close. His gaze dropped to her mouth. "Shouldn't we celebrate with a kiss?"

"I think we've already done that," she reminded him primly.

"Celebration is good for the soul, and don't ask me who said that, I might've just made it up. But I believe it if it involves you kissing me."

She raised her brows. "Oh, now *I* have to kiss *you*?"

He gestured at their surroundings with his free hand. "I just bought you a store, didn't I?"

"Trying to purchase my affections?"

His grin was boyish and unapologetic. "Did it work?"

"There's at least one dead mouse in here. That's not too seductive."

He sniffed the air. "Hmm, you're right. We're going to have to hire someone to clean this place up and do the repairs. Luckily, I know —"

"Someone who can do it," she finished for

him, sliding her arms around his neck. "Why am I not surprised? Now, about that kiss . . ."

It was long, lingering, and when they broke apart he said with obvious reluctance, "I'd better get back to work or there won't be any wine to sell. Let's lock up and go home."

CHAPTER TWENTY-TWO

His first clue that something was wrong was the pool of blood seeping under the door.

No, not blood, Mace realized after the first frozen moment. Red wine.

Relief.

Thank God.

Better than blood, but still . . .

What the hell?

The rustic door to the winery, original to the old bunkhouse they'd remodeled when they started the business, had been kicked in, the hasp of the lock snapped off. It swung awkwardly as he pushed it open, one of the old hinges clearly damaged. Mace stood there, arms at his sides, and grimly surveyed the destruction of the tasting room his mother had so carefully designed and decorated. Smashed glasses, the shelves now empty, torn paper that used to be lists of wine in soaked piles on the old plank floor, stools overturned. What infuriated him most was that the antique framed picture, which dated back to the 1800s — showing the ranch hands gathered in front of the building when it was a bunkhouse — had been ripped from the wall, the glass shattered, the photo itself soaked in wine.

There were jagged broken bottles, pools of wine everywhere, and the sheer malice of it made him so furious he could barely scroll through his contacts for Spence Hogan's number. He didn't even want to think about his office, but luckily he backed up all his files to an off-site account; he also kept them on a separate hard drive, which was at the house, and his laptop was in his truck.

Spence answered quickly. "Mace, what's up?"

"You know the trouble I mentioned that might swing into town? Well, it's my guess he's arrived, and with a vengeance — and that's no exaggeration. Either send a deputy out to the winery or come yourself. I won't touch anything here. I'm going back to the house now, so I'll meet you there. Slater's home today, and Grace, being a former cop, will be a big help."

"I'll be right there. Give me the details then."

Mace called Slater as he walked out to his truck. "I'll explain when I get back to the house, but make sure everyone's accounted for and don't let them out of your sight. Call Grace and tell her to come home. Where's Luce?"

"Up on the ridge. Mind telling me what's going on?"

He muttered a word his mother wouldn't approve of. "Tell Drake to get up there *now* and bring her home. I doubt our problem would know anything about the cabin, but I didn't think he could figure out how to get onto the ranch unnoticed, either."

"*Our problem?* He? Mace, what the heck are you talking about?"

"I'll explain. Spence Hogan will be at the house soon."

"You'd *better* explain! I'm calling Grace as soon as we hang up."

"Do it. I'm on my way."

The worst part was that he knew Kelly would feel it was her fault somehow, and it wasn't, never could be. Yet he was fairly sure that was how she'd feel. He didn't want her to fly back to California, even if Vreeman was in Wyoming. It was purely selfish on his part; he'd never be able to sleep if he didn't know with absolute certainty that she was safe, and that meant having her beside him.

He got to the house in record time. Slater was waiting for him on the front porch, brow furrowed, as he skidded in, a plume of dust fanning out behind his vehicle. His brother stalked down the steps, wearing casual dark slacks with the sleeves of his blue shirt rolled up. "Grace is on her way," he said curtly. "The baby, Kelly, Mom and Harry are inside. Ryder, too. I called Raine, and she and Daisy are home. I told them to lock the doors and not to trust anyone who comes knocking. So, what's this all about?"

"Someone broke in to the winery and trashed the place. It doesn't take much insight to assume it's one Lance Vreeman, who has a vendetta against both Kelly and me, since we sent him to prison for a decade. There's already been a cryptic — and untraceable — message to her phone. Someone knows where she is."

It was Slater's turn to use foul language, running his fingers through his dark hair. "Are you kidding me? Trashed how bad? Could it just have been kids?"

"Bad. And I doubt the kid theory." He slammed the door of his truck, still fuming. "How could a bunch of kids have gotten onto the property without a single hand seeing them? This was calculated to infuriate me, it was personal, and like I said, I know who did it."

"Grace told me about the guy who attacked Kelly. This Vreeman character." Slater looked white around the mouth. "I want my wife pulling safely down that driveway *immediately* if you're right."

His brothers, both of them, deserved the truth. "I'm not a hundred percent sure, but my gut says it's him. He was released last week. Maybe he's still in California, although I doubt it. Maybe he followed her here. More likely, I'm the one he hates the most. I'm the one who stopped him, beat the tar out of him and turned him over to the cops. I'm pretty easy to find, too. My testimony sent him to prison, and I don't regret any of that. I want to catch him so I can send him back there." He shook his head. "Sometimes, I wish I'd done a lot more damage to that son of a bitch when I had the chance."

His brother frowned. "Bliss County isn't exactly a place you can stroll into and stay anonymous. He'd better hope I don't catch him on this property."

"You or Drake, or even worse, Red. That old cowboy might just shoot first, ask questions later."

"Here comes Spence." Slater lightened up a little. "I'd be the last one to mention it, but I think he might've broken a few speeding laws getting here so fast."

"I didn't mince words when I told him how serious this could be." Mace wasn't concerned for himself as much as he was for Kelly and his family, and for that matter, her family. "If you saw the winery, you'd agree."

"I already agree. I'll stay here and keep an eye on things."

"Thanks."

Spence pulled up and got out, with the truck still running. He jerked his head sideways. "Let's go. Everything else okay?"

"Define *okay*." Mace went around and got in the vehicle. "We're talking about thousands of dollars' worth of damage. I stopped in the doorway and I saw the tasting room. I'm going to speculate that my office is destroyed, too. I have no idea about the room where we bottle the fermenting wines."

Some of those vintages couldn't be replicated. If they were ruined, gone, the winery was in trouble. The business was insured, but it would be hard to start over again, and even harder to open a shop without inventory.

Spence's reaction when they pulled up confirmed his own feelings as he saw the damaged door, hanging uselessly to one side. "Holy shit! Someone really went to town."

"Wait until you see inside."

Spence had his notebook device out and was making notations. "Well, it's no secret how he got in, is it? I really despise senseless destruction. Hopefully I can lift a few prints. Let's walk through and you can tell me if anything's missing."

"That might be a neat trick," Mace said in resignation. "You'll see why the minute we walk up those steps."

It wasn't logical to feel this was all her fault, and Blythe homed in on Kelly's sense of guilt with unerring maternal insight. "You've done nothing at all to make this person act like this."

Kelly picked up her cup of tea. "I walked across campus alone after dark. It was stupid then, and now I'm being shown just *how* stupid."

Blythe laughed ruefully. "Honey, we've all done foolish things that could've ended badly. I remember as a teenage girl I once ran out of gas. My father was always after me to make sure I kept the tank at least half full, so I felt like an idiot. That was before cell phones, of course. A young man stopped and offered me a ride home, and I got in his car, contrary though that was to everything I'd been told. Fortunately, he was just being nice and delivered me to our house safely. My father wasn't furious with me about running out of gas, but I got a tongue-lashing over getting in a stranger's car." She took a sip of the steaming tea in the delicate porcelain cup before she added, "I shudder to think of the things my sons have probably done that could have resulted in catastrophe. I remember taking Drake to the hospital for a broken arm, and not one of those three hooligans would tell me what happened. I suspect to this day it was a dare of some kind, because you've never seen such a sheepish bunch. Not one of them would look me in the eye."

In spite of the circumstances, Kelly stifled a laugh. "I can see them not wanting to incriminate each other and presenting a united front. My sisters and I had the 'Don't tell Mom' rule, too."

Blythe gently set down her cup and gave her a direct look. "My point is that while you made what turned out to be an unwise decision that set off this series of events, you *should've* been able to walk safely across campus. Was it a great decision to walk on your own? No. Does it make you responsible for the actions of a criminal?

The answer to that is also no."

Kelly appreciated the logical approach, but sometimes a person couldn't shut off the chain of events he or she had set in motion. She said two agonized words, "The winery."

"Is a thing. A building with wine in it. Everything can be replaced."

"Mace loves it."

His mother didn't disagree. "Yes, he does. But he's rational enough to know that the welfare of the people he loves is more valuable than physical possessions."

Mace *was* that practical. "I just feel bad. It's like his good deed has come back to punish him."

Blythe smiled. "Oh, I think if asked, he'd say he's fortunate to have met you. In fact, I'm sure of it."

She was grateful his family felt that way. "I'm the lucky one."

"Oh, we agree there, but then, I'm just his mother."

She had to laugh at that one. Fortunately, the man himself arrived at that moment, with the police chief. Kelly started to leap up, but caught herself. What was she going to do, fling herself into his arms like an actress in a bad soap opera? Instead she asked with credible steadiness, "How bad?"

Mace didn't look happy but he responded, "Mostly the tasting room and my office. It almost seemed as though he was interrupted." He turned to his mother. "Mom, that old picture of cowboys you love is ruined, and I know it can't be replaced. I'm so damn mad about that, I saw red — and it wasn't just the wine all over the place."

"Yes, it can," Blythe said serenely. "Be replaced, I mean. Well, technically no. But that print that was destroyed can be redone. I have the original in the safe."

He looked relieved. "I thought it *was* the original."

"Raine is a valuable person when it comes to art. She found someone for me who handles old photographs on a professional level, someone who retired from the Smithsonian. He did a beautiful job."

Mace glanced at Kelly. "I'll be putting in a security system here, and one at the winery store. Another one at the new store."

Spence Hogan agreed. "They make panic buttons on remote controls for some systems. That even protects you as you walk out to your car, because it pinpoints your location. I'll go back to the station and fill out all the forms, run whatever prints we can get, make a few calls. If any information turns up on this end, let me know as soon as possible."

"Will do. Thanks, Spence."

"Wish you didn't have to thank me, but I'll do my best."

As Spence drove away, his massive truck rumbling down the lane, Blythe rose. "I take it we need to form a cleanup detail. I have no doubt everyone will pitch in."

Blythe left the porch and Mace turned to Kelly, his stance as inflexible as his tone. "You aren't going to California."

Kelly wanted to sass him right back to lighten the mood — *You're not the boss of me* — but this wasn't grade school. "I *have* to. I've got arrangements to make. Winding down my job, leasing my condo . . . I can't just walk away from my life."

"Let me *be* your life. Starting now."

"You're rushing into this."

"Are you warning me about you?" He leaned against the post at the top of the steps. "I think you know I make up my own mind. Ask anyone. My family knows I've decided. In some ways, I might've decided this ten years ago, but you were seeing someone at the time. In fact, I had to call him for you," he added wryly. "Besides, you don't ask for the number of a girl who's just been through such an unpleasant experience. I figured I was out of luck. I knew where to find you, but it seemed all wrong just to show up at your door."

She'd been dating Ray, the guy she was involved with before Alan, so she was glad Mace hadn't dropped by. In all conscience, she would've had to turn him down and then lived with the regret of what-might-have-been. "Instead I showed up at *your* door," she said. "Well, in your town."

"I don't think I need to spell out that I'm glad you did. I hope you like carrot cake and pie."

Mystified, she stared at him. "What? Well, I love both actually, but . . . where did that come from?"

"I'll explain later." He held out his hand. "Let's go. My mother's always efficient and the troops are being deployed. Which is good, since there's a royal mess to clean up."

Red was already there when they arrived, standing inside the front door, hands on hips as he surveyed the destruction. He turned, and his expression was not that of a happy man. "Only a demented catfish stuck in a shallow muddy pond would do this sort of thing. It's totally pointless. Whenever I think I have the world figured out, along comes something else grazing on my land without permission. I'm so spittin' mad I could put out a forest fire."

Kelly decided right then and there that maybe she wouldn't marry Bad Billy; she'd snap up Red instead. She closed the door of the truck with a slam. "I'll spit with you."

"I knew you were a good girl." He looked at her with amused approval, then sobered. "This could've been a lot worse, but it's bad enough. Son, you need to sit on this front porch with a rifle by your side. Or else find some other way to fix this mess."

"Spence is working on it, and so am I," Mace said.

He turned to Kelly. "I doubt Vreeman drove past the house," he said, "but it's possible. So many vehicles come and go here that none of us pays too much attention. But I guess he couldn't find me, so he thought he'd get his revenge by wrecking the place instead." There was a meaningful pause. "Who knows where he is now — or when he'll be back."

"Don't even say that." It wasn't as though she didn't know firsthand that Lance Vreeman was capable of violence, and regardless of how well Mace could take care of himself, he couldn't prevent someone from walking up with a gun and simply shooting him. "Maybe *you* should come back to California with *me.*"

Mace gave her a look of derision. "Forget it. I'm not going to run away from this jerk, and I have so much to do I hardly know where to start as it is. Right now it'll be with a broom and some trash bags. How about if I sweep and you hold the bag?"

Kelly had to admit the mess was appalling, the sheer malice of it revealing the danger posed by one crazy man. She felt both helpless and infuriated as she looked at the carnage of broken bottles and the deep scratches on what had been quaint, polished tables. All the cushions on the chairs were slashed and soaked. She couldn't really see anything salvageable in the entire space.

Red, wearing gloves, had begun to pick up shattered bottles. She followed Mace with the open bag, and although she was as fond of wine as the next person, the smell was overpowering.

"What a waste," Red muttered. "Do you realize how much coq au vin Harry and I could've made with all this?"

Kelly's imagination was taxed by that question. Picturing Red fussing around with a pot of chicken and dashing in wine and spices was quite the vision, but maybe he wore a different outfit than his torn jeans and worn boots, and what might be the world's oldest hat.

Or maybe he didn't. He was a Renaissance man, according to Mace, all wrapped up in faded denim and plaid flannel. Despite his colorful sayings, he could quote Shakespeare, and — for some reason none of them could ever pry out of him — spoke fluent Castilian Spanish. The Carson brothers' theory was that it had something to do with a woman, but when Red didn't want to give up a secret, there was no getting it out of him. He could be a stubborn old mule.

At the moment, the stubborn mule was picking up shards of an antique mirror and tossing them in a bag. As he worked he muttered, "I hope those seven years of bad luck bite you in the ass, you destructive yellow-bellied slithering lizard." Immediately he turned to Kelly with a rueful smile of apology. "Will you pardon my language, ma'am?"

"I'd have said a lot worse," she replied as Mace deposited a dustpan full of broken bottles in the bag she held open. Reinforcements arrived then in the form of several ranch hands, plus Blythe, Drake and Luce. Their reactions were all pretty similar.

"I'll string him up from that tree by the river when we find the guy who did this,"

Drake said with deadly anger to Mace. "You know, the one we always wanted to climb but were afraid to try."

"Good choice. It's nice and tall." Mace picked up the ruined print, and Kelly winced as he dropped it regretfully into the debris. Even the frame was beyond repair. She felt his pain. It was reflected in his response.

Luce elbowed her husband. "I'll bring the rope. In the meantime, let's get this mess cleaned up. I brought a bucket, and I can't wait to see you with a mop, cowboy."

In a surprisingly short time they had things more or less in order, with the floors cleaned as well as possible. The old wood planks were stained with wine, but Blythe pointed out that it gave them even more character, and she could be right.

To Kelly's relief — the only positive aspect of the entire thing — they discovered that the poster of the mad scientist had survived the onslaught. She found it intact and practically jumped up and down with joy.

Mace saw her expression and sighed. "That image *is* going on a bottle, isn't it?"

"Oh, you bet it is," she said.

Chapter Twenty-Three

Kelly had left for California the following Monday morning, and Mace had driven her to the airport in Cheyenne. Red had been kind enough to return her rental car — one less chore for her to deal with. They'd covered the distance in tense silence. Granted, he couldn't dispute that she had responsibilities and he knew she'd be back, but he worried about her.

And he missed her.

Two Mondays later he *really* missed her.

There was no denying that if Vreeman actually was in Wyoming, maybe California *was* safer for her. Of course, it was just one plane ticket away.

He felt torn.

On the bright side, that had been one unforgettable goodbye kiss.

He'd have to satisfy himself with that memory of her, soft and willing in his arms, until she came back safe and sound. In the meantime, he could hardly concentrate, although he still was trying to repair the damage to the winery. That absorbed some of his attention. Because of all the spilled liquid, Spence hadn't had any luck at all in his attempt to lift fingerprints. They also discovered that a box of disposable gloves was missing, so they both assumed that whoever had done the damage had appropriated them. Another reason for the lack of prints . . .

Mace had hung Raine's poster in his office as a peace offering to Kelly, to apologize for arguing with her before she left.

"The place is looking back to normal. Sort of, anyway." Slater wandered into the fermenting room, hands in his pockets, his voice laconic. He glanced around, then got straight to the point. "When's Kelly coming back?"

Mace slapped down the ledger he had in his hand — it recorded the times he'd started various batches of wine. Yes, it was old-fashioned to use a pen and paper, but that was how he'd been taught by his grandfather, so that was how he operated. "I get asked that daily. Daisy asked me last night when she and Raine were over for dinner. The answer is the same. I don't know yet."

"Don't get testy."

"Don't be nosy."

Slater wasn't fazed; he simply folded his arms and leaned against the wall. "I'm not nosy. I'm concerned. You've barely been at the house except to grab an occasional meal. You're even sleeping here."

Mace pointed at the daybed. "I've slept here plenty of times before."

"You do realize Red brings that decrepit bedroll of his and his rifle, and sleeps on the porch of the house now. Spence couldn't definitively pin the break-in on Vreeman, so let's form a different plan. For starters, we'll place remote cameras around the house, the winery and the barn. Then we'll mount a search. You, Drake and I know this area. If he's back in California, we can't do much about it, but around here it's different. He's not staying in town or at the resort, which means he might be camping out if he's still in Bliss County. I think it would be time well spent if, instead of guarding the home front, we rode out and searched for him. If we can't find him anywhere close by, we'll put cameras in prime spots, because if I was him, I'd be moving around. Let's call it a combination of old-fashioned posse and modern technology. If we track him down, we can politely invite him to the police station to deal with Spence's questions about why he might be here."

"That, unfortunately, is not a crime," Mace pointed out. "He's allowed to be in Wyoming. Except for the actual attack on Kelly, he might be a suspect, but he's free."

"If he's trespassing on our land, or anyone else's, it's still illegal. Given the circumstances, I think most judges would agree he isn't here on vacation. There's no solid evidence — yet — that he wrecked this place, but I'd say there's probable cause if we can prove he's in the area."

True enough. "I'm more worried that he might be back in California. I know Kelly's wrapping things up there and working from home as much as possible, but somehow he got her cell number. He's probably figured out where she lives, and no one can stay inside forever. I'm betting someone at her office gave him the number and told him she was here in Wyoming. I haven't seen him for a decade, but he was a good-looking guy, prestigious family, smooth manners —"

"When he wasn't trying to choke someone unconscious and drag her off," Slate interrupted, his voice steely. "I get your point. Maybe he could convince someone he was a friend or a brother, or even that he represented a winery. Explain to me why you aren't on a plane to California right now, Mace."

"Good question, but I told her just to stay at the ranch, and she informed me in no uncertain terms that I wasn't going to tell her what to do. She used the word *dictatorial* about three times during that conversation. Tell me, Showbiz, do you feel comfortable telling Grace how to live her life? I can't force this. I don't know Kelly's ex, but there's an awkward situation on the job. He recently got a leadership role with the company — and that's one of the reasons she's leaving. I'm hoping it's for other reasons, too . . ."

"Reasons that have to do with you? Here's a thought. Go and ask her. And to answer your question, no, I'd never dictate to Grace, but I would make my feelings clear."

"Kelly knows how I feel."

Slater shook his head. "Do you understand anything about women? You have to tell her directly that you love her and want to be with her for the rest of your life. A ring might be a nice touch."

He was about to protest that first, he didn't have a ring; second, he'd already been warned he was rushing things; and third, that although they'd spoken on the phone every day, she hadn't invited him to visit.

Instead, he took a deep breath. "You really think I should go to California?"

"Absolutely. This is driving you crazy. Where's the guy who used a pilfered golf club for a rudder on a runaway sled?"

"I was a reckless kid, and by the way, I'm well aware that was a damn bad idea. I was read the riot act and had to muck out stalls for a month to pay for a new club."

"I remember." Slater gave him a half smile. "Served you right. Look, I'm just saying that you don't usually sit idle when there's something you want to do. Go and see her, talk to her. It's simple."

Not bad advice.

He doubted it would be simple, but . . .

"What would I say? 'Trust me, I know what I'm doing here'? That would be a lie, since I *don't* know what I'm doing."

"One of the things I can bank on in this world," his brother said with convincing sincerity, "is that you really do know what you're doing. You always have."

The next morning, he was on a plane.

Kelly heard the car pull into her driveway and glanced at the clock — 4:00 p.m. Janice had mentioned she might stop by tomorrow, but maybe she'd left work early and decided on today instead. It wasn't like her not to call; however, she lived the closest of all her sisters and had been known to drop by without warning. From the living-room window, she could see the driveway — and she didn't recognize the car. She felt a pang of alarm that faded quickly when she recognized the tall man who got out of the vehicle.

Mace.

He wore the usual jeans and boots, with a blue dress shirt that she suspected one of the females in the Carson household had picked out and presented to him as a gift, since it was same color as his unforgettable eyes. No hat, but then here in Los Angeles, he wasn't riding out anywhere.

He hadn't said word one about a visit, and she'd talked to him just yesterday.

She went into the foyer and opened the door as he came up the walk, managing a breathless "Hi." *Oh, good, Kelly. That was brilliant.*

His response was a lazy smile. "I have a different kind of greeting in mind."

He sure did. He came through the door, closed it behind him and kissed her thoroughly. If she was breathless at the sight of him, words weren't even possible after that hungry kiss. He lifted his head and surveyed the polished wood floors and library table.

A framed picture of her and her sisters in bathing suits on a Bermuda beach sat next to the heirloom crystal bowl her grandmother had given her one Christmas. "Nice place," he said casually, as if he hadn't shown up unannounced.

She still hadn't recovered, so her voice wasn't quite steady. "Thanks. Uh, Mace, what are you doing in LA?"

"And here, city girl, I thought you'd come to the correct conclusion that I'm here to see you, no explanation necessary."

"But you don't like the city."

"Apparently with the right incentive, I can overcome that." He let her go, amusement dancing in his eyes. "After telling me this is a pleasant surprise, show me around."

It was a pleasant surprise. If only he understood how frantically she'd been working to wrap up her projects at the office, including the purchase of his grandfather's business, trying to decide if she should lease or sell her condo — all the details that went into a major life change. She'd have to sell or give away all her furniture if she moved to the ranch. She was seriously thinking that maybe she should just buy a small house in Mustang Creek. It wasn't as if she and Mace were engaged or anything.

The man had turned her world upside down.

"I missed you," she confessed, meaning it.

"A good start."

"Follow me into the kitchen. It's a little early, but can I offer you a glass of wine?"

He walked behind her down the hall. "It's never too early, and I've been through three crowded airports today. I say yes to the wine. Besides, I came from the Mountain time zone, so for me it's five o'clock."

"Convenient thinking, cowboy."

"You look really good."

He had to be joking. She was wearing her hair up in a clip and had on pajama pants and an old T-shirt. Not what you'd call high fashion. "No, I don't. I never dress up when I work from home."

"Why would you?" Typical male answer. Mace shrugged. "And yes, you do, by the way. You might want to change for dinner, though. It's too much to hope there's a Bad Billy's here, but I want to take you out. Pick someplace trendy if you like, but make sure it's quiet enough so we don't have to shout to hear each other."

There was an English pub about two blocks away. It wasn't Bad Billy's, but it was casual and the food was fine, and it wasn't loud at all.

He was right; they needed to be able to talk. "I know a great place I think you'll like."

His grin was quick. "With my unsophisticated tastes, you mean."

"No, I didn't mean that at all. You happen to know a bowlegged cowboy who cooks French dishes but can shoot the warts off a toad, remember? That makes you the most interesting person in a city that celebrates interesting like no other. The Spotted Dog is quiet, and the food's not Bad Billy's but it's good." She pulled two glasses out of the cupboard and one of his wines out of the rack by the stainless steel refrigerator. "How do you feel about Cheyenne Chardonnay?"

He took the glasses out of her hands. "That I hope it has more body next time. It was lighter than I wanted."

"It's a bestseller!"

"This is a refrain, Ms. Wright. I make the wines to please me." He set the glasses on the table. Taking both the bottle and the opener from her, he deftly uncorked the wine. "It doesn't mean I don't want other people to like them, but that isn't really what I'm thinking about when I make them. I am sure chefs operate the same way, tasting a dish and finally deciding *they* think it's all it should be. That's the only opinion

they have, based on their palate and taste."
He paused. "Like I said, I thought it was
maybe a shade too light."

"You can't be critical of this wine!"

"Of course I can."

"Your perfectionism is going to be ex-
hausting, right?" She sat down at the oak
table and let him pour.

"Like Billy and the mushrooms? How
could he think anyone wouldn't like those?
I guess genius needs to be coddled."

"Don't even compare yourself to Billy and
those mushrooms." She accepted a glass.
"That's just conceited."

He grinned. "They were pretty outstand-
ing. I like these wineglasses. Very different."

They were lovely and made of pale green
glass with scenes of jungle animals peering
from the depths of the rainforest. "Hand-
painted in Brazil. My father was there on
business and bought them for me. He realized he couldn't check them with his bags,
or put them in the overhead compartment,
without risking breakage. He had to fly from
the southern tip of Brazil to Puerto Rico,
change planes there, change planes again in
Dallas, and finally on to LA, with the box
balanced in his lap the entire trip. That's
fatherly devotion, wouldn't you say?"

Mace looked alarmed, setting his glass

down very carefully. "Don't you have something else, preferably plastic? If I had a list of all the wineglasses I've absent-mindedly knocked over, it would be pages long. I can't meet your father and have to confess right away that I broke one of his hard-earned Brazilian wineglasses. I'm serious. If you want me to take another sip, get me a glass you bought at Wal-Mart or something."

Meet her father?

She got up, laughing, but with Mace she was frequently laughing and that was part of the attraction. It was easy to be happy around him, and while she normally thought of herself as someone who was satisfied with her life, lucky in many ways, she was startled to realize that contentment was fine, but happiness was different.

She got out a generic glass she'd bought a dozen of for one of her sisters' bridal showers and handed it over. "Feel free to demolish it. I promise I won't weep. I'd cry more over the spilled wine."

He gingerly made the transfer and returned the other glass. "Thanks. I can relax again. I bet Raine could do a design like that for the store. No anacondas or leopards, but mountains lions and bears."

She regarded her glass and decided that was a brilliant idea. "You're starting to sound like me, you know."

"There are worse things in my book." His smile faded. "Is everything still okay there, since the last time we talked? I've been going crazy worrying about you. Any sign of Vreeman?"

"No." She took what could be described as a gulp of wine and shook her head. "I hate this waiting for something bad to happen. Maybe it never will. You've been worrying about *me*? I've been worrying about *you.*"

He regarded her over the rim of his inexpensive glass. "Here's a thought. If you were in Wyoming, neither one of us would have to worry about the other one. Fly back with me? The store is now your baby. I closed on it the other day."

So things were rolling along. "I don't know. How long are you staying here?"

"I won't do the business any favors if I'm gone very long."

What an unfair card to play! "That's not an answer."

"When can you come back with me?"

"If you're asking whether I've given my official notice at work, then yes, I have. And no, I haven't seen Alan yet."

His answering smile didn't begin with his mouth, but the light in his eyes. "I was hoping that might be the case. Both of those things," he added.

Oh, she was so lost in that smile. Kelly equivocated. "As far as the job goes, it isn't as simple as just walking away. I still have some special projects to wrap up — and a major bonus is involved. Not something I plan to leave behind."

"Well, do what you have to do, so we can go home. I'd like to get back to the winery, and I'm definitely not leaving *you* behind."

CHAPTER TWENTY-FOUR

The Spotted Dog was one of those quaint little places that had dark leather booths and low hanging lights over polished tables, and if it was casual, it was definitely LA casual, not the Mustang Creek version. To Mace's relief, though, the music wasn't blaring, just playing softly in the background, and the clientele was mostly late twenties to midthirties. His boots and jeans didn't necessarily fit the ambiance of the pub, but he hadn't packed anything else. Kelly, of course, looked fantastic in a dark blue knit dress with cute little black boots. Although of course he preferred the cowboy boots she'd bought in Mustang Creek . . .

"I assume you're famished," she said teasingly after their drinks — two glasses of the house chardonnay — were ordered. "It's a sign of my affection that I didn't offer to cook for you. I was going to have a turkey sandwich, and yes, avocado on top. No bean sprouts. Don't tell Thelma, but I'm not a fan of bean sprouts."

"Hey, don't sell me short. I like turkey sandwiches."

She snorted. "Yes, you'd probably eat at least three of them. My condo is not the Carson household. I shop for one. I get takeout more than I should, but I've been working long hours." She paused and added quietly, her eyes suddenly luminous, "I can't believe you're here."

"Blame Slate. He told me flat out that I should get my ass to California and haul you back to Wyoming. I'd been thinking about it, anyway, so I went along with his advice."

"That's more than a little high-handed. On his part *and* yours."

"I want you to be happy. And he wants me to be happy. I wasn't once you left." Their drinks arrived, accompanied by embossed menus showing the outline of Tower Bridge over the Thames.

"I'm changing my whole life for you." She didn't touch her glass of wine or her menu. "I mean, not *just* because of you — but circumstances . . . came together in a certain way. And here we are."

"I have to believe it's where we were always meant to be. Sometimes the way those circumstances conspire is the best scenario."

"But it's all happened so fast!"

He understood her trepidation. He felt it, too, and yet that fear was overshadowed by his excitement and his optimism.

"I still believe everything's happened for a reason. And it's about you and me being together."

She looked away. "Don't try to simplify this."

"Don't try to complicate it."

"You country boys are so annoying." But she looked back and smiled, even if that smile wavered.

"Part of our irresistible charm." He lounged in his chair and searched for the right words. "What if I promise not to rush you and you promise to trust me?"

"If you think I don't trust you, think again. Let's talk about the store. You *already* closed on it?"

"Bob wanted to sell and I wanted to buy. His price was fair, so no bargaining on my end. Title work done and papers signed. It belongs to us."

"To *you.*"

"You and me both. You get to do whatever you want with it. I talked to my accountant, and he advised making us equal partners, fifty-fifty, with the understanding that I front the costs and provide the goods, and you do the rest. Agreed? I explained that you really know what you're doing, and he's on board. Andy and I are old friends. We went to high school together."

"Of course you did." Kelly took a sip of wine. "It's not as good as yours, but a decent California chard. So I can start talking to Raine?"

"Anyone can talk to Raine," he answered truthfully. "You'll get her honest reaction. If she isn't interested, she'll be up front with her reasons."

Kelly seemed reassured, but he didn't blame her for the cold feet. *Move to my state. Live my life. Start my business.*

On the other hand . . . *Come live with me because I'm in love with you. I want to trust you with a big investment and give you carte blanche to do with it as you will, and I swear to give you time to adjust.*

"If you have trouble with her straightforward approach, send her to me. We'll find a compromise."

He was convinced that she and the headstrong-but-creative mother of his niece would get along very well. "She's going to love your ideas. And I predict that Melody Hogan will jump at the chance to do the wine charms. Harry will offer to make appetizers for the wine-tastings, and Red will want to help. His contribution will probably be buffalo cheese puffs or something. Maybe elk. Your launch parties will be the talk of the wine world. I'll see you on late-night television and all over the internet."

Kelly rested her forehead on her hand. "Elk cheese puffs?"

"The man swears by elk meat. I bet they'd be good."

"You're not kidding, are you?"

"Nope."

Her eyes sparkled. "Maybe he can make those for when he and I get married. I always dreamed of serving elk at my reception."

"Hey, I thought you'd changed your mind and were going to marry me instead."

"What can I say? I'm fickle." She pretended to contemplate the idea, two fingers pressed against her chin. "It's actually a three-way tie — you, Bad Billy and Red."

"I don't see either of them hopping a plane and heading off to California. Surely that has to earn me points," he teased back, not sure if he'd been a complete fool to even suggest that maybe she could marry him.

One hand moved in an airy circle. "The night is young. Who knows who might show up." Her hand jerked then, enough that some of the wine in her glass slopped over the rim. Her expression went from light-hearted to fearful. "Oh, God. I shouldn't have said that. Mace, I think that's *him* sitting at the bar! He walked in with the last group of people but isn't sitting with them. His hair's a different color and he looks older, but I could swear it's Lance Vreeman."

Mace had heard regularly from Spence and his brothers; there'd been no sign of Vreeman. Given his absence from Bliss County, it wouldn't be surprising if the man was back in California.

The fact that he happened to be in the same restaurant certainly wasn't a matter of chance. Or coincidence. Mace turned around to peer at the new arrival. It looked like Vreeman to him, as well, but he wasn't confident enough to definitively say it *was* that scumbag. "It could be him," he said in a whisper. "I assume you've lost all desire to eat here. Should we finish our drinks — I refuse to let him run me off completely — and pick up something from the Thai take-out down the street as we walk back to your place?"

She nodded, and he saw her swallow. "That sounds better. I'm sorry, but I couldn't eat a bite with him sitting right there. I *hate* this! I feel like a prisoner. If I'm at the office, I only go to lunch in a group. I drive a different route home every night, and I bolt from the car to my front door with my thumb on the panic button for the car alarm. If the condo didn't have an alarm system, I wouldn't even sleep at night."

"I've been sleeping in the winery office, and Red's been camping out on the porch of the house. So, you aren't the only one on guard. I can't tell you how resentful and angry I am that one person can do this to so many other people."

"I'm kind of counting on what I call 'the Carson influence' to make it stop." Kelly had stopped watching the man sitting at the bar. "It's like a virus you catch on vacation. You think you're healthy, independent and fine, and the next thing you know, you need the Carson influence to get better. It's . . . it's like an inoculation or something." Her eyes were haunted. "Your mother told me to stop apologizing for the way this arrived on your doorstep. But . . . I can't help it."

Anyone in his family would point out that the bastard over at the bar was always the real problem; Vreeman was solidly to blame. Mace finished his wine, and stood. "I'm going to go pay our tab. I'll be right back."

"Mace, don't —"

Poke a bear with a stick? Well, here was the thing. This bear was already poking him. Maybe up close and personal, he'd be able to tell if it really was Vreeman.

He nudged his way through the gathering crowd — the place was filling up — and glanced over, as if waiting for the bartender to notice him. He knew at once.

The wavy chestnut hair was now blond, there were lines on his face that hadn't been there before, and he was wearing eyeglasses, but it was him. Kelly wasn't wrong.

Mace found himself looking into those cold eyes. "Fancy meeting you again, Vreeman."

"Yeah, fancy that. Small world, Carson." There was an underlying sneer in the response.

"Well, I have a friend who might point out this is Kismet in a garbage bag. Stay away from Kelly, stay away from anyone she cares about, and stay out of Wyoming. I hope we've come to a mutual understanding. I know you followed us, because I don't believe in coincidence, and I know you trashed the winery. Kelly's going to get a restraining order, but I'm not. I'd love to catch you alone. This conversation is over."

He laid a bill on the bar to pay for their drinks and walked away.

It wasn't as if she was some helpless female, but she was willing to admit that she was oh so glad to have Mace Carson sitting at her kitchen table, devouring chicken curry with appreciation. He'd ordered the hottest version possible, so there was a hint of sweat on his forehead. "There's only one thing I regret about Mustang Creek," he said, pointing his fork at his plate. "No Thai food, no Chinese, no authentic New York deli, no Greek place, the list goes on. This is what I miss about the big city."

She'd managed to relax enough to eat some of her food, a spicy beef noodle dish she ordered every time she stopped there. "Well, here we don't have Bad Billy's and we don't have Harry."

"True. And luckily Stefano makes fabulous Italian, and there's a good Mexican restaurant in Wallace, about twenty-five minutes away."

"See, it's not so bereft, after all," she said. "But no ocean. No beaches with girls in bikinis."

He shrugged. "We have the mountains, Bliss River and no crowds."

It felt disloyal, but she thought she was

going to like Wyoming. A lot. "Mustang Creek, the whole area, seems beautiful and relaxing," she said a little wistfully. "I won't miss my fifteen-mile commute, which can sometimes take an hour and a half."

He shuddered. "Yuck. I wish I could come up with a more sophisticated word, but *yuck* seems to fit."

"What did you say to him?" She pushed aside her plate and looked at Mace intently.

She didn't have to specify *him*. "That you're getting a restraining order, and he'd better leave you and your family alone. That I was aware he was responsible for trashing the winery, and that I knew he'd followed us tonight. I think I made it clear that if I got an opportunity to break his nose again, that would be fine with me."

"Men are so bloodthirsty," Kelly murmured. "But a restraining order isn't a bad idea. Until tonight, that hadn't occurred to me. Then if he follows me again, at least I'll have some recourse."

"Since you'll be coming back to Wyoming with me, it'll be more useful in case he decides to tag along. Then Spence can arrest him. There's no judge in this world who wouldn't give him the maximum penalty, considering that as soon as he was released from prison, he immediately started harassing you."

"Oh, I found out how he got my cell number. He called the office, claimed to be my cousin and said there was a family emergency and he didn't have my number. Normally that wouldn't work, but we have an older lady who only works one day a week as the receptionist, so he struck gold there. When our paths finally did cross, she asked me very kindly if everything turned out okay. I didn't have the heart to tell her she'd given my number to a convicted felon."

"He's dangerous, but no one's ever said he's stupid."

"He's not . . . normal." It was undeniable and frightening. Her voice was almost inaudible.

"No, he isn't," Mace agreed. "I'd say he probably fits the profile of a psychopath. Kelly, why do you think I'm here?"

"I'm just *glad* you're here."

He flashed a smile. "I am, too. It took some nerve to show up the way I did. I honestly didn't worry about that until I was on the plane. For all I knew, you had symphony tickets, or plans with family or friends."

"Symphony? I'm a girl who favors eighties-style rock. Don't tell me, Red listens to Mozart."

"Maurice Ravel." Mace managed to keep a straight face. "Some Buck Owens and Gene Autry to balance it out. A man can't get too immersed in culture, after all."

"Is that a direct quote?"

"If you want it to be."

"Save the facile charm for other women." Kelly rose to take their plates to the sink. "I'm immune."

He followed her, bringing their glasses, and after setting them down, kissed her neck. His hands slid over her hips. "No, you aren't."

No, she wasn't.

"If you're right, then chivalry's truly dead because you shouldn't take advantage of me."

"Let's see, I've admitted I'm in love with you, I've invited you to live with me in Wyoming, and I flew here just to make sure you're safe. I don't care about chivalry one way or the other, but I'd say you can count on me when it matters."

She believed that.

"Mace, that *is* chivalry."

"You'll have to dumb that down for me."

"Oh, right. You're one of the smartest people I know." She rolled her eyes. "Give me a break."

"That's what you call a compliment? *One* of the smartest? That's like saying you only *think* I'm good-looking."

She might strangle him. Or kiss him. "I'd suggest we watch a movie, but maybe you could tell me a bedtime story instead."

That won her a long, slow look. She knew he did it on purpose and, coupled with that wicked smile, it was lethal. "You and a bed? Now we're talking. But I invited myself, so if you asked me to get a hotel room, I wouldn't blame you."

Who was he kidding? She'd missed him so much. Abandoning the dishes in the sink — something she never did — she turned around and rose on tiptoe, wrapping her arms around his neck. The kiss seemed to last forever, a heated exchange of breath and touch, and when it was over, she suspected they *both* understood how much they'd missed each other.

She was a tidy person by nature, so even with his unexpected arrival, her bedroom was neat. The bed featured a cream coverlet embroidered with tiny violets. The room was fairly sparse, with a dark antique dresser and a chair and reading lamp — nothing frilly. She swallowed a laugh as Mace sat down on the side of the bed to shuck off his boots.

"What?" He glanced up and narrowed his eyes.

"You look cute sitting on a flowery bedspread. I've never had a cowboy in my bedroom."

"I hope not. Word has it they can't be trusted around beautiful women."

"Let me guess, Red told you that."

He unfastened the two top buttons on his shirt, then yanked it off. "I think he said that beautiful women were like fresh-baked biscuits with honey butter on top, and any cowboy worth his salt would ride a hundred miles in the blowing rain to get one."

Kelly fell on the bed, pretending to faint, and seconds later he was there, pulling her close. "You came farther than a hundred miles, though."

"Yeah. I guess I'm not in Wyoming anymore. I haven't seen a single moose since I arrived."

She snuggled into his arms. "You could try your famous call."

"Shh . . . Remember, I told you about that in confidence. Or I could just tell you a story? Isn't that what you wanted?"

"Okay." She smiled against his chest.

"Once upon a time," he began, "a lovely maiden traveled to a magical land. She had a nefarious plan to bamboozle an innocent alchemist, wrest his secrets from him and enslave him. But that backfired, and instead she succumbed to his incomparable allure."

Kelly hit his shoulder lightly. "Oh, right. Incomparable allure?"

"Hey, this is my story and I'll tell it the way I want."

"She wanted to *enslave* him?"

"I'm telling this from his point of view. His perspective is that she deliberately used her wiles to try to rope him in."

There was no avoiding it; she had to dissolve into laughter. Again. "Mace, you can't say 'rope him in' and use 'incomparable allure' in the same story."

"I can't? This is a Wyoming fairy tale. Anything goes there."

"Okay, I stand corrected." She ran a finger along his lower lip. "Go on."

"She roped him in. That's end of it. They got married and lived happily ever after."

"You could be the worst storyteller on earth." She trailed her hand down his stomach. "That's the most overused ending ever."

"I never claimed I'd be good at it."

He might not be good at storytelling, but everything else . . . yes.

CHAPTER TWENTY-FIVE

The next night her family descended like a herd of locusts.

Wait, was it a herd? Swarm, maybe . . . he wasn't sure. Perhaps he'd spent too much time out on the lonesome range.

All of Kelly's sisters arrived. Just his luck — Kelly was out. The first one showed up, opened the door with her own key and came in with dessert in a pastry box. Two children flew past him, glancing over their shoulders and grinning curiously.

"Come back here, you two, and say hello to our guest," their mother ordered.

They obeyed readily, greeting Mace with questions. Was he Aunt Kelly's boyfriend? Was he really a cowboy? How many horses did he own?

With a roll of her pretty eyes, Kelly's sister said, "Sorry," and sent the kids packing.

They went straight to the television, switched it on as though they'd done it a thousand times before and plugged in a device with a video game.

The woman giving him a thorough once-over was a slightly older version of Kelly with darker hair, a scarlet silk blouse tucked into perfectly tailored slacks and West Coast sandals. She eyed him up and down and murmured, "Oh. Very nice."

Somewhat nonplussed over the unabashed appraisal, he held out his hand. "Mace Carson."

She handed him the dessert box instead. "Ah, yes. Kelly's hero." She grimaced comically. "Sounds like a movie title. Anyway, I do recall you from ten years ago — the way you rescued our Kelly and then the trial. Never met you then, but I sat in the courtroom. I'm Janice. My sister's mistake was mentioning to me that this would be a bad night to stop by because she had company. I made an educated guess and began plotting immediately. You'd think the kid would know better than to be evasive with me, but apparently some people don't learn from experience."

Two more vehicles had pulled in, and the drivers were arguing before the doors had even slammed shut. "Why did you bring pasta? *I* brought the pasta."

"I brought more. Do you suppose we

won't eat it? Where have you been?"

"In a land where people also eat salad."

"The kids asked for chicken Alfredo. I think Sue's bringing a salad."

More children made a beeline for the living room, giggling as they raced by. The two new adult arrivals breezed in, and Mace got a double once-over. One of them said to the other, "Oh, yeah, he's cute."

"*And* he's a gen-you-wine hero," the other added.

A black SUV drove up then, and at least five little kids piled out, followed by what had to be the fourth sister. She had to be the closest in age, because they could've been twins, right down to those stunning eyes. "So you're my sister's cowboy. The one who slung her on his horse in that cute skirt I would've bought for myself if she hadn't spotted it first. I'd like to have seen that."

Sue hadn't brought a salad, after all, but judging by the covered dish in her hands, more pasta.

"Er, my brother actually slung her onto my horse. I just happened to be sitting on it at the time. Nice to meet you."

Rarely had he felt so outnumbered.

The women took over the kitchen and dining room, still squabbling, mostly laughing, the young cousins doing the same thing. Kelly was due back any minute, and he was anxious to see her walk through the front door. She'd run to the bank and her office, and as much as he'd wanted to go along, she was adamantly opposed, as if it would give Vreeman more power. He understood that, and yet he didn't.

No way could he protect her all the time, as she'd pointed out. And if she was afraid to be on her own, that fear was exactly what gave Vreeman some kind of hold on her.

When they'd gone to the county courthouse to file for a restraining order, she'd been visibly nervous. He couldn't blame her, but this seemed like a step in the right direction.

No, the right direction would be when they got on that plane tomorrow morning and flew northeast.

Watching as various women invaded cupboards, setting the table and putting out food, he felt like a trout pulled out of the Bliss River. The sisters resembled each other enough that he was hesitant to use first names, even though they'd introduced themselves in passing. When Kelly finally walked in, he couldn't restrain a sigh of relief. One look at his face and a giggle erupted.

"Quite the crew, huh? Now you know how I felt at the ranch. What, may I ask, is going on here?"

The tall one, Janice — he'd gotten that down, anyway — explained innocently, "Impromptu potluck dinner. Three pastas, since some of us can't take instructions and bring a salad, plus bread and dessert. If you want carbs, you've evidently come to the right place."

"I heard pasta dinner," one of them argued. "So I brought pasta. Is anyone going to pour me a glass of wine or do I have to feel like I've trekked across the Sahara on a hot day without a camel?"

"My pleasure." That he could handle. Luckily Kelly had a good supply, much of it from Mountain Winery, and he went to work. He uncorked a chardonnay, a merlot and a chianti and offered them in glasses that weren't hand-painted. The children came in for juice and bottled water, filled their plates and went back to the television.

Everyone else sat down around the table, and Mace became the recipient of speculative female observation.

At least he was wearing a decent shirt. A miracle. He'd washed the one he'd worn on the plane and for some reason put it on after his shower.

That was one redeeming factor in what he assumed was their assessment of his suitability for their little sister.

Four pairs of eyes regarded him over plates of linguine and angel hair pasta. They started to talk among themselves. "He's nice-looking and polite, but that isn't enough. Alan seemed good. He wasn't. Or at least not good enough."

One of them stepped up. "I don't know. I never got the right vibe from Alan. This one seems different."

"In what way?"

"Well, okay, there's the whole hero thing, but —"

Kelly stepped into his corner. "Hello! Don't do this. We're both here, listening to every word."

They ignored her. "Good different." One sister — he thought it was Elaine — took a bite of Alfredo and studied him. "I can always tell."

"Like you're some sort of oracle," Janice said scornfully as she took a piece of garlic bread from the basket.

Elaine retaliated immediately. "You dated that creepy Bruce guy in college, and I disliked him on sight. Was I right or wrong?"

All four of them nodded, even Janice, who said grudgingly. "Right."

"This one seems good in a sexy cowboy down-to-earth way."

"Thanks," Kelly said drily. "Unless you just scared him off. Most men would've run screaming from the room by now. Only a man who can capture a bull in dense fog would have the courage for this circus."

Live large. That would be advice from Red, from Slater and from Drake. He decided to go for it, crossing his arms on the table. "Since you're all here, what are your thoughts on a ring? I need advice."

Eyes lit up all around. Elaine said, "Good question. She's picky. Have you noticed? Very little jewelry."

"Well, no. Men are usually challenged in that department. That's why I'm asking."

Kelly whispered in obvious agitation, "Ring? Why are you doing this? Mace, I'm going to kill you. You're about to incite a riot."

"Okay." He'd been struggling with how to do it, and somehow this seemed to be the right time. He just needed to get it done. He eased off his chair and knelt, taking her hand in his. "Maybe I should ask the question first. Will you marry me?"

Damn him.
Straight to hell.

Asking in front of her sisters was unfair. Like out-of-the-ball-park unfair. On the other hand, he hadn't invited them; they'd barged in, albeit bringing some delicious food, but their nosiness was not to be believed. Unless, of course, you knew them . . .

He wanted to *marry* her.

She didn't stand a chance. Not that she hadn't already come to the conclusion that she'd say yes whenever and wherever he asked, but she hadn't expected such a public display.

Everyone was staring at her. She finally managed to say, "You have to swear you won't turn into a toad or I'll have Red shoot your warts off."

Her prince started laughing. Her sisters looked mystified. Mace said, "I swear it, although I think you mean a frog. I'm sure that for your sake, Red would take a bead on me. I accept your terms as long as that's a yes."

Her sisters didn't look any more enlightened, but they were obviously delighted when she nodded. "Yes."

The startling part was that she was certain this wasn't a mistake.

When Alan proposed, she'd said yes, believing she knew him as well as it was possible to know another person. Believing they'd always be aligned in their thoughts and feeling. Believing he'd keep the promises he'd made. She'd been wrong.

This wasn't like that. They were older, more experienced, more mature. Although it was rushed on both their parts, it seemed right, and maybe she *could* take a second chance.

"Yes." She said it again with emphasis. Mace was Mace, so he stood and picked her up, kissed her soundly in front of everyone, then set her back on her feet.

"Caveman style," Janice commented with a sigh. "So romantic."

In a reasonable voice, Kelly said, "It's ridiculous to get engaged so soon."

"We are, though." He had the audacity to wink at her. "You just said yes."

"You are," her sisters said in chorus. "There are witnesses."

Then, of course, the debate was on. "Ring? I say diamond. She's traditional." This was Sue.

"No, emerald." Elaine suggested. "To match her eyes."

"Ruby. I love ruby engagement rings," Janice countered.

"*You* like rubies, but maybe she doesn't. What about a freshwater pearl?"

"It isn't a precious stone."

"What the heck does that matter? I think it'd be pretty."

"See," Kelly muttered.

Mace sent her an empathetic smile. "I eat dinner at the Carson table fairly often. It isn't like I'm not familiar with this scenario. My brothers would look blank on the subject of rings, but they weigh in with no problem on just about everything else."

"The haggling will continue, as though they're trying to buy a Persian rug at a street bazaar in Morocco."

"They love you. So do I. We have a lot in common."

Suddenly tears were on her lashes. "Mace, are you *sure*?"

"Were you sure the first time?"

"Well, yes. I thought so. But things changed." That was honest.

"This time they won't. I know myself well enough to promise you that." It made her feel better, not simply because she was sure he was telling the truth, but because she could tell he was sincere.

"Kelly, don't cry." He brushed her cheek with the pad of his thumb and gazed at her in consternation.

"I'm happy, not sad. I tend to shed tears for both."

"I vow to get a handle on that dynamic one day." He squeezed her hand.

"Good luck." She dashed away another tear. "I've never been able to anticipate it. Sometimes I just cry."

"Maybe we could use a hand signal to help me out. Thumbs-up for happy tears, thumbs-down for sad ones."

She hiccuped out a laugh. "I'll try to remember."

Then she gave him a thumbs-up as another tear rolled down her cheek.

Chapter Twenty-Six

It was five days before they could leave.

Kelly had to meet for a final time with Dina, her previous manager and attend a farewell lunch. She had to hand in her formal resignation, finish up the sale of his grandfather's winery and a couple of other projects — and lease her condo. She quickly found a young couple interested in renting the place furnished for at least a year.

Meanwhile Mace took care of what business he could, via phone and internet.

Finally, they were back in Wyoming. The flight to Cheyenne was mostly filled with silence and what he perceived to be a settled contentment over her decision. *We are going to elope,* she'd informed him, and that news was music to his ears, anyway, regardless of what his family might think. In his book, most grooms would prefer that course of action. Short wedding, long wedding night.

Good idea.

"I want to go to the new store first thing in the morning," she told him as they waited for her luggage, since he'd brought three changes of clothing and a shaving kit in a carry-on. "I'm excited about getting started."

That could be true — and in a sense he knew it *was* — but she wasn't fooling him. "You're trying to protect my tender feelings by not saying that you're nervous about the move, about getting married and about changing jobs." He plucked her bag off the carousel. "It's okay. I've asked a lot from you."

"You've offered a lot in return. The store is the kind of special project I've always dreamed about." Her smile was delicious and innocent.

"Oh, great, I come in second to a musty building with a sagging sign."

She raised her brows as he wheeled the luggage toward the elevators. "Of course. I'm all business, remember?"

"You're right about that. I was seducing you so you'd move to Wyoming, because I wanted your expertise. I even threw in a marriage proposal. Nope, I'm not to be trusted."

Kelly gave him the look he deserved. "You

won't get an argument here on the 'not to be trusted' part."

"I plan to take advantage of you again," he said without apology. "Just as soon as possible."

Kelly had a truly melodic laugh. He was enchanted by it. "I'm duly warned," she said, opening the elevator door, so he could wheel her bag out. "And I really mean it — I can't wait."

No wonder he loved her.

They took the shuttle to the long-term parking lot where he'd left the truck. He would've been more than happy to get on the road to Mustang Creek, but . . . all his tires were flat. Not salvageable, either, but with deep punctures. And of course he had one spare, but not four.

They simply looked at each other and stayed calm. "Damn him," Kelly said quietly. "How did he even know this was your truck or where you parked it?"

"I'm guessing he followed me to the airport. We can rent a car."

"I know, but —"

"Don't let it get to you."

"This confirms to me that I'm not the one he wants to get even with, Mace. You are."

He was seething as they went back inside and arranged for a rental car and to have his fixed. The sense of personal violation was definitely there, enhanced by the knowledge that if the vendetta was aimed more at him than Kelly, she'd still be the perfect way to carry it out. Vreeman knew they were together in California; he'd followed them there. He'd obviously realized Mace was staying with her.

On his hands-free device, he called Slater once they were on the highway. "Headed home, and Kelly and I are looking forward to seeing everyone. I think our guy was hanging around the ranch until the day I left. Are the cameras still up?"

"They are. So far, we have a lot of footage of bears. There are more than I thought, by the way." Slater's laugh held no real amusement. "You have reason to think he'll show up again?"

"Well, he obviously followed me to the airport, because someone vandalized my truck, and he certainly followed me to California, so I'm just guessing he'll follow us back."

"Then we'll get him. Hey, I hope you realize you mentioned a puppy to Daisy and Ryder. Needless to say, they told Mom, who said something to Lettie Arbuckle-Calder, who arrived toot-sweet in her expensive car and took them off to the Humane Society.

You now have two dogs. They each picked one out. I can't tell if Delilah's a real dog or a dust mop, but Samson shows all the signs of becoming a small horse."

Two dogs? What?

At least Kelly was laughing now, but he sure wasn't. "I can't have a dog named Delilah," he said in mock horror. "No way."

"I'm afraid you do, brother. Here's some sage advice. Don't tell children they can pick out a puppy and then leave the state. All hell can break loose. Luckily, Harold's a patient dog. Delilah took an instant shine to him and wants to snooze on top of him. Here's this big German shepherd who's tangled with a mountain lion, and it looks like he's wearing a feather boa every time he lies down. Want to hear the funny part?"

"There's a funny part? Go ahead."

"Ryder picked out Delilah, and Daisy picked out Samson. There you go. It's life without reason. The teenage boy who wants nothing more than to ride bulls on the rodeo circuit is the one who selects the little mop dog, and Daisy, whose favorite color is pink, picks out what I suspect will resemble an English mastiff someday."

"English mastiff?" Mace groaned.

"Not purebred." Slater was enjoying this way too much. "He can sleep on your bed.

Maybe he'll only get up to a hundred fifty pounds or so."

"I want to state that this was *his* idea," Kelly said. "He said *puppy* with so much enthusiasm. He should be twice as happy now."

Slater thought that was funny. Of course. "I can make this into a documentary. Call it *The Mop and the Monster.*"

"I was about to suggest that," Mace said darkly.

"I'll take that into consideration. See you later." His older brother chuckled and ended the call.

Kelly held on to a half smile. "Now that you've met my sisters, I'm sure you'll agree your family is fairly normal."

"*Fairly* being the operative word."

He was so happy to see the Tetons, he was going to just forget about a potentially one-hundred-fifty-pound dog sleeping next to him. He decided to take a stand. "Samson will sleep on the floor."

"I agree. Delilah will apparently sleep on Harold. We're in the clear."

"Okay, I do admit I shouldn't have said anything to the kids."

"Except you're like a kid, too, so you couldn't wait."

"I'd take offense, but I revel in my youthful optimism. I have it on good authority that your family calls *you* 'the kid.' "

She made a face. "That's Janice's fault. I was stuck with it all through school. Even my teachers called me that. I wasn't too fond of it then, but as thirty looms on the horizon, I'm starting to like it."

"The kid, the mad scientist, the mop and the monster. At least our little family will be interesting."

"Maybe not so little." Her voice was so quiet, he almost didn't catch the inflection. Kelly took a deep breath before she went on. "I've been trying to figure out if I should say anything yet or not. But . . . here goes. I'm late."

Late? Oh, hell, *late.* He almost missed the turn he needed. "You're . . . pregnant? But we used protection —"

"Except for that night at the cabin." Her voice was hushed.

It wasn't as if he didn't know that having unprotected sex wasn't without possible consequences, so this was hardly all on her shoulders. In that moment, at the cabin, he hadn't cared. "How do you feel?"

"Like normal. Maybe more tired than usual, but I've been working so hard, that stands to reason."

When he got up early that morning, this

was not a conversation he envisioned would be part of his day. Mace drove almost on autopilot and reminded himself to choose his words carefully. "I do care how you feel physically, so don't get me wrong, but I was asking more about your emotional state."

"I thought men didn't like to talk about feelings."

"We don't like to talk about *our* feelings. That's different. I got the impression you wanted a baby."

"I do." There were those tears again, making her eyes glassy and threatening to spill over. "I wasn't ready when I was married to Alan. But I want a baby with you, Mace. I'm still cautious about believing it. We don't know."

"That's easily solved by a pregnancy test."

"True," she said without conviction.

She was vehement. Maybe his brothers were right, and he'd never understand women. He was definitely out of his depth. "Okay. Can you tell me why you're so hesitant?"

"I'm not sure I can handle the letdown if it's negative. It's only been a few weeks. Let's just wait and see. I've decided to become a pioneer woman and move to Wyoming, so I think we should play it that way. One day at a time. How do *you* feel?"

"I'm getting kind of hungry. Lunch was a while ago."

Kelly punched his shoulder. "Quit that."

But the tears were gone. He took that as a thumbs-up.

He was never going to be a traditional sort of husband, but since she didn't want that, anyway, it should work out.

He made her believe in true love.

There was a reason she hadn't told him about the pregnancy before he'd so boldly proposed. No, many reasons. She *wanted* it to be true, and she didn't want to jinx the possibility.

She'd gone ahead and told him, anyway.

"What if it isn't true?" She just needed to know.

"Then we'll be fine." He reached over to briefly clasp her hand. "I'll be the happiest man on earth, either way."

She settled back against the seat and blinked rapidly. "Don't make me cry again."

The fact that she was more emotional than usual didn't mean anything. Her life was changing at a slam-dunk pace and that would throw anyone off balance. Mace took it all in stride, or he seemed to, but she had a scary feeling that her hard-won sense of independence was flying out the window.

"I want to check on the winery, but we could go to the cabin tonight. What do you think?"

"The week in LA got to you, and you need a solid dose of the outdoors, is that it?"

"Something like that."

"Wolves howling in the background . . ."

"Can you make that happen?" He looked hopeful. "I need the fix. Back in the wild. If you're a pioneer woman, I'm a mountain man."

"You're ridiculous." She was laughing now, relaxed again, and that felt really welcome. "I doubt I have a wolf call that'll work, but I'm willing to give it a try. Maybe a rabbit will come running instead. Would you be willing to accept a fluffy bunny tail instead of bared teeth?"

Mace shrugged. "Well, okay. It's a compromise, but if you can't pull it off, you can make it up to me. You've given me the only promise I need. I'll let you slide on the wolf whistle."

"Make it up to you?" she asked skeptically. "Excuse me? Who showed up on whose doorstep? Who proposed to someone in front of four siblings, putting me on the spot? I think if there's making up to be done, the ball is in your court."

He didn't look guilty at all. "So *yes* to the

cabin? I thought I'd make it up to you there. Seemed to me you liked that sleeping bag scenario."

"Don't try plying me with wine. I can't do that until we know." Oh, hell, she was getting weepy again . . . This was not going to be an easy journey.

"I'll drink for you during the next nine months. It's a generous offer, don't you agree?"

"Oh, yes. I'm overwhelmed."

"The least I can do if you have to carry this baby."

"We don't know —"

"I just have a feeling it's true."

"We'll see," she said as lightly as possible. "In the meantime, the sleeping bag sounds promising. I've had my fill of traffic and city noise, too. Peace and quiet have grown on me like the Carson boys . . . how did Raine put it? She compared you to lichen on a rock?"

The gate to the ranch loomed, the metal arc of mustangs racing, with manes gleaming in the sun. "Yeah, that was flattering." He turned into the long drive, and she could see the tension ease from his shoulders. "Speaking of my family, what exactly do you want to say? If we tell them we're engaged, wedding plans will immediately commence, and that would nix an elopement. If there's even a whisper about a baby, you'll find yourself propped up on pillows and being spoon-fed whatever my mother and Harry think pregnant women should eat. Plus, the minute I walk into Melody Hogan's studio and order that ring, the jig is up. She isn't a gossip, but if people see my truck parked outside her place in a town like Mustang Creek, that'll set off bells. Your call."

Okay, so he'd proposed in front of her sisters. She also had a confession to make. "I mentioned it to your grandfather."

"Mentioned what?"

"That we might be engaged." She hurried on apologetically. "After the business part of the conversation, we started to talk about Mountain Winery, of course, and then you. I talked about the store, and then . . . I said something. No, implied. *Implied* is a better word."

"You blabbed, huh?"

"Not blabbed. I told a very nice elderly gentleman that I was engaged to someone he thinks the world of."

Yes, she'd blabbed.

Mace shook his head. "If he knows, my whole family knows. Brace yourself."

CHAPTER TWENTY-SEVEN

There was some sort of impromptu tournament going on in front of the house when they pulled up. There were dogs, children, quite a few adults, as well. He saw disks soaring, balls being thrown and the animals all running amok. In the pasture, the horses, too, seemed to find the antics fascinating, their heads thrust over the fence. Slater, Drake and Luce seemed to be having as much fun as Daisy and Ryder. They waved and went right back to it.

It was good to be home.

Slater was right about Delilah. Mace couldn't tell what breeds went into her genetic makeup, but she had long brown hair that touched the ground and she was about the size of an average house cat. Still, she seemed to have no trouble scampering around after a tennis ball and pouncing on it before the giant, clumsy puppy could get there.

"Check out the size of Samson's paws," Kelly murmured. "He really will be a monster."

"And she does look like something you'd find on the end of a handle in the housekeeping aisle."

"She's adorable. All that puppy energy."

"Hmph." She was pretty darned cute, but if he had to have a dog named Delilah, he refused to use the word *adorable* from a purely male point of view.

At that moment, Ryder scooped up Delilah and she wriggled with joy and licked his face. "How come I have the feeling that those aren't our dogs at all?" Mace said drily.

"Funny, I have that same feeling." Kelly's eyes were sparkling, the sun shining on her hair. "But those are two happy dogs and two happy kids."

He had no idea if it was possible to fall more in love with someone every time he looked at her, but he was starting to believe it.

His mother, Harry and Grace were on the veranda, watching the circus and sipping tea, the baby in Grace's lap. His mother merely said, "I'm glad you two had a safe trip. How was California?"

She knew. It was there in her eyes. Had to

be Grandpa who'd told her.

Trust her to give him and Kelly the needed space.

So he simply kissed her temple and said, "Fine. I think we're going up to the cabin tonight. We can take the dogs with us if you want — although I suspect I know what you'll say."

"So Delilah, Samson, Violet and Harold can't sleep on my living room rug together? That would be cruel." She shook her head, still smiling. "I'm sorry to tell you this, but I think Daisy and Ryder each got a dog, and if you want one, you're on your own. Territory's been established, and there'd be a rebellion if you tried to take those dogs anywhere."

"I was well-intentioned." Mace had to admit his plan hadn't gone as expected. "I thought Kelly and I could get a dog together and —"

"And then you mentioned it to Daisy and Ryder." His mother smiled again. "Kid instruction — don't say anything ahead of time. Children want immediate action."

"I'll make a note, but not to be disrespectful, I don't think I'm the one who said anything to Mrs. Arbuckle-Calder."

Harry chuckled. "He's got you there. It's like letting a tornado loose. I love Lettie,

496

but she's a force to be reckoned with when she gets an idea in her head."

It was wise not to point out that described Harry, as well, so Mace didn't. "She sure made the kids happy."

"She did put on the brakes, so give her some credit. I gather the kids were ready to bring home every animal in the shelter. They stayed for hours, debating their decision."

"You knew this would happen." It was an accusation.

"Well, I had a feeling it would." His mother just took a sip of her tea.

He turned to his sister-in-law. "Grace, are you and Slater resigned to this?"

"We don't have a choice." She grinned. "You'll need to find your own puppy, Mace, and my advice is just to go and adopt it yourself. Where's your truck?"

Figured Grace would be the one to notice that . . . "There was a problem," he said vaguely. "It's being repaired, so we rented a car." He changed the subject quickly. "I'm not sure about another puppy. It's already a zoo around here." But there was no denying that kids and dogs were having a ball. Shouts of laughter and wild barking came from the lawn. "Although I suppose one more won't make much difference."

Kelly wasn't helpful, either. She said with a straight face, "I'm sorry you can't have a dog named Delilah, but I've always favored the name Fifi. I can see you riding out to capture the Houdini bull in boots and hat, calling for Fifi, your faithful companion."

He sighed dramatically. "I sometimes find your sense of humor questionable. Let's go put the luggage away, throw a couple of steaks in a cooler and ride out. This place is as loud as LA at rush hour."

"I'll pack the cooler." His mother rose with alacrity and followed them inside. About two steps into the foyer, she grabbed Kelly and hugged her. "I'm so very happy for you both. Congratulations!"

"It's fast I know, but —"

"I knew I was going to marry Mace's father the day I met him. He felt the same way. Things were more traditional back then, so we waited to get engaged, but not because we weren't sure."

Mace had every certainty his mother and his fiancée were talking about *him.* He hurried to the back of the house as fast as he could carry the luggage.

The sooner he and Kelly headed for the cabin, the better.

Bronze was high-stepping, dancing sideways, restive against the reins, and Mace of course noticed because Stormy was the same way. "Up for a short run?" he said. "I think these two have missed us."

Kelly nodded. She wasn't an expert horse-woman, but practice had made her more competent, and she and Bronze seemed to understand each other. The horse was sending her definite signals. "Not a race," she insisted, since she knew she could never keep up with Mace and Stormy. "A nice comfortable gallop will be fine. I still have city smog in my lungs."

"Wait." He reached over and caught her reins. "Maybe we shouldn't."

"Mace, relax. I won't fall off, and even if I did, I'm sure the baby — if there is one — would be fine."

"Okay, then." He didn't look convinced, and she thought it was the most endearing expression ever. "Ladies first."

One nudge of the heel and they were off, definitely not racing. Mace was keeping their horses under control.

They pulled up in the meadow. She got there first and crowed, "I guess we were racing, after all, and I won!" She pretended to frown. "Oh, wait. You *let* me win."

"My horse let you win. He has good manners. If he'd wanted to, he would've been so far ahead you wouldn't see him for the dust."

"What a gentleman."

He patted Stormy's neck. "He is."

"I meant you, but, anyway. Are we close?"

"I hope so. We slept in the same bed last night, didn't we?"

Kelly threw him a quelling look. "I meant close to the cabin. Are you ever serious?"

"I'm serious about spending the rest of my life with you, and yes, the cabin is pretty close. We can walk the horses the rest of the way to cool them off."

She needed this break, this solitude, just as much as he did. Needed to take time to assimilate the enormous changes in their lives. Needed time together.

A calm evening spent under the stars.

Other than Blythe, his family might not have said anything about the engagement, but they all knew. While Mace was putting up the horses, she walked into the cabin and found a bottle of champagne and two glasses. Someone — it must've been Raine — had made a gorgeous picture of a wineglass beside a bottle of wine with a black bow tied around the neck. The bottle was surrounded by scattered white roses.

When he came in, she pointed at the display. "Okay, mea culpa. I don't want to hear about it. You proposed in front of my sisters. We're even."

He wasn't surprised, just went over to wash his hands. "I told you one word to my grandfather and there'd be a call."

"So . . . even?"

"I'm willing to call it a draw if you are." He grinned. "Now that's a picture we should hang in the store."

What a great idea. "Someone with good taste was very thoughtful. I love it."

"My mother packed enough food for fourteen people, so maybe she doesn't trust me to cook a decent steak over an open fire and wants to make sure you don't starve. I hope you're up for two different types of salad. There's some sort of cake thing, too." He took down a battered old frying pan he informed her was seasoned just right, according to Red. "I'll bet this has been around since the Civil War, and I'm only half joking. It should probably be in a museum somewhere, but it does cook up a mean steak."

It did look like it had seen some chuck wagon time, but it fit in with the cabin and a campfire. "I'm starving. All sounds good."

Everything was delicious. Tortellini salad and something with tomatoes and olives to start. His mother needn't have worried about the steaks; he cooked them perfectly over the open wood fire, and Kelly ate as if she were on shore leave from a long deployment. Then they shared Harry's decadent chocolate cake, which tasted even richer and more decadent as they ate under a sky full of stars.

"That's a hungry baby," Mace said with a laugh.

"Or it could be that my inner chubby self wants to be set free."

"I'd love you, anyway." He got up to clear their plates. "Why don't we go inside and I'll take care of the dishes."

"No, I'll wash and you dry. You know where everything goes. Mace, listen!"

The distant mournful howl came again, not as close as before, but at least she didn't need to trot out her nonexistent wolf whistle.

"I hear him. I think he's saying welcome home." Mace's blue eyes held a soft light. "I'll go get the hot water from the fire, and we can tidy this up and then maybe relive the experience of sharing a sleeping bag. It evokes fond memories for me."

She agreed. Wholeheartedly. "For me, too. But after these past few weeks, I could fall asleep on my feet."

"I'll catch you," he promised. "Always."
And she knew that to be true.

CHAPTER TWENTY-EIGHT

"I'm just going to trust you. Pick out something good." Mace looked at the work-table scattered with sketches, small tools and, at the moment, a spool of gold wire. Melody Hogan's comfortable little house had become her studio ever since she'd married Spence.

Melody was someone he'd known his whole life, and although her favorite clothes were jeans and a faded T-shirt, she still managed beautiful extremely well. "You don't have a preference on the stone?"

Mace had to grimace. "No, but I've tried. Let me put it this way. Kelly's sisters certainly had differences of opinion. My two sisters-in-law have weighed in, and they weren't in agreement, either. So, Mel, please, just choose something. It's your area of expertise. Go for it."

"What about topaz? She's blonde, and it'll set off her hair. I know a dealer who handles some that are really top-notch in clarity and depth. I've been itching to work with one of his stones. Topaz isn't usual for engagement rings, but that's the beauty of it." She industriously picked up a pad and started scribbling. "Two small diamonds on either side and a marquis cut. Don't worry, I won't make it too big. I met Kelly when she stopped by to commission the clock for the old store, and she's not the flashy type. She also has slender fingers. Must be an occupational thing, but I always notice people's fingers."

"And I pay attention to the kind of wine they like to drink." He was more than happy to let Melody make a selection or two. And at his expense — as a thank-you. "Again, an occupational thing."

"Well, you know how much I like your cabernet."

"It's yours."

"Thanks! Looking forward to it. Oh, I hear you have two dogs, thanks to Mrs. A-C." Melody clearly thought that was funny, tucking her pencil into her ponytail. "You were outmaneuvered, Mace."

"Not really," he said. "We planned on two dogs from the beginning, but if Mom and Lettie want to believe they're diabolically clever, so be it."

"Your mother is *kindhearted*." Her voice held amused emphasis. "The ranch is a big place. A few more dogs running around just adds to the general ambiance."

"So speaks the woman with multiple cats and energetic dogs running all over the place."

"I am that woman. Let's not forget the baby and the husband with unpredictable hours." She laughed. "Keeps life interesting. Why do I sense you need this ring soon — if not sooner?"

"No comment." He left, smiling, although that was short-lived a minute later when his phone rang. He answered it and heard Slater say with evident satisfaction, "Well, we got him."

"Elaborate?"

"Oh, your boy is back in Wyoming, and I have footage of him on Carson property. He's a tall blond guy with glasses, right?"

That hadn't taken long and didn't bode well. He and Kelly had been home only three days. "Yes, that's him. Where?"

"I put a camera by the grove near the far pasture. I have him on video with binoculars aimed at the house."

Mace took a breath and climbed in the truck, the one he'd just gotten back with intact tires. "This guy is off the grid. He's spent time in prison, there's a restraining order against him, and he's a convicted felon on parole. Call Spence and tell him he's here, will you? I'll go check on Kelly right now." He paused. "You're a genius, Showbiz."

"Don't I know it."

She was at the store this sunny morning while the floors were being cleaned and the old shelving removed. It wasn't as though she was alone, but he had to fight the urge to speed through town.

She was just fine, looking up as she sorted through boxes, her expression inquiring. There was an endearing smudge on her chin and, instead of her usual stylish clothes, she wore faded jeans with a hole in the knee and a plain blue tank top. The place was shaping up, the old coolers carted away, most of the rusted shelving unassembled and ready for the recycling company to pick up. Scrap metal was easy enough to get rid of, anyway.

"Hi." He kissed her. Pulled to her feet and *really* kissed her. To say he was concerned was an understatement.

She got it, too. She frowned. "Is there a problem?"

"Yes, and no."

"That's clear — as mud. Pick up a case of

wine and tell me about it. I prefer informative and useful rolled together."

"Good to know." He hefted a case of wine. "The next time we're making love, I'll be sure to give you the weekly weather forecast. Where do you want this, boss?"

"Ha, ha, ha." Her lips twitched as she picked up a broom. "The back room's where I had them start, so it's done. Let's just pile everything in there until all the racks arrive. I'm just cleaning and getting ready to organize the office. Now, what's the sort-of problem?"

"Vreeman is here in Wyoming."

She went still and briefly closed her eyes. "For the past decade, I knew this wouldn't just quietly go away. What do we do now?"

"Well, here's the good part. Slater set up cameras, and he's got pictures. I feel confident that Vreeman was smart enough to evade the surveillance cameras at the airport long-term parking lot, but he apparently didn't expect them on a remote ranch in Wyoming. Even though he hasn't technically violated the restraining order, he sure has trespassed. I think when you're still on parole, especially for a felony conviction, you're not supposed to break *any* laws. The best part is that we can prove stalking. He was using binoculars to watch the ranch.

We have it on video."

Her expression eased a fraction, but her voice was tight. "I'd love to see him go straight back to jail."

"All that has to happen, in my opinion, is for Spence to round him up and for us to press charges. Slate was going to give Spence a heads-up."

She sank down to sit on one of the boxes. "I've always thought hate was a useless emotion. I still do. Lance Vreeman had everything — looks, money, a family that tried to back him up in every way possible . . . but he's just set on a path of self-destruction."

"Red would say he's hell-bent on Hades, so why not let him mosey right on down there."

Kelly gave a weak laugh. "Red might say that."

His phone beeped, and he glanced at it. "I'm headed back to the winery, but even with the guys working here, keep the doors locked if you're alone for a second. I'll come back to help you this afternoon, okay?"

He was out the door about two seconds later, calling Drake back. "What now?"

"That's an impolite response to someone giving you a friendly call."

"My jovial mood has taken a holiday.

What kind of friendly call?"

"Well, the bull's gotten loose again. None of us have been able to figure out how he manages it. I've even called Jim Galloway, but we're all sitting around scratching our heads. That critter is pretty determined. Want to come help me rope him in again?"

"I don't have time for this, Romeo."

"Oh, I think you do. Usual spot and bring a rope." He chuckled. "That Thor is one predictable bull." Then he hung up.

Mace stared at his phone before he climbed into his vehicle. Drake was a man of few words, true, but he was usually blunt, not cryptic.

He discovered why when he got back to the ranch, saddled up and rode out to Thor's favorite pasture.

There was Drake sitting on the fence, legs dangling, and from the wrapper on the ground next to him, it looked suspiciously like he'd eaten a sandwich while waiting. Harold and Violet were lying in the long grass. Drake didn't turn when Mace approached, but just said, "I'm used to catching the bull, but not quite used to this. Our new bull doesn't like trespassers. Call your lawyer and find out if we're at fault if someone trespasses on our land and our bull is loose and decides to charge him."

Lance Vreeman. There he was. The Houdini bull *had* gotten loose again and had the man trapped near a small pile of wood that'd probably been split decades ago. The animal snorted if Vreeman even moved a muscle, and Mace joined his brother on the fence, swinging his legs over. "Well, I usually don't have a signal up here. How'd you call me?"

"I had to ride down the trail about five miles." Drake shrugged. "I figured Thor had the situation under control. He seems to think this is his pasture and an uninvited someone is in it. He doesn't like that at all. As for Vreeman, if this was a hundred years ago and I had a tree handy —"

"I'd do the same. Hmm. Eventually he'll have to relieve himself, and Thor could just take care of it for us."

"Bulls are straightforward creatures. My advice is to never attract their attention — unless you have a plan in mind."

Mace rubbed his jaw. "Slate called Spence. Normally, I'd feel bad about letting a man try to fold himself into a pile of wood so a bull forgets he's there, but in this case, he's not exactly my favorite person."

"Thor doesn't seem to like him, either," Drake observed. "Since I think he's smarter than you are, I went with his instincts."

"Our bull is smarter than I am?"

"Well, just sayin'. He has Vreeman cornered. You haven't managed to do that."

"Uh, I sent him to prison for ten years," he argued, enjoying the situation. The person in question didn't look comfortable at all.

"My bull got his ass rounded up in one afternoon."

That was all true. "We have a mutual problem. Your stubborn bull is loose. We have to catch that valuable animal — and also make sure the less valuable animal, being Vreeman, is delivered safe and sound to the people who'll impress upon him the need to change his ways. If you have a plan, Stormy and I are right here listening."

"That's easy enough. Help me get a rope on that giant pain in my rear, and then you can tie up Vreeman with help. I think you've done that before."

"One of my fondest memories." Mace pointed at the wrapper. "Did you really sit here and have your midafternoon snack while you were waiting for me?"

"Cut me some slack. I'm entitled to sustenance now and then." Drake grinned at him. "A man gets hungry watching justice being meted out. I was enjoying it, actually, and since I don't want my valuable investment to bolt or come to harm in any way, I need a second pair of hands. I'd have sent in the dogs if I wasn't worried about the bull raising an objection by kicking their brains in."

Mace shook his head. "Drake, here's my suggestion. You're going to have to cave on this. Fence in this particular section and let the bull graze here. It's obviously what he wants, and if it'll make him happy, just do it."

Vreeman finally called out, able at least to hear them. "Hey!"

They both ignored him, but at the sound of Vreeman's voice, Thor moved closer in evident displeasure.

"That's occurred to me, believe it or not," Drake said with resignation. "I just hate digging postholes. I tell you what, since my errant bull caught your man, if you'll help me, we have a deal."

Mace wasn't crazy about posthole-digging, either, but his older brother had a point. "All right, sure. I owe Thor."

"Spence is holding him?" Kelly looked sideways at Mace and was rewarded with a nod.

She was tired, she was dusty, her muscles ached, but she . . . was happy. And relieved, hopeful and about a dozen other emotions.

"Trespassing is usually just a fine," he said, "but stalking isn't a slap-on-the-wrist crime these days. Spence thinks he has more than enough evidence for the district attorney to take it to a judge."

She wanted to collapse in relief and from sheer exhaustion. She'd been working frantically because it needed to be done, and it took her mind off what was going on. "That's *such* good news."

"It's not a case of life being all wrapped up with a pink ribbon, but it improves my outlook. How are you feeling?"

"Like I could take a nap every five minutes." That was the hopeful part.

"Still no pregnancy test? You're firm on that?"

"Why can't we just take things as they come — let this be a mystery for a while? I know you're excited. So am I. But the truth is, I'm a little overwhelmed. In a very short time my life's changed dramatically. I've quit my job, moved to a new and completely different place, I'm getting married. Getting the store up and running is no small project, and then there's all the stuff connected to the partnership." She blew out a breath. "This is a positive kind of stress, but it's still stress, and that alone could've made me late and could be making me feel so tired and emotional."

"I hate to break this to you, but if you're pregnant, everyone will see pretty soon. I think that sexy black skirt is going to be hanging in our closet for a while."

She wasn't quite willing to tell him yet that she'd started taking vitamins and checked online for doctors in the area, because she knew he was as happy as she was at the possibility of a baby. And she loved the idea of *our* closet.

He went on. "I wish I completely understood why you're not ready to find out, but I'm willing just to walk by your side."

Maybe she was being unfair. "I just can't deal with the disappointment if I'm wrong. I realize it would be nice to know for sure . . ."

"You don't have to realize anything. We can wait."

"I'm furious with you." It just came out.

That stopped him cold. "Why?"

"Because I love you so much, it scares me."

"Well, hell, woman, don't you realize I feel the same way about you?"

"You do?"

The tension was broken when Mace suddenly laughed. "Yeah."

"You actually get scared?"

He was serious now. "Sure, I do. Sometimes. But I'll be damned if I'll let a little fear come between me and a lifetime of loving you."

"You're wonderful, Mace Carson," she said very softly.

"So are you," he replied. "I guess that means we have a lot more in common than our fondness for good wine and the new stuffed mushrooms at Bad Billy's."

She was grateful for the touch of lightness. "I'm glad you mentioned those, actually. The mushrooms, I mean. I'd like to serve them at the reception. We could do a sort of cook-off thing, like on the Food Channel — let Bad Billy and Harry go toe-to-toe."

"Bad idea," he said. "There might be bloodshed."

Kelly feigned alarm. She'd been kidding, but she wasn't ready to let him know that. "Surely not?"

"At least you're pragmatic enough to realize that elopement or not, there *will* be a reception. If you want a war, just pit those two against each other. Heck, why not throw Stefano into the mix for good measure?"

"I don't want a war, I want *mushrooms*. And if we have Billy make them, Harry's feelings will be hurt."

"We can't have that. So we'll order the mushrooms from Billy and give Harry free rein to whip up whatever she likes." He drew her close, took her into his arms. "So, lioness, what goes best with stuffed mushrooms. Zinfandel? Merlot? Chardonnay?"

Kelly kissed him. "You do."

FOREVER

The reception was the event of the summer.

They'd been married quietly the day before — no elopement, after all — with only her family and his in attendance. It was his mother's idea to combine the reception with the launch of the store, and that was a stroke of brilliance. People poured in, the place was decorated with flowers and, of course, the food was a hit. Ryder and Daisy enjoyed walking around with trays of canapés as potential customers checked out the wine on the newly installed shelves. And bought it. Bought a lot of it.

Then half of Bliss County showed up at the ranch, and Mace's grandfather made the trip from California to share in the celebration. Kelly's family was there in force, and her previous boss, Dina, came with *her* new husband.

The bride was absolutely radiant, shining brighter than the topaz ring on her finger.

All was right in Kelly's world. She'd worked hard to make sure the store reflected Mustang Creek, adding a touch of Western elegance. Naturally Mace was proud of her, but he was also pleased that she'd been such a great choice; she'd handled something he didn't feel equipped to pull off, and he certainly couldn't have managed it as well as she had.

He could tell she was pregnant because he saw her naked as often as possible, but today Kelly wore a full skirted ivory gown, so the rest of the world was probably still oblivious. Oops, strike that. Grace and Luce had cornered him a few minutes ago and asked.

"Something you aren't telling us, Mason Carson?" Grace asked.

"Give it up," Luce told him.

He'd defended himself with the truth. "I asked her to marry me *before* we knew."

Their smiles could've lit up the night sky. Both of them hugged him, and he felt just as excited, but he needed to tell Kelly that she wasn't fooling everyone, not by a long stretch.

Luckily, his wife's sisters took care of that for him.

"Kelly!" It was a chorus and a refrain. They circled around her like a wagon train.

One of them asked, "When are you due?"

How they'd taken one look at her and known was a mystery to him.

Janice — it would be her — immediately demanded, "Is it a boy or a girl?"

Mace tried to intervene. "We have no idea —"

"He's right," Kelly protested. "We don't know. It's too early."

They crowded around her, and he was just a bystander in the drama, which was fine. Kelly had finally gone to the doctor, who'd confirmed the pregnancy. Mace had accompanied her, and they'd both heard the heartbeat. She'd held on to his hand so tightly he was surprised none of his fingers cracked.

More tears from her, but his throat tightened up, too.

That wasn't the only wedding present he had for her.

"I have a gift for you. Be right back."

Lettie Arbuckle-Calder pulled up, got out of her expensive car looking like a million bucks in a suit that might have cost that much, and opened one of the back doors. As he hastened over to take out the pet carrier, he was informed in her forthright way, "I made an executive decision for you."

Lettie's husband, getting out of the passenger side, shut his door and agreed with resignation, "She did, son. This was out of my hands."

Mace heard a noise from inside that was definitely not a bark. A small paw came out through the front of the carrier and batted his arm. "A kitten?"

Mrs. A-C looked unrepentant, but he couldn't imagine her ever being repentant, anyway. "She's darling. Wait till you see her. She needs a home with a big veranda, so she can sleep in the sun."

Oh, hell. He had a feeling that Kelly would find it hilarious to name the critter Fifi. If there was anything worse than having a dog named Delilah, it was having a cat named Fifi. "Uh, well, thanks. I'll take your word for it." The die was cast, anyway. Children were already swarming, wanting to see what was in the pet carrier.

He let them peer inside, the dogs leaping around on all sides.

Kelly was at his side, instantly smitten.

"What did you do? Oh . . . Mace, how sweet!"

Naturally, the tiny feline was Fifi-worthy, with fluffy white fur and a little pink nose, blue eyes. It was the right choice, then, adding the small fluff ball to their brood of pets.

Then he caught sight of the expression of

wonder on his mother's face when she spotted the kitten and dashed toward them.

Maybe he was becoming an expert on love at first sight. He said to Kelly under his breath, "Okay, it looks like there might be a change of plans. Do I get points for trying?"

Fortunately, he'd married a very smart woman. Kelly had noticed Blythe's response to the furry little newcomer, and she murmured back just as quietly, "Sure, I'll give you the points, because I'm thinking the same thing you are. Your mom and this kitten are meant to be."

His mother scooped the tiny cat up in both hands, and it was hard to know who was purring the loudest, Blythe or the feline.

Naturally the kitten rubbed against her chin and cuddled against her. Love at first sight for sure. Yeah, that cat was *not* going to be theirs. So he did his best. "Mom, you love cats, and Mrs. A-C said this one's special."

Mrs. Arbuckle-Calder was either a natural actress, or else she knew his mother wanted a kitten and had pulled a fast one on him. "Blythe, I figured that with all the dogs around here, you wouldn't mind another cat."

Good save.

"I do miss my cat." Molly Malone, an

aged tabby, had died the previous year.

Yup, he'd been bested.

"However, there is someone else I brought along, just in case it might suit the newlywed couple. Randolph, would you mind?"

Randolph Calder was an austere, successful businessman, and it was comic watching him walk back to the car and emerge with a wriggling puppy in his hands. The heritage of this critter was questionable, but it was cute — maybe a mix of beagle, corgi, who knew what else? Mace was delighted when it made a beeline for Kelly. Closely followed by a full-grown female, probably its mother.

Mrs. A-C peered around and said serenely, "See, I knew they'd love you. And, anyway, I couldn't see splitting up a family. Now, I don't mean to be demanding, but I need a glass of wine."

Mace said with a smile, "Let me get you one."

The mushroom debate continued once the festivities were over and the newlyweds had retired for the night.

"I liked Billy's best because of the garlic." Kelly kissed him.

Mace argued with her, but this was going to be a lifetime of back-and-forth. He kissed her in return, his mouth moving down to her breasts as he slipped off her bra. "Please admit Harry's were a contender. The addition of the ground elk was magnificent."

"I think that was pork sausage," she corrected him. "I agree, though. Hers were also delicious."

"Well, maybe it was elk sausage. Ever consider that?"

"I think you're mixing up Red's fictional cheese puffs with the current conversation."

"That's possible." He took a nipple in his mouth and sucked lightly. She nearly leaped off the bed.

"I declare a tie. Why am I starting not to care?"

"Because you love me, and I love you *and* making love to you. The puppy is now snoring, which doesn't bode well for the future if he already snores at this tender age, but we can overlook it for the moment. And . . . we're alone."

"I'm really happy. With you, about you and because of you." She traced the outline of his cheekbone. All true. Every word of it.

"I'll take you anywhere you want for a honeymoon. You keep hedging on the location. Your sisters are going to tan my hide if I don't give you the honeymoon of your dreams, and I'm a little scared of them, even if Slate and Drake have my back. What are you thinking?"

She wasn't thinking about much at all, except what an effective job he was doing at distracting her. Kelly gasped, but his skilled hands were gasp-worthy. "I've always wanted a honeymoon in Wyoming."

"Done."

"And a puppy as a wedding gift."

"Got it already. Keep going."

"A business to run."

He licked her inner thigh. "Okay, cross that one off. Next?"

"A baby."

"I'm on a roll here."

"Yes, you are." He was taking care of her just fine. She shifted against the sheets because he knew exactly how to touch her. "A soft bed is nice when you have someone to share it with. That would be you, cowboy."

He lifted his head and looked at her intently, and she knew this was the real question. "The city girl doesn't need shops and people on their cell phones walking by? She's willing to trade her impractical sports car for something that might make it through mud and snow? Instead of trendy restaurants and glittering lights, she'll take mountains and the occasional moonlit ride?"

"Yes." She pulled him in for a languid kiss. "She's decided that maybe at heart she's a country girl."

ABOUT THE AUTHOR

The daughter of a town marshal, **Linda Lael Miller** is the author of more than 100 historical and contemporary novels. Now living in Spokane, Washington, the "First Lady of the West" hit a career high when all three of her 2011 Creed Cowboy books debuted at #1 on the *New York Times* list. In 2007, the Romance Writers of America presented her their Lifetime Achievement Award. She personally funds her Linda Lael Miller Scholarships for Women. Visit her at www.lindalaelmiller.com.